The New Hero
Volume 2

New Heroes for a New Age

Edited by Robin D. Laws

Published by Stone Skin Press 2013.

Stone Skin Press is an imprint of Pelgrane Press Ltd. Spectrum House, 9 Bromell's Road, Clapham Common, London, SW4 0BN.

Each author retains the individual copyright to their story.

The collection and arrangement Copyright ©2012 Stone Skin Press.

All rights reserved. No part of this publication may be reproduced, stored in a retrieval system, or transmitted in any form or by any means electronic, mechanical, photocopying, recording or otherwise, without the prior written permission of the copyright owner.

ISBN 978-1-908983-03-9

A CIP catalogue record for this book is available from the British Library.

1 2 3 4 5 6 7 8 9 10

Printed in the USA.

This book can be ordered direct from the publisher at www.pelgranepress.com

Contents

Preface: Where the Hero is Now **Robin D. Laws**	5
Alex Bledsoe **Finger Stakes**	11
Jesse Bullington **Saturday's Children**	24
Emily Care Boss **The King's Condottiere**	46
Greg Stolze **Dead Leather Office**	68
James Wallis **Alms and the Beast**	92
Jennifer Brozak **Iron Achilles Heel**	112
Will Hindmarch **Blood for the King**	124
Matt Forbeck **Friends Like These**	148
Robin D. Laws **Among the Montags**	171
John Scott Tynes **Footsteps in Limbo**	190
James L. Sutter **Guns at the Hellroad**	210
Jean Rabe **Stalking in Memphis**	233
Christina Stiles **Killing Osuran**	249
Tobias Buckell **The Rydr Express**	263
Biographies	286

Where the Hero is Now

A Preface

As you have no doubt intuited from the numeral at the end of its title, *The New Hero 2* continues Stone Skin Press's exploration of the iconic hero story. As these pages will further confirm, the precise demands of this timeless structure paradoxically offer writers a near-limitless variability.

Stories of iconic heroes pervade our culture. If anything, as genre storytelling undergoes an unprecedented resurgence, they've never been more omnipresent. The rise of the information economy tilted the mainstream to please a generation of tastemakers. Nerds and hipsters have converged. Your hairdresser digs vampire romance; your plumber rocks a killer videogame rig.

Key to this shift is a preference for the mythological over the psychological, for the symbolic over the naturalistic. Either set of modes can provide mere diversion or communicate depths of human experience. They demand, however, to be read in different ways. Inevitably, critical frameworks lag behind changes in the way we appreciate narrative, which remains at heart an instinctive and emotional process. Ways of understanding developed to explicate works of psychological naturalism may lead us to downgrade the fundamentally mythic expression that is the iconic hero story. Yet viewed from a remove, it is a container no more or less robust than the dramatic formula we've conditioned ourselves to value above all others.

Inner change defines the dramatic protagonist. He undergoes a transformative arc, moving from rise to fall or from degradation to redemption. His struggles chart out as a series of emotional encounters with those around him. That arc tells his entire story; when it ends, we need no more of him.

The iconic hero, on the other hand, is built for outward conflict. Her battles take place in the external world, which confronts her with a disorder she must rectify. Armed with a signature array of working methods that reflect the character's ethos, she tackles it. Crisis tests her, but she remains steadfast, or recovers her fundamental sense of self after momentarily losing sight of it. She resists transformation, instead cleaving to a consistency of character. This full-circle structure allows her to return for repeat adventures. From this repetition arises a satisfying sense of recurrence continuity.

Is life a line, or a series of cycles?

It is both, of course, meaning that we don't have to choose. We can enrich ourselves on the tales of both the dramatic and the iconic hero. Each mode is at its most fully realized in the hands of authors who know its ground rules, and best appreciated by audiences attuned to its expectations.

Here, working in various genres, voices, and tones, appear fourteen writers well steeped in this eternal rhythm, ready to divert and to disturb, to thrill and to please.

This *New Hero* outing serves as a snapshot capturing the present state of a fast-moving genre scene. Supernatural elements continue their invasion of other conventions. Mash-ups rule the day, reviving established tropes by smashing them together and seeing what weird resonances emerge from the collisions. Replacing the realist extrapolation from a fantastic premise is a post-modern arrangement of tropes and images, pitched to a self-aware reader ready to accept the sets of conceits they offer up.

The volume bookends itself with a pair of already-established recurring characters of recent vintage.

In "Finger Stakes", Alex Bledsoe brings us a deliciously mordant tale of hardboiled swords and sorcery featuring his genre-bending private eye, Eddie LaCrosse. Drawing equally from the wells of Fritz Leiber and Raymond Chandler, "Finger Stakes" partakes of the next iteration of heroic storytelling: the playful, knowing mythic mixmaster, borrowing elements as it desires them from disparate traditions.

You don't have to be fictional to be an iconic hero, as Jesse Bullington evocatively establishes by casting Weegee, the NYC news photographer who turned hard-hitting tabloid snaps into gritty art, as the protagonist of "Saturday's Children." The disorder he faces reveals itself as a supernatural one, leading him to partner with an old flame, seer Claire Simons. Reverberant with period atmosphere, this urban fantasy reads in high-contrast black and white and pops like a flashbulb.

Emily Care Boss likewise presses a real figure into service as her iconic hero, in this case bringing to swashbuckling life painter and mercenary captain Onorata Rodiana. "The King's Condottiere" plays its fifteenth century derring-do straight, bringing us a feminist role model we might not believe, were she not lifted from the history books.

When magic meets modern crime, either the unearthly quality of the former or the low-life credibility of the latter may suffer. Greg Stolze's "Dead Leather Office" not only nails both elements, but makes them seem like they always go together. Maybe that's because his no-nonsense protagonist, the "cold woman" Cadillac Anne, has a boot planted firmly on both sides of this duality.

James Wallis grounds his swords and sorcery excursion "Alms and the Beast" in a redolent sense of history, placing his unnamed pilgrim hero in England and burdening him with the emotional scars of the first crusade. By siting him in this specific place and time, James finds a refreshing new context for that most classic of iconic types, the enigmatic man of action.

The emergence of popular serialized fiction coincided with the opening of the American west, forever linking the frontier gunslinger to the iconic hero tradition. Today's weird west resurgence, as typified by Jennifer Brozek's "Iron Achilles Heel," puts a geek-culture torque on this longstanding connection. The relationship between a man and his weapon is never more acute than when the gun talks back.

Within the exacting structure of the iconic hero story a deft writer finds room to portray the grace notes of daily existence. In Will Hindmarch's "Blood for the King", those telling details just happen to convey the rhythms of a spacefaring future where humanity is in decline. Thus he situates the medical hero, here personified as Dr. Ariam Keown, amid deftly drawn signposts of the new space opera.

Students of genre mash-up will want to perform a compare and contrast between Alex Bledsoe's story, referenced above, and Matt Forbeck's "Friends Like These." Both combine fantasy with the hardboiled detective sub-genre, to notably different results. Matt populates his world of shotguns and sorcery with the outre denizens of post-gaming fantasy. A breakneck farrago of wisecracks, bar fights and elven corruption ensues.

Having asked twenty-seven other writers, in both this and the original volume, to tackle the sometimes-unforgiving structure of the iconic hero tale, I figured I'd better put myself to a similar test. "Among the Montags" plays with viewpoint, voice and identification with the protagonist as it follows its mute hero, Longthought, on a canine rescue in an exurban Toronto devastated by semiotic apocalypse. Were this an exploitation movie, the tagline would read: *One sword heals; the other one kills.*

In the Professor, a kindly but tormented psychopomp to other souls trapped in Limbo, John Scott Tynes presents an iconic hero unlike any other. In "Footsteps in Limbo", the world to which he restores order is an eerily depicted half-realm between life and death. As he investigates a series of strange disappearances, we are drawn into a melancholy reality driven by a passive, refracted logic.

James L. Sutter infuses the weird western with millennial anxiety in "Guns at the Hellroad." His hero, taciturn freelance gunslinger Jacob Weintraub, brings order to a world broken by a past Rapture and/or Singularity. The relationship between hero and his sidekick of the moment, a blind seer, brings a flicker of human verity to a shattered landscape.

Jean Rabe's hero, the summoner Sabine Upchurch, calls history's deceased greats to her side, to protect her beloved city from harm. "Stalking in Memphis" sees her confronting a mythic firebug with the aid of a deity more familiar with a different town of the same name. Jean's lighthearted touch finds the fun in the modern occult genre.

The originators of popular genres often find their prose styles denigrated even as the trappings and assumptions of their stories become touchstones for generations of imitators. Perhaps it's their unruliness of their craft that lent their work the energy needed to exert this effect. Christina Stiles recognizes this, attacking her sword and sorcery story "Killing Osuran" with a straight-faced intensity Robert E. Howard might applaud. The homicidal thirst for justice displayed by her not-quite-human hero, Kaja Dawne, manifests itself through the story's unnerving ferocity of viewpoint.

The anthology heads back to space for its final rip-roaring tale of futuristic ultraviolence, courtesy of Tobias Buckell and his recurring bad-ass, Pepper. Buckell plays gut-crunching id off against speculative superego in "The Rydr Express." Pepper's previous exploits can be found in such novels as *Crystal Rain*, *Ragamuffin*, and *Sly Mongoose*. In the end though, the true hardnose is Tobias who can make you take second person and like it.

The breadth of tone, voice and theme found in this collection testifies to the enduring strength and gaining momentum of the iconic hero form as we enter a transitional era in narrative. The way we consume stories is changing, as are our expectations for them.. Whether we learn to understand them better, or simply keep on enjoying them without looking too deeply under the hood, one truth remains incontrovertible: the hero is always with us, and the new hero is here to stay.

—*Robin D. Laws*

Finger Stakes

Alex Bledsoe

There was a bit more gray in Jane Argo's hair, but otherwise she hadn't changed at all since the last time I saw her. She was still taller than me, curvy in all the right places and quite capable of dismembering pretty much anyone, male or female, who crossed her path. She still wore a sword that most men, including me, would have trouble raising past the horizontal. This made her high, little-girl voice even more incongruous, but I knew better than to laugh. Men who laughed at Jane Argo tended to end up with even higher voices.

She sat across from me in my sparsely-furnished office above Angelina's tavern in Neceda. She crossed her fur-fringed boots on the edge of my desk and tilted back her chair. She explained her request with the term, "Professional courtesy, Eddie. One sword jockey to another. We're so much alike, you know."

I almost *did* laugh at that. We became sword jockeys for vastly different reasons. I'd been raised at court in far-off Arentia, and had the best education and martial training before I left home following a tragedy for which I felt responsible. I began a long stint as a mercenary, until I grew weary of killing on someone else's say-so. I then discovered that my mix of skills and experience made me a perfect sword jockey, hiring out to solve problems too delicate or difficult for official channels.

Jane grew up in the woods, a peasant girl who married young and, faced with the prospect of a life of nothing but bearing children and backbreaking labor, ran off to sea at the first opportunity. She'd been a privateer, then a pirate, then a pirate hunter. She was the one who caught Rody Hawke, the most vicious and successful pirate who ever sailed, and who was now sealed in a cell at the top of a tower until he revealed the location of his treasure. She became a sword jockey when she tired of the ocean and returned to her husband, finding she too had a set of abilities that had few other uses. I liked her and trusted her, but I could also tell she was yanking my chain.

"We're about as 'alike' as a monkey and a breakfast roll, Jane. And 'professional courtesy' doesn't put ale in the mug. You know I get twenty-five gold pieces a day plus expenses, same as you."

"Don't you have a special rate for friends?"

"Sure, if they don't want me to work very hard."

Metal and gems glittered as she waved her hand in defeat. I'd seen marks left by those rings on the faces of many a punk over the years, but not on the one face that needed it most. And that was the reason she said, "Okay, fine. Drive a poor working woman to poverty. You're hired. Now go get him."

"Not so fast," I said, and refilled both our tankards from my office bottle. Outside the sounds of Neceda, the small riverside town I used as my home base, came through the window. It was early summer, and the markets were suffering as they awaited the first harvest, which made everyone short tempered as their money ran low. It might be a good time to get out of town for a while. "If you know where your husband is, and the kind of trouble he's in, why don't *you* go get him?"

She took a drink and looked down at the floor, at the wall, out the window, anywhere but directly at me. Finally she muttered something into her ale.

"Beg pardon?" I prompted.

With careful pronunciation she repeated, "Because after the last time I did that, I promised him I would never do it again."

And there it was. Jane Argo, the toughest female sword jockey around, who could slice a bumblebee in half in mid-buzz, was genuinely in love with her no-account husband Miles. Of all the mysterious things I'd witnessed over the years, the way love made people act remained the strangest of all.

Miles Argo was the kind of man you couldn't turn your back on even if he was up to his neck in dried mud. During the years Jane had been at sea he'd been too busy surviving to get into too much trouble, but once she came back he was proof that free time was a bad thing. When she began actually earning a living, he became essentially useless. Using her money he whored, gambled and drank; she saved his ass and took him back each time.

Clearly Jane had serious blinders on when it came to Miles. But as a newly-committed partner myself, still marveling at the intensity of my feelings for red-headed courier Liz Dumont, I was in no position to mock. Who was I to say it *wasn't* true love?

Jane tossed a bag of coins on the desk. "That should get you through the week. If you need more, we'll talk then."

I picked up the bag and put it away without counting the contents. I always felt a little nervous working for a friend, but money was money, and Jane definitely understood the nature of the job. "All right, I'll go get him and bring him home. You're right, it won't be quite as embarrassing as his wife doing it, although I won't go out of my way to shield his tender feelings. But you know he won't stay. He'll be out hound-dogging around again as soon as your back's turned."

"Oh, I know," she agreed with no hesitation. For a moment I saw, beneath the extraordinary façade, the very ordinary woman with an everyday broken heart. Then it was gone, and she smiled ruefully. "Believe me, I've lived with the son of a bitch and heard every excuse you can imagine. I *know*."

◇

I started at Long Billy's tavern, Angelina's competition across town. Angelina had banished Miles years ago after he made a drunken pass at her; since she was only slightly less intimidating than Jane, I suppose it meant Miles stayed true to his type. But I knew he sometimes spent his meager winnings at Long Billy's, so I sought out Billy himself.

"Miles slip his leash again?" Billy asked from behind the bar. As his name implied, he was very tall and thin, though he claimed the sobriquet "long" had an entirely different origin. His eyes never left the ample cleavage of a very young girl well on her way to drunkenness at one of the nearby tables.

I said, "You've got boots older than her, Billy, you should be ashamed of yourself."

She caught him looking and tugged her top down even more. He smiled. "Shame is momentary, Eddie. Memories of love are forever."

"You call that love?"

"She will. When I'm done with her."

"So did Miles say where he'd won his money?"

"Someplace called the Diamond Hole in Four Chops. Old mining down at the foothills of the mountains. He said the cards there were smoking hot for him. His exact words." He paused, and tried to make the next comment sound casual. "And how's Angelina these days?"

"She's right across town, Billy. Why don't you go ask her?"

"Ah, that's okay," he said. "Just curious."

There was some history between Angelina and Billy, but neither spoke about it in anything but vague terms. Unlike Miles and Jane, Angelina and Billy were equals, which might explain their estrangement. But I thought the same about Liz and me, so what did that portend? I shook my head, finished my complementary ale and left Billy to his conquest of the moment.

I headed out through the forest toward the mountains on my latest bad-tempered, recalcitrant horse. Two first-timers tried to waylay me, and I thought I was going to have to kill them both, but instead I left them with marks of my sword's flat across their

Finger Stakes

backsides that wouldn't fade for a week. I'm not sure why I let them go; either my tolerance of amateurs had grown, or I just already had enough blood on my hands.

A silver strike six years ago brought a boom to Four Chops that had since dwindled down to a loud clap, with only a brothel, two taverns and a lone gambling house still in operation. The unused buildings had begun to collapse, and in five years the whole place would be abandoned to the forests and the winds.

For now, though, it was livelier than it should have been, especially after midnight when I arrived. That should've tipped me off. A half-dozen horses were tied outside the whorehouse, and both halves of a broken Boneslicer single-edge cavalry sword lay in the mud in the middle of the muddy street. As I passed one of the taverns a man staggered out, cursing in a language I didn't know, with a dagger imbedded in his thigh. He went past me into one of the abandoned buildings on the opposite side of the street and crashed into something wooden that broke beneath him. No one pursued him.

I carried my reliable Eventide sword, with the extra-firm grip wrap on the hilt, in a Grand Bruan-style scabbard across my back. I chose that blade despite the fact that it shredded the lip of the expensive scabbard whenever I drew it, because it was light and sharp enough to bisect a sneeze. Hopefully, though, the only metal I'd need to wield would be Jane's money.

Miles might be in one of the taverns or the whorehouse, but that would mean he'd won some money first. I decided to start my search in the Diamond Hole, the gambling house where he'd won in the past. It was at the other end of town, a low flat-roofed building with torches blazing on either side of the entrance.

I tied my horse alongside eight others and went to the door. A big, broad-shouldered man opened it. "Yeah?"

"I have money I want to lose," I said. "This looks like the perfect place to do it."

"Are you some kind of funny guy?"

"Some kind. But my gold isn't a joke." I took out a coin and held it so the torchlight sparkled on it. "I'm also looking for a pal.

Squirrelly little guy named Miles. He wouldn't happen to be here, would he?"

"Nobody's here. I'm not even here."

"Lot of horses for nobody," I pointed out. I extended the coin. "Mind if I look around for myself."

He took it without a word. "You have to check your sword with me before you go in."

I did so, receiving a little metal chit with a number on it. I noticed mine was the only sword hanging from the pegs. I thought of those horses and wondered what I was walking into.

It appeared to be an empty room. The only light came from a lamp over a table in the far back corner. All the other tables were empty, and there was no one behind the bar. The normal smells of sweat, ale and desperation had faded to a rancid background odor.

A tired-looking woman with frizzy hair approached me out of the shadows. She wore clothes more appropriate to a younger, fuller figure. She said, "Hello, stranger. You're traveling late. Buy a girl a drink?"

"I'm more interested in a deck of cards," I said.

She gestured toward the back of the room. "That's the only game in town right now, handsome." She slid her hand inside my jacket and pressed it against my chest. "Unless you count the games where everybody wins."

I pulled her hand away and pressed another of Jane's coins in it. "I'm a sore loser at those kind of games. Nothing personal."

She scowled, torn between the money and my disregard for her ragged feminine charms. The money won, and she faded away into the darkness.

I approached the sole illuminated table. There was Miles Argo, all right. Experience had taught him to sit in the corner so no one could slip up behind him. That didn't matter in his case, though: the threat was all in front of him, in the form of a deck of cards so cold they might as well have had icicles. The tiny pile of chips in front of him, and the much larger pile before his opponent, told the story.

Finger Stakes

Miles Argo had once been a good-looking guy. Now he was skinny, balding and middle-aged, with trembling hands and dark circles under his eyes. The other player at the table, a corpulent woman in expensive clothes, daintily sipped her drink and slid some chips to the center of the table. There was no way Miles could call the bet, so that should've been that. But guys like Miles didn't become guys like Miles by knowing when to quit.

He placed his cards face-down on the table and said, "I can't believe I have to fold with a hand like this." He turned to a well-dressed man with a blank face leaning against the wall. He was clearly the boss, and I wondered why he put up with this.

"You know my credit's good, Walter," Miles said, sounding like a teenage boy pleading with his father. "Get me through this hand? My luck's turned, I swear it."

"You credit's shit," Walter said calmly. "And so is your luck."

"Please, gentlemen, language," Miles' opponent said archly. Her type was easy to classify: slumming minor royalty from one of the bordering kingdoms. Part of the fun was reminding the rabble that her gold made her better than them and that she deserved their deference.

I looked around again. Where *were* the people belonging to all those horses? Sure, some would prefer drink and/or whores, but there had to be a few who wanted to gamble away what little money they had. I peered into the shadowy corners, but they were empty, and there were no secondary rooms for private games.

"So I have to fold," Miles said, and shook his head. "And me with a hand like this."

I tossed enough to cover the bet onto the table. It was Jane's money, anyway; it seemed appropriate. The jingle got everyone's attention, especially Miles'.

"Eddie LaCrosse," he said when he recognized me. "What a surprise. What brings you to Four Chops?" He sounded sick to his stomach.

"You do. Finish this hand, then you're leaving."

Miles swallowed hard, glanced at Walter, then said, "It's, uh ... not that easy."

He tilted back his chair and raised one ankle. A manacle and chain were around it. "I'm pretty far in the hole. They let me keep playing, though."

I looked at Walter. "You have the key to that?"

Walter gave me no visible respect. "Yeah."

"So how far down is he?"

Walter told me.

I said, "Come on, he'll never play his way out of that. You're just keeping him around for giggles."

Walter's eyes narrowed. "I don't giggle about money, friend. And I don't recall anyone saying this was any of your business."

There was no way I could pay off his debt, and I wouldn't even if I had the scratch to do it. Yet Jane had paid me to bring him back. I didn't expect to find him literally chained to his bad habits, though.

My options were limited. I could simply kill everyone except Miles, but that seemed an over-reaction, not to mention difficult to do without a sword. So instead, I said, "All right, then. I'll play you for him."

Walter turned his head to look at me. The motion was stiff and mechanical, as if few things ever roused his interest. "What?"

"One hand. If I win, he leaves and makes good on his debt when he can. If you win, he stays."

"He's already staying," Walter pointed out.

"But he's also losing. That doesn't put any gold in your strong box, does it?"

"You're mace-addled," Walter said.

A hidden door opened in the wall beside the table, and in an instant I understood everything. Through the opening I saw a well-lit counting room, the light glittering off neat stacks of coins. Two men bent over vellum scrolls as they noted amounts with long, ragged quills. Three additional men, tall and professionally grim, stood guard. Something similar was probably going on in the other establishments as well: scribes and accountants taking stock of profits, while armed guards both protected them and kept them honest. That explained all the horses.

Finger Stakes

But it was the man who opened the door who held my attention. Chills ran up my neck. I knew him and, unfortunately, he knew me.

"No, Walter, I think that's an excellent idea," Gordon Marantz said.

Marantz was immaculate in a tailor-made tunic and trousers, and boots so expensive they wouldn't dare scuff. His hair was combed back from his face. He looked vaguely amused, as he tended to whenever he wasn't actually killing someone. It figured Miles would pick Marantz's collection night to end up short.

Marantz smiled at me. I felt like a rabbit looking at a wolf. He said, "If it isn't Eddie LaCrosse, Neceda's favorite sword jockey. This is unexpected."

"Oh, isn't it," I said flatly.

He came around the table toward me, and it took all my self-control not to back away. He nudged the rich woman opposite Miles. "Get up, Mrs. Farnsworth. This night just got a lot more interesting." As Mrs. Farnsworth quickly gathered her winnings Marantz said to me, "I think it's only fair that you and I play this hand."

"Why doesn't that surprise me?" I said.

Confused, Miles looked from Marantz to me and back.

Marantz laughed again. "Come on, Eddie, if I wanted you dead, you'd be tasting sword metal right now. So would your red-haired girlfriend. You have to know that."

I knew it, although the threat to Liz was new. Marantz must really dislike me. "Do you want me to say thanks?"

"Not at all. I like knowing you're always looking over your shoulder." He sat, picked up the deck of cards and rippled them between his hands. "Here's the game, though. We're playing for finger stakes."

"Finger stakes?" I asked.

He nodded at Miles. "His."

Miles sat up straight. "Now, wait a minute."

"Shut up," Marantz and I said in unison.

Miles' voice grew high and desperate. "Like hell I will, you can't just treat me like I'm not here—"

Marantz continued as if Miles hadn't spoken. "Best of five hands, which means you have to win three, Eddie. If you do, I'll cancel his debt and let you take him home. But for each hand you lose, he loses a finger."

Miles looked as if he might be ill. "Mr. Marantz, Eddie, please, I can get myself out of this."

"No, you can't, Miles," I said, but my gaze stayed locked on Marantz. To the gangster I said, "You're doing this for fun, aren't you?"

He shrugged. "Like you said before: giggles. He's a bum, and I'm tired of messing with him. You, though ... I'm looking forward to messing with you."

"Let's play for *my* fingers, then."

Marantz shook his head. "No, Eddie. I understand how you think. You're tough: if I chop off a few of your fingers, you'll just figure out a way to swing a sword with your toes. But you'll hear the knife cut through *his* skin and bones in your dreams for the rest of your life."

I really didn't like the idea that Gordon Marantz knew me so well. But I also saw no other choice. "All right," I said. "Best of five. But I want some changes first. Let's have a new deck." I kicked two chairs away from a nearby empty table, picked it up and inspected the bottom for anything untoward. "And a new table. This one will do."

"Hey," Walter said, "I could take that personally."

"Good," I said.

A flunky appeared and lit the lamp over our new table, directly beside the current one. The front door opened and a half-dozen of Marantz's men entered. They froze and fell silent when they saw their boss. He gestured for them to stay where they were.

When we stood behind our new respective chairs I said, "Miles comes, too."

Marantz's eyes narrowed. "Why?"

"He deals."

"I don't think he's objective enough."

"That breaks my heart. He deals, or I walk."

"That's sort of an empty threat, Eddie."

Finger Stakes

I shrugged. "Maybe. Call my bluff, then."

Marantz's face gave nothing away as he pondered. He might know things about me, but that went both ways. I knew his vanity was as wide as the Gusay River, and now that he had a crowd of his own people watching, he wouldn't want to deprive them of a show.

At last he shrugged. "Sure. Why not? Walter, unlock the ferret and bring him over."

Suddenly Miles was beside me, his hand on my arm. "Eddie, we have to get out of here. There aren't that many, you can take them—"

"You have a gag handy, Walter?" I said.

"I do," Walter agreed.

"All right, all right," Miles said, raising his hands in defeat. He pulled out his chair and dropped heavily into it. "Let's get this over with, all right?"

Marantz sat at the new table, put his hands flat on it and said, "Walter, get us that new deck our friend asked for. And bring me a drink." He looked a question at me, but I shook my head. He laughed. "Mr. LaCrosse doesn't trust us to give him unpoisoned ale."

I took my seat. "Mr. LaCrosse doesn't trust you to give him unpoisoned *air*." I glanced over at Miles, which was a mistake. I did not need to see the fear in his eyes.

Walter brought Marantz a drink and a fresh deck of cards. He gave them to me to shuffle, which I did. Then I handed them to Miles. He dropped the deck twice, scattering the cards on the floor the second time. As he picked them up, I tried to calm the pounding in my chest. I was only partially successful.

At last Miles got the cards under control and dealt them carefully, practically handing them directly to us. I felt his sweat on them when I arranged them in my hand. Marantz was as cool as a mountaintop in winter.

I won the first two hands. Possibly Marantz threw them, just to get to the good stuff. The next hand would either send Miles home intact, or start him down the road to wearing only shoes he didn't have to tie.

Miles knew it, too. He was breathing so loudly I could hear it. He practically had to shake the cards free of his trembling, clenched fingers.

I looked at my cards. Marantz looked at his, then at me. We were both professionals at keeping things off our faces, so there were no tells to spot. It was a matter of smarts and nerve.

"Do you think," Marantz mused, "he'll wet his pants when we take his thumb?"

"You're starting with his pinky," I said.

"I don't recall agreeing to that."

"If you want your fun, you will."

"It's purely a business decision. He loses his thumb, he won't be able to deal cards any more. Considering what a bad investment he is, I'd be foolish not to do it."

"Hey," Miles said, "I'm sitting right here, you know."

"Shut up," Marantz and I again said in unison.

"Or," Marantz continued, "I could take his nose-picker first. You pick your nose a lot, Miles?"

Before Miles could answer I said, "You're taking his pinky first. End of negotiation."

Marantz leaned over the table toward me. His smile disappeared, and his voice dropped to a whisper meant only for me. "You need to think this tough-guy thing through, Eddie. You're sitting in one of *my* establishments, a long way from home, surrounded by folks a whole lot more scared of me than they are of you."

"I'm scared of you, too," I said simply. It was the truth.

This took him by surprise, although he hid it so well I'm not sure anyone else saw it. In our previous encounter, I'd bluffed him into doing what I wanted by appealing to his honor, which at the time had amused him no end. Perhaps he thought it gave me an inflated sense of my own invulnerability, and he anticipated the fun of correcting that in front of his people. Now I'd just taken that away from him.

"I've got a question for you, Eddie," Marantz said. "Why are you doing this? For him?" He nodded at Miles. "You have to know he's a turd. Really. Look at him. He'd sell you out in a minute if it got him off the hook. So what's in it for you?"

Finger Stakes

"Twenty-five gold pieces a day, plus expenses."

"That's all you're worth?"

I smiled. Marantz didn't understand as much as he thought. He'd never comprehend why naming your own price was important. "That's *what* I'm worth."

He chuckled and shook his head. "You always surprise me, Eddie. Do you want any more cards?"

I looked at my cards a final time and shook my head.

"Then show me what you got." He tossed his own cards to the table.

◇

"It hurts," Miles whimpered.

"Oh, shut up," I said. "It's just a damn pinky. You'll be lucky when you get home if Jane lets you keep both your balls."

We were halfway back to Neceda, and the sky in the east was now gray with impending dawn. Birds tittered in the trees around us. The road was deserted, but the closer we got to town, the busier it would become, as farmers and tradesmen started their long days. I led Miles' horse beside my own, while he wobbled in his saddle and cradled his bandaged right hand against his chest. The white cloth was thoroughly soaked with blood.

"You threw that hand on purpose!" he wailed.

I snapped, "Hey, jackass, I *rescued* you, remember?" But I wasn't entirely sure he was wrong.

I'd had a decent hand back at the Diamond Hole, but could've discarded and made it better without losing anything. Maybe secretly I *did* want Miles to suffer for everything he'd put Jane through over the years. I'd stood shoulder-to-shoulder with her in battle, something I knew Miles had never done. Or ever would do. She deserved better than this wheedling little toad.

"It hurts," he said again, drawing out the last word.

I was sure it did. But not, I suspected, enough.

Saturday's Children

Jesse Bullington

There's this moment before they show up where all the church talk and ghost stories seem a sight realer than usual, when the traffic outside and the rats in the walls go quiet, when anything seems possible…and then it is. I seen him settle onto her, saw it in the way her shoulders relaxed, all her fear pushed out or down or wherever she goes when one of them gets on board. I backed away from her…no, from *him*, careful not to smudge the symbol on the floor…it looked like he was already here so maybe it wouldn't matter but the first thing she taught me was never ever screw up one of their whatchamacallits, those symbols, because that was what they needed to find their way here…into the real world.

Eyes still closed, he reached across the desk and plucked up the tinted glasses, planting them on what was now his face. He smiled, her teeth looking sharper, her lips redder, and behind those specs I saw him open his eyes. I tried to think about all those poor kids, how we had to do this, but when I seen the recognition blaze up in those shaded eyes I couldn't help thinking my number might've finally come up.

◇

July of '42 was what the wisenheimers fanning themselves with reubens at Ernie's counter called a Scorcher, and what the toughs who hung around the Carousel called One Hot Sunuvabitch. Those hoitie-toities at Elmo and the Stork probably had all kinds of other names for it, but I thought One Scorching Sunuvabitch summed it up pretty okay. Not as bad as the summer of '40, but what was? The summer of '39...lame punchline, but if you were living in the city those years you knew it weren't no laughing matter.

Kind of weather made me happy to keep the hours I did...and hoods or not, the clubs like the Carousel made a decent office when I wasn't hanging around the Shack with the boys...except for the weekends, when the clubs get too loud to hear my police ban. But on a Tuesday night, say, I wouldn't trade Sammy's or the Carousel for anything on Fifth Avenue, no thanks...even with the hoods. Kids...same kind of riff-raff thought they were bad news for going up to Connie's back in the day...not for the music, like me, but to be bigshots braving Harlem after dark...never mind blacks weren't even allowed in, unless they were on stage...and they didn't call them blacks then, neither.

Anyway, I'd left Sammy's at nine trying to get some butter to go with the bread I'd shot that evening...I hadn't put together a *PM* piece in a while, but I knew the *Post* was paying better for Fire pics at the moment, and I could always mail them non-exclusive to *Life* afterward. It was only midnight-ish and I was hoping for a Murder before the presses ran, and with this weather somebody was bound to pop...and probably pop somebody else in the result. I'd got a nibble and quit Sammy's, but after scooting all the way up the island it turned out to just be a bindlestiff croaked from the heat, and to top it all they'd already carted him...so I camped at the Carousel and waited for my luck to change or the clock dial to push me down to the *Post* with just the Fire pics.

"Got a misper at 23 Mount Morris West, corner of 122nd," the ban crackled and I froze, halfway up to get another rickey…I've got a radio in the car but came into an extra and fixed it up so it could go where my jalopy couldn't, say inside a club…but anyway, the call.

A misper wouldn't mean nothing to me most nights…think about it, if a person's missing what's there to shoot? But this was the third night in a row I'd heard a misper come over the line, and it wasn't too far to Garvey Park and so next thing I knew I was evened up and out the door, sweating like you wouldn't believe. Something sour was in my belly, twisting all around, but I figured it must've just been the egg in my last rickey being a little off from the heat.

Twenty-three Morris was a big ugly tenement, but at least it had a view of the park. More than a few bodies were laid out there in the shadows, and I thought of all the nights I spent there myself before things came together…not in Marcus Garvey, I wasn't crazy, but down in Bryant, lucky if I had an old newspaper for a pillow. Dark days, and if I'd set up the Invisible Light ahead of time I would have nabbed a few of the park sleepers, but I don't want to bust up nobody's dreams with my flash bulbs…if you're sleeping in the park, dreams is about all you've got.

I beat the officers there, but that wasn't too queer…a misper isn't going nowhere, and it was Harlem to boot, so it's a wonder they showed up fast as they did. I took some snaps of the mother while I waited, and she was a real mess, wailing and hair-pulling, the whole bit…got some good ones, but didn't press my luck…a lot of neighbors out in the street with her, and I'm not some clod…I got respect for people's feelings, and the shots I had of her crying kicked me just like they always do. The fire escapes were crowded with folks, some of them shouting at her to shut up, others shouting at the shouters for *them* to shut up.

"Whattya know, Fellig," I heard behind me, and that queasy kind of feeling in my gut got worse…I knew the voice, and Detective Harris wouldn't be out there at one in the morning on a Tuesday for no simple missing person.

Saturday's Children

"This might be a shocker, but word on the street says it's One Hot Sunuvabitch," I told Harris, turning around to get a look at him. He didn't look good, suit not rumpled enough, eyes not red enough...I wondered if he was waiting for this, or something like it. We didn't shake. We don't shake, Harris and me...I don't think he takes cream, he just rub me wrong.

"Don't go nowhere," Harris said, blowing smoke in my eye as he dropped his butt. "We're gonna have a chat, Fellig."

"Sure," I said. "Sure thing."

I overheard what I could and when they moved inside I went to my car and started developing the sobbing mother pictures in my trunk. It's a decent set-up, and since I strapped things down real good I haven't spilled nothing. After backing it up out of the streetlight I didn't even have to bag the film. I was finishing up when Harris came over, and screwing the last lid on I tried to close the trunk before he saw the 8x10s sitting in my dark-boot, as the boys call it. Don't know why I got spooked about him seeing the glossies, I mean, I'm the only guy they let keep a police ban in his car so it's not a secret what I'm doing at the scenes.

"Whattya got here, Fellig?" said Harris, catching the trunk and flicking it back up. "The Negress in Despair?"

See, that's what I mean about Harris...I wouldn't give him a glass of water in a desert. He snatched out the pictures but I didn't say nothing until he started folding them up.

"What gives, Harris, those—"

"Open investigation," said Harris, as if that changed things. "No pictures and no running that kraut mouth of yours 'til you hear from me personally, got it?"

Austrians ain't krauts, but try telling that to a bigot, especially with the war and all, so I oughta just take it and nod, sure, okay, officer, but instead I hear myself saying, "I ever call you schweinehund, detective? I ever run my mouth about me and my buddies at *PM* invading Greenpoint?"

"I am goddamn serious, *Weegee*," he says, like it's some kind of insult or something instead of what every other badge in the city calls me. "You sell a picture like that, you gotta tell them what's going on with it, and they run it with a caption, and next thing I know there's a goddamn panic down here in the jungle. Stay outta this."

"I didn't see you last night," I say, putting a few chips down as he turns to head back to the station...and he folds without even looking for a tell or glancing at his hand.

"I don't come up here every time a pickaninny runs off," he says with that trademark compassion of his. "And remember, it's for their good nobody makes a scene out of this."

Looking past him where all the neighbors were finally going back to the mattresses they dragged out onto the fire-escapes and rooftops and, for those unlucky saps without either, their broiling little rooms, I just shook my head...the scene already happened, and as for word getting around, well, it'll do just that fine without me. I wished I'd paid attention to where the last two nights' mispers were, but from what I overheard Harlem's already had a few, and recent. Kids, too, little kids, trying to cool off by sleeping outside on the roofs or escapes...I used to worry sometimes, shooting them up there, about some baby rolling off or something, but it looks like there's something worse going on than freak accidents. Kids are going missing, and in this town that means somebody... or something...is taking them.

◇

"Hey Weegee-man," says Kameela when I walk into her place, and I give her a big old wink for her trouble.

"What's the rumpus, Ms. Simons?" I say back, knowing full well she was in nappies when that turn of phrase was anything near to hip.

"She's waitin' for you," says Kameela, and I get the little twinge I always get when she looks at me like that. Girl is a solid bombshell, no doubt...drop her on the Hun and they'd be pledging allegiance in nothing flat. Hair like cotton candy under the pier at midnight, skin like the kind of cocoa you only find in the real deal Austrian dives, little Alm huts for us poor damned refugees stuck in Alphabet City or Yorkville. It's not the first time I think about kissing her like a sailor home from the Pacific, and it's not the first time she laughs like she knew what I was thinking... that girl...

"Come on in, Arthur," says her mother, and I'm probably blushing. "Kameela, you leave him alone."

"You don't gotta leave me alone," I stage-whisper to her but she just rolls her eyes, done with me the minute her mom opened the office door.

I leave behind the posterboard saints and symbols, the incense and rosaries, and go into the back office. You walk in the front door of the Lenox apartment Claire Simons shares with her daughter and it's all hocus pocus, Houdini-land, but that plain rear room is where the real weird goes down.

Nice mahogany desk, poster behind it of Frankie like you were in a bobby-soxer's bedroom, and *her*, but she makes all the difference. Mrs. Simons got the looks of her daughter, only aged real nice, and with that, I don't know, seasoning comes something else, something intense...she's a little big, but not as big as I'll be when I'm her age, God willing. We kissed once, way back when, and it was one of the greats, you know? I've had girlfriends for years on end that didn't make the impression that one kiss did...and even realizing after the fact she weren't herself when it happened didn't sour the memory...not too much, anyway.

"Good to see you, Arthur," she said.

"You too," I said, sitting my big butt down and trying not to stare at her fireplug lips. I can't look at that woman without... jeez, I sound like some kind of pervert, but really it's just...if you ain't met her there's no point...good looking as Kameela is, she's Eleanor Roosevelt compared to her mom, and run that on the front page, it's gold. "You too."

"You were there last night," she said like it was no big deal, her knowing where I was at one o'clock in the morning on a Tuesday in all of Manhattan. "At Garvey Park, where that little boy got nabbed."

"Yep," I said, wriggling a little. "You got your ghosts on the case?"

I always feel like a twerp, saying stuff like that, but no matter how hard I try it always comes out wrong when I try to talk about her...Stuff.

"Mr. Himes isn't a ghost, he's a slumlord," said Mrs. Simons, smiling like she always does around the time I'm feeling like a capital jackass. "He come by earlier, told me all about it. Said he saw the great man himself taking pictures, but I didn't see nothing but the arson in the *Post*."

"Goddamn *Post*," I say, like it's their fault Harris smothered my scoop. I shift a little in my seat and repeat what I eavesdropped the mother saying to Harris, what we both know she already knows: "Little boy went missing from a third storey fire escape. Sleeping 'tween his mom and sister and whammo, gone."

"Not the only one," said Mrs. Simons and I just nod, wondering like I always do if I'd even be here if I hadn't taken that shot of the weeping mother...the Negress in Despair, how Harris pegged it. The horse's ass. But Mrs. Simons isn't done yet. "But you wouldn't be here if it was just one, would you, Arthur?"

"You wanna grab a drink tonight?" I say, cutting to the chase and giving myself a cheap little kick at the same time...thinking how nice it would be if I was saying this without some kid gone missing, some *gaggle* of kinder snatched by who knows what creeper...and me thinking the same kind of thoughts about her daughter...I'm a dog, no doubt.

"Sure, Arthur, sure," she says, but she ain't smiling. She knows way more than me but I know not to push, not yet...she needs my police ban and I need her if I'm gonna get a decent night's sleep...I get up to boogie but she queers me by saying something else, makes me go all cold...we both know she don't need to tell me to leave the camera at the apartment, that if I want to be in any shape to chase my bread and butter I better not mix business with...This. No, it's the other part that puts the chill on me, something she never asked before in a friendship full of the kind of requests that'd get you fitted for a nice new jacket at Bellvue Hospital, you weren't asking someone who knew you real well... and trusted you not to be a damn loon no matter what calls you made over the pond at midnight: "Leave that camera at home, Arthur, but see if you can't scare up a piece. See if you can't get iron slugs, too."

My apartment is above a gunshop and I got fifteen bucks in my pocket, so it ain't nervousness about finding a piece that's got me sweating as I step back onto Lenox, wondering how a nice Austrian boy like me got himself mixed up in all this voodoo.

◇

I met Mrs. Simons down at Coney Island, way back. I'd just got a new lens and wanted something special, something permanent, so I went over to the row where all the sailors got their ink done, and the first parlor I poked my nose in had this beautiful colored girl getting done up...she had her shirt pulled up over her head and was lying on her stomach, staring out past the tarp the artiste had instead of a door. She stopped my heart, and when I saw the size of the piece the bearded wonder was doing on her back I knew I had to get a shot...it was big, with a crazy kind of cross in the center and some weird square-ish shapes floating over toward her ribs, and I could see the bulge of her breasts crushing down into the table...love at first sight? Forget about it.

The thing is, I knew the girl...the guy tattooing her was talking at me but I was just staring, trying to figure out where I'd seen her...she was looking right past me, out the gap in the tarp where I'd come in, wearing a spooky kind of smile, a cigar burning down in an ashtray set on the table next to her face. She didn't even seem to mind the needle scarring up her back, let alone the smoke coiling round her face like a wispy snake... anyway, I'm ignoring the guy inking her 'cause it comes to me where I seen her, and I'm so excited I'm about to flip.

"Claire Simons!" I say, having heard her a week before at the Cotton Club, and a month before that at Connie's. Most of the crowds didn't like her but I took that to be on account of her being local, and leave it to some fool-headed Society clowns and cheap hoods to dismiss talent on principle if it happened to be from the island...everyone's a critic. "Ma'am, I just love your voice!"

"What?" she growled at me, and I realized I must have made a big faux pas in calling her ma'am...I thought that was how you talked to older black folks but I should have known, I thought, no lady...black, white, whatever...likes being called old by some schlub barging in on her getting tattooed.

"Sorry, Mrs. Simons," I said, holding my camera between me and the glare she was throwing my way...Jeez Louise, I thought, here she is with her shirt over her head and you're calling her ma'am and just acting like your shaking her hand after a gig. I started backing out but not quick enough, the bearded tattoo man shouting now but not stopping with his work...A real class act, a consummate professional.

"Get the fuck outta here, Usher fucking Fellig," said Mrs. Simons, snatching up her cigar and flicking it at me. "Get now, motherfucker!"

"I'm sorry," I said, stumbling backward into the tarp, the murder in her eye nothing I wanted no part of. "I'm so sorry, Mrs.—"

"Shut the fuck up!" She roared, rearing up. The tattoo guy fell back but bless his dedication, held onto his needle.

"Damn!" I said, getting caught up in the tarp. "Mrs. Simons, I'm sorr—"

"Fuck!" came like a bus tire blowing out, and I brought the tarp down on top of me...next thing I know it's getting pulled off and Mrs. Simons is dragging me down the boardwalk with one hand while she's pulling her shirt back on with the other, all the time saying stuff that'd make a marine blush. Finally she remembered I was there and turned my way. "What's your name?"

"Arthur," I said, more than a little scared...the only thing worse than her knowing my birth name back there was how different she looked now, beat down and sweaty like a hansom horse at the tail end of tourist season, and not knowing my name any better than she should have in the first place. I got the goose-in-the-graveyard chills like never before...though I've had them since. "Arthur Fellig."

Saturday's Children

"Well, Arthur, that's one I owe you," she said, her voice nowhere near so deep as it had been. Touching her back with a wince, she screwed up her face and with a tone to make me feel like she'd actually walked in on me and her old lady, added, "Mother*fucker*."

I didn't hear her curse much after that, except when she was being ridden, and even then there wasn't so much of it. She said Saturday was the worst of all, and no way was she letting him back on her back after the stunt he pulled. Ghost or demon or whatever he is, that Baron Saturday has some serious sand to try Mrs. Simons, I tell you what.

◊

Rolling up Lenox that night, I felt about as comfortable as sand in your socks. I didn't have my Speed Graphic, which put me off, and I *did* have a .38, which put me even further off...I hadn't got iron bullets for it because they didn't make no iron bullets for it, and wasn't I a cowboy for thinking they did? What put me off most of all was I'd had to leave the SG as collateral with Jovino, who runs the gunshop under my apartment. He just laughed when I told him I needed a piece and had fifteen bucks on it, and that's me out of my baby, at least for the night...but who am I fooling, that wasn't what put me off most of all. What done that was knowing a bunch of kids were missing and it was up to me and Mrs. Simons to sort it all out.

Kameela was just leaving as I pulled up but she was with a couple of girlfriends and didn't stop to chat, just waved and hoofed it down the sidewalk. Going was about as nice as coming with Kameela Simons, and watching her melt down Lenox I thought of my buddy Pat over at the *Gazette*, does Cheese Cakes...he could do her justice, but no way I could...even if I had my Speed Graphic with me instead of that damn piece weighing down my pocket like a bottle of cheap hooch, kind of weight to your jacket that lets you know life ain't going the right direction at present.

The house was dark but I let myself in, locking up behind me. When the lock clicked Claire's door opened in the back, giving me some light. I picked my way through Kameela's office with all its Conjure Woman props…the candles out, the cards stowed, the table with my namesake board on it pushed to the side so I don't bang my shin on it like usual…nice of her to clean up for me.

"Shut the door, Arthur," Mrs. Simons told me. I just stared at her like some bumpkin getting his first look at the city. It weren't what she wore so much as who was going to be wearing her, something I could tell at a glance…it wasn't the suit she got on, that could be for any one of them, it was the stovepipe hat on the table, and the tinted glasses like the lifeguards wear down at Coney.

"That's, uh, he, uh," I stammered…she had warned me if I ever seen her in specs like that to book it away from her, and if the hat was on to book it double-time…bitter as he likely is on her, he's got even more cause to do me some mischief.

"It's got to be him," she said, and didn't look any happier than I was about the prospect. "I've had a busy day, Arthur."

Her desk was moved against the wall so it was only me and her and Frankie on the wall, and as I set my radio on the table she took a mixing bowl and started laying the powder on the floor. I'd seen her use cornmeal and ash before, sawdust, gunpowder, you name it, but this was something else entirely…this was dirt, and from what she'd told me before about this joker I can imagine what kind. Between the gear on the table and now her getting started before we'd even overheard anything on the ban I was getting real nervous and said, "Don't you want to wait? We don't know if another one's going down tonight."

"We know it's not, because we're gonna stop it," she said, and I got the shakes something fierce to see that I was right and the damn thing she was drawing up on the floor matched what was half-finished on her back. "I had a busy day, Arthur, and there's no question what we need. Who we need."

"Right," I said. "Sure, Claire, no question. I'll just be out in my heap you need me. Why the heck you didn't just have Kameela stick around and—"

"She does *not* need to get mixed up with him," she looked up at me and I wish she hadn't, the fierce on that pretty face like nothing you'd ever want mixed up, like a good cup of creamed coffee got old sausage grease poured all in it. "You get the babash out of the top drawer and pour us out some while I explain, alright?"

I did as she told me, the rum smelling just as hot and mean as I remembered. Pouring out two fingers into the glasses she kept in the drawer, I tried to keep my stomach from getting angrier about what I was about to dump into it...I couldn't blame it for being cross, considering.

"So what's the story, then?" I said, seeing she'd stopped over the almost finished symbol drawn in gravedirt on the floor. Considering she hadn't called him down in the ten-plus since we'd met at Coney, I couldn't blame her...this whole night was bad news as my belly... normally we'd be halfway to a scene, and with any luck we'd beat the cops and she'd scope it, get her info, and *then* we'd be back here so she could get rode and get the answers. Next I'd drop the anonymous tip off at the station...so-and-so's been bumping hobos for kicks, or that nogoodnick's been shaking down old ladies for their pennies is holed up at this address...and then we'd be done until the next time she let me know she'd need my police ban or I let her know the island might benefit from a spot of her charity.

"Seventh sons," she said, shaking her head and finishing the diagram. Coming on over, she took her glass and had a little sip, crossing herself and scowling as she put it back down. "Six of them in as many nights. I only got to the three families up here, but I gather the rest came from the Kitchen."

"Yeah, well, leave it to the Irish to have seven sons," I said, but seeing her expression I took a sip of that evil drink by way of penance.

"Seventh sons of seventh sons," she said, and I caught the nervousness in her voice. "I knew, Arthur, soon as Mr. Himes came by, I just *knew*. Saturday's boys, each and every one. It's got to be him. He'll know, and know what to do. If he doesn't, nothing will."

"Right," I said, "so he comes, I ask him who's been doing it, where they are, yadda yadda yadda."

"That's it." She nodded. "But I expect he'll have other business with us. If he comes at you, or tries to make me leave, to finish what he started, you've got to push him off me."

"Yeah," I said, taking another sip and almost yakking on it. "Yeah, easy, I'll push him off you."

"You can do this, Arthur," she told me, laying her steady hand on my shaking one. "He comes at you, you just do what you did last time. Say my name three times, and if that doesn't work—"

"Doesn't work!"

"If that doesn't work, you shoot me with that iron I told you to—"

"Jesus, I'm not gonna do that! Jesus!" I pulled my hand away from hers...never thought I'd do that.

"Not in the face, dummy" she said, frustrated. "Just my foot or something, it'll knock him loose like nothing. But just saying my name ought to work."

"Jesus!" It felt good, so I said it again. "Jesus!"

"Not tonight, Arthur," she smiled at me. "Not even close."

◇

"Usher!" he said, smiling with her pretty teeth, snapping her pretty fingers at me. "You meddling motherfucker!"

"Hey," I said, suddenly wanting another sip of that babash but not willing to take my eyes off him. I had the gun out. "How, uh, how, uh..."

"How I been?" Baron Saturday took his top hat from the table and put it on, the glasses and now the hat covering up whatever bits of Mrs. Simons remained after he got on her...or in her, I guess was how it really was, but she always talked about it like he was riding her, and I guess it was less disturbing to think of him being *on* instead of *in*. A little less, anyway. "Just fucking fine, Usher, just fucking dandy, sitting fucking pretty while some piece of whoreshit motherfucker kills my boys, and all on account of you, *motherfucker!*"

He was madder than I'd thought, and I pointed the .38 at him. "I got iron here, Saturday, and I'll say her name before you—"

The gun was flying across the room, the hand that had held it numb, and her fingers were tight around my neck, the floor slapping me on the back like a doctor whopping a newborn, and he was all kinds of on top of me. He was still smiling, which only made it worse...I'd screwed the pooch, *bad*, and then, as sudden as he had me, he hopped up and grabbed the rum.

"That's a lesson taught, Usher," he said, guzzling from the bottle as I tried to catch the breath he'd knocked out. By the time I could even think about saying her name three times or going for the gun he had drained half the bottle. Then he reached down into my suit and plucked out one of my cigars, and as I staggered up to my knees he snapped her fingers again and the end of the cigar lit up like a headlight. "Iron my ass, you bullshitting meddler. I could've killed you there, and be wearing Claire forever-like by cockcrow. That's one you owe me, plus the one from before makes two."

"Two?" I was gasping for air, and had a lump rising on my scalp. "What I—"

"One for knockin' me off her back in the day, and one for not killing you tonight, you stupidass motherfucker," said Baron Saturday, blowing a plume of smoke in my face. "You're gonna get right with me, boy, startin' now. Get to drawing a circle over there in the corner, but fuck with my veve and see what happens."

I thought about kicking the gravedirt symbol anyway, maybe making a break for the gun, but instead I just stepped around the cross-and-floating-coffins design on the floor while he dug in the desk drawers. Before I could start asking about circles he'd pulled out a piece of chalk and threw the white nub my way, pegging me in the forehead with it...I'd met some of the others before and always gotten along okay with them, I guess, but this guy... no class. I did what he said anyway, though it took a while to get the diagram he wanted drawn just right. Looking down at it, I seen it was one of them star shaped things but he just laughed when I tried to explain I didn't go in for the hoodoo stuff myself.

"Tell me another one, Usher boy, tell me a-fuckin-nother one. Now here," he said, passing me a piece of paper with some crazy nonsense words scribbled on it that he'd banged out while I was drawing up his circle. Wagging the bottle at me, he said, "Lemme finish this jankro batty and we'll catch up with the motherfucker what's been killing my boys."

"Killing?" What he'd said before finally sank in. "The kids—"

"Dead, motherfucker," Saturday leered at me but there was no humor in the smoke-leaking smile he pointed at me like an ivory knife. "Every one of them boys is dead, thanks to you and fuckin' Claire. Why you think I was tryin' to get a decent saddle on her? What kind of asshole you take me for? I was tryin' to stop all this, so I could come in when my boys needed me, but you fucking kids cut me out, didn't you? Didn't you!"

I allowed that maybe we did, which is the only way you can deal with folks like Saturday.

"You meddling motherfucker," Saturday shook his head, and under the wrath in those eyes I actually felt bad for waking Mrs. Simons up when she was getting tattooed. "So much goddamn blood on your hands. We'll get square fore it's all done, Usher motherfucking Fellig, yes we will, but first you stop this bullshit never should've started in the first place. Now get to summonin' the demon, dumbass!"

"Demon?" Whatever was going wrong in my guts took another twist in the opposite direction of right. "But you're already here."

Baron Saturday laughed like I'd told him the funniest line in history, like I'd told a joke that would've made God himself slap his knee, and then he became serious as a grieving father facing the man who killed his only child. "Not yet you haven't, motherfucker. Read the words."

◇

I never summoned a demon before, but it weren't as hard as you'd think. I read the words, and next thing I knew there it was, crawling around in the circle looking like that damn Feejee Mermaid that scared the piss out of me when I seen it at Barnum's, a kid fresh off the boat…but that weren't half as scared as I was then, with the real deal giving me the hairy eyeball. Nah, the summoning was easy…what got me about the whole demon thing

Saturday's Children

was when the ugly mug started talking to me, and damned if it didn't have a Teutonic accent to match the one I'd tried so hard to smother as I grew up in the naked city.

"How dare you summon me, Usher Fellig," the demon said, its claws clicking together as it reared up on its snake body. "How dare you interfere—"

"Motherfucker doesn't dare *shit*," said Baron Saturday, pushing past me and stepping into the circle.

The demon fell back, its big old monkey eyes widening with shock, and it scratched at the air at the back of the circle...but it was like there was some wall I couldn't see, and then Baron Saturday snatched it around the skinny neck and started shaking. Its claws came around and scratched his face, Mrs. Simons's blood splashing my wingtips, but before I could run in there to help... and probably mess everything up, looking back on it...Saturday was gone, and the demon with it. All that was left was Claire Simons, looking like something the cat dragged in, if the cat was one mean sunuvabitch. I caught her before she fell over, and before I could try to explain what had happened she upchucked all that rum he'd drank...which kind of summed up the whole experience, if you ask me.

◇

It was a couple of hours later when we called the Baron back. Mrs. Simons made me tie her to her chair before she let him return, on account of the stuff he'd said about getting even with us. Talking it over we figured he wanted to fix whatever demon was killing the kids more than he wanted to fix us, but once he settled that score there wasn't much stopping him coming after us.

"At least we know we've done some good already," she said with a weak smile. "Saturday's got a funny way of looking at death. He wouldn't get involved like this if the kids were just being killed. Something worse must've been happening."

"Worse?" The idea got me all queasy, so I asked, "What does he mean about them being his sons?"

"He's their met tet," she said, like that explained everything... she was still out of sorts. We'd got the cuts on her face iodined and all but she still weren't quite back to looking the belle of the ball. "We've all got one, and he was theirs. Mine too. He's smart, Arthur, they're all smart, in ways we'll never know. Why he thought he'd need to, what'd you say, saddle me, probably means he knows something about me I don't. Or maybe his crazy ass just saw that I'd try to keep him off me when I was older and never thought that might have something to do with him getting me all tattooed like some sideshow attraction, who knows. Important thing is, we'll have our answers when we call him back about who's been doing them kids."

"But he got it," I said. "I seen it, the ugly bastard. He got the demon and—"

"Not that simple," she said, kind of sad about it. "You had to call it up, right? Means someone else did the same, and put it on those kids. We got the knife, now we need the knifeman. Put that hat on me now, Arthur."

◊

It took me a couple of minutes to work up to untying her after he'd left. I guess part of it was my being unsure how it all worked, if he could be tricking me even though she seemed to be talking with her own voice again...but part of it was also me being nervous to talk about what Saturday told me, cause it weren't no good news. When I did untie her I just said the name Saturday had told me, and let that sink in. Instead of getting all gaga like I did, she just cocked her head and said, "Who?"

"Society fatcat," I said, amazed anybody wasn't familiar with him. "Forget fatcat, fat-tiger, fat-lion. He's in all the papers on account of being a horse's ass—I got a picture of him in a carriage with one and the same in the foreground, come to think of it. Anti-Semite, anti-Colored, anti-American piece of shit. Nazi-lover."

"Mind your language," she said idly. "And he's some kind of warlock or something on top of all that?"

"Don't you know? Like, what that, uh, veve and words Saturday had me use to summon it is all about?"

"*That*," she said, pointing at the chalk circle, "is *not* a veve, that's something else—I don't know what, and I don't want to. I think it's how they do it over in Europe, whole different kind of thing. What else did he say about it?"

"He said, the Baron, I mean, he said this bastard was using the kids for some kind of…ritual…killing one of them a night for seven nights, and if we hadn't nabbed the demon what was stealing them boys when we did something real bad would've happened. Not here, but somewhere over in Germany, he wasn't real specific… this Society sorcerer was doing it to help his Nazi buddies, but I didn't really get all of what Saturday was saying. He was spitting mad about being tied up, and on account of the kids that already died—us saving the last, and whatever other good we did by busting up that ritual, apparently don't cool him off much." I shrugged. "No pleasing some people."

"But what's to stop this warlock from just trying again," Mrs. Simons said, sounding about how I felt. "From starting over tomorrow night, or the next?"

"I'm telling you, Claire, we did good," I said. "Seems the way this stuff works, he wouldn't be able to try the ritual again even if he had his pet demon back, which he don't, and he won't, the Baron told me that much. I asked."

"But what you're telling me is the one who did all this, the one who killed those kids, we can't touch him, not with the police and likely not with my ways, neither. What you're saying is those six little boys died, and the one that did it walks. Is that what you're saying?"

I didn't say nothing, like that would help…it didn't. I was mad enough about it I thought about driving over to Long Island that very night and popping him with my .38, but I was too damn tired… and besides, anyone capable of summoning demons and impacting world events with his wicked ways and all was plenty match for some mook who'd never fired a gun in his life.

"Poor little thing," Mrs. Simons looked like she was about to cry. "Poor, poor little thing."

"Them kids? Yeah, I know, it cuts me up, too."

"I was talking about the demon," she said. "But yeah, it isn't the only one. Maybe we should have let Saturday mark me up with that tattoo, maybe he could have stopped this before—"

"Hold your horses, lady!" I couldn't believe what I was hearing. "You calling that ugly demon *poor little thing*? That goddamn *monster* I seen—"

"Was enslaved by some rich motherfucker and forced to steal children, Arthur! I don't know much about that…that *method*, but I do know the loas, demons, or whatever else we call up aren't the kinds of things that are all evil or all good, they're just…they just *are*. And yeah, this *poor thing* got itself bound by someone who *is* pure evil, and got *forced* to do pure evil, and now on top of it all Baron Saturday's caught it and it'll know nothing but agony until the end of time. Those kids it took, you told me Saturday said they'll be at rest now, with the ritual broken, but that…that poor thing won't ever know rest, not even when the last star burns out and everything's dark as the goddamn deep."

We sat for a while in silence, both of us staring at the smudged up symbols on the floor, the gravedirt and the chalk, and then she walked me to the door.

"He say anything else, Arthur?" Mrs. Simons asked me on the stoop, looking more than tired, more than upset…she looked scared. "Anything else at all?"

◊

"Usher Fellig," the Baron had said after giving me the Society sorcerer rundown. "You did good by me, my bitch, and so that's one of the two you owe paid in full."

"Well, y'know—"

"The second I shall collect upon forthwith," said Saturday, and he must've seen something on my face because his eyes narrowed and his lip curled. "What could possibly be bothering you, Mr. Fellig? Is it perhaps the shift in tone I have adopted, now that I am in a calmer place and have need of maximum clarity?"

Saturday's Children

"Well, I—"

"Perhaps it confounds you that I no longer speak like some gin-headed nigger looking to roll your white ass?"

"Hey, now, *Saturday*," I said, done with his malarkey. "I never said such a thing in my life—I don't give a fig if you talk pretty or not, say your bit and amscray."

"Alright, then," said Saturday, and all that confidence I'd had a second before went poof, gone. "Untie me from this chair so that I can finish what I started. This whole mess confirms the utility of having an open stall where Claire is concerned, as you both took your sweet, pardon me, *fucking* time in conjuring me down to assist."

"Not a chance," I said.

"Her or the girl," said the Baron, and he made her smile so wide I worried Mrs. Simons' cheeks would split. "Your choice, Usher motherfucking Fellig, but I *will* have a mare prepared for my convenience. If you do not give me Claire now I shall claim Kameela at a later date, and on that you have my word. I must add that if you insist upon inconveniencing me by way of postponing my establishment of a permanent mount upon this world, I shall, in addition to claiming the daughter instead of the mother, *most assuredly* fuck you up six ways from Saturday. If you catch my drift."

"Drift is right," I said, but my mouth was all clammy and my stomach was right back to where it started. "Six ways from Saturday, real funny. Go on and drift then."

"Not so long ago my mambos and hougans would weep for the honor of bearing my saddle," said Saturday, a whiff of melancholy to his voice. "My own children turn their backs upon me, no longer trusting, no longer—"

"Jeez Louise," I said. "Who wouldn't trust a nice guy like you?"

"Usher mother—"

"Mrs. Claire Simons!" I shouted in his face. "Mrs. Cla—"

"Don't you—"

"—ire Simons! Mrs. Claire—"

"Get you fuckers! *All* of you!"

43

"Simons!" I finished, and she was back, panting in the ropes. I sat and stared and wondered if he was really gone…and what I'd tell her if he was.

◇

"No, Claire," I told her on the stoop. "He didn't say nothing else. You go on and get a good night's sleep."

"You too, Arthur," she said as she closed the door. "You too."

Fat chance. Sitting in my car, I was shaking so bad I dropped my keys, and picking them up I heard footsteps outside my door. For a second I had this panic that it was Detective Harris, that the Society sorcerer had sicced him on me and I was about to roll downtown…or maybe he'd just bump me right there, I'd gets some bullets and he'd get a medal…but no, those were heels clicking on Lenox, and my guts got even worse than if it had been Harris with the pie wagon. I told myself I hadn't had no choice, that Saturday hadn't left me a lot of options, but I still got kind of choked up.

"Hey Weegee-man," Kameela said as I cracked the door to let her holler at me. Her breath could've peeled paint.

"Hey," I said, trying not to imagine her face twisted up with a cigar jammed between her teeth, those hazel eyes hidden behind tinted glasses…I didn't do too good a job of it. "What's the rumpus?"

"Ask you the same," she said. "The stuff you and her get up to…"

"Hey now, hey, jeez," I said, happy to be plain old embarrassed for a second.

"She's gonna start letting me in on it. No more of this cold-reading hocus pocus bullshit," Kameela said with a drunken grin. "Get into the family business for serious."

"Hey, you know, maybe it ain't such a good—" I started but she yawned in my face and rubbed her eyes like some kid busting up her folks' rummy night, and walked away before I even finished.

"Night, Weegee-man. You have a good one, now."

Like I said, fat chance. I watched her fumble with the lock and disappear into the house, no backwards glance…I was glad, I didn't deserve one. Turning the jalopy back to the Lower East Side, I thought it all over…it was the kind of night that belonged in the funny books, and I ain't buying no funny books, even if they are two for a damn nickel…but who am I kidding? I good as got myself a subscription.

The King's Condottiere

Emily Care Boss

Guttering torches sent shadows of the dead chasing over the battlefield. Onorata Rodiana pushed her dark hair out of her eyes. She bent over the images on the courtyard wall, her paint brush flickering in the fire light. Sketches stretched across the plaster. In miniature a gilded horseman spilled off his mount, his spear tearing a hole in another man's stomach. One shadow lingered where others ran. She looked toward its source. "Well, if you're going to watch, you should at least do something helpful. Come here and hold the paint for me would you?"

A tall man with a sword at his side moved away from the gate. She recognized the bleak smile of Micheletto Attendolo, his hand feeling along the scar below his eye. He took the narrow wooden tray and watched as she dipped the fine hairs of the brush into a pool of vermillion.

"Is this the battle of Brescia?" He walked along the line of the wall where reds and golds faded to black, smudged lines of faces and hands.

"It is." Onorata gave him a neutral look. "I feel like there is something not quite right, yet. What do you think?"

"The action is dramatic, the details of the keep excellent, but..." Micheletto trailed off.

A mischievous gleam appeared in her eyes. "Yes, what's wrong here?"

"Wasn't it a siege?"

"Not according to his Grace. Or rather, not as he would have it remembered. The slow starving of a few thousand men and women is not romantic enough for his liking, so instead we get what we have here: a battle of twenty thousand and the Lord personally skewering Niccolò Piccinino."

Micheletto stared at her, mystified, "Piccinino, dead?"

"That's my favorite part. Some poetic license to go with the hubris."

"Well, then you'll thank me for taking you away from this. I've a commission for you and your men. Sforza is calling for reinforcements for his defense of Anghiari, and I'd like you to join me. He's marching from Florence now. My men and I leave tomorrow, and we'd have you follow as soon as possible. We need all we can muster. What's your price?"

She took the paints and moved back to the fresco, completing the running leg of a stallion. "500."

Micheletto asked warily, "Ducats or Florins?"

"Florins, of course."

"500 Florins!?" He swore. "That's twice what I'm paying the others."

She turned to look at him across the battlefield. "You'll get twice the sweat and the blood from mine."

Footsteps echoed, and a young servant ran toward them. Light from the lantern he held revealed his panicked eyes. Storming behind him came the Doge of Venice, Francesco Foscari. In the darkness, light glinted from the labyrinth of gold thread winding across his deep red, velvet mantle. His eyes narrowed with anger as he saw Onorata.

"Rodiana! Why isn't this done?"

Rising from her deep curtsey Onorata addressed the Doge.

"Your Grace, I am working night and day to complete your masterpiece. It is my only wish."

His frown deepened. He walked towards her. "Your contract stipulates that it will be completed by the day my daughter is married. That is one month from now, yet here I see blank spaces, colorless lines." A great emerald glittered on the accusing finger he thrust toward her work. "You're violating your terms!"

Clenching her skirts with paint-stained hands, Onorata said, "I cannot do in six months what was supposed to take a year! My Lord, you must argue with Fate, that brought your beloved daughter's husband back from the wars so soon. Or his passionate heart, which can't wait until the date originally named."

"My Lord!" Micheletto knelt as he addressed Foscari.

Turning toward him, the Doge said, "Rise, address me."

"Your ally the Duke of Florence has begged that Venice come to the aid of the Italian League. The city of Anghiari, three days ride to the south, is threatened by your enemy, the Duke of Milan. We need Rodiana and her men to defend the town."

The Lord whirled around to face Onorata, startling the Page. "You cannot take a commission for battle while working for me. Send your second, Bernardi. That trumped up merchant di Medici won't know the difference and it's no matter to me if Bernardi dies. But if you die in the battle who will finish this fresco?"

Onorata said, "My Lord, your care for my well-being is touching."

"Don't try to humor me, Rodiana." Stepping away from the painting, Foscari straightened his gloves and gestured his servant on ahead of him. "Leave and you'll never get your 100 Florins. You'll stay here and finish this fresco if I have to chain you to the wall." He took their leave and accepted their obeisances, following the bobbing light into the night.

Onorata turned cold eyes to Micheletto. "Bernhard is expendable, is he? His offer, can you add that to my price?"

Shaking his head in disbelief, he traced the path a sword had narrowly taken past his eyes long ago.

"That's my only hope of taking you with us, isn't it?" She nodded.

"I can, but it means your men take the place of others we would have hired."

"So they will." Onorata said.

"What of the Doge's anger?" Micheletto asked.

"I've had a price on my head before and lived to tell the tale." She curtsied to the disappearing light. "My Lord, I take my leave."

◇

The sharp clang of the bells of San Marco rang out over the Piazza of Venice, crossroads of Europe and Asia. Heavy-laden boats crowded the canals, life's blood to merchants and lords fattened by trade. Waving away flies, Rodiana picked her way past a trader offloading wolf pelts and honey. She strode across the square, heading toward the pillars of the saints. Beneath the pillar of St Mark, a dozen men circled around a large ashy-blonde giant of a man. Sitting on a stool behind a small folding table, the tall warrior switched from German to broken Italian to address four men standing before him.

As she approached, Onorata sized up the bearing of the four. Three wore clothes worn from travel and carried the tell-tale, short-bladed *baselard* of Swiss fighting men. The fourth was a younger man with a heavily embroidered cape. He wore a sword that showed far more use than his fine clothes. As she approached, the richly dressed one threw up his hands and walked away.

Behind the table, a slight, rangy fellow carrying a *baselard* pointed her out to the German. The other men in the circle greeted her, straightening up as they saw her. All except one, a man in a dark blue doublet and brimmed hat in the French style, wearing the sash of an *arquebus* gunner. She arched an eyebrow at him; he nodded reluctantly to her.

The tall German deferentially offered her his seat, bowed and asked her in German about her health and state of affairs since last they spoke. She answered in Italian, "There's no time for that,

Bernhard, tell me news of the men you've found." She scanned the book, reading the printed names of those who had signed on. Most had a large 'X' beside the name.

The blonde man answered in heavily accented Italian, "Then Micheletto gave you enough to hire on new blood?"

She smiled, self-satisfied. "What he doesn't know won't hurt him. What prospects?"

"Aside from the rabble who think owning a sword and riding a mule makes you a knight? I found five. These three Swiss: Yves, Brandt and Georges." They bowed as he introduced them. "Good men, though none to match our Guilhem." The rangy man beside him smiled. "But they'll do. Also a couple of Germans I hired on earlier. And there was one young noble brat I turned away." He made a chuff of dismissal.

"Noble? Not that fine fellow who stalked off just before I arrived here?"

"Yes, he was persistent. Took a devil of a time getting rid of him. He wanted to talk to 'my captain'."

"So, you told him to talk to me?"

"Trust me, he's not worth the time." He dropped back into German. "He's as green as a shoot and thinks he's somebody. I don't want to pay him, just to have to cut the purse off his dead body to send back to his grief-stricken, high-blooded Mother."

Shifting to German, she said. "Bernhard, you have gone soft. Where did he go? I want to meet this young pup."

"I'm sure that gnat will be back. Perhaps you can convince him that he should go back to making money from trading furs to Bishops, and leave the real fighting to his betters."

As Bernard spoke, the young man returned, and addressed Rodiana "Excuse me, do you know who this barbarian's senior officer is? I can barely understand him through all his grunting."

"What business do you have with his captain?"

He glanced at her dusty hose and doublet, then shook his gloved hand at her dismissively. "It's surely none of your business, but I'm told that the Red Mark are the bloodiest, most vicious, and daring of all the *condottieri*. I've come to learn from them.

The King's Condottiere

Someday I will be a *condottiere*, and lead my own troop to glory for Venice, and perhaps even our Emperor and King!"

Guilhem said, "You do realize who the King is, don't you? Albert, King and soon to be Holy Roman Emperor of the *Germans*. Don't be so quick to insult one of your beloved Emperor's countrymen."

"That's just a title," the young man snapped.

"We don't serve the King or the Emperor. We serve the royal hand who pays our bills," Onorata said. "Today it is the Duke of Florence, tomorrow it may be the Duke of Milan. We fight our best. We live, we die. But we are our own masters. Free to choose whom we fight under and what we fight for. The King does not know our names."

The young man turned to her. "The important thing is that we know his! We can regain the glory of ancient Rome if we are united again under our King and Emperor."

Onorata leaned forward and said, "Do you know who is the duly appointed servant and regent of these lands by dear King Albert? The Duke of Milan!"

"If you want to serve the King so much, switch sides," Bernhard said. "I'm sure he would want a prize stripling like you." The tallest Swiss patted the noble on the head. Several of the men laughed.

"I don't care if you don't believe me, I will become a force to be reckoned with. I could fight any of you!" the young man yelled.

Onorata frowned at Bernhard, and motioned her men to stop laughing. She stood up and walked up to him.

"What is your name?"

"Emanuele di Francesca Moresini." He gave a short, elegant bow.

"Fight me, my young friend."

"You? But you're the smallest of the lot. Let me fight him." He pointed to Bernhard who pretended to cower in fear. This started the men laughing again.

Emanuele turned pink in the face. He turned his wrath on Onorata. "You're as thin and as frail as a woman!" With dawning comprehension he looked at her again. "What are you doing dressed as a man?"

He raised his hand to slap her. She easily caught his hand, and he found a half a dozen blades pointed at him.

"Appearances can be deceiving. You asked before who this *barbarian* reports to? He reports to me. Draw your sword or move along and go seek glory for your King elsewhere. If you can get a touch on me, then you get a chance in battle. You will join us at Anghiari."

He nodded quickly as the blades were sheathed. "A touch? Not to best you?"

Bernhard said, "Believe me, if you get a touch on her, you're doing well."

Rolling up her sleeves, Onorata took Guilhem's halberd. Emanuele pulled his sword from its sheath. His gloved hand gripped tighter as he stepped into the ring of onlookers. He took a moment to untie the strings of his cape and hand it off. The French gunner stepped forward to take it. Making a brief prayer, and holding the hilt like a cross to his forehead, Emanuele bowed to Onorata.

Facing him from across the circle, Onorata bowed in return. With a sprightly movement, she twirled the halberd above her head, and hailed the Red Mark. Her company erupted into the repeated cry, "Fight hard, live free!" The new recruits joined in the chant. Startled, Emanuele first extended his sword defensively, then an incredulous smile stole over his face as he took in the joy of the men around him.

As the cheers still sounded, Onorata let fall the halberd, and arched the axe blade in semi-circular flourishes past Emanuele's head. He hurriedly jumped back, only regaining his footwork in the midst of her attack. Coming to the edge of the crowd, Emanuele began circling. He ducked to avoid a blow to the face by the halberd's sharp spike. Continuing his circle, he maneuvered her into a pair of maroon-clad Germans who'd been calling out epithets. Emanuele took advantage of this moment of distraction and pressed forward, reaching into her guard. Onorata swiftly swung the tail of her pole back around, blocking Emanuele's blow.

"*Bravissimo!* Use your enemies against one another, on the field and in court." Onorata forced him back with successive sweeps to his feet and head. "Match your actions—to your strengths and their—weaknesses."

Harried backward, Emanuele shouted, "Suitable advice from the weaker sex. Your weapon's reach makes up for your shortfalls!"

Onorata's eyes tightened with rage. From the ring's edge, Bernhard called: "Son, you're not fighting your mother with a switch, here!" and the men erupted into laughter once more. With the sound of the laughter, Onorata became calm again.

Regaining the center of the ring, she made a strike at Emanuele's head, swinging the blade down in a long, powerful blow. Emanuele readied a parry but was staggered back by the impact of the axe. The momentum of the blade falling carried Onorata close to him and Emanuele saw an opening in her guard. But as he raised his sword to exploit it, Onorata stepped back, trapping his sword with the beak of the halberd. The momentum and leverage snapped it neatly out of his hand. She swung the pole up to his shoulder and gave a shove that sent him spinning face down in the dust.

To the sound of cheering, Onorata moved away, and handed the halberd back to Guilhem. "Let us move from *Gioco Largo* to *Gioco Stretto*, from the long game to the short game. I hope you don't mind getting a bit closer to this poor member of the weaker sex." She retrieved her own blade from Bernhard. Despite its length, she unsheathed it with a light and mobile movement. She held it in both hands, her fingers resting beyond the guard but protected by a ring of steel. She raised the sword to her forehead and saluted Emanuele.

Gathering his senses, he pulled himself to his knees and looked about for his sword. A shadow fell upon him and he saw the Frenchman extend his hand to him. Looking guarded, he hesitated, then took the hand.

"You will be looking for this, I think." The fellow handed him his sword. "My name is Joseph. Don't think you're alone here."

Heartened, Emanuele took his sword in hand again, and turned to face Onorata. "A second round then?"

"As you say. This time, you lead." She took a defensive stance, her body facing to the left, sword held high, above her head, pointing toward him.

Emanuele stepped forward cautiously, feeling out her responses. As he made a thrust, she stepped to the side, letting him move past and struck his backside with a booted foot. Anticipating another sprawl on the ground, she glanced at the men and saw Joseph glower at her. She tipped her hat to him. While she was distracted, Emanuele rolled forward over his sword. He leapt to his feet and charged her.

As she fended off a series of furious blows, Onorata heard Joseph call Emanuele's name, over the cries of the other men. Swords clashing, she blocked a slash. "Young man, you have made a conquest! *Frère* Joseph hates everyone, but the Monsieur cheers for you!" Emanuele looked confused. She dropped her leg beneath his, and grabbed at his shirt to pull him down again but this time, he saw it coming.

Before she could trip him, he broke free, circling slowly, looking for an opening. She matched his speed, moving toward him making lazy explorations of his reach. He held his free hand outstretched, looking for purchase on her clothes as she moved near.

"Yes, exactly. You are learning! Now, let's show you the final lesson." Dancing out of his reach, she tossed her sword to Guilhem who snatched it from the air. Now bare-handed, she approached Emanuele and matched him pace for pace. He hesitated, drawing back as she drew near.

"Don't be alarmed. This is all part of the game." Onorata maintained her aggressive movements, stalking him around the circle. "If you come with us, you'll face knights on horseback with your sword lost, tangled in someone else's ribs. They'll not consider the dishonor of striking an unarmed man, they'll be too busy killing you."

Emanuele took a half-hearted swipe at her. She dodged easily.

Bernhard called out, *"He Junge, mach das nicht!* She hasn't lost all her tricks!"

Closing quickly as Emanuele thrust his sword in earnest, Onorata pulled a short triangular blade from a sheath at her back. She parried a blow and moved into his guard. Snaking her left arm in and around his right, she trapped him. Emanuele fruitlessly attempted to bring his sword around to strike, but she stepped in closer, holding the long knife to his eyes.

"Do you yield?"

"If I do I cannot come with you, can I?" He held his face away from her blade.

"If you don't, what will you lose, an eye? An ear?"

"What if I yield my share to you instead? I don't need it, and you could use my help." He gulped then took a deep breath and continued. "My family has influence in many places, Milan as well."

Onorata changed her grip. She held his wrist with her free hand and moved her blade fractionally away from his eyes. "You mean you might be able to bring some...persuasion to the field?"

"Yes, there are more than one means to end a battle."

"And many times in battle when the word can be more important than the blade." She stepped away from him.

"Yes, young man, you may join us. You just may have in you what it takes to be a *condottiere*."

◇

Taking the winding road south from Venice, Onorata's men traveled quickly. The fields of Lombardy gave way to the mountains of Tuscany and the hills above Anghiari. Waking early in the morning and riding far into the night, scouts led the way. They kept watch for Milanese troops laying in ambush or unexpected obstacles that could cause a costly delay.

As the group headed down the narrow mountain trail, silence followed them. The creak of saddles was all they could hear. Emanuele rode up alongside Bernhard at the head of the forces and asked him why they were traveling in the dark.

"Bernhard, what's the use of this? Is the time so pressing? If they've hired us on, they must expect we can make it in time."

"If we don't it's no pay, and the loss of all the money we've spent for provisions just getting us here. Son, you never get to a battle late unless you're more concerned with keeping your skin intact than you are with eating. If we can make it in time, we can beat Piccinino and his force to Anghiari. The fortress there is the key to this valley. If they take it, Florence will be open to them next, and we'll not be able to stop Milan from controlling the whole of Tuscany. They've the most men, the richest fields. Some think it's just a matter of time—"

"And others think that's only if we let them walk all over us." Onorata reined her horse beside Emanuele, cutting off Bernhard's words. "It's been said that they'd take over their neighboring kingdoms since 1426, and they are still at it. I'll believe Milan will rule the northern states the day I see a mercenary on the seat of the Viscontis. Wait—"

A figure came out of the gloom ahead of them. Guilhem's face grew clearer as they approached. He held his hand before his mouth. Emanuele recognized the signal for caution and stillness he'd been taught on the first day of their journey. They stopped their horses, and Bernhard shot his arm out in a gesture that was passed back and brought the line of mercenaries to a halt.

Onorata spoke in a near inaudible whisper. "What news?"

Guilhem said, "A contingent of scouts. Camped at a bend in the road a thousand paces on. They haven't heard us yet but we need to go cautiously. They've a guard at the ready, I believe, to report our presence to a larger force."

Onorata and Bernhard traded a look that Emanuele could make nothing of. He saw Onorata nod to Guilhem, then she turned her horse's head around to head back toward the other troops. "*In bocca al lupo*. Fortune go with you then."

Before he could stop himself, Emanuele cried the response, "*Crepi!*" Guilhem and Onorata shushed him. Bernhard reached out and clapped a hand over his mouth, whispering, "*Buben*, do that again and we will feed you to the wolves."

The King's Condottiere

Quietly, Onorata said, "He's not ready. Emanuele, follow me." But Guilhem raised his hand. "I'll vouch for him." Looking at Emanuele, he said, "If you promise to keep your mouth shut, you'll learn a lot, *Buebä.*"

Guilhem looked to Onorata for approval. She gave the young noble a long considering look, then nodded once more.

She said to Bernhard, "If he disobeys any order, you have my permission to strip him and send him back on a pack horse with a skin of water and a roll of *porchetta.*" Addressing Emanuele directly, "You can remember this and give the same warning to a young *condottiere* in your command someday." She set off toward the others.

Bernhard and Emanuele followed Guilhem on foot down the track. The trees crowded over the road. The night deepened before Emanuele's eyes. He tried to focus on Bernhard's great sword in its sheath before him, but if he slackened his pace at all, his eyes lost the image of the blade. Bernhard stepped lightly, more quiet than Emanuele would have guessed he could. Guilhem was a silent shadow before them. Emanuele could catch no glimpse nor hear sound of his passing.

Bernhard stopped abruptly and raised a hand to Emanuele. Guilhem appeared near him and a silent council of gestures and nods took place. Emanuele stepped close to them. At first all he could see was the still form of trees before him, until he realized that that was no illusion. The road took an abrupt turn, a new switchback begun. Emanuele caught the sign "horse" and strained his senses to tell how the mountain-raised Swiss had realized there was danger ahead. In the silence he heard the muffled stamp of horse shifting far away. Guilhem nodded and mimed wrapping something around his hand. Cloth wrapped hooves. Emanuele stepped closer waiting for his orders.

Guilhem took them slowly forward. Once past the bend, they heard the sentry, only perceptible from the shush of his mail. He was awake, but as blind as they in the night. Guilhem stationed them here, ready to run to the camp to rush the sleeping scouts once he accounted for the guard. As they waited, for a moment

Emanuele felt the reassuring pressure of a hand on his shoulder. He counted the moments, waiting for the next signal, the low cry of a night bird, or the death cry of the guard which would pitch them pell mell into the fray. Twelve, thirteen. Bernhard's slow breath beside him. Twenty-five, twenty-six. His own heart. Thirty-one, what was that? A sound as a branch breaking, a whump on the ground. Silence. Then the quiet whistle of a bird they'd heard a hundred times before, but not this close tonight.

Bernhard was moving before the whistling cry failed. His steps less quiet now, but with great strides. Emanuele followed behind holding his hands before him, his dagger in his right hand pointing down, to ward off trees, soldiers or to keep him from crashing into Guilhem or Bernhard. His heart now pounding, visions of himself riding a pack horse naked vied with the image of a soldier on the ground, with heart's blood pooling at the base of a tree and Guilhem in the darkness above him. He came to a clearing and the first glimmers of moonrise showed two men running down the road beyond. He saw a man slumped against a rock, his arm at an angle that would have been strained and strange in life. Emanuele moved past, crossing himself, and followed, the hilt of his dagger digging into his palm.

◇

Passing the great Lake of Montedoglio, the Red Mark arrived early the next day. Descending to the Tiber River Valley, they saw the town of Anghiari beyond, nestled in the folds of mountains. Dominating the town, the great Convent looked out over the city walls. The fortified place of God watched over the rich plain filled with fields and cattle.

Camp tents now dotted the plains. Everywhere flags were flying, cook fires roaring, and armed men crossing the fields. Onorata picked out Micheletto Attendolo's colors and headed her group towards his position. They rode their horses between straggled camps. Florentine troops' tents sprawled along the length of the road. Troops marked by the Papal keys abutted the town, camped in the shadow of the city walls. Onorata picked their course through fluttering flags with the three-leaved red lilies of Florence to Micheletto's troops flying the red and gold winged lion, symbol of Saint Mark and Venice. Their smaller encampment was in good order. The neat rows of their tents contrasted starkly with the haphazard placement of the others.

Onorata sent Joseph to find provisions for their horses, and a place for her men to settle their own tents. She spoke to a village woman traveling back to town who said she would show the way to the well and livery yard. In the camps, sounds of merriment and cheers rang out, traveling raggedly across the plain. Onorata entered Attendolo's encampment with Guilhem and bid the others wait at attention. "Bernhard, keep the men in good order. This hilarity before the battle is won seems misplaced."

As she and Guilhem walked on toward Attendolo's headquarters, Emanuele ran after them. Onorata allowed him to come, saying, "Your mouth stays shut, *bambino*. Your record is good so far. Don't spoil it."

Onorata headed toward a large tent, set centrally with a table placed before it and guards at attention. She strode purposefully toward them and spoke to one who ducked inside.

After some time, Micheletto Attendolo appeared. He was followed by a tall man with a round face, unprepossessing in his worn and battered red hat. But the way all eyes snapped to attention on him marked him out as Francesco Sforza, commander of the Florentine armies. "Micheletto, we have important issues to settle. The town is ours, but the position is one we must hold. The time for celebrating is over. We have the town but the battle has yet to begin. We expect Piccinino to reach here in the coming days. Give your troops their orders, then rejoin us to discuss strategies for our engagement." Dismissing them with a glimmer of a nod, he strode back into the tent.

Attendolo took Onorata aside. "Your work starts now."

"Damn well believe it. The troops are in disarray. No discipline in the ranks, with Piccinino arriving any time. The Florentines are too far from the city gates to make it inside if defense is needed."

Emanuele's eyes opened wide. "Will we be besieged?" Guilhem cuffed his ear.

Onorata said, "Only if we want to suffer a long slow death. Though the Milanese would be far from home, the Florentines could supply us only if they could make it through the surrounding troops."

Micheletto nodded. "We're looking to avoid that. We'll pick our place of engagement carefully."

"We can scout for you. We will set up a perimeter and give advance warning so you can bring the troops into formation at the strongest sites."

Micheletto said, "I'm sorry to send your men out immediately after their arrival. I will free up some of my men when I can to aid you."

"Just look for our banner. If we see anything we'll send a fast rider to you. The rest will be up to you."

◊

"You did well last night." Onorata addressed Emanuele as they headed toward the river. "Guilhem tells me you helped him catch a scout who woke and leapt on his horse to flee."

"If scaring the horse by appearing under its feet so that it dropped him from the saddle is helping, then yes. I did my utmost."

"You are learning! Humility is a proper start."

Bernhard said quietly, "We are all walking in the footsteps of giants here, you realize. The river we cross is the great Tiber, who birthed Mother Rome herself. "

The river rushed beneath their feet. Before them the plains dotted with brush and shrubs transitioned into neat rows of crops belonging to the nearby town Sansepolcro. Riding forward, Onorata turned her horse to contemplate the dark hills in the distance that sheltered Anghiari. She watched the river drifting between its banks.

"Ah! I can see it now. Brescia had a river running by it, too. It affected the flow of battle. I can still incorporate the river in the fresco, if the Doge will let me return to finish it."

Emanuele pointed toward Sansepolcro. A shadow stretched across the horizon, dark in the daylight. "Is there a storm rising?"

Onorata looked at the trees, calm in the morning air. She looked back at the cloud, then abruptly pulled her mount's head in, making him rear up and whinny. "Look where it's rising from. That is no cloud. It's Piccinino heading this way!" Turning to the others, she assessed the riders. "Joseph, take a banner and ride to Micheletto. When you are in sight, fire to alert him and he'll spread the alarm to the others. Our men who went to the south and west will hear the shot and ride back to join us. We'll stay here and see if we can buy you all some time."

Joseph, sprang to his mount's saddle but stayed. "Twenty men against an army? You're mad! You'll never hold them off!"

"All we need to do is to give the main force time to arrive. Get to Attendolo *tout de suite*, and we'll do our part. Now go!" As he hesitated, she struck his horse's haunch with her whip. "Go!"

The stallion pounded over the bridge, leaving a wake of dust behind. Onorata watched them go, then turned to the others. "Follow me." She lead the way away from the river, towards the cloud.

The sun climbed in the sky. The crickets keeping time gave way to the thunder of horse's hooves. Onorata arranged her men, a dozen on horseback in a line behind her, Emanuele holding the red banner of the Mark. Two groups of horse swept toward them. A call rang out and the riders halted. The white banners held over their heads settled in the calm air, the snake of the Visconti family eternally swallowing the child in its mouth. A trio of riders broke from the ranks and approached them, one a small round man with grey hair, wheezing and blinking at the dust in his eyes. The second, long-limbed his dark hair tied back beneath his helm. The third, holding the flag of Milan, looked to the others.

The tall warrior said something to the standard bearer and laughed. Onorata saw Emanuele watch them closely, but she watched the older man. He kept quiet, his eyes calm as he held a handkerchief over his mouth while the dust settled.

"Piccinino, you are an uninvited guest," Onorata said. Emanuele started as the older man replied, "Rodiana, you do not hold the keys to Anghiari. You speak for your betters. Though I am sure you speak true."

The young man with dark hair spoke. "Father, do we fight women and children here? There is no glory for kingdom and Emperor in such conquest. The cause of Milan will be shamed if we strike down such as these. They had better take cover in the convent beyond."

Piccinino's head tilted back. He gave a long bellowing laugh. "Francisco, have I taught you nothing? You have the honor to meet Onorata Rodiana. If you can call her troops children after meeting them in battle, I will join this lady and cower with them in the house of God that you suggest."

His son reddened, and put his hand on his hilt.

Still chuckling, Piccinino turned to Onorata, "You know this is a lost opportunity. And such a waste. You'll be crushed in this battle. I have 8,000 men from Milan. The Visconti's finest. And our ranks are swelled by the men of the neighboring city Sansepolcro. They will be on the side of the powerful when Milan finishes the childish rivalry that Florence contends. From there, we shall march on Naples and Sicily. Then Rome will have to acknowledge the ascendancy of the kingdom of Milan, and recognize the Holy Roman Emperor, King of the Romans: Albert, crowned with the Iron Crown of Lombardy. Come with us and be part of this new kingdom. There is no reason for the crown to lose such warriors as yourself. You know just as well that it could have been on our side that you were brought into this war. Why sacrifice yourself for the Florentines and their Pope?"

"And what about Anghiari? Shall I abandon my post?" said Onorata.

"What of them?" Piccinino said. "What are they but pawns in this war? They are but a way station and will neither care nor perhaps even know who rules, be it King or Pope."

"And my commanding officers? My employer, the Priore of the Republic of Florence?"

The King's Condottiere

"You mean Cosimo di Medici, don't you? There's nothing done in Florence that doesn't have his fingers in it. Their precious democracy holds a spider at its heart. When they once roused themselves to send him packing, he pulled his secret strings to make the merchants leave the city, one by one. So what did they do? They went crying to him and called him back to weave his webs once more. What are you doing working for these weaklings? You can come be part of the *Holy Roman Empire*. The glory of ancient Rome can be ours once more."

Onorata nodded to him thoughtfully. Then she turned to the men behind her. Guilhem held his halberd at attention. The Germans loosened their blades in their sheaths, watching for a sign. Onorata gestured to Emanuele. "Come." She waited as he moved to her side, the plain red banner at his side hanging like a dead thing in the quiet air.

"Emanuele, this is your chance. We are being asked to fight for our King and Emperor. All we need do is switch sides now and you can fulfill your dream of being the King's *condottiere*. What's your assessment of this situation?"

The red banner shook. Emanuele spoke with the hint of a quaver. "We are badly outnumbered."

"Your student speaks the bald truth, Onorata," interjected Piccinino.

"I concede the point. We are overpowered. We would take many of your knights before the infantry with bows and artillery reach us, but we would all die if we fight now. Proceed."

Emanuele's eyes widened and his grip on the flag staff tightened. "We have not yet been paid by Micheletto—"

Piccinino barked with laughter. "A telling detail," he said. "Micheletto Attendolo is here? I'm surprised he made it from Venice before we arrived. Though that explains your presence as well."

A sound like a waterfall in the distance arose. Onorata saw the glint of light on the tips of pole-arms, and the sea of faces beneath them like a daylight forest of shining trees.

Onorata said, "Your advantage there, Piccinino. Though, your intelligence must have told you Attendolo had been engaged."

"And yours did not tell you where I would approach from, since this is your attempt to delay us from reaching the other side of the Tiber. Come, Onorata, choose your side now."

"Emanuele, what do you think of this offer?"

Glancing back at Guilhem, then out at the waving staves in the distance. "Captain, I choose what you choose."

Onorata smiled. "There is your answer, Piccinino. Emanuele's loyalty stays with the one who led him here, and the soldiers who fought at his side. That is our only path to honor, Piccinino, though you may know it not. We do not fight for the Doges, the Priors, the Viscounts. Nor the Pope, nor the Holy Roman Emperor himself. We fight for each other, and for those we choose to ally with. Our contract is our word and our bond. We fight for them, and we may die for them. We fight for the Red Mark and for each other. Not for your King."

Piccinno's eyes grew darker as she spoke. He looked to his son, and gestured to his horsemen to come closer. Onorata flicked out her hand and gave a snap, and her men brought their weapons to hand. Onorata gestured Emanuele to drop behind her and, bringing her horse rearing up on his hind legs, gave a cry, "Now!"

From the ditches by the side of the river, six archers stepped out of hiding, firing as they went. Piccinino's men scattered. One horse fell screaming, crushing its rider beneath it. Piccinino and his son flattened to their mounts' necks as the flight of arrows flew by, then unsheathed their weapons and charged forward. Onorata's men quickly turned their horses and raced back to hold the bridge. Bernard and Onorata stood their ground and met the leaders of the enemy. Piccinino warily circled round Bernhard who, with his great sword with both hands, nudged his horse in counter-circles with his knees, tracking the small man. Onorata clashed swords with Francisco. Grasping the blade of her sword for extra leverage, she pushed past his sword to hold the blade to his throat.

Guilhem dismounted and sent his horse over the bridge. He attacked Piccinino's knights from the ground, pulling soldiers from their mounts. His halberd clanged on their helms and breastplates. He swung and ducked beneath their comrades' swords. Beside him the two Germans fought with pike and sword, spilling horsemen where they could and rounding off against those rising from the ground.

Swept apart from Francisco by the chaos of riders and men afoot, Onorata bellowed: "Kill the men, spare the horses!" Her arm raised above her head, her sword a leading edge of death, she charged a knight fighting Emanuele. She saw the banner fall from his hand. As she killed the mercenary, she saw the tallest of the three new Swiss go down. The man at his side picked up his halberd and straddled his body. Emanuele toppled from his horse. He clutched a bright line of red on his arm. Onorata dropped from her horse to defend him, giving him time to tend his wound.

"I'm sorry you lost your chance to fight for the King."

"He lost his chance in the mountains. It's you and the men I fight for, not Pope or King."

"Now you're talking like a true *condottiere*." Onorata parried a blow from horseback and shifted away from Emanuele. She saw him grab a fallen halberd and put his back to the edge of the bridge before he was lost from her view once more. The infantry were now reaching them. She swung, blocked and yanked a man off his horse, slaying him as he fell. The blood on her sword was redder than it could ever be in a painting.

She heard another sound. The sudden fervor of the man she fought with told her what it was. She saw the red trefoil of Florence and the golden lion of Venice. Sforza and Micheletto had come in time.

The bridge was taken and retaken by each side many times. Onorata's troops joined Micheletto Attendolo's mounted knights, pushing through to the other side only to be repulsed by the waiting ranks of infantry there. Archers and arms wrought havoc, though their aid was cut short once the armies mixed to fight hand to hand. The turning point came late in the day. Piccinino seized an opening and sent his riders across the bridge in a tight wedge, followed by infantry running en masse. The wearied troops on the other side haltingly resisted. Sforza, instead of rallying the men, led them backward, slowly giving Piccinino ground.

As the troops fell back Bernard and Guilhem rounded up the Red Mark. They looked to Onorata to see if they should join the retreat. She nodded, but signaled them to follow her and circle around to the north edge of the line. There she could see Cardinal Trevisan's troops readying themselves. When the cry rang out for the charge, red banners snapped in the wind beside papal keys, hurtling toward the vulnerable juncture of the bridge on the Anghiari side of the river.

◇

Emanuele came to with a jolt. His head was pounding. Aches spread through him everywhere, and a searing pain lanced through his side. His moan brought someone to his side, and hands helped him bring a water skin to his parched lips. Too lost in the pain to care who helped him, he croaked, "Was the battle lost?" but nearly slipped into unconsciousness before he heard the answer.

"No, young pup. We were victorious." He startled at the sound of Onorata's voice, and tried to sit up. She went on, "Though we nearly lost you. You're lucky Joseph pulled you into a ditch by the river so you wouldn't get trampled. Rest or his work is wasted."

Pain shook Emanuele again, and the smells of burning flesh and blood came to his nose from the battlefield. "I owe him my life now, as well as my friendship. How did the others fare? I saw Brandt go down."

"Georges and Yves are mourning him today."

"But we won the day?"

"Yes. Cardinal Trevisan's troops came down like the hammer of God on the Milanese and cut a full third of the force off from the other part across the river. After that, Piccinino's force broke and we gave chase. We have most of them now, imprisoned at the base of the city wall."

"What's to be done with them?"

"Sforza and Trevisan were all for killing them. But their men will have none of it. They're to be released once they've been disarmed and made to swear not to re-join Piccinino."

Emanuele shook a triumphant fist, then winced. "Piccinino was wrong then. Milan's plans are foiled."

Onorata nodded. "Though if you spoke to him today, I'm sure his offer would still stand." A sound of footsteps came near. Emanuele saw Joseph, walking towards them followed by Bernhard and Guilhem whose arm was in a sling. Emanuele shook his head. "Would the king mourn with Yves and Georges?"

"Emanuele!" As the others warmly greeted him, she said, "The great forget the common soldiers who die for their glory. It's up to us to remember our own."

Dead Leather Office

Greg Stolze

It was full on dark by the time I pulled in at Stacy's. I was just checking the address when a light flared on the stoop.

It wasn't a big tall apartment building in a downtown area, more like one of those small square ones with six apartments on two floors and everyone has their own outside. Like a motel, not a high rise.

That spark wasn't just someone stepping out for a smoke, either. It was a thin woman lighting a candle, which she held under her chin to put the spookiest possible shadows on her face.

"Cold woman," she called to me, as I got out of the car. "Your coming was foreseen."

"How about that," I said. "Call me Anne instead of 'cold woman' if you don't mind."

"Your name is of little concern to me."

I rolled my eyes. I couldn't really help it, I had been on the road all day and kind of had to pee, and here this gal's going for her daytime Emmy. I had to mess with her. It was like a moral imperative.

"Who sent you, the ouija or the cards? I'm guessing cards because you didn't call me by name, but the precision timing points the other way and, honestly? Most of the time I can't tell you jokers apart."

Her nostrils flared at that one. "Your blindness is as profound as your stupidity," she said, taking two steps down to get right in my face. I blew out her candle and then she popped me one in the throat.

I didn't have the first clue it was coming. She just opened her hand like she was sticking it in a baseball mitt and whipped it in. Hit me on the breastbone, slid right up into my neck. I was gagging and coughing, stumbling back down the steps and I noticed the big rings on her knuckles when the door behind her opened and Stacy rolled out.

Stacy is a big woman, arms like hams. Her right hand popped down on the skinny bag's head like Scottie Pippen palming a basketball, and then those banana-thick fingers really dug in, gripping the hair right next to the scalp. I didn't see what she did with the left. I'd guess a kidney punch, because the candle-gal arched her back and whinnied like a horse.

Stacy marched her down to the sidewalk and pushed the oracle's hips up against the car. "Not on the caddy!" I rasped, which is probably what stopped Stacy from slamming the bitch face first onto the hood. Instead she chucked her to the side, none too gentle, like those luggage guys at the airport.

"Didn' see *that* comin', didja?" Stacy cried.

"You made a bad mistake…" the woman snarled, on all fours, right before I scooped up the candle and threw it at her. It went end over end but missed. I made her jump anyway.

"Git!" Stacy said, and she scrambled off.

◇

Twenty minutes later I was soothing my throat with some decaf tea while Stacy made up a sofa bed. "Gosh Anne, I'm real sorry about that," she said. "Riff raff. You sure you're alright?"

"Yeah," I croaked. "It's just like a bad cold."

"Here's some towels and such you can use," she said. "Bathroom's first on the left, you sure you aren't hungry or anything?"

"Ate on the road."

"Want a beer or something?"

"Tomorrow," I said, and something made my look at her *Sideways*.

Lots of people can see the future and the past. Okay, not lots, and most have to use a crutch like the cards. Most have to sign up with the higher or lower forces to get the sight, too. Looking *Sideways* is related, but not the same. It's all about the big What If.

Stacy's break was a good thirty-five years back, and it was a man. She went with one and got here. *Sideways*, I saw what she'd be if she'd gone the other way. Wow.

"Nothing else you need?"

"Wanna tell me why I'm here?" I said.

"If… if y'ain't too tired." She twisted my washcloth between those huge round hands, then spread it out and primly flattened it, knuckles dimpling. I decided not to tell her about that *Sideways* self with the big diamond ring, skinny neck, any laugh lines botoxed to death, or just moved down to the mouth as prissy old lady scowl-marks.

"It's my boy John," she said.

"Up in Chicago?" I said, wary. She shook her head.

"That's Johnny Bees," she said. "He's my oldest. Jack, the young one, he lit out for California a couple years back. Looking for giants, y'know?"

I didn't, but I let it go. "Which John is this, then?"

"Crooked John. The middle child. He's been arrested."

◇

Long John Crawson was a story man from way back, a trucker hauling up and down I-55. When he married Stacy she was normal as dirt, which is probably why they worked out. He named his three sons after himself and stroked out in 2003.

I got on Johnny Bees' bad side after his daddy's funeral, which is never a good time to cross anybody. Not my finest moment or his either. I remember the hornets crawling through my hair, dozens of tiny wings scraping and fluttering at my lips as I tried to get to the water... even years later, thinking about that gives me the willies.

I got along fine with Crawson, never found out exactly what his story was but, like a lot of weird parents, he had weird kids. When Stacy needed help, she decided to look outside St. Louis, and I immediately wondered about that. But that's not what you ask.

"What he get took for?"

"Bank robbery," she said.

"He done time?"

She shook her head. "Jailed seven times, arraigned twice, never convicted. Those cops," she said, mouth flattening. "They just won't leave him alone."

I dropped my chin and gave her a glance over the glasses. "And this is entirely the police department's fault?"

"Oh, he looks the part," she conceded, "but honestly."

"Hm. So what's my role in all this, then?"

"An innocent man's in jail," she said. "That ain't right, is it?"

"Nobody's innocent," I said, but with a yawn instead of any particular heat.

◇

"Mph! That is one fine automobile!" the man exclaimed. It was the next day and after Stacy went to work I'd gone to visit some old haunts. I figured I'd see the bank after the lunch rush, then stop by the jail during visiting hours.

"You can touch the fender if your hands are clean," I said. He laughed. White guy with heavy features and dirty fingernails, a flannel shirt and jeans and work boots. The day was clear, but the weather was chill and there weren't many other people sitting out on stoops. Or, in this one's case, sitting on the steps of a boarded-up church.

"I'm Arvil," he said, standing and coming to my window. The Dead Leather Office was on a one-way street, so I could park with my window by the sidewalk.

Looking at it, you wouldn't guess it'd been a church once. Even the tall, pointed ceiling, the double doors and the stone steps and arched windows just begging for stained glass... you wouldn't think it. If someone told you it'd been a business once, or anything other than an empty husk full of rat turds and debris, you wouldn't believe it. You'd know that buildings don't get built abandoned, but the Dead Leather Office, formerly Stamwicke's Fine Leather Tanning, formerly before that Our Lady of Perpetual Sorrow, looked like it'd been driving people away since before its foundation was dug.

"Anne," I replied.

"Cosby said something about a 'Cadillac Anne' once or twice," Arvil said, eyes lighting and narrowing.

"Where is Cosby?"

For a moment, Arvil's grin faltered and he looked over his shoulder. "He went in," he said, finally. "Couple years ago."

"That's a shame," I said, looking at the church. I'd made sure to come in the morning when the sun was on its face. I didn't want to park in its shadow, or even walk there. "Still, no one's come to put it to work?"

"People've tried," he said, and I didn't need to look front or back or *Sideways* to figure out how well that had gone.

"Hop in," I said.

"Thought you'd never ask."

As we pulled through a stoplight I asked what Cosby had said about me.

"He said you were one dynamite lay, if I recall correctly."

That bastard. "I guess my reputation preceded me. You know Crooked Johnny?"

"I could show you a crooked Johnson, if you like."

"C'mon Arvil, focus. Stacy's boy, middle son."

He ran his hands over the wood panel in front of him. "This is what you call a luxe interior. Shouldn't it be pink though? Like that Pointer Sisters song? 'I wanna ride in yo' piiiink Cadillac'."

Dead Leather Office

"Does that ever work on anyone?" I asked, giving him a look when we pulled up at a stop sign.

"A gentleman don't kiss an' tell."

"More than Cosby can say," I muttered. "Get out."

"What, just like that?"

"Unless you got something to say, we're done. I didn't come down here to get hit on, though I'll keep you in mind if I ever need motivation to shower for a whole week."

"Mm, I could spend a week with you in a shower," he said, "gettin' squeaky clean and *dirty* at the same time..."

"Yeah, bye bye."

"All right, hold on." He sighed. "I know Crooked John's in stir, but that's about it. I'll ask around though. I can be very persuasive. People tell me things."

"Yeah, you're all charm Arvil."

"I'm a master of Tongue Fu."

"Ick."

◇

"Pleased to meet you," the bank manager said, shaking my hand. "You can call me Lou." He held out a card. It read "Lucius Gil Sexknife."

"Um," I said.

"The middle name rhymes with 'eel.'"

"I have to say, the 'Geel' part wasn't what caught my attention."

He gave a weary, practiced shrug. "It's just a name."

"Okay."

"My parents were Ed and Mary Sexknife."

"So it's pronounced just like it looks. Right." I tucked the card in my purse, pulled out a notepad and said, "What can you tell me about the robbery?"

"There's not a lot to say," he started, and then paused as the light jazz drifting from overhead was interrupted by a harsh squawk. "STOCKER TO PRODUCE, STOCKER TO PRODUCE." Every "P" sound made a thudding noise.

"Um, yeah," he continued. "The guy came in through revolving door, pointed a gun at me and said I should empty the cash drawer. I did it—I mean, that's policy—and he took off."

"Was he wearing a mask or anything?"

"Nope. He had a hat, so we didn't get his face on camera, but I saw it."

"How much did he get away with?"

"Two thousand, four hundred and eighty-eight dollars."

"That doesn't sound like much," I said. "If you don't mind me saying."

"It's not," he replied. "We're a micro-branch inside a grocery store. He probably would have done better if he'd cleaned out the checkout tills."

I tidied up my notes and shook his hand.

"So, which paper did you say you worked for again?"

"The Tribune," I lied, and got the hell out of there.

◇

Crooked John Crawson had his mother's heavy frame and his father's delicate features. From afar he was all broad shoulders and meaty arms, and then you got close and saw wide-spaced, sky-blue eyes under unbelievably long lashes, blonde dangling hair that just begs a woman to sweep it up behind his ear. Full, baby-sweet lips. Put that all together with an orange jumpsuit and the obligatory "LOVE" "HATE" knuckle tats, you get an irresistible classic Bad Boy.

"It's nice to meet you, Miss Anne," he said. "My mama told me you were going to come help." He had just the voice you'd expect—warm and innocent, so much so that you found yourself listening for a mocking edge.

"Umph," I said, consciously pushing his charisma away. "Hear you have all sorts of police trouble."

A hooded chill fell over his features, instantly. "Nothing I can't take."

"How'd you get fixed for the bank job?"

"I dunno. I was doing some stuff…"

"Stuff?"

"Helping a buddy move some books and records. Furniture," he said. "You know. Then the cops showed up. Took me in, stood me in a pickup line. I guess the guy fingered me, the witness."

"That would be Mr. Sexknife," I said.

He smirked.

"It's just a name," I told him. "You have any idea who did it?"

"Sounds like a dumbo snatch an' grab to me."

"And if you were to rob a bank, it wouldn't be some nickle-ante grocery branch?"

"I never stole nothin'," he said, and that mocking tone was in the voice now, for sure. "'Cept maybe a heart or two."

"Ever steal anyone's identity?" I asked. He just raised an eyebrow, which I think was as good as a yes. I gave him the *Sideways* look.

The big decision, of course, was to change himself into Crooked Johnny. Or not. *Sideways*, his blockiness was mostly fat and his face, while exactly the same, was also as different as a handshake from a fist. The glimpse I got put him in a cheap brown suit, working his hands in a nervous gesture that wasn't quite wringing them but would get there in a few years.

"When I came to your mama's house, there was a white-blonde woman waiting for me. Buncha rings, candle, high-strung disposition."

"Ugh," he said. "That's Tasha. She's a psychic," he said sympathetically, the way you'd say "she's HIV-positive."

"You think she's got a horse in this race?"

"She's boards. The boards are the big winners around here," he said. "You hardly see any tarot at all. Tasha and her bunch chase 'em out. If they're in anyone's business, well, we don't know about it."

"How about a guy called Arvil? I guess he watches the Dead Leather Office now that Cosby's gone?"

"Arvil owns a bookstore, record store, second-hand kinda place," he said. "That's who I was helping move stuff."

"Right. The cops don't know where the money is, do they?"

"No one does."

"If you did," I said, "you wouldn't tell?"

"If I knew who robbed that bank, I wouldn't tell," he said. "Omertà."

◇

Bruce Bunce entertained me in his home, which was entirely decorated in red and black. I mean *entirely*. When he offered me coffee, it was poured into a red cup and stirred with some kind of black metal spoon.

"Cadillac Anne," he greeted me. "It's been a while."

"Not since the Crawson funeral," I said.

"Mm, I can see why you didn't want to come back."

"I've made right with the family," I said.

"That's good." The whites of his eyes were so bloodshot they looked red, the pupils black. His mouth was completely toothless, just a wavering line of red gums.

"In fact, Stacy asked me down to help Crooked John out of stir."

"Huh."

"I couldn't help wondering why she didn't reach out to locals. Long John's old people. You, for example."

He narrowed those red-black eyes at me and said, "I don't like your tone."

"Sorry." I wasn't.

He grimaced. "You know how it is. People drift apart. Sure, she knows a little bit of what's going on, but she doesn't have any goals, you know? What's she going to do, anyway? If she gets involved? Get hurt, that's what." His toothless s-sounds were a bit mushy, made him sound faintly drunk.

I couldn't see anything about him. No past, no future, no alternate selves. Nothing but red and black.

"Her son had 'em though," I said. "Goals. What was he up to? Stealing third base, or people's ideas?"

He tapped his spoon delicately on his coffee cup, watching the white sugar blacken. "Stolen glances, yeah. That sort of thing."

"Not snatching bank money at gunpoint?"

"I wouldn't say it's his style but what're you going to do? The boy's pure gangsta, as they say. Wouldn't snitch to the cops if his life depended on it."

"I suppose a spell in the joint won't do his rep any harm, will it?"

"You know how stories get around," Bruce said, looking idly away. His face was as wrinkled as a rock star's hotel bedsheet, but there wasn't a single white hair on his head. All curly, glossy black.

"Does he even want out, do you think?" I asked.

"If he doesn't, you can just pack it in, right?"

"It don't work that way," I said, and he must have caught something in my voice because he said, "Too bad."

"I hear Cosby went to church," I said.

Bruce was tough, but that made him shudder. "Damn shame, that."

"Now this Arvil character is keeping tabs on it?"

"We all pitch in. There's more to Arvil than you might have seen on the surface."

"There would have to be," I said. "Then there's this Tasha woman who poked me in the throat."

Bruce chuckled, then immediately held his hands up apologetically. "I'm sorry, I'm really sorry."

He wore fine black leather gloves. He said it was because his hands had been burned, but I think it was to hide red nail polish.

"That's more apology than I got from her," I grumbled.

"Tasha is just... Tasha. She's crazy, and you know I know crazy. Has a dozen or so puppets on her string, people who don't dare squat for a piss without her casting their horoscope." He pronounced it "pish."

"Cards or board?" I asked.

"I shouldn't say," he said. I dropped my head and looked at him over my glasses.

"Fine," he said. "Cards. You happy now?"

"The Death Church must make her crazy," I said. "Why isn't she setting up shop, getting herself a set of Major Arcana embossed on rawhide? You guys stopping her?"

"We don't have to," Bruce said. "You know as well as anyone. She doesn't because she doesn't. It's not her wyrd, her fate, her destiny."

"And the rest of you?"

"Who bells the cat?" Bruce asked. "You know how many people that black hole's gobbled up."

◇

Arvil's bookstore was a hole, but an interesting one. Not just books, but vinyl records and old toys in their boxes. Everything dusty and reeking of the past. The kind of place where people think they can find anything, if they think they can find the past in things.

"Cadillac Anne!" he called out as I entered.

"Arvil," I said. "Crooked John had some words for you."

"Just like I got words for you, words like luscious, irresistible, *hot*..." He waved his hand as if he'd just touched a stove burner.

"He was helping you move some furniture when the robbery went down, isn't that right?"

"I'd like to help *you* move some furniture, preferably a bed but I have a chaise lounge that would do in a pinch."

"Okay, that's enough," I said.

"You're no fun," he pouted. "All right, yeah, I think he was."

"Why didn't you tell the police? Alibi him?"

"The less I have to do with the cops, the happier I am," he said. "I got whatcha call underworld contacts."

"What, you know someone who shoplifts?"

He rolled his eyes and shook his head and I just kept my face steady and unamused. Eventually, his lasciviousness faltered, then died.

"Okay, honey, you're queering an 'everybody wins' deal here," he said. "Crooky J. gets f'real penitentiary time to beef up his cred. As a bonus, he stays alive."

"You think he's safer in jail?"

"Are you kidding? With his story in play he'll run that place within a week."

"His mama…"

"His mama's getting him back in nine years even if he *doesn't* skate," Arvil said. "She should count her blessings."

"Count her…?" The penny dropped. "He was going to take down the Dead Leather Office, wasn't he?"

"No," he said, looking away.

"He was going to try. What, was he going to use simony on it? Robbing the place of its charm?"

"In the 1930s, pickpocketing was 'lifting leather,' I guess," Arvil mumbled. He put down the Terry Pratchett paperback he was fiddling with and turned to me full face. "It's all water under the blood gutters and baptismal font now, isn't it? I hate that place more than anyone. Cosby and me, we were tight, understand? But you don't just de-consecrate the Death Church and turn it into a pizza place. That place eats order, and identity, and craps out ruin. All anyone's been able to do since Stamwicke stopped skinning people in it is… is containment. At least this way, everyone wets his beak a little."

"Crooked John gets his legitimacy," I said. "The real bandit gets his thousand bucks and change."

"Bunce," Arvil said.

"Bunce? The gunman was Bruce?"

"Think about it."

"How'd he pass for Crawson?"

Arvil laughed. "He didn't. The branch manager just lied about it. You think a guy managing a bank pulls teller duty all the time?"

"Why?"

"You might want to ask Mrs. Sexknife about that."

"Aw Jesus," I said. That bad boy appeal. "John stole the manager's wife. Could it get more sordid?"

"Well, if you and me was to…"

"Give it a rest," I said, then stopped as the sensation hit. Icy, like water running down my whole body just behind the skin, from scalp to heels, pushing out gooseflesh and shivers.

"What?" he said, too startled to even leer at my stiff nipples.

"The future," I said. "You... oh God, we do it."

"Oh ho?" the same overdone, lecherous-not-really-humor snapping back into his tone. "You an' me doin' it, huh?"

"Because I'm grateful," I rasped. "Because you step up and kill it."

Easy come, easy go. His words and face were suddenly cancer-serious. "Me? I'm 'sposta kill the Office? No, that's got to be some mistake, I... I mean, promising your body if I take a stab at it, that's one thing, but..."

I slapped him.

"I'm not offering you a goddamn thing," I said. "But it looks like you're the one who figures out something."

"You expect me to come up with an idea when I've been racking my brain for years? Just suddenly figure out how to stop the ever-eating Death Church like that?"

"Figure it out any way you like," I said, and staggered out. Should've stayed and put him on the track to his destiny but, honestly, I couldn't stand to look at him.

◇

"I can't make heads or tails of it," I said.

"Bruce Bunce is the scum of the earth," Stacy said, hands in fists so tight you could see her bones through the padding. "Calling himself Long John's friend and then scheming with some, some *outsider* to put our son in jail!"

"For all we know, it was Crooked John's idea."

"No, he wouldn't take the fall for anyone unless he had to. He was set up. I should call his brother..."

"Which one?" I said, getting a little nervous.

"Why not both?"

"Let's not let this get out of hand."

"That's easy for you to say, he's not your son!"

We just sat in silence for a bit, then got back to eating. She'd made meatloaf.

"Did Crooked John ever talk about the church?" I asked.

"Hm? We're not what you'd call traditionally religious," she said, and then she got it. "Oh." She set down her fork, like she'd lost her appetite, and something that big's hard to misplace.

"He talked about it after his dad died," she said.

"Long John was involved?"

"The Dead Leather Office is a stain." Her voice was low, almost murderous. "Live here long enough and it touches you. It gets on you. You live with the stink long enough and you don't realize you're making it too."

I nodded. "Okay. This is deep. Can you find Tasha?"

◇

There's a neighborhood, not all the way downtown, but close by the brewery. There's some crap stuff all around it. Urban blight, or whatever you want to call poor neighborhoods. Food deserts, I guess. But in the middle of it there's this one stretch of blocks where the brownstones are all getting renovated and bought up by retiree couples, gays, and mid-range professionals. It's centered around an organic grocery store, a coffee shop and, right between them, a tiny store front psychic. No sign, just this big vintage palmistry poster in the window.

It was late but the lights were on, with a BMW parked right in front. We pulled into a tiny space right behind—I could barely parallel park the caddy in it.

A brass bell rang when we entered and even though the surfaces were all clean, I could see spiderwebs forming in the corners. A young woman with vacant eyes smiled up from her laptop, sitting at an antique roll top desk.

"Hi, I'm afraid we're scheduled full for the evening but if you'd like to make an appointment for tomorrow…"

"We'll just head on back," I said.

Her smile faded and she nervously got up. She couldn't quite bring herself to block the doorway, though, and I didn't break stride.

"She's with somebody!" the receptionist said, alarmed.

"Nah, she's expecting us," I replied. "I mean, isn't she?"

Her fingers plucked at my sleeve. "It's private," she whined, but then I was past. If she didn't stop me she wasn't even going to slow Stacy down.

The back room had the mood lighting and the mysterious scents and in the middle of everything, a round table with some truly beautiful astrological crap carved and inlaid on the top. A coiffed woman of about my age was frowning down at the table, at little marble representations of the planets, at yellow scraps of paper with numbers scrawled on them.

Tasha looked up from saying something about Venus, then stood, nostrils flaring.

"You've got a lot of brass coming in here," she said.

"You're one to talk."

"Excuse me," the woman said, turning and standing. "I was in the middle of a consultation!"

"All B.S.," I told her.

"All right, I think you'd better leave," she said firmly. Tasha smirked.

"We have business with the hoodoo lady," Stacy said. "You can reschedule."

Stacy grabbed the client's arm just as I got an icy sensation and said "Don't!" but it was too late.

I was seeing things in an overlay, real time blurring into a just-glimpsed future. It was finished by the time I heard the slap and the oath. Stacy crashed down to the floor and the client was forcing fat Stacy's hand into the most uncomfortable position I can imagine.

"Beatrice here studies the martial arts," Tasha said, pleased as punch.

"She teach you that thing you did to my throat?" I asked.

"No, that was pure intuition."

"You think I'm some gullible fool?" Beatrice hissed at Stacy. "Some weak little thing you can push around? SHUT UP!" she shouted, right in Stacy's ear because Stacy had started to howl and kind of blubber as Beatrice kept pushing her hand.

Dead Leather Office

"Okay, that'll do," I said.

"Who the hell are you?" She glared at me and I sighed.

"Lemme guess. You came to Tasha here and she knew stuff about you no one else could have figured out, things you maybe didn't realize about yourself…"

"Oh no," she said. "Are you another debunker? What *is* it with you people? I know all about Barnum statements and playing the odds and…"

"*It was cold*," I said, raising my voice and that stopped her. "It was cold, wasn't it? That first time, that incredible insight? Even if it was the middle of summer you got a chill, maybe even shivered?" I leaned in and my whole front felt like ice, I realized my breath was starting to steam. "That's the real deal. Some people think when information travels backwards in time, it has to suck out heat to defeat entropy or some damn thing. I don't know. All I know is, if she's read your horoscope without a slick of ice on the table, it's just her telling you what you want to hear. Or what *she* wants you to hear."

Stacy had quieted down to sobs. Later she told me Beatrice seemed to just forget about her while I was talking.

"She said…"

"I really don't care and it really doesn't matter," I told her. "You're going to do fine in your career, you don't get a raise this year but you make out all right with the Christmas bonus. Your mom's going to give you a health scare in October, but she survives. You're going to have to be real patient with her for a while."

"T… Tasha?" she stammered, but she didn't look away from me. I was looking right in her face but I was seeing *Sideways*.

"That's not what really kept you coming here though, is it? You want guidance? We all do. Don't trust your judgment? Well, most people with confidence don't deserve it. I think, though, you have one question you don't dare ask."

She half shook her head, but she wouldn't look away so she couldn't complete the gesture.

I frowned. I felt bad for her. "Well yeah. You both would have lived. I'm sorry."

The sound she made right then... it was hardly human. Or maybe it was too human, more human than most of us want to hear.

She hid her face in her hands and ran out the door.

I looked over at Tasha.

"You tarot or ouija?" I asked. Then I looked down and saw the gun.

◇

Later, in the caddy, Stacy kept sneaking glances up at me.

"What?"

"What did you mean," she asked, "when you told her 'you don't kill me'?"

"Just what I said. She doesn't kill me. I know just how I die and she ain't in the picture."

"You know... wait, you know how you're going to *die*?!?"

"How, when... the whole megilla. It's not as great as it sounds."

"It sounds *awful*!"

"Well then, I guess it's not as *bad* as it sounds."

Now it was my turn to look over at her. She was crying, a little. We'd gotten a cup of ice at a Carl's Jr. and she was rubbing it all over her wrist.

"What are you and Tasha even trying to do?" Her voice was plaintive, confused, like a little girl who just walked in on her parents doing it.

"All right. You want the metaphysics? Here's a the metaphysics. Two primal cosmic forces, okay? Some people call 'em progress and decay. Others say stagnation and renewal. Or order and chaos. But if you want a neutral description, say fate and destiny. You with me?"

"You're talking about the future."

"Futures, there's a ton of 'em. Lots of competition to get real, y'know? The forces, the principles... I don't know if they're actually intelligent and conscious the way we are, like god and a devil. They may just look that way, or maybe we project... anyhow,

Dead Leather Office

they're always in conflict. One of 'em speaks through the ouija boards, mostly. The other through cards. That's why I needed to know how Tasha does it. I had to know what side she was on."

"And Tasha?"

I pointed up at the sky. "Progress, stagnation, 'order.' The big cosmic puppeteer, the spider's web."

"What about you, Anne? Where do you fit in all this? Whose side are you on?"

"Neither side. I'm just a valve between 'em. A necessary midpoint. I didn't really look for it, but I didn't say no." I shrugged. "Which is why I'm what I am."

"The cold woman."

" Karmic plumber, more like."

"It's why you know when you're going to die," she said.

"Yep."

Right at that moment, a vintage mustang pulled up next to us, radio blaring. Stealers Wheel. *Stuck in the Middle With You.*

Hilarious.

◇

I told Tasha that she didn't kill me and she pointed the gun at Stacy, so I interposed myself between them and then we probably would have had a royal slap fight if her receptionist hadn't stuck her head in and gasped something about guns being bad karma. Just by instinct, Tasha hid the gun and told the receptionist—whose name, it turns out, is "Lotus"—to call the cops. That's when I saw the family resemblance between the pair of 'em, too.

Well, I took a peek at *Sideways* Tasha and saw her doing a tarot reading on top of a human sacrifice, the blood starting to freeze on the cards as the guts and skin-peels steamed. Hard to believe the version I was dealing with was the *nice* one. Anyhow, that vision was a lucky catch. I knew she was Team Ouija, which meant Bunce had lied to me.

"Get everyone to the Dead Leather Office," I told her as I helped Stacy to her feet. "Make sure you call Arvil."

"That piss-ant? Why should I?"

"Because it's where I'm going at midnight and I know everyone cares."

◇

I was disappointed, but not surprised that Arvil wasn't waiting. What surprised me was Mr. Lucius Gil Sexknife. He was loitering—no other word for it, really—and he tried to slink into the shadows of the church steps when the caddy's lights hit him.

"Hey, SEXKNIFE!" I called and he started to run. I floored it and beat him to the cross-street. He wasn't a fast runner, so I was able to turn without even squealing the tires. He stopped, spun around, and ran for the entrance.

"Don't be an idiot!" I shouted, pulling a three-point-turn and driving the wrong way back, but he was tugging the door as I stopped at the curb.

He was looking at me as he went in, so he didn't see how the shadows inside were stretching out for him. Stacy managed to haul herself out by the time I made the sidewalk.

"You don't have to come," I told her.

"Isn't that the one that framed my boy?"

"Um…"

"Yeah."

She did let me go first though.

Nobody's 100% clear on the Dead Leather Office. There's a hundred rumors, every one plausible if it's bad enough. Indian burial grounds, Satanism, various stories about octopi. It first turned up in the news in 1952 when a nineteen-year-old congregant came into Easter Sunday service with a rifle and a shotgun, killed the priest and nine others before topping himself on the altar.

It was closed, de-consecrated and vacant for years before Clive Stamwicke moved in and started the foulest-smelling tannery in St. Louis. His gloves and purses fetched luxury prices even as the stench cleared out the neighborhood. It wasn't until 1982 that the cops bumbled onto an 82-year-old Stamwicke having a seizure while attempting to abduct a teenage runaway. They found human bones, some decades old and some far more recent, in the building's furnace. No trace of human skin was ever found on the premises except for one bongo drum in Clive's office.

Murder, madness, foulness and corruption. A few attempts to exorcise or neutralize or cleanse the place of its energies were made, but it was like wood too wet to burn. Nothing could make it right.

Inside, it was too dark, even for midnight. The windows were smashed, work tables overturned, walls spray-paint vandalized. Typical urban wreckage until you noticed that a lot of those graffiti tags were left unfinished, and that despite all the bird, bat and rodent droppings in evidence there was not a single spiderweb. Not one.

"What're you doing?" Bruce Bunce demanded, turning halfway around as Sexknife's footsteps flap-flapped up the center aisle. Bunce had a red light, a tiny bright LED, throwing his face into scary relief and failing to show more than the shape of the black pot he'd put on the centermost table.

"Bruce, someone..."

"Shut up," he said, turning fully as he saw us behind Lucius. Now he was just a dark shape, limned in crimson.

"Sorry Anne," he said. "I'll try to keep it off you if I can get it on a leash."

Then he struck a match and threw it into his bowl. A lot of things happened at once.

First off, there was that "whump" sound you only get when fumes catch fire. A scarlet cloud rose, carrying dollar bills upwards as they flared, igniting. Secondly, a broken window broke further as Tasha cleared her way in with a hammer handle. She couldn't enter, but she could aim her little gun inside. It didn't sound as loud as it should have when she fired, because the church itself... convulsed.

It was like an earthquake, only not really. My instincts told me the floor was roiling and tipping, that the ceiling was crumpling in, but there were no cracks, no dust, no splinters and flakes as things fractured because things *weren't* fracturing. All of us inside were sucked towards the center, towards the table that only *looked* like a table while I knew it was an altar. It felt like matter was moving, but maybe it was space itself breaking and folding.

Bunce staggered and screamed as Tasha got a hit. Red red blood spattered the altar and his burning cauldron, and the church started screaming. But just as nothing broke during its spasm of space, this howl was felt more than heard, until it ripped itself out of our four throats.

"Get him out of here!" I shouted at Stacy, shoving Lucius into her arms. The banker was stunned and Stacy wasn't much better, but she was strong and heavy and there are few things more absolutely real than a 260-pound midwestern mother of three.

"Crimson blood!" Bunce cried. "Midnight black! The red of Tasha's wrath and the blackness of my heart!"

"It's eating you, Bruce!" I said, trying to pull him back from the altar. It didn't have a bowl of burning money on it now, it was something else, something you couldn't look at directly. Something red and black.

"No," he said. "I'm eating it."

He lunged at the hole and I didn't think, I grabbed him.

We got sucked in.

◊

We weren't bodies in there, just selves. I could feel myself being drawn down, unmade, and I realized this was real danger to me. Lots of bad things can happen without killing you, but I guess my whole *déjà memento mori* situation had made me complacent about survival. The vortex couldn't kill me. Nothing could before my time. I knew that.

What I hadn't known was that I could be unmade. I wouldn't die, I'd just cease to be, forward and backward in time, edited out like a cosmic typo. The church could do that, or Bunce could, or whatever they were turning into together.

Dead Leather Office

And then there was a book with me.

No eyes to see or hands to grip it, nothing but disembodied consciousness in conflict and peril. Then suddenly a book. Specifically, a copy of Tom Phillips' A *Humument*. A copy with a coffee stain on the upper left corner of the cover and I knew that book. It was Cosby's book.

Cosby's *favorite* book and I remembered lying on his bed on a lazy Saturday afternoon paging through the surreal, kludged together image of Bill Toge's quest for love, or something. I never got it, but I didn't have to, because then Cosby was there.

You have to get out. He didn't say it, there weren't words there any more than there was time, but I could tell it was Cosby. The church might have pulled him in, but it hadn't quite chewed him to pieces. Not yet.

Help me. I didn't say it either, and then I knew that he was never getting out, he was too deep and within a year at most he'd not only be gone, he'd never have been and I wouldn't even remember his kind eyes and stubby hands. I felt the chill down in my bones and knew this was too certainly true. Then I emerged.

I fell backwards onto the crap-dusted floor, Bunce lying beside me, and up by the altar Arvil was stabbing the black pot with a cardboard box, about the size of a Monopoly game.

"Gag on it!" Arvil screamed. The box had a cloaked figure printed on the dark paper, under the white letters "OUIJA."

The board disappeared with a pop and Bunce cried out in pain and despair. We were just in a dirty, abandoned building with a broken black pot on a table and an angry bookseller stomping out the flames on singed currency.

"You prick," Arvil said to Bunce, and switched to kicking the prone man in the face for a bit before I said, "Okay, stop that." Between the two of us we got the sobbing red and black man to his feet and walked him out, one arm over my shoulder and one over Arvil's.

"What'd you do to it?" Tasha demanded as we came out.

"Choked it," I said, letting Bunce flop down on the sidewalk.

"With what?" she asked.

"Meaning."

"That Ouija board was a collector's item, dammit," Arvil said. "A William Fuld Mystifying Oracle. I paid sixty bucks for it!"

I felt a weird flash of affection for Arvil. There was something… not noble, almost the polar opposite of noble about his relentless focus on his money, his lusts, his plans. It was honest and human and reliable. You couldn't admire it, but you could count on it.

"Listen up," I said, and to my surprise, everyone did.

"Tasha," I said. "You ain't gettin' rid of the Dead Leather Office. Sorry, that's just so."

She nodded. I think she saw, finally, how strong it was.

"Lucius," I said. "You saw that thing, right?"

"Uh huh… kinda…"

"You want more of that?"

He blanched. "No ma'am," he whispered.

"Then you and Bunce take this back and make it right," I said, shoving a handful of burned banknotes at him. "That a problem, Bruce?"

When I looked at Bunce, there was a vacancy in his eyes.

"Bunce?"

"I don't think everything came back," Arvil whispered, but I couldn't really pay attention because I was suddenly smothered in Stacy.

"My boy's coming home?!?" It was half question and half ecstasy.

"I think so."

"Oh, thank you thank you! If there's any way I can repay you…"

"There is," I said. "You're going to help the church's new guardian find meaningful stuff to sacrifice to it."

"Guardian?" Arvil asked, but he already knew.

"Anne," he said, "I hate that place."

"Yeah," I said. "I think that's what got you out."

He looked as lost and sad as a motherless child, just for a moment, and I think it was helpless fear that made him slip back into his tired old seducer routine. "You said you'd be grateful,"

Dead Leather Office

he said. "But I know how tricky foretelling is, you probably saw yourself being grateful for my hot lovin' and plenty of it."

"Not tonight," I said. I'd have to wait until Cosby was all the way gone, but I didn't see any reason to tell him about that. I didn't bother to tell him how disappointed he'd be. I'd seen that too.

He shook his head. "I thought we were going to fix everything," he said.

"I never said I'd make things happy," I replied, "just that I'd make 'em right.

Alms and the Beast

James Wallis

It was Lug Finer who met him first.

It was late in the day and the boy was tilling the hard earth of his father's strip in the barley field. He was the last person still working, the scrape of his hoe the only sound breaking the early evening tranquillity. The other serfs had gathered up their tools and headed back to the village as soon as the sun had dropped below the trees of Fordham Woods to the west but Lug, with less than half of the strip finished and weeds flourishing between the stalks of the ripening crop, told himself that the risk was worth the reward. If there was blight in the barley it needed to be grubbed out, and there was enough light to spot any telltale black patches on the green ears of the tall stalks. His hands were blistered but the job had to be finished tomorrow: he owed his work on Thursday and Friday to the reeve.

The last of the sun slid below the horizon, and something in the way the light changed made Lug look up. The air was still. All the birds had stopped singing. The hairs on the back of his neck were prickling in a sudden chill.

Something was looking at him.

There, in the copse of trees at the edge of the field, something had moved just out of sight. He could sense it. Some thing was staring at him. No shape, no sound, no smell, just an unnameable sense of danger from that patch of shadows.

Why had he stayed in the fields? He knew it was dangerous. He'd seen the ripped corpse of Peter the miller's son a fortnight back. He hefted the hoe in his hands and didn't take his eyes off the spot at the edge of the wood. Was there a dark shape behind the rich green of the midsummer leaves? Was that branch swaying in a breeze, or because something had touched it?

Now it was darker. How long had he been standing there? He had no idea. He couldn't see the thing in the wood, but he knew it was there as certainly as he knew his own name. His blood pounded in his head, roaring, drowning his senses. He felt himself held in the thing's thrall like a rabbit facing a fox. He couldn't move. Any moment darkness would fall and it would rush—

A voice came from behind him: "Don't look at me." Lug jumped an inch, and stumbled in a half-turn.

"*Don't look at me!* Keep your eyes on it. Look away and it knows your defences are down.'

Lug dragged his gaze back to the edge of the wood. "What— who are you?'

"A traveller. A friend. I want you to get behind me. Move slowly. Don't stop looking at it. Then move as I move."

"What if it attacks?"

"*Do as I say!*" and Lug did, unable to refuse the command. The speaker was half a foot taller than him, the side and back of his head hidden by the hood of his studded leather cloak. He carried a heavy pack on his back. One hand rested inside the cloak, probably on a weapon. The rest of the details were lost in the twilight.

The stranger moved sideways to the earthen path between the wide strips of barley, and Lug moved with him.

"How close are we to Alburgh? Which way is it?"

"Four furlongs, maybe five." Lug pointed without taking his eyes off the wood. In the corner of his eye the steeple of the church was just visible against the darkening sky.

"I'm going to walk backwards till I reach the old road. You must move too, but keep me between it and you."

"I'll try." Lug said.

"You've got a name?'

"Lug.'

"Do as I tell you, Lug, and you won't die today."

Lug swallowed, his throat clogged with fear and the day's dust. The stranger took a backwards step and he took one to follow, stumbling on a clod of earth.

"Pay attention, Lug, and keep moving." There was a note of humour in the man's voice. It was strangely reassuring. "Tell me, this thing watching us, have you seen it before?"

"No."

"But you know what it is?"

"We call it the beast."

"When did it come here?"

"Last full moon. It's killed two men." They had reached the road, the weeds between its ancient stones dry from the lack of rain. Other than their footfalls there was silence: the breeze was gone, the insects quiet, the landscape still. The smell of dry grass and ripening crops filled the evening air.

"Now turn round," the stranger said, "and be my eyes to lead me to the village. Don't look back."

Lug stared down the shadowed road towards Alburgh, and took a step. There was a crash from the wood beyond the field, a great black shape exploded from the undergrowth, and a guttural roar split the gloaming. The stranger pulled on a leather strap and his heavy pack fell to the ground, then he tore a strange curved sword from under his cloak and raised it to strike as the beast charged through the barley towards them.

Lug threw his hoe aside and sprinted away, down the road towards the village. Behind him the sounds of desperate fighting faded until all he could hear were the slap of his shoes on the ancient flagstones, the ragged rhythm of his breaths, and his sobs of fear.

Alms and the Beast

It was only later, as he sat in the reeve's hall cradling a cup of ale and telling his story for the third time, that he realised the roar had not come from the thing in the wood, but from the man who had saved him.

At the head of the hall the reeve John Kiteley sat, with his sons on either side, listening. When Lug had finished and the hall had emptied, the villagers heading back to their homes in scared groups, the reeve spoke.

"What do we make of this stranger?"

Robert, the younger son, spoke first. "A brave traveller, no more. We bury his remains tomorrow."

"No." Edward raised a hand. "Maybe not dead yet. And tonight is a bad night to find strangers in the lanes."

"Bad?" John asked. "Bad for whom?" But Edward had lowered his face and said no more. John turned to Robert. "I want no terrified villeins, not with harvest so close. We three take watches from the church tower tonight. Robert, you first. This beast may be able to kill a peasant or traveller, but we'll see how it fares against three good swords."

As their father leaned forward to rise from his seat, Edward learned back and caught his brother's eye.

"This is the sequence I have told you of," he said.

"What?" John asked. But Robert just nodded and turned away.

◇

Will Godley woke to a sound of knocking. The room was dark, and no light came from the window — of course, there was no moon tonight. He slipped from under the blanket and made his way through the dark hut to the front door. His hand paused on the heavy bar that held it closed. What if the visitor was not some parishioner troubled by dreams of devils and things in the wood, but something darker? But man-killing monsters were not known to knock on doors, and it was his work to serve to all God's creatures.

"Who is it?" he asked. "What do you want?"

"Alms and aid," came a man's voice, ragged and weak. "Aid for a pilgrim."

That was not a response he had expected. Will lifted the bar and opened the door. Outside a dark figure clung to the doorpost. Even in the starlight Will could see the blood on his face, and the deep wound it welled from.

"God welcome you, come in!" He grasped the stranger by the arm and half-carried him across the room to a low bench, then rushed to stir up the cooking-fire, making new flames send light dancing across the room. He poured a beaker from the water-jug and turned back to the stranger, who was peeling off his blood-soaked clothes. Will passed him the cup of water and he swigged it, then splashed the rest across his face. Bloody water splattered over the straw on the floor, more blood welling from a deep cut across his forehead. There were other wounds on his chest and his left arm. They looked like bite-marks.

The stranger held out the empty cup. "Can you heat some more? I must clean my injuries."

Will filled a pan and set it on the fire. "Are you the man who saved Lug Finer?" he asked.

"The lad in the barley field?" The stranger grimaced. "I am, and lucky he is. I was afraid there might be more of the things along the road."

"Did you kill the beast?'

"No, only wounded it. It was wanting an easy kill, not a fight, and it ran after the first good cut. Sprained my leg badly before it went, though. I had to crawl most of the way here." Now clean of blood, his strong features and proud nose showed the touch of Norman lineage. Dark eyes stared out from under heavy brows. His voice was low and rich, his accent not local but still familiar.

"We must tell the reeve," Will decided, turning to the door, but stopped as the stranger's hand closed around his arm.

"Tell me about this beast first," he said.

"It has killed two people in as many weeks," Will said. "We hear it howling in the woods at night. People say it's the devil."

"You agree?"

Alms and the Beast

"I think the devil has more important business than a village of poor farmers." He turned to face the stranger. "Have you come to deliver us from it, then?"

The man's face was unreadable in the shadows as he scrubbed his cuts clean. "Something like that."

"I have prayed for divine aid," Will said, "but I am not so naïve as to believe in angels. Who are you?"

"Just a pilgrim."

Will shook his head. "Too close to harvest-time for pilgrimages."

"See my cloak if you don't believe me."

Will picked up the heavy, bloodied leather from where it had fallen and the silver badges, brooches and buttons gleamed up at him in the faint light, thickly studding the back of the garment: scallops and ampullas by the score, and among them the badges of St Giles from Winchester, St Cuthbert of York, and Thomas Beckett of Canterbury. He saw the Virgin of Walsingham and the beheaded martyr from the great abbey at Bury Saint Edmunds, and others he didn't recognise. So many badges, so many pilgrimages, so many miles walked. This was either a man of great faith, or a man with a great sin to atone for.

"What's this?" Will asked, pointing at a figure of a woman.

"Saint Catherine, from Rouen." Will looked blank. "France," the stranger clarified.

"This one I know—Saint Peter of Rome. One of my tutors wore it. But this I've not seen before."

"Croix Bellaert, from Sinten. Here is Saint Barnabus, from Cyprus. And this," the stranger touched a gold crucifix, crudely cast, "this I made in Jaffa in the Holy Land. We melted down jewellery we had looted and fashioned pilgrim badges for ourselves. So close." He paused. "We could see Jerusalem from its walls, but we did not go there. King Richard led us back."

Will understood. "You're a crusader."

"I was."

"Our lord went. Geoffrey of Wilton, with his sons. Did you fight with him?"

A grim laugh. "I did."

"Some men from the village too. Robert and Edward Kiteley, the reeve's sons."

"They went to the Holy Land?"

"Yes."

"You hesitate. What are you not saying?" the stranger asked.

Will paused. The reeve was his friend and protector, and as the village priest he owed his loyalty to him and his family, not to this vagabond with uncertain motives.

"They came back different men," he said finally.

"As did I. War changes all."

"Not like that. Edward—his faith has changed."

The pilgrim's head jerked up, his eyes focused. "Say more."

"I cannot. He does not speak of it in public." Only in the confessional, he thought, and that is between him and his god.

"But you know something," the pilgrim said. "You must tell me."

"I will not."

"You will," and in a movement the sword was in the man's hand, pointed at Will's breast. "I have to know. Your life may rest on it."

Will said nothing. His mind was calm, calmer than he could possibly have expected. Nobody had ever pointed a sword at him before, and he had no doubt that this taciturn, bloodied man would use it to get what he wanted. But his faith was strong.

There was a lump of fear in his throat. He tried to ignore it.

He walked forward, a slow step at a time, until the point of the curved sword was pressed against his ribs, sharp against his skin.

"Are you really so fearful that you cannot trust anyone?" he said. "Or is your pilgrimage so personal that you must do it alone? You asked me for aid. Do you now turn it away?"

There was silence in the low hut. The pilgrim's sword did not move, and neither did Will.

Finally the stranger sighed and lowered his sword. "You are right. I beg your forgiveness, but this night, this matter..."

"It taxes us all," Will said.

"This is not the road I thought my life would follow," the pilgrim said.

Alms and the Beast

Will was about to respond but suddenly the stranger reached across and grasped his wrist. The meaning was unmistakable: *be quiet*. He stopped abruptly.

Something was moving outside the cottage. Something, not someone. Heavy feet padded slowly around the outer wall, and moments later a sound of snuffling came from the crack at the bottom of the door.

A dog? A loose pig?

Will looked at the bloody water on the floor, trickling towards the threshold, and knew it was something worse. Something had tracked its wounded prey here.

The door swung inwards as the creature outside brushed against it. *He hasn't barred it shut.* He cursed himself silently.

The door began to open, pushed by something unseen. Will sensed its presence: heavy, alien, malevolent. It made a sound from deep in its throat, half grunt and half chuckle.

In a single movement the pilgrim threw himself across the room to the fire, grabbed the water-pan there and flung it towards the doorway. The main force of the water hit the intruder full in its face. There was an inhuman shriek, the thing reared up and for a moment it seemed that it would leap into the room, but then it was gone, fleeing back into the darkness.

Will slammed the door shut and pushed the bar back into its place. The stranger lay sprawled on the floor where he had fallen. The priest helped him to a sitting position.

"That was the beast?" Will asked.

A grimace. "As a man of God shouldn't you ask me how I am first?"

"I'm sorry. Are you—"

"I'll live, but I twisted my leg again as I went down. Have you studied Galen? Do you know the healing arts?"

Will knelt before the stranger, his hands feeling the man's thigh, knee and shin. "This hurts, here?"

"It does."

"The bone is damaged below the knee. Not broken but twisted, almost sheared." He looked up at his face. "If I asked you to rest it you would not."

"Not tonight."

"I thought you wouldn't. Well, I can splint it and bind it and rub teasel-root and horsetail into it, and it'll hold together if you don't do anything stupid like starting a fight."

"I'll do nothing stupid."

"No fights?"

"No stupid ones."

Will sighed. "It is the best healing I can offer. For more you must talk to the witch." He went to the shelf and got down some salve and strips of willow-bark to fashion a splint.

"A witch?" the pilgrim asked, surprise in his tone.

"Call her a wise woman then. Mother Oatley. She lives by the river. She can aid you."

"You're an odd one, priest, consorting with witches."

Will shrugged. "While my wife was dying, Mother Oatley helped her when prayer did not. You are a man of learning—you know faith is not as simple as good and evil. God works through all of us, even if his ways seem strange to our poor understanding. So it is with this woman."

"Then let us go to her."

"Why such haste?" Will asked, rubbing a thick paste onto the pilgrim's leg. "The beast is still out there. The door is secure. We are safe for the night, and you need rest."

"I cannot rest," the pilgrim said. "Not this night."

"Why not?"

"You know what today was?" Will looked blank. "It was the solstice, Will, the longest day of the year. The old Saxons called it Litha. Tonight is a powerful dark, the last moonless night before the harvest comes in. Such a night comes only every thirty years."

"And what happens on that night, do you believe?" Will asked.

"It is hard to say. An opening of ways or a channelling of powers, perhaps. There would have been a ritual a few weeks back, maybe under the new moon, to bring the beast here."

"Someone called the beast here? To what end?"

"Protection. To keep people away from whatever tonight's purpose may be."

Alms and the Beast

Will grimaced, trying to recall a conversation he had dismissed at the time. "Mother Oatley said she heard something strange a fortnight back, a high keening in the woods. Said her mother had spoken of such things."

The stranger stared at him, pulling himself to his feet. "That was it. Come on. Pass me my cloak. I must talk to your witch this minute."

Will helped wrap the cloak around the stranger's shoulders, then moved to unbar the door. He could see a faint glow through the cracks between the wooden planks. His hands lifted the bar.

But this night is moonless, he thought. So what light—

The door thudded inwards, knocking him off his feet. Something rushed towards him with great arms outstretched to grab him as he fell. He felt himself lifted and flung against the wall, his limbs flailing. His skull cracked against the rough plaster and he fell to the floor.

A great shaggy form stood above him.

It had not fled into the night, he realised. It had stayed outside the door, waiting.

Its breath was foul. Everything about it was foul.

So this is what the beast looks like, he thought absently, as its huge claw descended and ripped his throat out.

◇

Robert Kiteley had seen the fire from the top of the church spire and had sprinted down the stairs. A hut was ablaze, over by the river, its dry thatch sending high flames into the night sky. He needed to wake the village and get help. Whose hut was on fire? Not many people lived over by the mill.

He reached the ground and ran from the church, through the graveyard and past the priest's house. As he approached he saw strange lights and shadows leaping on the ground, thrown from inside. A second house afire did not bode well, and his path would take him past the door. He stopped for a moment, then drew his sword and moved on, uncertain of what he would find.

But then there was a flash and a roar of flame from within the hut. Fire flickered through the doorway, and a tall inhuman figure rushed out through the door, smoke trailing from its body. It ran for the woods and was gone into the darkness.

"The beast," Robert whispered.

Behind it came a man with a limp, a body in his arms. Robert did not recognise them, but ran towards them.

"All safe?" he called.

"It killed him," the man said. "Don't go in. There's nothing left." As if in answer something inside the house fell with a crash and a rush of flames and sparks. Robert threw up a hand to protect his face from the sudden heat. When he lowered it the stranger had laid down the body he carried, and was making the sign of the cross over it. Both men moved away from the blaze.

"God rest him," Robert said. "Who are you?"

"A pilgrim. The man who saved Lug Finer. The beast followed me and killed the priest. I drove it off with fire. You?"

"Robert Kiteley. I was standing watch. Another hut is on fire, by the river."

"The witch's?"

That would make sense. Robert nodded. "How did you know?"

"It fits. If she is a witch, then she may know what is to happen here this night. We should try to save her."

"We should," Robert said and hit him as hard as he could.

The first blow went to the man's face, the second and third were punches to the stomach, the fourth tried to knock the sword from his hand but—as the stranger doubled over—went too high and caught him on the shoulder. The fifth was an uppercut aimed for the face but missed completely, as his target slumped to the floor. Robert pulled back his leg to kick hard at where he knew the man's head must be, and pain exploded in the knee that carried all his weight. Bone and cartilage crunched, he was thrown off balance, and fell.

He hit the ground badly, trying to break his fall with one arm, sending ugly shocks up the bone to his shoulder. He tried to roll away, realized too late he'd chosen the wrong direction, and a

Alms and the Beast

moment later had the breath knocked out of him as the stranger's bulk crashed down onto his chest, pinning him down. The curved end of the sword's blade pressed hard into his flank, below the ribs, ready to gut him. The stranger's outline loomed overhead. Blood from a broken noise dripped onto his cheek.

"Who told you I was your enemy?" the man hissed. Robert made a token effort to throw him off, but felt the sword's point break through his clothes to his skin. He gave up the struggle.

"My brother." Another prod. "Edward."

"Good," and the weight was off him. The stranger was on his feet, holding out a hand to help Robert up. "Your brother I knew about, but I needed to be sure about you. What did he tell you?"

"He said a stranger would come tonight. He told me you were in thrall to the beast, and I must find you and stop you."

"What would your brother be doing while you sought me out?"

"He would be calling on God's power to banish the beast."

The roof of the priest's house collapsed inwards, sending fire shooting at the sky. There were more screams in the distance. The sudden light revealed the pilgrim's face and the grim realization on it.

"God speaks to him? Since the Crusade?"

"So he says. He calls it his blessing and says it has given him the power of an Apostle."

"Something speaks to him," the pilgrim said, "but it is not our Lord. He has been tricked, as a friend of mine was tricked, but he can be saved. Do you trust me?"

Maybe. "Yes."

"Then come with me." He stooped to offer Robert his hand and Robert grasped it to pull himself up, noting with a soldier's eye how the man took the weight on his right leg. Behind them, villagers were leaving their houses and running towards the church. The fire was spreading, moving from cottage to cottage, illuminating the village.

"Where are we going?"

"To the river. There's a ford?"

"Yes."

"It makes sense," the pilgrim said. "A ritual where ancient channels cross their paths."

Robert nodded silently, inwardly happy. His brother had been right. The sequence was being followed.

The stranger broke into a jog, and Robert followed, keeping a pace or two behind. Their feet beat a rhythm on the flagstones of the ancient road. The man's limp was more pronounced now, the injury clearly at the knee. Robert smiled to himself.

Behind them something roared, the sound cracking the night with the cry of a predator sighting its prey. The stranger increased his pace, moving out of the circle illuminated by the burning village and into the edges of the wood. He was limping harder now. To anyone already in the dark they would be obvious targets, silhouetted against the fires. But ahead of them something else glowed through the trees with a strange shadowless aura.

Another sound. Heavy footfalls were approaching from behind them, large and catching up. Robert pushed his legs harder, drawing ahead of the stranger.

"Stay back!" the stranger cried. "You do not know what lies ahead!"

Robert ignored him, sprinting on. He did know what lay ahead: the ford, where his brother was waiting for him.

The light grew as the trees widened out where the road approached the river, with scrub along the bank. The surface of the river was afire. Pale flames flickered on the water as it approached the old ford, growing a foot high where the Roman road dipped under the river, and then dying away as they floated downstream on the current. In the centre of the water-fire, thigh-deep in the river, stood a figure he knew well.

Then a shaggy form he had seen before leaped from the bushes beside the road, took two long loping strides, and hit him sideways with the impact of a carthorse. He slammed into the paving stones, the rough surface scraping skin from his face and arms, his sword flying away into the undergrowth. An instant later his world filled with matted black fur and the smell of raw

Alms and the Beast

meat. It had him in its grasp, pressing his face against its pelt, suffocating him. He struggled, flailing, pushing against it, feeling its huge arms crushing the air from his lungs.

Something about the smell reminded him of the desert.

It was no good.

He was dying.

The beast atop him lurched to one side, and then further. Its grip loosened. Something spilled down across Robert's face, hot and acrid. He pushed against the beast one more time and it fell away from him to sprawl across the road. Its body was not as big as it had expected, and then he realised its bestial head was lying six feet away. The skin around the face was bubbled and raw, one eye the colour of a boiled egg. Dark blood or something like it covered the flagstones.

Beyond it the pilgrim stood in profile, sword raised.

Beyond him, a second beast.

From where Robert lay on the ground, staring up at them, the two figures looked like things of myth, giants of legend, representatives of the ageless, eternal conflict between virtue and evil. He believed he had left that war behind on the bloodied sands of the Holy Land. He had been wrong.

Ribs and joints scraped in pain, but he pushed himself to his knees, then to his feet. The beast did not turn its head to look at him, but he knew it was watching him to see if he was still a threat. With no weapon, his lungs still aching and his body bruised, he didn't feel like much of one.

At that moment the song began.

It was a weird high sound, a rising and falling like a shawm or crumhorn, but vocal and ululatory. It did not come from the tongue or the throat but somewhere else, deeper in the body. It came from behind him, from the figure stood in the river. From Edward.

The flames on the river blazed up, and the beast hurled itself at the pilgrim.

Robert waited for the man to raise his sword, to fend off the blow or slice at his attacker, but the man did not. He half-turned and ducked down, presenting his shoulders and back to the beast. The thing flung its jaws wide and bit down on the pilgrim.

The man flipped his sword in his hand and threw it, low and hilt-first, at Robert. Startled, he fumbled the catch. The sword clattered to the stones and it took him a second to scoop it up and adjust his hand to the unfamiliar grip. When he looked up he expected to see the pilgrim torn in half, the beast ripping into his corpse. Instead they seemed locked together. Then the weird light from the river glinted off the myriad metal badges, the silver scallop-shells and saints and crucifixes, so close together that the leather of the cloak was almost hidden from view, and he understood.

Not a mark of faith or penance, but armour.

"Strike!" the stranger shouted, and Robert struck. The blade buried itself in the creature's shoulder and it turned and roared, the movement wrenching the sword from his grip. Beyond the beast, the pilgrim threw his cloak off and backwards, covering the monster's head.

The creature ripped the garment away, but the distraction was long enough for Robert to grab the sword and pull it free. A gout of ichor followed its exit. Beyond, the stranger ran into the ford, his legs kicking up sprays of water and cold fire. The song did not cease. Then the beast lunged again, and all his attention was on this fight.

Even with the wound in the beast's shoulder, it was the hardest opponent Robert had ever fought. It deflected his sword-blows with disdain and came back at him with blows so solid that parrying was like striking the sword against a tree. A claw caught him across the arm, ripping through his jerkin to the flesh, and a few seconds later a thick fist slammed his ribs, throwing him several paces back..

It was not like fighting a man, but not like fighting a creature like a wolf or a bear either. It had reason and cunning, it blocked and feinted, and it used the length of its arms like a cudgel, but there was a pure ferocity to its attacks that transcended any intelligence. Its body, muscles, claws, instinct, essence were created to overpower and destroy men like him.

Alms and the Beast

And at his back was his brother, in a struggle of his own.

The creature came at him again and he turned its first two blows away, knowing already that his sword would be too high and wide to parry the third. The end was inevitable. The creature's left arm was poised to swing in and gut him, there was nothing he could do to block or duck. The fight was over, and so was he.

Then there was a great splash, the fires on the river flared and the chanting ceased abruptly. The beast hesitated for an instant, but an instant was enough for Robert to bring his arm downwards in a scything hack and watch as the stranger's blade sank deep into his attacker's neck. He let go of the sword and stepped back as the beast faltered in its swing. It reached up with one claw to grasp at the blade, trying to pull it loose. Then its legs crumpled and it toppled backwards. On the ground, it twitched. Thick fluid poured from the wound.

Robert stepped forward and bent to pull the sword free. The beast's eyes blinked and fixed on him as he did, and its expression curved in a rictus that could almost have been a sneer. The sword came away with a burst of blood, and the beast shook and died.

He stared into its hideous animal face. Its eyes, he could see now, were black flecked with gold. There was a disdain to them, something that spoke of contempt, of how little this death mattered, how little he—the beast's killer—could understand of the sequence in which he had played his tiny part. You are insignificant, the eyes said. My death is as immaterial as you are. The sequence continues.

Robert spat into its dead eyes and turned to the river.

The water still glowed with cold light, but the fire had gone. In the shallows on the far side two men were fighting: Edward and the stranger. Both were warriors, both accustomed to battle in many forms. The stranger was winning.

Robert started to splash his way across the ford, watching as the stranger landed two punches to Edward's upper body. Edward swung in retaliation, missed, and took a full-force blow to the face. He went down with a spray of water. The stranger jumped after him, grasping him around the neck to drag him half out of the river. Then he bent, grabbed Edward by the lapels of his jerkin, lifted his head up, and shouted, the same phrase over and over. On the third repeat Robert was able to make out the words.

"Who taught you the chant? Who taught you the chant?"

He was nearly there. The stranger was shaking Edward, making his head bob, water running from his dark hair. If his brother said anything Robert did not hear it.

"Who taught you the chant? Who taught you the chant?"

Robert came up out of the water and ran a few short paces down the bank to where the two figures were. Neither looked at him.

"Who taught you the chant?" the stranger demanded again. Robert kicked him on the injured knee with all his strength. The leg collapsed and with a shout the man fell back into the river with a mighty splash. The waters closed over him.

Robert looked down at his brother, and Edward looked up, caught his brother's eye and smiled. His eyes were dark and knowing.

It was the smile that Robert had seen on the face of the dead beast on the other side of the river.

"Remember the sequence," Edward said.

Without knowing why he did it, without thinking of anything at all, Richard raised the pilgrim's sword, brought it down with all his force, and beheaded his brother.

Arterial blood, red and bright, rushed from Edward's neck. The severed head rolled onto the slope of the bank and trundled down with increasing speed until it met the river with a muffled splash. The moment it did the last of the light in the water vanished and the night enveloped them. The darkness was broken by the stars, the flames of the burning cottages in the distant village, and lights that bobbed and moved among the trees on the other side of the river. People were coming, bearing torches.

The stranger had hauled himself up out of the water. He tested his weight on the leg Robert had kicked, and winced. Then he noticed the torches.

"We haven't much time," he said. "Will they believe that your brother summoned the beasts?"

Alms and the Beast

Robert felt his grip on the world returning. "They may," he said, "if we tell them so. He has been changed since we returned from the Holy Land." *They will believe you killed him too*, he thought, *my word against yours, and nobody here knows you from Adam*. But as he looked at the man's face in the faint light he had a sudden flash of how he would have looked with the dust of the desert and the long fruitless road to Jerusalem on his skin, a gold badge from Jaffa on his cloak, and thought again.

"He was your older brother?" the pilgrim asked.

"Yes."

"I'm sorry. You travelled back from the crusade with him?"

"Yes."

"Did he visit towns or villages, or meet people on the way, that seemed odd to you?"

Robert stared at him. "Is this what you do?" he asked. "Walk the roads, chasing ghosts, killing for scraps of information? Who are you?"

"Tell me the towns you visited!"

"What happened here? What was my brother doing?" Robert shouted. "Did we stop it?"

"*I don't know!*" the pilgrim cried. "I must find out! There is a great darkness coming and I must know how to stop it!"

"It is no good," Robert said. "They are here."

The men from the village were splashing their way across the ford. Silently Robert handed the bloody sword back to the stranger and turned to face them. The light from their torches cast jumping shadows across the banks of the river. His father John led the group, his sword drawn. Many of others carried staves or cudgels.

"Robert!" John shouted. "Where is Edward?"

"Here," Robert said. He moved aside so his father could see the body. There was a confusion in his mind on how his brother had died.

"God's blood!" John said. "What happened here?" Then the light from his torch fell on the pilgrim's face. "You!" he said.

"You know him, father?" Robert said. "He saved Lug. What is his name?"

"He has no name," John said. "Sir Geoffrey took it from him, along with his title and lands. This is the man who killed his son."

"Killed Thomas Wilton? In Acre, on the crusade?" Robert had heard the stories and the rumours, the tales of sorcery and intrigue, of blasphemous doings and a funeral at midnight.

"I did not kill Thomas," the pilgrim said in a low, sad voice. "If I had, Sir Geoffrey would have had me executed. Thomas was my friend and bosom companion, led from righteousness by—" His voice petered out.

"Geoffrey could not prove you killed Thomas. But he still stripped you and made you an outlaw. And now you have killed my son." John stood over the body of Edward, his pose rigid with hate, waiting for an excuse to strike the strange man who stood opposite him. The energy and power that had sustained the pilgrim were gone, and he stood like a man awaiting the gallows.

"He did not kill Edward," Robert spoke up.

"No? Then who did?"

"The beast did," the pilgrim said. John looked at him with disbelief, then at the shaggy corpse on the far side of the river.

"The beast?" he said. "Robert, is this true?"

"Yes," Robert said. It seemed the easiest answer. Perhaps it was true.

John gave another to the far bank. "Who killed the beasts?"

"We did."

"He saved my life," Robert said.

John exhaled slowly, turning so he did not have to look at the body of his dead son. "This is a sorry state," he said. "I hope the dawn will make all things clearer. Meanwhile," he turned to the pilgrim, "you are a wanted man, but I owe you a debt for saving Robert. I cannot let you go, but I cannot let you stay." He paused and stared at the pilgrim. The man looked back but said nothing. "Tell me why I should let you live."

The stranger said nothing for a long time. Then: "I am as you see me: a pilgrim. I travel to the holy shrines to atone for my deeds, and to learn from the scholars. In Acre we met a power of evil that killed Thomas and set me on this path. The beasts are part of it. Your son was too. I live to defeat it. That is why I came here: I heard of your beast and recognised the signs. Such is my existence. If you end my life, that which I fight will grow stronger."

John was silent, thinking. "Well then," he said finally. "As I am the reeve you are in my custody, and if you escape then it is on my head. Go now. At dawn my men will come after you, and if they catch you then you will answer to Sir Geoffrey. Do we have an understanding?"

"We do."

"Then go." He pointed down the road that led into the wood.

"No," the pilgrim said. "That way leads to Wilton and I cannot go there yet. My cloak and pack lie in your village and I shall go that way." He moved away, wading into the river, pushing against the water, and Robert watched him go. He could see the man was limping hard.

"I think I met him in the Holy Land," he said to his father. "Maybe Edward met him there too." He realised his father was not standing beside him. John Kiteley had retrieved Edward's head from the river and was kneeling over it, head down, weeping silent tears. Robert watched him. Suddenly the night and the deed crashed in on him. His brother. The song. The beast. The river. The sword. The blood. His brother. He fell to his knees and wept too.

When he raised his head the fires of the village still burned in the distance, but lower now, the steeple of the church lit by the flames. It would never be the same now, it could not be. He stared across the river at the body of one of the beasts, cold and dead, stripped of all its terror. Men were gathering wood to make a pyre and burn it. Between him and it the river flowed on, silent and relentless, as it had done since before there was a village or a road here. Of the pilgrim there was no sign.

Iron Achilles Heel

Jennifer Brozak

"You ready?" Eric asked as he glanced from the sounds of gunshots and screams towards the spirit on his right and back again.

"I'm always ready to do God's Will," Joseph said. He looked through the bank office window and nodded.

Eric did not have to look again to know that Joseph had disappeared from his side. He could already feel the avenging spirit taking control of his body and let it happen. He knew all he had to do now was watch, listen and learn. If necessary, warn Joseph of something the spirit had not already seen.

Like an experienced thief, Joseph slid the boot knife blade up between the window panes and flipped the latch. He swung the windows open and pulled himself into the bank's back office. There, he crouched behind the desk, waiting to see if any of the bank robbers had noticed him. Considering they were in the front with the terrified bank patrons and there was no backdoor, Eric wasn't surprised none of them expected an attack from behind.

Joseph and Eric had tracked this band of robbers for the last hundred miles or so through towns too small to be remembered on any map. Once they got the gist of where the robbers were headed, Palmer, Arizona and the site of the most profitable of the small towns in the area, they had hurried on ahead with the intention of stopping the robbers before they made their mark there, too. However, only a day off the trail and just long enough to get the lay of the land, the gang had ridden into town and struck again.

But this time, there would be an accounting for their crimes.

"Please, mister, you have the money. Please, just go!"

"Never tell me what to do!"

The crash of the gunshot was followed by a surprised gasp of pain that faded into a weak whimper.

"Dammit all, they're shooting people."

"Not for long," Joseph murmured as he stood and moved to the office doorway, no longer hiding himself. In front of him was the teller's countertop. Beyond that, a score of frightened folk and the four bank robbers he was set to stop and bring back—alive or dead. Joseph's first shot took the bank robber at the end of the counter between the eyes. His second shot swung wide as one of the robbers, the one closest to the front door reacted, shooting Eric's body in the chest.

"Move it, Daniel!" that robber ordered.

Daniel, the original target of Joseph's second bullet and the robber who had just murdered the bank manager, cursed, shot wildly in Joseph's direction and ran towards the door. Joseph leveled his gun but stopped as Daniel grabbed the nearest woman and used her as a shield. Both men backed out it, Daniel still holding the crying woman hostage.

The fourth bank robber, to the left of door, the one who had seen Joseph shot but not react, stared as Joseph used his left hand to pluck the bullet from his chest and his right to aim and fire. The fourth robber gurgled as he dropped his gun and clutched at his throat to staunch the blood that spurted forth. He went to his knees, still staring at Joseph, before toppling over.

Eric knew the bullet to the chest had to have hurt but Joseph was a master at ignoring pain. When you could heal all wounds within a matter of moments, all you had to do was wait it out. And all Eric had to do was mend yet another bullet hole in his shirt. Fortunately, his body rarely bled while Joseph spirit-rode him.

Joseph headed towards the front door but stopped as one of the womenfolk, a girl from the General Store, frantically shook her head, "No!"

"What is it?"

She drew back from him as if understanding that Eric wasn't exactly himself. "Those two are the Marlin boys. They wait and shoot anyone who comes after them."

Joseph nodded, curt and polite. "Thank you, ma'am." He turned from her, walking towards the back of the bank, stepped over the first robber he shot and returned to the bank manager's office. He slid himself out of the window and crouched down, listening. There was a cry of a woman, not a mortal cry, but one of distress and outrage, followed by the sound of men's rude laughter and the pounding of two horses pushed into a gallop.

"Looks like it's chase then."

"Better for the townsfolk. Less likely to get killed."

Eric, suddenly in charge of his body again, knew what was expected. He whistled for his horse. In all the time he and Joseph had been together, the spirit still had not learned to whistle.

◇

Eric never thought he would get used to being a passenger in his own body, watching the gunfight with a sleepy eye, like a man who has seen the same vaudeville act one too many times. But here he was; nothing more than a human vessel for the Lion of God, Sheriff Joseph Lamb, doing his sworn duty to smite sinners and bring justice back to this wild land. It was the pain that broke him out of his complacency; pain in his hand and pain in his neck. Something he had never felt before while being spirit-ridden by Lamb.

Then he was falling.

Iron Achilles Heel

As he hit the dirt, the pain in his hand and neck was replaced with the jarring sensation of his teeth clacking together and the scrape of rocks against his cheek. The sounds of his horse galloping toward parts unknown covered the other man's groans until Eric rolled over and saw Joseph lying in the dirt, blood streaming between fingers clamped to the man's throat.

"Joseph! Holy God! What happened?"

"My gun," Joseph croaked. "What happened to the gun?"

The gun in question was a Colt 1851 Navy revolver with a series of intricate flame engravings on the barrel and a well worn handle. It was the Sheriff's weapon. Decades ago, it was used to murder him. Eric saw it lying in the scrub a few feet from where he landed. He limped over to it, picked it up and saw the deep notch in the barrel of the pistol where the bank robber's bullet must have hit it. One in a million shot.

Eric turned back to Joseph as he held up the pistol. "It's here. A bullet hit it." He rubbed a finger in the bullet groove and Joseph gasped in pain. Eric frowned and touched the bullet groove again and saw Joseph wince at the same time. "You didn't tell me you could get hurt," he said as he walked over to where Joseph was.

"Didn't know it until now." Joseph struggled into a seated position.

"Huh. The almighty Lion of God is not invulnerable after all."

The spirit looked up at his companion with a wry expression, "Appears not."

Eric hunkered down next to Joseph and stuck an experimental hand through Joseph's incorporeal arm. "That hurt?"

"No."

He touched the bullet groove on the pistol and did not have to repeat his question. Joseph winced in pain. "Well, hell and damnation, Lamb. How am I supposed to get you fixed? Your body isn't of this earth and any touch to the gun makes you weep like a child."

Lamb shrugged a little. "I don't know. Never been hurt like this before. But the bleeding's stopped. I think I'll live. It'll just take time to heal. A lot of time. More time than we have. We've got a job to finish."

Eric holstered the revolver and stood. "Not like this we don't." He turned in the direction the bank robbers went. West, towards the setting sun and the Mexico border or maybe a slight turn north and they'd be in California in the same amount of time. Either way, the Marlin boys were home free. "You're too hurt."

"You're right. *We* can't do anything. *You* need to finish the job."

"Like hell." Eric turned on Joseph, only to find him gone. The next words Joseph spoke were from inside his head.

"If you let these men go because of your yellow streak, it'll be one more step on your road to damnation. We made a promise. The words you spoke were your own. I did not force you."

"Damn you, Lamb."

"Not likely. We don't have much time. I'll be with you the whole way. You aren't helpless. You're not some mewling child. Now call your horse back. There's work to be done."

Eric resisted the urge to pull leather and bash that Colt revolver with a rock until it, and the spirit of Sheriff Joseph Lamb, were no more. Instead, he took a breath and whistled for his horse, Dusty; he used the whistle that promised the gelding a treat even though it was a lie.

◇

As the fire red coal of the sun touched the horizon, Dusty picked his way through the darkening desert landscape. Eric kept an eye out for leg-breaking holes. He also scanned the line where the fading light met the blackness of earth, looking for sign or silhouette of his quarry. All the while, he tried not to think of just how frightened he was of facing the Marlin boys alone.

No, not really alone. He had not been alone since that day in the church a year ago. There, in that haunted place, he had sought refuge from outlaws, found the gun, and with it, the spirit of the murdered Sheriff. He agreed, fearful and shaking, to do the Lord's work at the threat of his immortal soul, rather than die at that moment with his place in heaven assured. He wondered, and not for the first or last time, if he had made the right choice.

Iron Achilles Heel

"You'll need to dismount soon and go on foot."

No. Never alone. "You want me to keep going in the dark?"

"I'll help you to see as best I can. With all the ground we lost, this is our best chance to catch them before they cross the border."

"How you feeling?"

Joseph came forward just enough for Eric to feel the aching throb in his right hand and the searing pain in his throat; a pain so great he had to muffle a groan and tears stood in his eyes.

"I've felt worse."

"Really?"

"Honestly, no. This is bad but I don't think I'm gonna die... again. I think the Lord still has work for me to do."

Eric dismounted and tied his horse up in a loose hitch. If he died, he wanted Dusty to have a chance without him. He took a breath and continued following the trail on foot. There was nothing left to do now but go forward.

It wasn't long before he and Lamb spotted the faint glow of a campfire in the distance. It was low and unobtrusive in the gloom. Just enough coals to warm some food and keep the night from getting too cold. It was also the last mistake the Marlin boys would make, Eric thought. After the shooting they did this afternoon, he was going to shoot first and demand surrender second.

"Ill thoughts from a man doing good works."

Eric wanted to curse Lamb for his eavesdropping. "You said it first, 'sometimes a man has to do bad in the name of good.' These men are stone cold killers and think I'm already dead. I'm not going to give them another chance to actually put me in the ground."

"Watch that hole."

He looked down and saw he was moments from plunging his foot into a leg-breaker that would have stopped this foolish quest as well as his life. Eric stepped over it, balancing with one hand against a stone still warm from the heat of the day. He kept close to the rocks and the scrub to keep his own silhouette from announcing his presence.

"In any case," Eric said, "there's two of them and one of me."

"You get the drop on them and they might surrender."

"Or they might blow my fool head off."

"You never know, but we're about to find out."

Eric halted his careful steps through the darkness and unfamiliar land to look up. Before him was a small hill—a mound, really—with the silhouette of a man propped up against a rock at its apex. The glow from the dying campfire gave the man scant details: Stetson pulled low, a bushy beard and both hands limp upon his chest.

Remembering to pull his ordinary pistol from his left holster, Eric moved with swift, silent motions. Revolver now in his right hand, Eric acted on instinct. He took cover behind a rocky outcrop, cocked his gun and aimed at his target. However, instead of shooting first, he yelled, "Hands up! I've got you covered! Hands up or I shoot."

The Marlin boy—the older one, Jebadiah, Eric thought—did not move. For a moment, he wondered if the man was asleep and where the other one, Daniel, was. Then Jeb twitched. Instead of reaching for the stars, the man's right hand came down towards his thigh.

Eric fired twice. Both chest shots hit and Jeb fell over.

His heart pounding, Eric waited to hear what he would hear as the echoes of his shots died away—the scrabbling of Daniel fleeing, the crunch of rock underfoot, the yell of an angry, grieving brother or the clack of a pistol being cocked.

Nothing.

The seconds ticked by.

"I think you need to come up here and see this."

The voice was Joseph's and Eric could see him now standing above the still form of Jebadiah. Eric hesitated, looking around, flash burned eyes still seeking the other Marlin boy.

Joseph nodded with approval, "You're learning. It's clear. I wouldn't lead you into danger."

"What do you think you've been doing for the last year?" Eric scoffed as he put his normal pistol back in its holster and

Iron Achilles Heel

clambered up the mound to the makeshift camp. Immediately, he saw what Joseph wanted him to see: Jeb's throat had been cut, and deep. The wound had been hidden by his beard. Now, the almost dried blood glistened black in the light of the coals.

"Congratulations. You just shot a dead man and let his murderer know we're on his trail."

"Daniel did this?" Eric's eyes traced the outline of the gash in dead man's neck before looking at Joseph. He saw that Joseph had tied a kerchief around his throat and, while the blood was staunched, he saw the blood on the cloth and Lamb's neck was also black in the light of the firelight. Once again, he wondered at how a spirit could bleed. "Why?"

"'For the love of money is the root of all kinds of evil. And some people, craving money, have wandered from the true faith and pierced themselves with many sorrows,'" Joseph quoted. "In short, he got greedy. Money does funny things to a man. Guess he decided he wanted the bankroll for himself. From the looks of it, he planned it that way. Snuck up on Jeb here and cut his throat while the man slept. Then he ran." Joseph pointed towards the place where the last shades of red met black.

"And now he knows someone's coming for him."

"Yep."

Eric gave the camp a brief look over, saw that everything worth taking was gone and nodded. "Then we'd best go get him."

◇

They did not immediately chase down Daniel as Eric wanted. Joseph pointed out that it would be best to wait until moonrise as it was a clear night and the moon would give them better light to follow the trail. Instead, they argued about Jebadiah's ring.

With time to kill, Eric inspected what was left of the Marlin camp. Daniel had done a good job of ransacking it. There was nothing useful left. Then he saw a glimmer of light from Jeb's left hand. Upon removal and some squinting in the scant starlight, Eric discovered that it was a wedding ring.

"Huh. I didn't know he was married." He turned the ring over and around before reading, "With Love, Anne."

"Even outlaws find love," Joseph said. "You know you can use that as proof of your kill."

"My kill?"

"There's still a bounty on Jebadiah's head—dead or alive. That ring you just pocketed proves you deserve it."

Eric scowled, "No, it doesn't. I didn't have anything to do with Jeb's death. I'm not a murderer."

"Ah, but you are."

"No." He shook his head, "You spirit-ride me. You do the killing."

"While you get the reward and accolades?"

Eric swung his head from side to side. He wasn't hearing Joseph's voice in his head. That meant the Sheriff was around but, for some reason the spirit stayed hidden. He wanted to face his accuser, but suppressed his growing anger at the man's accusations. "That's not why I do this."

"Then why'd you take the ring?"

Eric's voice was quiet. "Even an outlaw's wife deserves to know her husband's dead and who really killed him."

Joseph did not respond. He remained quiet until they were well on their way to finding Daniel Marlin.

◊

Once the moon rose and turned the desert landscape into a myriad of dark and light silver tinted shadows, it was easy enough to follow the double horse track trail to the darkened camp recently fled by Daniel. Finding nothing but an abandoned pot of water over smothered coals, Eric and Joseph continued on. But this time, the double horse track was rushed and spoke of panic. Eric did not like it. A panicked man did risky things…like push a horse through a desert full of leg-breakers after dark.

"There is something up ahead."

Joseph was back within Eric and he could feel the Sheriff's lingering pain on the edges of his senses. He pushed it away and concentrated on the moving thing in his path. His heart sank as he got closer. It was a downed horse. A live one, in pain.

With his pistol drawn, he approached, looking all around. The horse groaned loud when it saw Eric. Its eyes begged him to stop the pain. To help it, somehow. There was a touch of a squeal in its next, more urgent groan and Eric could see the front foreleg was broken. "That bastard left you to suffer."

"No. I think he left her here as a way to tell how close you were getting."

Joseph was right; Eric knew it and did not need to question his mentor's comment. The choice was to either immediately end the horse's suffering with a bullet in the brain or to cause more pain and a slower death with a cut throat.

"What will you do?"

"I don't know. What would you do?"

"This is your hunt. Your choice." Joseph paused and added, "Choose with your heart."

"Are you testing me again? Because if you are, it's starting to irritate me."

"*What will you do?*" Joseph asked again.

"The right thing." With that, he put his pistol to the suffering horse's head and told the outlaw exactly where he was…and also told him the kind of man who was tracking him.

◇

They both knew it was a trap when they saw the next horse left in the dirt. This one whinnied and tried to toss its head at their approach but the bridle and bit held the horse's head close to the ground. Eric pulled leather as soon as he saw it and searched the shadows for the outlaw.

Sounds came from all around Eric. Pebbles thrown to distract him. Adrenaline pushed into him, honing his abilities. He listened for the scrabble of boot heel on rock and the cock of the gun. His eyes searched as he moved in closer to the horse. He was distantly aware of the horse's struggles to get up and the pain from Joseph's wounds. None of that was important. What *was* important was—

There. The scrape of spur on rock. That was all the warning he had before Daniel opened fire on him from the base of a nearby cholla cactus. Eric dove to the ground, firing two shots at the muzzle flash off to his left as he fell and heard Daniel grunt in pain. The sound of metal hitting the earth told Eric that Daniel dropped his gun. He listened to the man's moans of pain for a few moments before walking over to where the Daniel lay.

Daniel Marlin was a slight man. Young, in his early twenties, but had the weather beaten face of a man ten years older. He was curled up on the ground with his hands to his chest. It reminded Eric of Jebadiah's death pose. He could see the fresh blood, black in the moonlight, staining the front of Daniel's shirt.

"Help me. You've got to help me," Daniel wheezed at him. There was a high pitched sound of escaping air coming from the man's chest.

"Help you like you helped those people back in town? Helped the banker even after he gave you the money? Helped your own brother?" The righteous anger built up as Eric spoke, softening his words into the threat they were.

"You got to, lawman. Your… duty."

"Don't got to do anything, Daniel. Not a lawman, just a bounty hunter." It was the blood on Daniel's spurs that made him do it. Blood from the horse he ran until it faltered. Then left to die, leg-broke and keening in pain. Only Eric wasn't going to take that kind of chance with this kin-killing outlaw. He fired twice more: another shot to the chest and one to the head. "I do God's work."

He looked down at Daniel's limp body and watched the last breath escape already dead lips. Watched as the man's chest fell and did not rise again. "That's what you've been trying to tell me, hasn't it, Joseph? I really am a killer. Like you. Like him. Have been for the last year…no matter how much I've told myself I wasn't."

"No, Eric. Not like Daniel. He killed for the joy of it. You kill because it is God's will. You, too, are a Lion of God or you never would've been chosen to wield me."

Iron Achilles Heel

"Wield? All I do is sit back and watch you work."

"You do more than that and it was time you understood. We are cut from the same cloth."

"How do you know?"

"Look at your hand, my friend, and see that it is God's will."

Eric looked down at his hand and saw that he had not pulled his normal pistol from the left hand holster. He was holding the God blessed revolver. Its engraved flames danced along the now unmarred barrel of the pistol in the moonlight. To be certain, he raised the pistol up and swung the cylinder out to confirm what he already knew: it was not loaded. The last two shots he made, the ones that had killed the outlaw in cold blood, had been his choice but they had also been God's will. It was something to think about.

"Are you well?"

"By the grace of God, I am now."

But not tonight. Tonight was reserved for freeing the trapped horse, recovering the bankroll and backtracking his trail to his own horse. Later, after property was returned and a widow was informed, Eric would think about this revelation. Until then, he would soothe himself with the mundane tasks of being a famous bounty hunter.

Blood for the King

Will Hindmarch

The incoming ships first register as a pair of blips on a holographic display wrapped halfway around an operator's froglike head. In his native tongue he declares two vessels on his scope. The commander stomps over on pachyderm feet and makes a gesture in the interface. The hologram swells so it fills the flight-control room with bands of bright green light. Two yellow blips move through the air between commander and operator.

Too fast, the commander thinks. *The ships are coming in too fast.*

Out there, miles away from the station, both ships are drifting down out of the flight plane toward the planet's icy ring system. The ship in front is a slender thing, shaped like a needle with a booster rocket strapped on, big enough for just one or two pilots. The ship behind it has an angled, swollen hull, like something over-inflated, big enough for a dozen crew and pulled along by four forward-mounted, shuddering engines.

As they descend toward the rings, icy debris explodes in jet wash, sending buried rocks and metals spinning into space. The ship in back draws close to its prey. Magnetic grapplers unfold from a forward hold.

If they don't change course, they'll send debris lurching out of the ring system to rain down on the space station ahead of them, which hangs underneath the rings of ice. The station's flight-traffic commander adjusts the display goggles on his raised eyes and makes an uncertain sound. With a gesture, he tells the weapons operator to deactivate her safeties. He wants a warning shot to break up this chase.

Just then, the forward ship jukes toward the planet, kicking up debris from the rings, then swoops back through the debris for cover. The chaser plows ahead through the floating slush and T-bones the needle ship. Engines collide, throwing ribbons of burning fuel into space. Locked together by twisted metal and the magnetic grapplers, both ships tumble into the ice and dust.

The two yellow blips become a single red blip, drifting deep into the icy ring.

The commander keys the microphone on his throat and declares an emergency.

◇

"Here," says Gwoma, tossing a bag of tortilla chips, "I brought you some human food."

Ariam turns the bag over in her hands. "Where'd you get these?"

"From a salvage captain who found them on a derelict Earth ship. He told me they were 'edible triangles.' I thought it had probably been awhile since you ate human food."

"I wish you wouldn't say it that way. Makes me think of dog food. Like kibble."

"These are no good?"

"No, these are fine. These are good. I like edible triangles."

"They're from your people, yes?"

"They're from humans, yes. Not my people, exactly, but they were, you know, pretty ubiquitous."

Gwoma's frog eyes stare blankly back at her. On a quiruth face, no expression is an expression of emptiness, meaning either contentment or confusion.

"Ubiquitous," Ariam says. "They were, you know, all around. They were available almost everywhere."

Gwoma's wide mouth splits his domed head almost in two. The top half bobs up and down once. "Ah."

"Thank you for these," Ariam says, waggling the bag in the air. "I'll save them." She looked for a date stamp but found none. "You said these came off a derelict?"

"Yes, I'm sorry," he says. "On the old transport route coming out of your solar system. Still no sign of survivors."

Ariam puts the chips into her messenger bag. "No, it's all right. I didn't expect… anything like that." She downs the rest of her bitter tea, gets to her feet, and puts on her messenger bag. After keying a gratuity into the tabletop computer and tapping her card against the reader, she points with her head toward the train station at the end of the crowded plaza. "I'm going home. Walk to the train?"

Gwoma shrugs, cranes his short neck in a shallow circle—a quiruth nod—and stomps along next to her.

The plaza is crowded with quiruths bustling beneath an inverted dome ceiling with narrow, angled slats in the dome revealing more of the space station's webbed sprawl above, crisscrossing against a white ceiling of still ice, like a snowy upside-down plain.

From below, the space station resembles three thirds of a spider's web, stacked on top of each other and fanned out like a hand of cards. The overlapping layers of interconnected branches link to a single core tower running perpendicular to the icy rings above. All this orbits a stormy gas giant the quiruth had officially named with a collection of sigils and numerals that did little but file the place in a chronological database of stellar bodies. In practice, they call it Loyagrammer, after one of their lesser-known gods. The station is called Loyagram—the city of Loyagrammer.

Ariam and Gwoma cross the plaza. The place is toasty, as the quiruth like it, and loud with their layered murmurs. Shops and kiosks line the plaza, selling hot teas and cold soups, cheap electronics, and downloadable media. Steam carries out of one shop, beeping quiruth electronica drones out of another.

Blood for the King

No major hub in the space station's urban plan, this neighborhood is just a buildup of shops and services around the train stop. Called Goyamira (a quiruth word for Little Joy), this has been Ariam's neighborhood since she arrived on Loyagram, just one stop up the train route from her flat. The quiruth here work in the nearby service branches of the space station, like Ariam. These are city workers, mingling after the second watch at local power stations and the nearby hospital.

Ariam arrived a year ago already. Loyagram admins were waiting for her to formally renew her lease on her flat. It just took a thumbprint. She was two weeks overdue with it.

"How's work?" Gwoma asks in the quiruth trade tongue.

Ariam hasn't been paying attention. She searches for a quiruth word and, not finding it, replies in the trade tongue with, "Work is work." She shrugs.

"Ah," says Gwoma. "You're not working tonight, is that right?"

They stop in a crowd waiting for the next train.

"I worked the second watch. I'm on again tomorrow." She pauses, then asks in English: "Is that right? Did that sound right?"

Gwoma does the quiruth nod. "Very good," he says in English. Over the sound of the approaching train he adds, "You sound more natural than you did just a few weeks ago. Much, much."

Ariam smiles and moves toward the train. "You, too."

"Shall we watch movies tonight?"

"Not tonight," she says, stepping backwards into a train car amid a crowd of blue-green quiruths. "I'm just going to drink some alcohol, eat some triangles, and get some sleep. Have a good night."

Gwoma waves a webbed hand as the train doors whine shut. With a lurch, the cars carry Ariam along one short branch of the station, toward the hotel-like corridors of her residential building, caught in Loyagram's web.

Ariam swipes her card, enters her flat, sets down her bag, and feels her phone shudder in her pocket. It's the hospital texting her the emergency code. She runs her hand over her close-cut hair and looks at the ceiling. The flat's still dark. Through the kitchen porthole comes a band of light the color of an Earthly sunset, reflected off the planet's amber storms. She cusses to herself, texts the hospital that she's on her way, and heads back out to the train.

◇

On her ID card, Ariam Keown still has the swept-back afro she wore when she came to Loyagram. Now, as she waves the card at an identity scanner at the outer edge of the hospital, her hair is buzzed down close to her scalp. Quiruth don't like hair.

She slips on her augment glass as she enters the hospital and immediately receives telemetry from patients on the other side of the security barrier. Signals tell her square monocle the names of patients in nearby rooms, the ambient temperature when she eyeballs a vent, the time—deep into third shift, now—and the name of the quiruth doctor on his way down the corridor toward her: Kybek.

"What's the emergency?"

"We had a collision in space, not far from the station. Our rescue and salvage units are scanning the wreckage, still, but we've brought back only two survivors, one from each ship." Kybek speaks in the trade tongue, for Ariam's benefit, but he goes a little too fast.

"How bad is—"

"One is fine, as near as we can tell. The other is in some danger."

"Two patients and you needed me? Where is—"

"We were expecting more survivors. But we didn't call you off, because we thought you might want to see this patient." Kybek is about half Ariam's height. He pries his goggles off and lets them hang around his neck.

"You want me to operate?"

"You're welcome to weigh in on the injured patient, but it's the other one, the stable one, you'll want to meet. He's human."

Ariam turns her head but not her eyes. "Out here? Is he—"

"We're still waiting on tests, but he says he's infected, the same as you."

Blood for the King

Ariam walks around Kybek, deeper into the white-and-yellow hospital. Kybek hurries to keep up.

"He's in Secure Exam One."

"Dangerous?"

"He was being pursued by a ryric crew and until we learn more we're assuming he's wanted for a reason."

"What does he say?" Kybek starts to answer, but Ariam cuts him off. "Oh. I'm the interpreter."

"Right."

They walk past the admit desk, where quiruth of various heights mingle and murmur, past scanner suites and exam rooms to the secure ward.

"He's sealed?" asks Ariam.

"Yes."

She keys the door with her ID card and enters Secure Exam One. Inside the chamber is a smaller chamber, glass and plastic and metal, with isolated atmosphere and sensor rigs running in through conduits at the ceiling—a high-tech terrarium. The human inside is white, fit, shorter than Ariam, and dressed in a pilot's kit; his flight suit top tied around his waist, his T-shirt stained with sweat. The shirt reads *Hemingway Aerospace* in worn-out type. Amid all the signals reaching her monocle—information scrolling by from the isolation chamber systems all around—this human is a weird gap in the data.

Ariam taps the communications button on the side of the isolation chamber and asks, "You can hear me?"

The man smiles. He aims his voice toward the ceiling. "Hell yes, I can."

Kybek touches Ariam on the arm and she releases the button.

"He understands," she says. "Give me a minute." Then, back into the intercom: "I'm Dr. Keown. I understand you've been in an accident. Do you know where you are?"

The man smiles again. "I'm outside of ryric territory, right? I figure this is quiruth space?"

"That's right."

"Then I feel better already."

"What are you doing out here?"

"I wandered into ryric space in pursuit of a derelict human ship. Once it crossed the border, I guess they claimed it for themselves. So, illegal salvage. That's why I'm running. If you ask them."

"I'm asking you."

"Legal salvage. Until I drifted into ryric space, at least. Why? What are they saying?"

"Haven't asked them yet. I, also, I have to ask: You're a carrier right?"

"Am I infected? Yes, ma'am."

"Symptoms?"

"None yet. Is that what all this is for? I heard quiruth weren't—"

"It's *quiruth*, like quiet. Like choir. And, no, they're immune. This was for your benefit. To protect you from me."

"Ah."

"Yeah." Ariam turns to Kybek and switches to the quiruth trade tongue. "He says he's running from an illegal salvage charge because he drifted into ryric space by accident. He's infected, he says. So we can let him out of there, unless you want to hold him as a prisoner for the ryric kings."

"You believe this man?" asks Kybek.

"I don't know. But unless the port masters want to hold him on behalf of these ryric people—"

"They might. The other patient? *Is* a Ryr."

At first, she thinks he said *liar* in English. "That's…"

"A ryric king, like you said."

"Yeah, I get that."

"If that Ryr dies, his people will come looking for vengeance on this man. Right or wrong."

"That's—"

"Right or wrong."

Ariam activates the intercom again. "What's your name?"

"Daniel. Lowry."

"I need to go check on the other survivors from this crash, Daniel."

He makes a commiserative face and nods. She switches off the intercom.

"Show me this king."

Blood for the King

◇

The Ryr is in an exam-room terrarium like Lowry's, with bright lights and a hissing atmospheric regulator. When Ariam walks in, the room is white and clean and spare, but when she lowers her monocle the place comes alive with scrolling data from sensor equipment and transmitters all throughout the room. The Ryr's data comes scrolling up away from his body in semi-circular arcs where an embedded transmitter monitors his vitals and announces its findings in a ryric script. That signal hiccups and stutters as it struggles to interface with the quiruth instruments in the room.

The Ryr himself is big, almost twice Ariam's size, and curled on the bed like a sleeping dog, all four limbs tucked in under him. He's dressed in a quiruth gown, not unlike Earthly scrubs. He'd look forlorn if not for his face, if not for his eyes, staring out steady and unafraid. He makes Ariam think of a wounded animal, wary and threatening at the same time.

Kybek waves his webbed hand and activates the patient's chart in their monocles.

"He's suffered some internal injuries and has lost a lot of blood."

"Type match?"

"We're waiting for the computer to tell us if anything we have on file is compatible."

Data passes through the air before Ariam. She holds out a finger and scrolls back through it. "He'll need surgery to repair those blood vessels."

Kybek does the quiruth nod. "Can you do it with the autosurgeon?"

Ariam does the human nod. "Yeah. We shouldn't waste any more time, either. Get him prepped?"

"That's proving difficult. He's difficult."

Ariam touches the intercom on the Ryr's chamber. "I'm Dr. Ariam McKeown," she says in the quiruth trade tongue. "What can I call you?"

Kybek says, "He doesn't understand you," and the Ryr gives Kybek a dirty look.

"Oh, he understands me," Ariam says. "He just doesn't like us very much."

The Ryr unfolds a forelimb and makes a motion with his squat digits, like fingers on a keyboard. Ariam releases the button.

"Can we get him a keyboard?"

Kybek rushes off.

Ariam turns the intercom back on. "Keypad is coming. I understand you're in some pain. We're going to take care of you. Until your people arrive."

The Ryr blinks once.

Ariam wonders what a ryric nod or thanks would even look like and if she'd recognize it. She almost smiles, then stops, not knowing how that would be received either. Then, in English, she says to herself, "Just hang in there, your highness."

The Ryr is off the bed and at the glass in one quick four-limbed dash. He hoists his head up high and looks down on Ariam. His breath fogs the window. One canine lip is snagged on a yellow fang.

Ariam goes back a step and freezes there, hand off the intercom. The Ryr's mouth moves. She steps toward the glass and presses the intercom button again.

"Human," he says. "Human."

Ariam nods, then says in quiruth, "Yes."

The Ryr's forelimbs fold up in front of his chest. He's oozing through a bandage. "Human," he says again, his head swaying side to side, his gaze fixed.

Kybek comes back. "What is this?"

"I don't know," says Ariam.

Kybek puts the keyboard into the pass-through airlock in the Ryr's chamber. The Ryr's ears move as the airlock cycles, then he reaches out one long forelimb and picks up the keyboard. For the first time in a minute, he takes his eyes off of Ariam. He pecks out a few characters on the pad, which translates and projects his words to their monocles and a display in the chamber's window. It reads: *My people will come.*

Blood for the King

Kybek says into the intercom: "They're already on their way."

"Your injuries," Ariam says. "We need to get you into surgery. To help you."

My people will come.

"Not in time," Ariam says.

The Ryr looks back to Ariam. *No humans.*

Kybek looks at Ariam.

"What?" she asks.

No humans. Humans are sick. Humans are thieves.

"The operation is done by telepresence. By remote. She won't—"

The Ryr slams a forepaw against the glass.

Kybek shrinks. "It won't be a human. I'll do it. I'll operate."

Ariam looks away.

A human caused this. A human fugitive.

Ariam shakes her head.

"No humans," says Kybek. "Quiruth. I'll operate."

The Ryr lowers his head to get eye to eye with Kybek and stares.

"What do we call you?" asks Ariam.

The Ryr drops the keyboard into the pass-through and pads back to his bed.

"Nice," Ariam says, removing her finger from the intercom.

"What's nice?"

"You're going to operate? No offense, but at least get Gomig, she's the only other class-three surgeon that's logged a lot of hours on the—"

"I can do it. I can't force a patient to—"

"You backed off as soon as he had a problem with me. That feels great. As if I'd even be in the same room as him during the procedure. Do patients get to just—"

"Calmly. Choose their physicians? Yes."

Ariam flips up her monocle. "Fine, then. Good luck." She heads for the door.

"Where are you going?"

"Home."

"Stay here, logged in. In case we need you."

"What about—"

"Gomig came off a double shift two hours ago. We may need you. Please."

Ariam makes a gesture meaning *fine*.

"You can examine the human pilot? You know better than anyone else what—"

"Yeah, okay."

"We can probably let him out of the secure chamber, too."

"I don't think that's a good idea," Ariam says, stopping in the doorway.

Kybek tilts his head.

"Just…" Ariam shakes her head again, then looks out across admin toward Secure Exam One. "Let me talk to him, first. We don't know who he is yet." She walks out, leaving Kybek alone with the Ryr.

◇

She's on her way to Lowry's chamber when she dials Gwoma on her mobile. He appears on the tiny screen as a face in a dark space, lit by monitors and instrumentation from a dashboard. Reflected screens bend into letter Cs in his eyes.

"Ariam," Gwoma says. "You at work?"

"Yeah. You?"

The quiruth nod. "We'll be out here for hours yet, gathering debris from the crash. That ryric ship was pulled right apart. How are the patients?"

Ariam stops at a data kiosk in an alcove and ducks into the space it affords, getting her out of the corridor's regular traffic of patients and nurses. She pries off her monocle and pockets it. "I don't know yet. Too soon to say. What's the crash site look like?"

"It's a mess. Of course. Why?" Gwoma's squinting, which means he's concerned.

"And the smaller ship?"

"It's a wreck. Utter. What's going on?"

"How big was that smaller ship?"

Blood for the King

"It's a runabout. A rover. Tiny."

"Room for a passenger? Cargo?" Ariam's not looking at her mobile. She's looking into her imagination, trying to picture the ship.

"Not at all. Just the cockpit—ejected—and the engines. Ariam, what're you thinking?"

She turns back to face the mobile in her hand. "Nothing. Not really. Not yet. Except, Gwoma: who makes that ship, the rover?"

Gwoma turns his eyes upward. "It's a cheap faster-than-light craft. Commonplace, until a few years ago. Hemingway Aerospace, I think? A human company."

"Yeah," she says. "I've heard of them."

◇

The airlock cycles around Ariam on the edge of Lowry's chamber, air shushing against her face and across her knuckles. She's dressed in Earth scrubs and her big brown boots. The inner door opens and she steps inside the cleanroom with Lowry.

He waves. "Welcome to my humble... cell."

She gives off a half-smile as she opens her medical bag. "It's just for safety's sake," she says. She pulls a scanner out of the bag—it's flat and banged up, with a screen on one face and lens-like sensors on the other, ringed by four plastic grips.

"For plague?"

Ariam waggles her head from side to side. "Sort of. Quiruth are immune to it, but we're waiting to hear about the Ryr." She snaps her fingers, fishes her monocle out of her pocket and dons it again. "Tests should be back soon."

"That sort of thing isn't on file somewhere? Which species are susceptible and which aren't?"

Ariam smiles again. "We don't get a lot of data on the ryric body, despite them being so close by. The quiruth didn't have much on us, on humans, until I got here."

"When did you get here?"

"About two years ago." She steps up to Lowry, puts the scanner near his face, thumbs a button. It chirps to life.

"Why did you—can I talk? While that thing runs?"

"Yeah."

"Why did—how did—you end up out here?"

"How do any of us?"

"I'm here because I had an FTL failure. By chance. While the Ryr's ship was chasing me. I'm guessing you didn't get here quite by accident."

She considers it, taps a few keys on the scanner, and drags it through the air down to Lowry's torso. "I came here on purpose. I stayed by accident."

"What does that mean?"

"I came to study the quiruth, to see why they were immune to the plague, to see if we could learn anything from their physiology." She moves the scanner to her hip, types in a few notes. "Just a few more scans."

"So what happened? No breakthroughs?"

"It turns out I'm not a research scientist," she smiles.

"You said you were a doctor."

"I'm a surgeon—a trauma surgeon, by trade. The last licensed human surgeon, as far as I know. In exchange for a two-year contract manning autosurgeons for the quiruth, I got a few quiruth cadavers sent off to our research scientists. No breakthroughs."

"And your two-year contract is up."

"More or less." The scanner beeps. She logs a reading, starts a new scan. "I'll be out of here in a few days."

"What about me?"

"What about you?"

"Can I go?"

"Why don't you tell me more about how you got here first. You were running salvage?"

"Yeah, I was in pursuit of a human ship, drifting, and it went across the border into ryric space as I was trying to land in it. The Ryr, there, claims everything in his turf, and I didn't want to be a prisoner. I ran, they followed."

Blood for the King

"What kind of ship was it?"

"What's that?"

"The salvage. What kind of ship?"

"Old transpo hauler, for passengers and ore. Ghost ship."

Ariam nods, makes an adjustment on the scanner. "How does salvage work on a ship like that?"

"What do you mean?"

"Your ship's awfully small. What were you hoping to get as salvage?"

"The ship itself. Right it, fire it up, steer it out of there."

Ariam lowers the scanner, looks Lowry in the eye. "The whole ship? That's quite a score."

"Hell yeah, it is."

She nods, expressionless. "Okay. I'll let you know how your scans come back."

"You can't tell from—"

"You're still in the incubation period. You're not manifesting symptoms the scanner can detect."

"So how long do I—"

"Still no way to be sure. Some incubation periods last upwards of thirty years."

"I've heard."

"How old are you? Twenty-five?"

"Twenty-eight."

Ariam nods. "You inherited?"

Lowry nods.

She looks him in the eye again. "You want to see something?"

He shrugs. "Sure."

She goes back to her bag, packs in the scanner, and pulls out the rustling plastic bag she got from Gwoma. She tosses it to Lowry.

"Hey!" he says. "Nice! I haven't seen these in years."

"I know, right? A, ah, a quiruth captain got them for me. From a salvage team who found them near Earth."

Lowry moves to open them.

"Whoa, whoa," Ariam says, taking the bag back. "I'm saving these."

Lowry smiles. "Traces of us all over this part of the galaxy, still."

"Still," she says. Her mobile beeps, so she fishes it out and checks it. "I've got to take this. I'll be back." She hits *standby* on her device and heads for the door.

"I'll just stay here," Lowry says, sitting down on the chamber's bed.

On the other side of the airlock, Ariam keys her mobile. It's Gwoma.

"I'm on my way back early," Gwoma says.

"What's up?"

"Not on the mobile. I'll meet you there for tea."

◇

Ariam's sitting in the hospital's tearoom, reading quiruth reports about ryric culture, when her monocle squawks. She slides it over her eye and eyeballs the report from the Ryr's tests, CC'd to her by the lab. She's still reading when Gwoma stomps over, in his flight-crew gear, minus the helmet and hardware. He pulls up a stool and sits down at the chromed table with Ariam.

"You," he says, "look concerned."

"I am," Ariam says. "Blood-type matches came back on the Ryr. Generic artificial type-G plasma is a match. So are three kinds of blood in our records."

Gwoma waits for it.

"Two species are further away than the ryric ships on intercept and the third... is human."

"That's a shame."

"Yeah," she says, taking a sip of tea from a tiny cup. "It gets worse."

"Ah."

"Kybek is into the second hour of a two-hour procedure that's going to take him three. The Ryr is bleeding out internally while he works." She looks into her teacup, sets it down, looks back at Gwoma. "Kybek's going to run out of artificial blood, I just know it."

"What happens then?"

"Then," Ariam says, "the Ryr bleeds to death. The thing is, his species doesn't even need that much, but supplies are so low and the only possible donors are me and Lowry."

"And the plague—"

"Doesn't affect his species the same way, according to these findings," she taps her monocle, "but it would still probably kill him."

"Ah."

They sit in silence for a few minutes. Gwoma pours himself some tea, puts it to his mouth, and freezes when Ariam says:

"The thing is…"

"Yes?"

"There's this thing that human doctors do. It's called the Hippocratic oath. It's basically a promise to act ethically as a physician and do no harm. Named after the human we think of as being our first doctor. More or less."

"So it's old."

"It's real old."

Gwoma sips his tea, sets down his cup, folds his hands. "And you're thinking about violating that oath."

Ariam looks away. "The surgery with Kybek may mean I don't have to worry about it. If Kybek's online right now, he knows what I know. He's probably conserving blood as we speak. It'll be fine." She pauses. "What about you? What didn't you want to say on the mobile?"

"I can get you access to the human ship."

Ariam looks back at Gwoma, excited. "Really?"

"More accurately, I can let you watch me access the human ship."

"I can't leave the hospital for another—"

"It has to be now."

Ariam makes a face. "Dammit. Why now?"

"The salvage is being held until the ryric ships get here. I know the agent at the hangar right now, but she goes off shift shortly. We have to act quickly."

"You're just going to hand the ship over to the Ryr's people when they arrive? Both ships?"

"Not me. But yes."

"That's—"

"The Ryr's people will bomb this place apart if their Ryr dies here and we don't cooperate. The station authority will give up both ships and your human pilot, unless we can prove that he's—"

"That's not what I—forget it. Go and check the runabout's storage drives. Let me know what's in there."

"What are you looking for? You're not exactly entitled to—"

"I don't need copies of anything. I just want to know what sort of data is in there."

"Okay." Gwoma considers. "Okay. What if—"

Ariam's monocle squawks again. She holds a finger to pause Gwoma and activates her display. "Shit," she says. "Dammit."

Gwoma squints.

"Kybek's almost done," she says.

"Isn't that—"

"And he's out of blood for the Ryr."

◇

Kybek strips off his telepresence rig—gloves, goggles, mic—on his way out of the operation room up in surgery. He catches sight of Ariam on the other side of the glass sliding doors and braces himself. She stands there, in her scrubs, arms folded in front of her, a complex look on her face that Kybek still can't quite read after two years.

The doors slide open as he approaches. He holds a blue-green finger up to Ariam—a human gesture he's seldom used before—and speaks first. "Don't say it." Kybek sits on a bench outside the operator's room and puts his head in his hands.

Ariam stands next to him.

Kybek looks back toward the surgical room, where the alien king still lays, anesthetized and bleeding. "I nicked a blood vessel late in the procedure. I think it's repaired, but he's oozing blood.

Blood for the King

His system will keep cycling what we've given him, but it's only a matter of time until he bleeds out now. I've called Gomig."

Ariam nods. "I'm here. Now."

"And?"

"Wake him up. Let me convince him."

"You want to operate?"

Ariam considers. "I want to convince him to let me save his life."

Kybek looks at her. "You saw the lab report?"

Ariam waits a second, then: "Yes."

"I can't let you—"

"This is a quiruth hospital. It's the patient's—"

"No."

"It's his decision."

"He'll say no."

"Let him. If that's his choice, after I've talked to him, then fine. But don't leave him there dying while you assume."

Kybek weighs it. "Gomig will be here soon."

"Good. If I'm right, I'll be too busy to operate anyway."

Kybek looks Ariam up and down. "You can't donate enough."

"Not just me, no."

Kybek blinks. "Oh." He makes a low rumbling noise, a brief laugh. "The Ryr won't agree to that."

Ariam is still. "Let me talk to him."

◇

The Ryr awakens in the bright white operation theater with a start and a snap of his jaws. Kybek flinches, almost drops the injector he's used to dose the king into consciousness.

On the other side of the glass, in the observation room, Ariam keys the intercom. "Sir," she says, not knowing how else to address an alien king in the quiruth tongue, "I need to talk to you."

Kybek hands the Ryr a keypad with monitor. The Ryr takes it; he's still groggy, still aching from the wounds of surgery.

Ariam taps her mobile's keypad, forwarding the lab report to the Ryr. She's headed to the observation room door and into the surgical theater when the Ryr is done reading.

"You understand that?" she asks.

The Ryr stares at Ariam as she enters, in her scrubs and messenger bag, with nothing between them now but Kybek and the wires holding the Ryr to the vitals monitors. The robotic arms of the autosurgeon hang overhead. The Ryr doesn't reply.

"It means you'll die without blood. Blood I can give you. Blood that's infected with our plague."

The Ryr types: *Humans are sickly. I am a king.*

"Without human blood, you'll die before your ships even get here."

The Ryr regards her. The room has the chemical smell of disinfectant.

"With human blood, you might die years from now, unless—"

The Ryr types: *I do not fear death.*

"So I've read. But do you look forward to it? We can give you years of life back."

And a terrible death.

"A slow death, yes," she says. She walks toward the Ryr. "Unless your people find a cure."

The Ryr turns his head but not his eyes. Kybek looks from the Ryr to Ariam and back. *There is no cure,* texts the king.

"Not yet. But your people are great and wise, are they not? Perhaps they can find a cure when their king's life is at stake. Perhaps you can show them that you're not afraid of human sickness."

I'll be contagious. You have infected me already.

"You'll be contagious to a point. It's not the same among your species as it is for mine. No sexual contact. No sharing of blood. You can do that."

You are trying to trick me.

"Are you willing to bet your life on that?"

The Ryr licks his teeth. The Ryr looks at Kybek. The Ryr types out: *If I die, my people will take revenge on the human fugitive. That is all you are trying to avoid.*

Blood for the King

Kybek says, "We are willing to—"

"We are trying to avoid your death, Ryr," says Ariam. "Above all. If you live, you can work with the quiruth authority to get satisfaction in this case. If you die, you die here, alone, and the human pilot outlives you."

The Ryr snarls to himself. *I want that fugitive and his ship returned to me.*

Ariam looks the Ryr over, trying to decide whether to make her play now or wait. She thinks of Lowry, withering away in a ryric prison for the last few years of his life. She thinks of him disintegrating into dementia and dying amid uncaring ryric prison guards. She thinks of him in that little ship, alone in space, his face lit only by his scanner console. "You mean you want the data he stole to be returned."

The Ryr snaps his mouth shut. *What data?*

"Whatever signals he intercepted out there in your space. Whatever his ship has on its memory drives." She folds her arms and leans back on her heels. "Am I wrong?"

And the pilot. I want the pilot.

Ariam looks at Kybek, then back to the Ryr. "That's not—"

The Ryr makes a face that resembles a smile, but Ariam doubts that's what it is.

"The pilot is a separate issue," says Ariam. "You can take that up with station control and local law enforcement. If you live."

Kybek looks at her with wide, worried eyes.

"Do you want to live?"

The king, still staring at Ariam, slowly types out: *Yes.*

Kybek coughs. "You'll accept human blood? Infected blood?"

Give me the blood.

Ariam's mobile beeps for her. "Thank you, Ryr," she says, turning to leave. When she's back outside in observation, she looks to her mobile. It's Gwoma. "Gwoma, please tell me I'm not a liar."

Gwoma's little pixelated face tilts to one side. "You're not. Lowry's memory drive was loaded with signals intercepts from ryric space."

Ariam exhales.

Kybek comes out of the surgical theater. "I didn't think—"

Ariam holds up a finger to Kybek and says into her mobile, "I got the Ryr to agree to human blood but he'll want us to return that data. Will station control agree to that?"

Across the room, through a glass wall, Ariam sees Gomig signing in to the surgical operations room.

"I'm still sorting that out," says Gwoma. He looks off-camera. "I have to go."

"Call me when you've talked to the precinct officers and to control." She thumbs her mobile off and pockets it. She looks at Kybek.

"You did it," says Kybek. "Now you just have to get the pilot to agree to it."

"That'll be no problem," Ariam says. "The Ryr had easy math to do—a few years is more than zero—and Lowry's got nothing to lose. It'll be no problem."

◇

"No way," says Lowry.

Ariam and Lowry sit on opposite edges of the bed in his terrarium. Kybek watches them from outside.

"Lowry," she says. "There's no danger to you—"

"I'm not worried about that. I just don't see why I should save the life of something that wants me dead."

"Saving the Ryr's life would be a show of good faith to the quiruth, who might be in a position to protect you."

"They'll let me go?"

Ariam looks him in the eye, considers it. "No. That'll just make the Ryr's people furious and spark more trouble."

"Then screw that—"

"But the quiruth can arrest you for reckless endangerment, and have you serve out your sentence among the quiruth instead of sending you back to face ryric punishment."

"That's not right. I haven't done—"

"Lowry."

Blood for the King

He gets to his feet, zips his flight suit shut. "No! Screw that! I was trying to avoid a wrongful—"

"Lowry, knock it off." Ariam looks away, looks back to him. "Do you think we're stupid?"

"What do you—?"

"Your ship's memory drive is full of ryric signal intercepts. You weren't salvaging human tech or artifacts, you were spying on the Ryr's people so you could sell their data."

"Where did you—"

She tosses him the bag of tortilla chips. "My friend is a salvage captain and his people are always on the lookout for transponder signals from human ships near the borders around here, so they can snag them before the ryric get to them. No human ship came by. The closest one he's found in months was one on a vector out of our solar system, and it was way off. That's where he found those," she points to the bag of chips.

"The transponder on the ship was dead. I just—"

"Dead like your RFID tag?"

Lowry smiles out a mixture of shame and acceptance. "Shit."

"Even the Ryr's personal transmitter was read by the systems in here. But you're a blank space on my monocle. You disabled your transmitter so that you wouldn't be giving off signals the ryrics could trace. Am I right?"

"Maybe it's just not working right," Lowry says, but even he doesn't believe it.

"Lowry, you're a thief, just like the Ryr says. Now you can live out the rest of your life on a quiruth penal colony or deep in a ryric prison barge. You can let a creature die, that you have the power to save, and do yourself a favor at the same time. Or you get petty revenge, I guess, and suffer for it."

Lowry comes back and sits down. He opens the bag of chips. "My dad used to say that we're approaching the end of a human era. Living inside the ellipsis at the end of the human sentence. Maybe there's more coming we just can't see, or maybe we're closing in on the end for real."

Ariam nods. "Yeah."

"So now I have to live out the rest of my life in captivity?"

Ariam looks away at nothing. "There's just thousands of us left. What we do now defines how our species will be remembered. We have just a few years, in the grand scheme, to save ourselves or make our legacy as a species—as a people. You're an ambassador for a vanishing culture. But you chose to spend the years you were given, these few years, stealing. And you caused a terrible accident." She looks back at him. "You're not helping to save your species. You're not making us any better loved in the galaxy. I think you're getting off lucky."

Lowry fishes a chip out of the bag then offers the open bag to Ariam. She takes one.

"Yeah," he says.

"So now you can do something else. Something that might tell the Ryr and his people what humans can be like. Right?"

"Yeah." He licks salt off the chip. "Yeah."

"So you'll do it?"

Lowry nods.

Ariam bites into a chip. It bends in her mouth, soft and stale.

◇

The door to Ariam's hospital room slides open as Gwoma enters wearing a heavy, ugly sweater and coveralls.

"Doctor Keown," he says.

"Gwoma," Ariam says, delighted. "Tell me you brought wine. With the amount of blood I've given, it won't take much."

"No." He sits down next to her bed. "I have news for you, instead."

"I heard that the Ryr is going to be all right."

"His ships are inbound. Won't be long now. The human pilot is going to be held by the quiruth authorities for the flight accident."

Ariam nods.

"And station control," Gwoma says, "has decided to suspend your invitation for another term at the hospital."

Ariam smiles to herself. "I don't think I was staying anyway."

Blood for the King

She and Gwoma sit in silence for a while. A nearby monitor shows a quiriuth nature show about microscopic life in Loyagrammer's atmosphere. They pretend to watch it together.

"I was thinking about something you said," Gwoma says.

"Yeah?"

"About your oath?"

"The Hippocratic?"

He nods.

"What about it?"

"'Do no harm,' you said."

"Yeah," she makes a face. "Here's the thing. I never took the oath. I was never sworn in by any human institution. Human hospitals were in shambles when I was a kid. I prefer to think of my vow as 'do net good.'"

"And you think that's what you did?"

"I saved lives today and maybe helped to save a lot more."

"You spread a fatal disease."

"I turned the resources of a rich and powerful nation toward finding a cure."

"A hostile nation."

"Yeah, well. One thing at a time."

Friends Like These

Matt Forbeck

I was just about to toss everyone the hell out of the party when the Imperial Dragon"s Guard came busting through front door of the Quill and took care of that unpleasant detail for me. One minute, everyone was hunting down my last nerve and jamming it with red-hot brands The next, the door exploded into the main room, nearly taking off Thumper's head.

You've never seen a room clear out so fast.

You can hardly blame them though. The Quill isn't one of those high-class open-air places you find higher up the mountain here in Dragon City. You know, the ones with the wrap-around balconies that give you a clear view of the blue sky and the distant sea.

No, the Quill is a real dive, the sort that accommodates all types, by which I mean the scum of the scarred earth. It's not stuck down in Goblintown, mind you. The clientele's halflings or humans mostly, with the occasional elf or dwarf slumming it down here with us short-timers. The kind of folks that the real powers in this world don't much care for if they bother to think about us much at all. You know: my friends.

We'd all gathered around that night to toast the memory of Gütmann on the anniversary of his death. We hadn't gotten that far into it before we'd started in on each other again. There was a reason we didn't get together much after he died. None of us could stand each other any more.

Honestly, if we'd stood together against the squad of crimson-coated guards that stomped into the room, we would have been able to laugh them away. We had them outnumbered and outclassed. There's something about seeing a bunch of jackbooted elves in uniform come storming through a door, though, that stabs the fear that you've done something horribly wrong right through your heart until it jabs you square in your fight-or-flight button.

Of course, the fact that every one of us was guilty of something or other countless times over didn't help. Just being in a bar like this where they served dragonfire was enough. The question wasn't whether or not we deserved to be locked up. It was which of our many crimes we'd be charged with in the end.

"This is a raid!" said the captain of the squad, a humorless elf by the name of Yabair. "Freeze, or we'll fire! No one needs to get—Hey!"

No one listened to him. Not one of us. We scattered like cockroaches before an uncapped light. All except for Kai.

Righty slipped out the rear window. Never mind that it looked out over a six-story drop straight into the cesspool into which every bit of this sector of Dragon City's sludge ran. Even without the fingers on his left hand, he'd still be able to scale that wall better than I could walk across the floor.

Danto spat out a horrible word and then disappeared. Whether he turned invisible or disappeared or just decided to blink out of existence entirely, I couldn't tell, but I knew I couldn't duplicate the effort.

Thumper disappeared behind the bar, and Kells and Cindra—who'd been waiting for him to serve up their drinks—vaulted over the polished wood surface to join him. They knew about the trapdoor hidden back there, just like I did, the one through which most of the tavern's dragonfire deliveries came. Keeping low, I charged after them, hoping to follow them to safety.

That damned orc Kai, though, chose that moment to stand up and square off against the guards. He produced a double-barreled shotgun he'd been hiding under his table, hammers back and ready to fly. Without a word, he leveled the gun at the captain's chest and let loose with both barrels.

The buckshot glinted hot and white as it ricocheted off the captain's enchanted chestplate. The force of the impact alone knocked him back off his feet and sent him sprawling through the doorway behind him.

That's when the bullets started flying. The rest of the guards spun their pistols toward Kai and started firing. The gunshots cracked louder than thunder inside the Quill's rock walls. One of them pointed a wand at the orc instead. It was a military-issue model, straight and uniform, milled by a machine, with a handle encased in some creature's scaly skin.

I didn't want to stick around to see what it might do.

I dove over the bar, crashing through a pair of half-full steins, and smashed into wall behind the bar. It hurt a lot less than a bullet would have, I'm sure.

I landed on my back, and before I could turn over onto my knees, something else came over the bar and kicked me right in the gut.

"Sorry, Max," Moira said as she scrambled off me and toward the trapdoor. I tried to answer her, but I was having too much trouble breathing right then to manage it.

The tow-headed halfling grabbed the iron ring on top of the trapdoor and yanked. It didn't move. She turned and snarled like a cornered dog. "Some dragon-damned friends," she said. "They bolted it from the inside."

"Bastards," I said. In my head, I made plans to beat my inevitable fine out of them when I found them.

More gunshots rang out. A bottle burst open over our heads and showered us in shards of glass and expensive dwarven rum.

"Cease fire!" someone shouted.

Friends Like These

The barrage kept going.

"Stand down, you jackasses! I said, cease fire!"

I put a hand over Moira to protect her. "Keep your head down," I said. "Once they run out of bullets, they'll stop. Then they'll scoop us up and take us downslope."

I'd never seen Moira's bright blue eyes so panicked. She scrambled around behind the bar, searching for a way out. "You don't understand," she said, her voice rising to a keen. "I can't get caught. Not now."

She pulled a switchblade from her pocket and popped the stabby part free. She jammed the tip into the seam of the trapdoor and tried to pry it open.

"You've been picked up in a speakeasy before," I said. "You know the score. It's just a slap on the wrist."

She glanced at me, and the guilt shone in her eyes. She gave the knife one last try, and the blade snapped in half.

"CEASE FIRE!"

The bullets stopped. All I heard was the stomping of boots and the low groan of someone who hadn't managed to get out of the way of all that lead.

"Moira Erdini!" someone said. "Come on out! You are under arrest!"

I goggled at Moira. "What did you do?" I wasn't asking about her knife.

"I'm in serious trouble, Max," she whispered as she turned toward me. "You can't let them take me."

I've seen Moira face down a vampire. I watched her spit in every one of a hydra's faces. I'd never seen her so scared.

"All right," I said. "Hide."

I put both hands over my head and waved them above the edge of the bar. "Don't shoot!"

"Stand up!" a hoarse voice said. "Slowly!"

I did.

Yabair stood there in the center of the room, flanked by guards on four sides and circled in an expanding halo of smoke. Two carried pistols. The one who'd been responsible for most of the destruction carried a rune-encrusted submachine-gun, the barrel of which glowed as red as a blacksmith's forge. The fourth held a wand with a cold-iron tip.

Holes pocked every wall in the room and the floor and ceiling as well. Tables had been tipped over and glasses smashed. The smell of spilled beer and liquor wafted through the place, cut by the sharp, distinctive stench of brimstone and cordite.

Kai still stood at his table, frozen as solid as a statue. He'd been reloading his shotgun when the guy with the wand had zapped him with a paralysis spell. His face had frozen in an ugly twist, the kind you see in candid photographs when you're caught with your eyes half closed. It takes a lot to make Kai uglier than he is, but that did the trick.

Everyone else was gone, and that scared me more than anything else. If the guards had allowed the others in the bar to slip away, then they really did have only one damned thing on their minds: Moira.

Despite that, all of the guards had their weapons leveled at me.

I ginned up my best grin. I knew I was doomed. If they couldn't find Moira, they'd probably take out their frustrations on me. Hell, they'd probably do that either way. The only satisfaction I'd get at this point would come from helping her escape their claws.

"Where is she?" Yabair said.

"Who?" I did my best to look confused.

"The halfling who dove back there with you." The elf glared at me with perfect green eyes. They said, "I've already seen more years than you'll ever see months, boy. You cannot fool me." But I wasn't so easily dissuaded.

"Gone," I said. "Slipped out through a trap door."

Yabair sneered at my lie. "And why did you not follow her?"

I grimaced. "She locked it behind her. That little sawed-off bitch."

Moria kicked me in the shin for that one. I didn't take offense. I'd only said that to see if she'd managed to find a hidey-hole. The pain in my leg said "Not quite yet."

Friends Like These

"This 'bitch' of yours is implicated in the death of one Chiara Selvaggio. Anyone who stands between her and the swift prosecution of justice will share in her fate."

My breath caught in my chest. The Selvaggios were one of the oldest, wealthiest, and most powerful families on the planet. Chiara was the eldest daughter of Constantine Selvaggio, the clan's patriarch.

I heard a soft whimper, and I had to double check that it hadn't come from me.

"By now, this halfling you're hunting must be halfway back to her burrow," I said with a mouth gone dry.

Yabair bared his teeth in what only his mother might have charitably called a smile. "If so she'll find a cold reception waiting for her. But perhaps she is not so far gone as you say."

Yabair nodded to the elf with the wand. He made a smooth gesture that hurt my eyes to follow, and electricity arced from the tip of his wand, forking into several branches as it went. One of them speared me right in the chest, causing every muscle in my body to contract at once and nearly blanking out my brain. I collapsed over the bar an instant later.

Other arcs from the wand crashed randomly into tables and bottles. A spectacular one lit up the cash register behind the bar and blew it wide open. The last one found Moira as she tried to cram herself into a small safe and zapped her good. She cried out in pain and surprise, giving herself away.

With fingers still numb from the electric shock, I went for my wand.

I never had a chance.

The guard waved his wand at me again, and I froze. His spell had petrified me solid before my wand had even cleared its shoulder holster. I could feel everything—including Moira scrambling past my legs as she went to give the trapdoor one last desperate and futile try—but I couldn't move a muscle, not even to blink.

I didn't see the guards grab Moira and haul her away. They never passed in front of me, and I couldn't turn my head. She screamed bloody murder at them though and fought them all the way. She even managed to stab one of them in the gut with a hidden knife, but they shot her in the back as she tried to flee.

"Quickly," Yabair said as they carried her out of the tavern. "We need her alive for questioning. Not until then can you permit her to die."

Moira keened like a banshee as they took her, more from anguish than in pain, her voice fading with every step away. "Max!" she said. "Help me!"

And then she was gone.

By the time the petrifaction spell wore off, the squad of guards had long disappeared. Kai loosened up a moment before me, and he picked his way through the wreckage to come over and stare at my face.

"Least you stood tall 'steada rabbiting like the rest," he said with grudging respect. The fact that I couldn't speak saved me from having to correct him. "Save yourself the grief though. She's gone. Let 'er go."

The paralysis wore off then, and I lurched forward and stabbed my wand into the bar, nearly snapping it in half. Kai didn't bother to conceal a snigger.

I ignored him and headed for the door. He grabbed me by the shoulder and hauled me up short. The circulation was starting to return to my limbs, and it stung. It hurt worse where he touched me. I shrugged him off.

"I said, forget it." He shook his head at me, maybe out of pity, maybe out of disbelief.

"If I can get to her before they lock her in the Garret—"

"They'll kill you." Kai held up his hand to cut me off. "They took you right out, and that was after I softened 'em up for you."

I stared at him. Something was wrong, but I didn't know what. Then I figured it out.

I had my wand out and at his throat in an instant. He glanced back at his shotgun, still sitting on top of his table, unloaded.

He grunted at me. "You want to die, I can kill you right now."

Friends Like These

"You sold her out." I muttered a word that increased the heat coming out of the tip of my wand to an uncomfortable level. Kai squirmed against it. He knew better than to make a move though, at least if he wanted to keep his head above his shoulders.

"I shot them!"

"I saw Yabair after that. He didn't have a scratch on him. That breastplate of his doesn't cover everything. He knew you'd shoot at him. He was ready for it."

Kai snarled at me. For a second, I thought he might try to rip my throat out with his bare teeth, and I wondered just how smart I was to put this orc into a position in which all he had to do to save his reputation was murder me. I was too angry to think straight. I snarled right back at him.

The fight drained out of him.

"They came after me first," he said. "Caught me in my home. I had to do it. I cut them a deal."

"You didn't have to do *anything*."

"It's a murder charge, Max. You know what they do to orcs charged with murder? They stake us down outside the gates and wait for the zombies to come eat us."

My guts somersaulted at the thought that Moira might share that fate. I must have twisted my wand farther into Kai's throat. He winced in pain.

"Come on, Max. She's a halfling. They won't do that to her. The Dragon thinks they're 'civilized.' Worst they'll do is electrocute her."

"You're not helping!"

I pushed him away and lowered my wand. I wanted to kill him. I needed him to give me a good reason not to.

"What happened?" I said.

Kai rubbed a reddening spot on his neck. "I just told you. They came after me for the murder."

"I meant the murder. What happened?"

"I wasn't there. I didn't have anything to do with it."

"Dragonshit!" I shook my wand at him. "If you're so innocent, why'd they come after you?"

He put up his hands. "All right. They traced the stuff that killed Chiara back to me."

I jabbed my wand at him. "So. How can you say *you didn't kill her!*"

"I didn't! I swear on my balls, I didn't have anything to do with it. I only work with top-shelf dragon essence, and I cut it perfectly. There's no way it was too pure."

I whistled at that. Dragonfire was one thing. Just about everyone drank that magical hooch. It wasn't legal, sure, but the guard mostly turned a blind eye to it, especially the ones who were paid off well enough. Straight dragon essence, though, was much stronger stuff and much harder to come by.

"She OD'd on it?"

"Coulda happened, but I doubt it. Moira told me Chiara had been using for over 500 years. She knew her stuff. I set her up with her first hit from my supply a week ago, and she loved it."

That stepped me back. "Moira sold it to her?"

Kai sneered. "Now you see. I had to give her up."

"No, you didn't."

I punched him in the face. He'd been watching my wand and didn't see my incoming left until it was too late. He dropped to his knees and clutched at his nose. When he brought his hand away, it was covered with blood.

He looked up at me, something even uglier than his face burning in his eyes.

"Give you that one, Max. Hit me like that again, though, I'll kill you."

I grabbed him by the front of his ratty shirt and pulled him up so I could snarl in his face. "I put it on the streets that you snitched on one of your own people, and you won't live long enough for me to worry about it."

Kai's green skin went pale.

I pushed him away, disgusted. As I headed for the door, I spoke at him over my shoulder. "Don't come back here again. At least not until Moira's out of trouble. I see you, I might forget how much I like you."

Friends Like These

I didn't wait for him to reply.

I walked through the cobblestone streets of the city, people on brooms and carpets and in the occasional mini-blimp scudding overhead through the moonlit night sky, visible as silhouettes there, even beyond the light from the glow globes in the street lamps. I kept my head down and ignored them all as I thought about Moira.

The damned thing about it was that Kai had been right. I had no chance of saving Moira now, short of mounting an armed assault on the Garrett—the best-defended prison on the planet.

I tried to tell myself to forget about her and just let it go. She'd have done the same for me, I'm sure. But I couldn't manage it. Having started the night remembering the loss of one friend, I didn't think I could stomach losing another.

I legged it up the stairs to my rooms over the Barrelrider, the smell of halfling cooking wafting up from below. The letters painted in gold on my door read "Max Gibson, Freelance." Freelance what, they didn't go on to say.

As I reached for the door, I saw that it was unlocked and that someone had uncapped the glow globes in my office. I drew my wand and braced myself to kick open the door and take out whoever was waiting there for me. Then I heard Nit's voice call out.

"Save the furnishings, Max. It's just me."

I stifled a groan. I didn't want to deal with the old halfling just then, but he wasn't about to give me that choice.

My door creaked open on hinges that hadn't seen oil since before I was born. My desk sat directly across the floorboards, right in front of the one large circular window in the room, the top portion of which had been pivoted open, letting in the night air. Nit stood there in his bare feet, right on top of my blotter, which brought him up to eye level with me. He swirled a snifter of dragonfire about in his left hand, stirring tiny bursts of cold blue flames out of the mahogany liquid.

"They got Moira," he said.

I moved into the room and glanced around. It didn't seem like he'd brought any friends, but then Nit didn't need them.

He raised his voice. "Did you hear what I—?"

"I was there," I said.

"And you didn't save her."

"She's a big girl."

"She's my girl."

I shrugged at him. "Then you should tell your daughter to quit selling dragon essence to elves who turn up dead from it."

He didn't flinch at that.

"You knew about it."

He looked away. "Like you say, she's all grown up. She heard this elf needed a new supply, and she wanted a piece of that action, some quick money. She could get into places that other people couldn't touch, quiet and discreet. So that's what she did."

"You could have stopped her."

"I'm here to hire you."

"She's already in the Garret by now."

"To clear her name."

I allowed myself a bitter laugh.

"This is important to me, Max. She doesn't come home, her mother will kill me."

I shrugged at him again.

"I'll give you the deed to this place, Max. Your office. Your rooms. Your's forever."

"She's supposed have killed a Selvaggio. They invented the word for revenge."

"You think I don't know that? They'll come for me next, Max. And my wife. And the rest of my kids too. And if I'm going down, I'm taking everyone with me. Everyone."

At that moment, Nit seemed older than I'd ever seen him. Weak. Tired. He gave me a hard glare, then drained his glass and licked away the magic flames that danced along his lips.

"You're not *asking* me to help out here, are you?"

"You're the right man for the job, Max. The only man. She didn't kill that elf, and you know it. Figure out a way to prove it, and we're all in the clear."

"And if I screw it up?"

"Then we're all dead."

Friends Like These

I got Nit to give me the key to Moira's place, and I hoofed it over there, double time. She'd moved out of their family burrow ages ago and into a snazzy place upslope, on the edge of Gnometown. I'd never been inside before, but I'd carried her home to it more than once.

It wasn't just that her place wasn't built for someone my size. It was actively hostile about it. To even get up to her apartment I had to crawl on my hands and knees through a twisting tunnel too narrow for me to turn around in. Fortunately, the key worked, and I got straight in.

I'm sure Moira thought of her place as spacious and friendly, but she only stands a hair over three feet tall. The ceiling of her apartment was only five feet from the floor. I found it easier to remain on my hands and knees rather than try to walk hunched over through the place and smack my head on every lintel.

I'd always thought of Moira as clean and neat, but her place was less of a burrow and more of a pit. Food containers from her parents' restaurant stood arrayed on the dining table and around a sink stacked near to toppling with mold-crusted dishes. Dust stood thick on counters and sills, and the floor was sticky enough that I reconsidered my position and got back on my feet, back pains be damned.

Scraping my scalp on the ceiling, I moved through the place slowly, looking for something—anything, really—that would give me a clue about what had really happened to Chiara Selvaggio. I didn't have much hope that I'd find anything. I didn't even know for sure how the elf had died. I wasn't about to just take Kai's word for how it had all played out.

After a while, I gave up, unwilling to endure the filthy place any longer on the off chance that something useful would leap out at me.

And then it did.

Or rather, he did.

He, in this case, was a fat, greasy, unshaven halfling with a rusty meat cleaver in his hand. He came at me with a strangled scream that sounded something like an elderly cat that had fallen into a blender. He swung the cleaver in front of him like he was shooing away a stubborn fly.

I brought up my wand and pointed it at the cleaver. Its blade began to glow red, and the wooden handle started to smoke. The halfling dropped it with a yelp.

"You bastard!" he said. "You'll pay for that!"

He started toward me again but hauled up short as I leveled the wand at his chest. "Back off, Stubby," I said.

"How did you know—?" He peered at me through greasy locks of hair that had fallen over his eyes. "Wait. You're Gibson, aren't you?"

"What the hell happened to you?"

"Nothing! What do you mean?" He looked down at himself and seemed to realize how awful he looked. "I don't—Ah, hell."

He slumped over, dejected. "I—I didn't—I haven't been out much lately. I'm sorry." He picked up the cooling cleaver, considered it for a moment, then pitched it into the sink.

"What happened here?" I asked.

Stubby flushed with embarrassment. I could barely hear his voice when he spoke. "She left me."

I sat down on the least sticky part of the floor I could find. I kept my wand out and ready though, just in case. "What happened?"

He shrugged. "I dunno. When I moved in here, I thought things were great. I mean, sure, she was always nagging after me to help clean up, but I figured we'd work it out. Instead, she just stopped coming home."

"What, at all?"

"I think she snuck in sometimes when I was out. I never actually saw her though."

I nodded. "She's good." Not good enough to hide in plain sight from a squad of the Imperial Dragon's Guard hunting for her, but sharp enough to get past this guy on his best day—something that had to sit in his distant past.

"At least I know where she is now," I said.

Hope rose in Stubby's eyes. "Where?"

"The Garret."

Friends Like These

His eyes widened far enough for all the hope to spill out of them.

"She's been picked up for the murder of Chiara Selvaggio."

Stubby growled. "I knew it. That bitch!"

"Hey—"

"I'm talking about that damned elf. I warned Moira about getting involved with her. I knew nothing good could come from it."

"Involved?"

"You know what I mean."

I shook my head. I'd always thought of Moira as interested only in male halflings, despite her tendency to wind up with winners like Stubby. The thought that she might have switched her tastes for both gender and race made my head spin.

"She was selling her dragon essence," I said.

Stubby smirked at me, and I wondered which one of us was being willfully ignorant here. "That doesn't explain where she's been for the past few weeks. It doesn't take that long to smuggle a little DE upslope. Not for someone like Moira."

I had to admit that Stubby had a point. The other possibility was that she hated his guts and was just avoiding a confrontation with him until he took the hint and left, but I didn't want to raise that for fear that Stubby would go hunting for the cleaver again.

Also, I'd never known Moira to avoid someone like that. She might flee from the guard, but Stubby wasn't in the same class. I would have guessed she'd have slipped a knife into his back before she'd let him ruin her place like this.

"Where's her room?" I asked.

Stubby jerked a thumb toward the back, and I hunkered over in that direction. The round door to the place stood open, and the smell from it hit me before I could see inside it. Breathing through my mouth, I poked my head in.

The bedroom was a pit. It looked like Stubby had spent most of his time here, unwashed and miserable. The sheets were twisted into a greasy knot on the bed. A stained blanket lay on the floor, half-buried beneath piles of dirty clothes. Books lined the shelves, but they'd been taken down and reshelved at random, pages spilling out of their broken bindings. Plates of rotting food and overturned mugs had been strewn throughout the place, giving the stench a wide variety of means of assault.

I pulled my head back out and fought not to gag. As my head spun, I glanced around the rest of the apartment. The only clean thing in it was a door that sat in the rear part of the place, the farthest from the grimy windows. The door was painted green and had a golden knob set into the center of it.

"Where's that go?" I asked.

"Her office," said Stubby. "She doesn't let anyone in there."

I slouched toward it. "You haven't tried it?"

"Just the once," he said, staring at the palms of his hands. "It gave me such a shock I never came near it again."

I knelt in front of the door and peered at it. I didn't even see a keyhole for a lock in it. If she'd spelled it to keep out unwanted intruders though, the door wouldn't need a lock, would it?

I waved my wand at the door, and it glowed an electric blue from the central doorknob out past the edges of the frame.

"What are you doing?" Stubby squeaked.

"Just seeing what I'm up against. There's a bastard of a charm on this thing."

He shook his hand as if trying to fling off a ghostly pain. "Tell me about it."

I stared at the door. With a protection charm like that, Moira could be as general or as selective as she liked when it came to who it would keep out. She might have only targeted Stubby, although I knew she was more paranoid than that. Most people just set up the charm to zap away anyone who wasn't them. It made it tricky to get into if the owner wasn't available, but not impossible.

Still, I didn't have the time to undo the damned charm. It would take me hours that Moira didn't have. The penalty for murdering a noble—especially someone from a clan as powerful as the Selvaggios—could only be death. Every minute Moira spent in the Garret was another minute's worth of torture for her to endure until her coerced confession, another minute closer to her execution.

I reached out for the door.

"Hey, wait!" Stubby said.

As my fingers closed on the knob, the blue glow blinked away, retracting into the edges of the doorframe. It pulsed there, waiting for the moment it could flow forth again. For now, though, it would let me pass.

I pushed the door, and it glided open on silent hinges.

"Wait!" Stubby grabbed me by the shoulder.

I glared back at him and fought an urge to hammer him down with my elbow. He let me go.

"How come she let you in?"

I moved into the room. "You'll have to take that up with her. Right now, though, I'm going to trust her judgment."

I closed the door behind me. Stubby threw himself against it and started pounding on it. Then the blue glow snapped back into place, and the pounding stopped, punctuated by a sharp yelp of pain.

The inside of the room was as black and cold as a tomb. I waved my wand and uttered an incantation that made the entire shaft glow white from end to end. I held it up to push back the inky darkness.

The room was little more than a hole carved into the mountain's stony crust. It featured no windows and had no glow globes for illumination. Maybe Nit had set it up as a safe room for his daughter, a place she could to go escape from her enemies—or from his if they tried to get to him through her. There weren't many things inside it at all, but I had to assume that Moira wouldn't have bothered to store something inside there that wasn't valuable or vitally important.

The few things in the room had been set on shelves carved out of the rock or simply leaned against the bare wall.

I found a stack of gold bars, a few sacks filled with coins, a small bag stuffed with diamonds, and some pieces of art I was pretty sure had been stolen from the Imperial Dragon's Museum about six months back. Behind the art I found another small bag of red velvet that had not stones in it but a snowy-white lock of hair tied with a crimson bow. I stuffed it into my pocket.

I also found a small glass hookah, the kind used for smoking drops of dragon essence. I knocked it off its shelf and then accidentally stomped it into dust as I stumbled about the place. I can be so clumsy when I need to.

I reached for the door, and the blue light reeled back from my touch again. I put out the light on my wand, and then slipped out the door and shut it behind myself. The glow snapped back over the door again. With a dismissing wave, I let my spell that had exposed the charm expire, and the glow faded into invisibility again.

"What did you find in there?" Stubby asked.

I ignored him and started for the door.

"Where are you going?" His voice rose with every word.

"Get out of here," I said. "Grab your things and go."

"You can't kick me out of here."

I looked back at him as I reached the door. "Within a few hours, Moira's either going to come here and do it herself—or the Imperial Dragon Guard will sweep through here and either burn or confiscate everything in it."

Stubby blanched. "Where are you going?" he said. "No one can break her out of the Garret."

"I'm going upslope," I said as I crawled out of the place. "I'm going to pay a visit to some of her friends."

It took a lot of fast talking and name dropping, but I've never been shy about either of those things. Soon enough, I managed to wheedle myself an audience with the Selvaggios I most wanted to talk to.

"I can't believe you let one of them in here." Oscuro Selvaggio glared at me with ice-blue eyes, his perpetual snarl disfiguring what should have been a handsome face. "And after one of them killed my sister—your only daughter. Is our home no longer sacred?"

I ignored the bigotry. I was a human in Dragon City. I was used to it.

Friends Like These

"Drop the revulsion act," said Faustina Selvaggio, the matriarch of the clan. Despite being at least five times my age, she was impossibly beautiful and graceful in a way that made me embarrassed by every crude thing about me. "It doesn't suit you."

"I came here to discuss the death of Chiara," I said. "The wrong person was arrested for her murder."

"What do you know of it?" asked Faustina. "Word of her death has been kept under a tight wrap. Not even the Dragon Emperor has been made officially aware of it yet."

"Moira Erdini is a friend of mine. I was there when she was arrested."

"I'll have to speak to the guard about being so lazy in the execution of their duties," said Oscuro. "Without much of a struggle, I'm sure they could have found something to charge you with as well."

"Do you always rely on using trumped-up charges to get the guard to do your dirty work for you?" I asked. "I think I'm starting to see a pattern here."

The elf's blade was out and at my throat faster than I could see it move. I scanned the walls of the room instead of giving him the satisfaction of flinching.

This was likely the brightest room I'd ever been in at night, certainly one of the highest points on the mountain to which I'd ever aspired. We stood in a plain but beautiful natural chamber formed by the patient weaving of living trees into walls and ceiling. The southern face of the room lay open to the thin and chilly air that often seemed to blow straight through the tiniest seams in the woven branches. While it didn't bother the two elves in the room with me, it was everything I could do to stifle a shiver.

From our vantage point, I could see the lights glowing like distant stars in most of the southern portion of Dragon City as it splayed out below us, sprawling all the way down the mountain's slopes until it reached the massive Great Circle, the giant curtain wall that enclosed the entire mountain and protected us from the undead dangers that hungered beyond it. I'd been born and raised here. The glowlight glittering off Oscuro's long thin blade reminded me that I'd probably die here. I just hoped it might be a little later.

"Desist." Faustina spoke with an edge in her voice that seemed sharper than Oscuro's sword. He resheathed his weapon as quickly as he'd drawn it.

"I've known Moira for a long time. She's many deeply disturbed things, but she is not a killer."

"And we are to simply take the word of someone like you for that?" Oscuro rested his hand on the hilt of his blade still.

"No," I said. "Of course not. Why would you?"

Faustina cleared her throat. "I, for one, would like to learn the truth of the matter, no matter how it may come to us."

"The truth is simple to see," said Oscuro. "That filthy halfling creature hooked my beautiful, darling, beloved sister on illicit drugs and then killed her with an overdose."

"Or not."

"Explain yourself," said Faustina.

"Let's be honest. Most of the elves in this city are doing drugs of one kind or another. Something about relieving the ennui, I believe."

Oscuro began to object, but Faustina cut him off with a chop of her hand. "Continue."

"Chiara had been doing drugs for centuries. For some reason, she needed a new supplier. That's where Moira came in."

"So you admit it!" said Oscuro.

"That Moira brought drugs to Chiara?" I shrugged. "I suspect so, but I don't know for sure. That's not the important part though. As old as Chiara was, as much dragon essence as she'd probably used over the centuries, you don't think she knew how to get high? Without killing herself?"

"So it must have been murder," Faustina said, lowering her eyes. "I don't see how this helps the case of your friend."

"Of course it was murder," I said. "But it wasn't Moira who did it."

Oscuro began to object again, but a glare from his mother cut him short.

"Figure this," I said. "Chiara had to be Moira's biggest customer. Moira would have seen her as a gateway to supplying other gold-drenched elves with Kai's product. What would she gain from killing her?"

"She's vermin," Oscuro said. "What other reason does she need?"

Only Faustina's presence kept me from punching the smugness off Oscuro's face. That and the fact he'd have sliced me to pieces. "Like I said, the drugs aren't important. It's what happened after she started coming here."

"What do you mean?" Faustina said, intrigued.

"Moira and Chiara fell in love."

Oscuro scoffed at this, a little too hard. "Preposterous! To think of a Selvaggio partnering with a halfling? It's just absurd."

I pulled the red velvet pouch from my pocket, and I opened it up to spill a snowy-blonde lock of hair into the palm of my hand.

"That's not hers," Oscuro said. "You could have gotten that from anywhere."

"It's elf hair for sure," I said. "Too fine and silky to belong to anyone else."

"There are many other elves in the world."

"Silence," Faustina said. She held her hand out for the lock of hair. I deposited it in her palm.

She brought it closer to her eyes and examined it in the moonlight.

"Mother," Oscuro said, "you can't possibly—"

"And why wouldn't I?" Faustina said. "You children think that because you have the privilege of your birth you can fool anyone? I can hear you talking to each other at night through the walls."

"That proves nothing." Oscuro favored me with a devastating sneer. "She could have taken that when she killed Chiara."

Faustina ignored him and held me in her steady, brilliant gaze. "But if your little halfling didn't kill Chiara, then who did?"

I didn't know for sure. Honestly, I didn't know at all. I just decided to play a hunch.

"It was you," I said to Oscuro. "You waited until a night she'd had a bit too much, and you pumped enough extra in her to make it look like an overdose. Like an accident she was too smart to have."

Oscuro flushed, his pale skin turning a bright pink. "And why would I do something like that?"

"Why not? Chiara, your beloved sister, was sleeping with a disgusting halfling—" Then I realized what Oscuro's real reason had been. Why he'd been willing to risk everything, including the future of his family, on this murder. The timing—when Moira had first started up with Chiara, when she'd started supplying her—it all made sense.

"You were jealous. Chiara slept with Moira," I said, "instead of you. You used to supply her with dragon essence—probably had for decades—but she broke it off with you despite that and took up with Moira instead."

Oscuro went from pink to pale again. "I—I did no such thing."

Faustina's face curled into a twisted and miserable thing. "Don't lie to me anymore, Oscuro," she said with as much composure as she could muster. "I could always tell when you were lying. You've been lying to me all day. Only now I know why."

Oscuro drew his blade and lunged at me. Faustina waved at him, and a gust of wind raced in from the window and slammed him into the room's interior wall.

"We can't let this get out!" Oscuro bellowed over the roar of the wind. "We must kill him either way."

"If you let Moira go," I shouted at Faustina, "drop the charges against her, I will make sure that none of the evidence in this case ever reaches the light of day."

Faustina lowered her hand, and the wind expired. Oscuro fell to the floor. "Tell me," she said to me. "Why shouldn't I kill you and let your halfling friend die?"

Looking into her eyes, I knew this was a legitimate question, one for which I had better have a good answer.

"Because I'm here to help you. How do you think I found that lock of hair? Moira knew that it might someday come to her word against someone else's, so she squirreled things away against that. I found it in one of her safe houses. You can bet she has other mementos hidden around the city, each with their own bit of damnation for you and your family if they're found. Which they will be, after her death."

I didn't know if any of that was true, but it sounded exactly like something Moira would do. I just had to hope that this powerful elf matriarch might believe it too.

Faustina stood as still as a statue, considering this.

"Mother," Oscuro said. His voice trembled as he reached for her.

She spun on him, screaming. Her voice was so loud and brutal that he fell to his knees in pain and his ears began to bleed. Even standing behind her I had to clap my hands over my ears and plug them tight just to keep from joining him on the floor. When she finished, she drew another breath as if she might scream again. She held it when she saw that Oscuro had begun to weep.

She turned back to me then. "You will go to the Garret to retrieve your friend. You will bring her home. You will tell her that if she strives to damage the reputation of my daughter or anyone else in my family—if she ever darkens the doors of my estate again—I will tear her inside out and feed her to the falcons."

She glared right through me. "Are we clear?"

"As crystal."

I double-timed it out of there and hopped a flying carpet out to the Garret. By the time I got there, the warden had already gotten the word that Moira was to be released. I'd never seen a dwarf so astonished.

Dawn broke in the east as I escorted Moira out of the cold,

gray prison. The dew-coated city was waking up all around us. I could smell bread baking somewhere.

Battered and bloodied but still unbroken, Moira staggered out of the place, weak on her feet. After a few steps, I picked her up and carried her to the waiting carpet.

"Thank you, Max," she said, wrapping her arms around my neck and burying her tear-streaked face in my shoulder. "I thought I was dead."

"Hey," I said, "we're friends, right?"

"I didn't think you liked me."

"I don't."

Among the Montags

Robin D. Laws

A hunched figure, draped in rags and bits of carpet sample, drags himself across the cracked tarmac of fucking Vaughan Mills. Cold wind slices across the damaged parking lot. It whispers of buddy cop movies, steroid scandals and Apple product launches.

The man totters on gammy legs toward the safe end of the superstore complex. Before, his name was Wyatt Dean Moler. He used to be a professor of social work at the University of Toronto, with a PhD in community planning systems and development. Now he's Cripple.

Every place like this, he many times has thought, has a guy like him. All named Cripple.

He's making do without a cane. He had one, his original from Before, but then the motos took it from him. He's tried to makeshift one from old boards and once a construction rebar, but they were never right. For a few days he had a shopping cart to lean on, but an old man's not gonna hang onto a treasure like that for long. And sure enough some guy in a grimy red toque took it off him two days later, waving a .22 and claiming there was a bullet in it. Bullet didn't matter; Cripple couldn't stand a pistol-whipping, as was plainly obvious to both of them. Still, damnfool didn't make it more than a hundred yards before a gang of jerseys jacked him for it and the pistol. Which he sure didn't fire no bullets out of.

That was before Smoky. Smoky wouldn't have let no dirty-toque dickweed take Cripple's shopping cart.

Cripple makes it to the steeled-up door that bulwarks the entrance to the safe end. Above it looms signage in the shape of an enormous lake bass. The safe end used to be a giant sporting goods store, its focus fishing, hunting, and the outdoors. The huge fish on its sign is surreal enough in its original form that the semiotic winds have left it as is.

Some say the fish is in the process of coming to life, or at least gaining animation. Occasionally opening its mouth. Goggling its eyes. That sort of business. Others say it's not the case, but will become so if enough people believe it. Cripple is pretty sure that both statements are BS. It's weird out here, but not that weird, not yet. Though based on prior events, who can say what can't happen anymore?

He bangs on the door. After some scuffling around noises from inside, the peephole slides open.

"What you want, Cripple?"

"Need to see Longthought."

"Everybody needs to see Longthought."

"Just let me talk to him, please."

"Go away before you attract something."

"I brought stuff."

"What kind of stuff?"

"You don't do the negotiating."

The guardkeep cogitates. "I'll go get Laws," he finally says.

Cripple waits.

The slot reopens. A squint through cloudy prescription lenses.

"What kind of stuff?" Cripple recognizes the voice. It's Laws. Before you talk to Longthought, you have to talk to Laws. He's as old as Cripple, maybe older. Unlike Cripple he has a gift that justifies his upkeep and protection. To render himself doubly indispensable, he's wormed his way into an unofficial post as Longthought's intermediary.

"Good stuff. Cans."

"More specific."

"Six cans refried beans. They're low-fat, but they're refried beans."

"Name brand or off-brand?"

"Name brand. Let me in and we'll talk."

The door clanks open. Guardkeeps step out with sweeping crossbows. One of them, pointedly, pointed at him.

Cripple ignores the slight. Hobbles quickly in. He fishes into the frayed pockets of his long wool overcoat. Pulls out the promised stuff.

Laws examines it, struggling to place them in the right focal length for reading. Like anyone who relies on glasses, he hasn't had a new prescription since the collapse. He feels the cans for dents.

He's gray-haired and shaggy. A scraggly van Dyke surrounds his lips and chin. His eyes are brown, his eyebrows thick and dark and untended. A colorful Hawaiian-style shirt hangs on malnourished shoulders. It's faded and discolored and threadbare. Old-fashioned Japanese courtesans, drawn in woodblock print style, repeat across the surface of the shirt.

"So what do you want with Longthought now?"

"Six cans does not buy me in?"

"It buys you in to talk to me. Selling me gets you in."

"If Longthought could just hear me out, he'd agree."

"So sell me and you'll get your shot."

Cripple sells him. Laws nods his head. His Before name is the same as his After name, or so Cripple has heard. He gets to keep it, because it's a metonym. Cripple still remembers words like metonym.

Laws leads Cripple down aisles formed by denuded shelving units. They once held lures, boots, flotation vests, boat covers, GPS devices, seats and steering wheels for all-terrain vehicles. He takes Cripple into a storeroom. The smell of sweat and breath tells Cripple that this is where the people of the community live. He thinks he smells bacon and tries not to look desperate.

Two rangy women, skin leathered by sun, wind and barthesdrift, block their path. The taller, younger, dark-haired one is North, which is short for Magnetic North. The diminutive, older, artificially copper-maned one is Detector.

Cripple has dealt with them before. He creeps behind Laws.

North strikes a demanding hip-cocked pose. "Who let him in here?"

Laws pulls a face. They aren't the boss of him. "What's your real question?" He tosses Detector the first of the cans. When her arms are full he offloads the rest on North.

"He's not staying," Detector says.

"Who said he was?" Laws huffs. Making an impatient show of his patience.

"Well then," says North. "Good."

They step aside. Laws steers Cripple away from the encampment, down a warren of cardboard boxes. The two plot a circuitous route through the aisles. Like they're afraid Cripple will watch and remember where the community stores its food.

"Don't tell him you paid," Laws warns.

"I won't."

"I'm serious."

"Promise," says Cripple.

Laws takes him into an anteroom. Longthought strikes a fencing stance, a wooden sword outstretched. Practicing against an invisible opponent. He wears a ragged karate keikogi stitched from low-thread count bedsheets.

Everybody says he's seven feet tall but that's two to three inches worth of exaggeration. His mutations are highly advanced. Physically Longthought is leaving humanity behind. His skin is rubbery and lemon-rind yellow. A dome of hard cartilage covers the top of his head; its lower edge forms a thick, uniform brow that runs all the way around. His unblinking eyes are four or five inches across. Thick muscles fight each other for space beneath his hide. Imagine an elephant's foot, cloven in two—that's what he has on the end of his legs. And of course there's no mouth in his face. Up close you can see the tiny screen of perforated skin above his chin. But Cripple isn't that close.

"Cripple has a sob for you," says Laws.

Longthought puts down the wood sword and stands facing Cripple. He isn't sitting down or anything but even so sinks into a posture of total relaxation.

Without further pleasantries Laws turns his back and leaves.

"It's Smoky," says Cripple. "My dog. Someone's got him. It might be the vicks but I'm afraid it's Dogmeat Drew. Smoky saved my life a bunch of times. Kept watch over me when I slept. Protected me and my stuff. But more important, he was a friend to me. I don't mind being out there. Or rather, I can understand why that has to be. Why the community figures I can't pull my overhead. Fine, that's it, this is the post-world. The companionship of that one creature, who asked nothing from me but a few scraps, kept and keeps me going. I understand reality. I realize permanent harm might have already come to him. But I got to do all I can to rescue him, if he can be rescued. And all I can is coming to you, Longthought. You probably don't think it's worth the bother, saving animals, when you can't even save all the people. It sounds selfish and corny and soft in the head for me to ask. But I got to ask.

"He looks like a German shepherd except for the coloration, which is gray, like you'd guess from the name. He has green eyes and you can also recognize him from his greeting bark. It's this yip, like this." Cripple imitates the bark. "Smoky has a way about him, he can tell the good people from the predators. When he sees you, you'll get the friendly bark, you can be sure of that.

"I woke up as they took him in the night. I saw legs, in jeans and sneaks. They were grabbing him up. Putting something over his muzzle—chloroform I'm thinking. There must be places you can still find chloroform. Then they coshed me. When I came to it was daylight. Of course they took all the stuff at my campsite. And of course I have backup caches where I could go to and reclothe and get the—anyway, that's neither here nor there.

"I owe him this much, to come here and tell you this, and hope you'll help."

Longthought communicates, as he does, in units of emotional impulse. Signs and signifiers ripple out through barely perceptible shifts of posture and via pheromonal emission. He sends this to Cripple: sympathy, comfort, affirmation. Resolve.

The towering lemon-skinned man waves for Cripple to follow him. Longthought stops to grab a brown suede duster from an off-kilter chrome coat-rack. Hanging under the coat is a leather belt, to which a pair of scabbards are attached. Longthought buckles this around his waist. From the scabbards jut the curved hilts of Japanese-style short swords. Wakizashi they call them.

Thus equipped, he goes to Laws' cubby-hole. The old man sits inches from a flatscreen monitor, typing into his keyboard.

The Internet doesn't exist anymore. All servers down. Nothing to power them. The parts purloined and repurposed. Or simply trashed. Yet this is the old writer's gift: he can still access it. Fitfully, unreliably, but for him it's there. If he fucking swears at it enough.

"Unsurprising," he mutters, when he sees Cripple standing there.

Laws attaches a wind-up juicepack to the printer. Its cartridge filled with a mixture of soot, egg yolk and screech, it rattles up a floor plan. He hands it to Longthought, who studies it.

"We don't know where Dogmeat Drew is at, so I'm thinking you wanna start with the vicks," Laws says. "Everybody knows where they hang out. This floorplan is my guestimate based on the Google Street View of their hideout. Your basic industrial park business unit layout."

The area around the mall is filthy with industrial parks.

"Before," Laws goes on, "it was a wine agency. There were other adjacent companies, too, but I can't make out their awnings. Cripple, you think you can see any better?"

"I don't see anything on your screen at all," says Cripple. "In fact I don't believe your computer's turned on."

"Bullshit," says Laws.

Among the Montags

Longthought folds up the map and places it in his pocket. As Laws does not need to explain, the image from the Internet won't take into account reconfigurations that post-date the collapse, whether mundane or from the S-winds. It's a start, anyway.

Laws sits impatiently as Longthought beams emotional indicators at him: compassion, fellowship, the altruism impulse. "We're to take care of him here?"

Longthought nods.

"Okay, but not permanently. You get that, right? Not permanently, not without a vote of the full community."

Longthought departs. He heads out through the secret exit, which takes him deeper into the mall. Moving through gaps in its shattered plate glass, he steps out of a ransacked athletic shoe outlet. He eases into the food court. A pack of situations catch wind of him. They're down by the information court, snurfling aimlessly around in search of food scraps. A couple of the bolder ones stride his way, wifebeaters tight against ripped pectorals. All threat and menace, they strut in baggy flowered beach pants.

They get close enough to see that it's Longthought. They throw up submissive arms. "Sorry bro," they say. "No harm, bro." They turn, preserving the remnants of their collective dignity, and cower behind the info kiosk.

Longthought exits the former mall. He lopes into the winter air. Somewhere a chainsaw screams. Longthought pays it no mind. It's not a real chainsaw. It's an emotional echo, a dreamcatcher of latent unease. In other words, a trap.

In front of the vick hive, pickups and vans are sloppily parked. Waxy driblets of dried greasonol leak down from their gas caps. Ferocious snarls echo from the back of a white junker SUV. Its roof bears the dents of multiple rolling incidents. Burly vicks drag sheet-metal carrier cages from the truck. Inside, heavily muscled dogs insanely leap. They buck and turn and try to bite the vicks' gloved fingers. Flat-faced sentries lean against the archway of the HQ's main door.

They tense, pushing off from the brick, when they see Longthought coming. The dog handlers gingerly drop their cages. The creatures inside howl and froth.

The doormen blast on whistles. More vicks pour from the doorways. By the time Longthought reaches them, there's a good two dozen of them. All the same body morphology: stocky, squat, wide-shouldered. Foreheads slope back. Jaws jut out. Skin tone runs a spectrum from Yaphet Kotto to Elric. The vicks wear hand-painted football jerseys and necklaces made from shredded aluminum cans. They pose and front, brandishing mockguns carved from wood and painted black.

Longthought approaches. He broadcasts calm, non-confrontation, inquiry.

A vick appoints himself leader and moves to meet him. "Get out of our heads, lemon man."

Longthought emits more calm.

"Turn around and go back the way you came," says the vick leader.

Longthought stands firm.

"We don't come to your hidey to fuck with you. Don't you come to ours to fuck with us."

Longthought broadcasts non-fuck-withitude.

"Your uninvited physical presence here is problem enough, lemon-rind. This is not the Before. There is no public space anymore. Every encroachment outside of your own zone is trespass. You know that."

Longthought settles in.

"Don't think that we won't go to combat mode. Because we will, to defend our hidey and the honor of our sport. It ain't like Before. Don't you go judging us. These animals weren't just bred to fight. They were made to fight. They are made of fight. Form and figure. That we celebrate their expression of their Platonic selfhood, that is no business of yours."

Longthought transmits an image into their minds: a vision of Smoky, plucked from Cripple's memories.

The leader reels back. "I told you not to do that, fucker!"

Another of the vicks stumbles back into a dog cage. His pant leg gets caught in the latch-bolt. He ducks down in an attempt to free himself. He pulls the cage door open. The beast inside barrels out, scattering the assembled vicks.

It looks as much like a shrunk-down lion and/or baboon as a pit bull. With bounding leaps it propels itself through the air. It lands on a vick standing at the leader's right hand, pulling him down to the broken pavement. It digs six-inch canines into the downed vick's throat.

The vicks groan in horror. Blood jets all over.

Longthought bends down to grab the beast. He pulls on its haunches, tearing it from its victim. The frenzied mutation whirls to attack him. It bites down deep on his arm. Its canines pierce his duster and the bleached arm of his bedsheet keikogi. They can't penetrate his rubbery hide. He wraps his arms around the wildly resisting lionbaboondog. Struggling it into place, he positions it into the crook of his arm. He chokes the fucking thing out. Once limp, he gently lays its unconscious bulk on the tarmac. The dog's owner runs over to slap a chloroform rag on its lips. He drags the limp beast back into its cage and locks it firm. He locks an angry gaze on the bozo who clumsied it to freedom. The guilty vick backs off, envisioning his future shit-kicking.

With the dog out of the way, the wounded man's condition can easily be seen. The jugular gouts open. The guy is flat-out done for.

Longthought crouches over him. He withdraws his left wakizashi.

"Whoa whoa whoa," says the vick spokesman. "If there's mercy-killing to be done, it's us who's gonna do it."

Longthought hits him with a punchy wave of disagreement. He's got it all wrong. That's not what this is.

The sword blade glows orange. He plunges it into the wound. It impales the neck. Comes out the other side. The vicks have not yet had time to react when he pulls it back out again, just as quick. The torn throat is whole again. The injured man, already in cardiac arrest, sputters back to life.

Longthought sheathes his blade.

He does not attempt to explain. That would require too many abstractions. Longthought has two blades. The sword of killing and the sword of healing. He can't use the kill-sword until first using the heal-sword. And vice versa. To take a life, he must preserve a life.

Astonished vicks haul the reviving man into their hidey. Longthought grips his big hand onto the leader's shoulder. Beams him again with the image of Smoky. Glances significantly to the chloroform rag, lying abandoned in the gravel.

"You think us sentimental," tries the spokesman. "You think we value our lives higher than we do our battle-beasts. As if that's such a big favor, leaving him alive to starve and suffer another day. But if you don't tell people we're pussies, if you don't say this is how you got us to cough up the word, fuckit, I'll tell you, all right? Because let's say we don't want to find out what that other blade does. Let's say that. Understood?"

Longthought nods.

"Okay so yeah we traded the mange you want to Dogmeat Drew. He had one we wanted—a blooder, high fight in him, mangler breeding balls. For some reason he was hot for Cripple's mutt. Probably as a soup or curry. So don't get your hopes up. So yeah, Dogmeat Drew. Now leave us be."

Longthought: anger, interrogative.

"I told you who. I'm not comfortable spilling the locale also. Find him yourself."

Hand drifts to other blade. The universal language.

"Shitrocks, man. Okay, okay. Construction site. Down Fish Road. Don't tell it was us who narked. We might need further trade relations with him. Unless you cap him. Tell him whatever you want if you cap him afterwards. Dogmeat's moderately useful but not to give you an impression vicks give a crap."

Longthought turns and goes.

"Yeah no pleasantries on this side either, Lemonhead!" shouts the vick after him, hands cupped around mouth.

Longthought trudges down Fish Road. Over its broken swelling pavement. Snow whitens the air. Small bullet flakes from nowhere. These days storms come on faster.

Snow is a foot deep and squeaking beneath his boot heels by the time he reaches the chainlink surrounding the construction site. It's surprising that Dogmeat Drew has the pebbles to hidey here. It's got the haunt on it. This is where the Howler ate those children. Before Longthought ended him.

Longthought steps through the hole in the fence he made the last time he was here. Every footfall in the complaining snow announces his approach. Clumps of gathering flake cling to the gray sides of a half-finished concrete shell. It thrusts up for four boxy stories. Holes for windows. No roof. Longthought hears scurrying inside.

He strides in, moving through a narrow doorway. A clattering net drops onto him. He fights it. Sharp edges of tin cans and sharpened tools, attached to the nylon net, are meant to cut and scratch. They don't do that, but they do confuse the issue. The more Longthought struggles, the more he entangles himself.

Footsteps pound in the snow outside. The net is a delaying tactic. While he's stuck in it, Dogmeat is peeling out the back, across a flat expanse.

Longthought leaves the net on as he pursues. The storm's fucking up visibility. A few seconds makes the difference between keeping Drew in sight and losing him. Once lost, it could be ages to find him. Too late, assuming Smoky isn't already stewing in a pot. Longthought barrels on. Leaps over a ceramic conduit. Skids across a pallet of warping lumber.

Dogmeat Drew is a sideswiping dark blur in the whiteout ahead. Longthought speeds up, pouring strength into his leg muscles. Drew makes the mistake of turning his head back to look. Loses ground. Longthought topples onto him. Lands on him with a thumping and a grunt from each man. Dogmeat Drew gets the wind knocked out of him. Is cut by the shrapnel he tied to his own net. Longthought wrestles off the net. Rolls it up. Wraps it around Dogmeat's wrists, then his ankles, then brings the two loops together in a crude hog-tie. Drew squawls, face-first in the snow. He tries to kick, drawing the net tighter around him.

"I din't do nuthin'!" he whines.

Longthought makes him see Smoky. Makes him see the chloroforming rag, the hands of the vick who captured him.

"I swear to bones I din't eat that dog!"

Longthought beams him skepticism. Impatience with his bullshit.

"No no seriously I din't I din't. Those vicks. Those damn vicks gave me up. Freakin degenerates is what they are. They are devo. D-E-V-O."

Longthought balls his fists.

"No no I only acted as a broker in this arrangement. I got no investment here. No reason to be hurt. And besides, what do you care about Cripple or Cripple's dog? Your community red-lined him. Wouldn't let him in. That makes him fair game, don't it? *Ouch!*

"Okay okay, I gave the dog to some new guy. Doesn't even have a metaname yet. Said his name was Anderson. Though maybe that is a metaname. An actor who played the boss of the Six Million Dollar Man reference. Also the guy who played MacGyver, a reference to that maybe.

"Why did he have a jones for the dog? How do I know? What am I, a wiki? All I know is it wasn't fighting and it wasn't eating.

"Where is he? Don't you know? He's in your own freakin' mall, lemon-head. I mean, Longthought! *Oww, don't!* He's set up in the bad end. Yes, that's right. Deep in the freakin Baby-Mart. Among the montags. So he's got to have powerful essence. True mojo, for them to leave him alone. No, to rally around him as his guardkeeps. You don't pack that kinda mojo, do you, rinder boy? No disrespect."

Longthought lets go of him. He rolls in the snow, wriggling against his bonds. Longthought draws a wakizashi. He slices Dogmeat free. Heads back north.

Dogmeat Drew calls after him: "You don't got to do it. Whatever you promised Cripple, you didn't say you'd descend into a montag den for him." He gets to his feet. "Hold up and listen to me, lemon-head! I don't like you. You get into my shit. Every time we meet, I get humiliated. But don't go get yourself wiped, lemon-head. We need you around here. Do you hear me? You're a stabilizing influence!"

Among the Montags

Longthought crosses a berm littered with shattered cars and then the charred foundations of a drywall warehouse. He stalks across the roadway to a field thick with Chinese sumac saplings. In a few years, if it keeps going like this, all of Vaughan will be a forest of the things. Tree of heaven, they call it.

Between the snow and the chin-high forest, it's picky going. He hops a fake-rustic wall made of bricks meant to look like stone. He's into the parking lot.

Around the entrance to Baby-Mart montags lurk and growl. They bend at the waist, weighed down by pendulous pseudo-implants. Their eyes glow red. Hard nails glint and sparkle. Matted peroxide hair cascades over long, slack-jawed faces. The drool of lost fame-dreams drops from airbrushed lips.

Amidst them are others of like ilk: lohans, kardashians, even a few of older resonance: a zadora, an angelyne, a pair of headless mansfields. The glam-slammers, the body-image victims, hungry and vengeful.

This won't be cakes and ale, but going through the mall would be more dangerous still. For every guardian here, there are three inside. Plus the traps and the reality bends. The hanging chains and the cascades of water dripping from nowhere.

Through overturned vehicles Longthought creeps. They smell him in the air. The montags fan out through the labyrinth of wreckage. A bikinied specimen launches herself frothing upon him. He leaves swords sheathed. He lets her hit, twists, uses the impact to direct her into the side of an immolated Hyundai. She gasps and goes down, but now a dozen of her sisters mob around him. He clambers awkwardly onto a half-ton's wheel-less chassis. He leaps down, running. They follow, shrieking murderously. Maenads, he thinks, footnoting when he should be fucking fleeing.

He gets to a swathe of cleared pavement near the Baby-Mart entrance. Surprises them by whirling, holding his ground. Clotheslines one. Kicks another into a crumpled garbage bin. He takes their blows as they crowd around him. Longthought lets their savagery build. He turns from the hardest of the hits. Claws rake him. His coat shreds. He waits opportunistically, until they tangle into one another. Takes them out when they're distracted. He punches with all of his strength. With the heel of his hand, he drives montag noses up into montag skulls. They can take it. They'll collapse, then regenerate. The idea behind them is too numinous, too resilient, to allow them to die. Not while Barthes winds swirl.

Longthought falls to his knees. There are too many of them. He takes a kick to the jaw. Another, another. One has climbed on his back, is trying to drive pointed forefingers into his eyes. He flips her onto her back, crunches a boot into her throat. The eruption of savagery earns him a moment to reposition. Then the flurry of attacks resumes. Under the pounding, his vision ripples.

He sees the dog. Smoky. It's not the same memory he got from Wyatt Moler, the so-called Cripple. This image is blurrier, fresher, current. A self-image from within, as a person pictures himself. The dog is inside. Communicating. In his mind's ear, Longthought hears the friendly yip Cripple spoke of. Determination surges through him. He rises. Shrugs off the kicks, the punches, the clawings. His fists become precision missiles. They fly to throats and temples. Montags fall. Lohans scatter.

Like retail greeters more shuffling montags await him at the Baby-Mart foyer. Seeing him spacked in their sisters' the blood, they rear back. He explodes through them, paying a toll in further clawings.

The store is mold, wet, gloom. Fluorescents erratically flicker. Lohan puke slicks the floor. The brown dust of broken acoustic ceiling tiles lies like sawdust on every surface. Baby monitors, long stripped of their batteries, cough and crackle all the same.

Canine whimpering beckons him from the second-floor office. Longthought thunders past strollers, over bassinets, down aisles still stocked with jumpers and pacifiers. He mounts the steps. A kardashian springs at him from a stockroom. Longthought seizes it by the shoulders and hurls it to the sales floor below. Its spine snaps. It crawls on its broken back, meeping forgotten catch-phrases, seeking a sheltered place to regenerate.

Longthought kicks down the door. Screws fly from ripped-out

hinges. Instinct, or something in the dog's low keening, warns him to duck. A bullet from a gun—an actual bullet from an actual gun—ricochets off the metal-shod door.

Furling up like a wave, Longthought smacks the shooter in the jaw. The attacker's finger clicks the trigger. Nothing more in the cylinder. Longthought roundhouses the gunman. He skids across the polished floor of an office-turned-laboratory.

One light source illuminates the room: a 42" plasma screen. Grass-green reflections play across the slumped, stunned figure. Nothing about him indicates mojo. Fiftyish, balding, the drooping face of a formerly well-fed man who's learned starvation. The vestiges of a double chin still hang around his jaw. Dots of stubble darken his cheeks. He wears a drab business suit, dress shirt, black unpatterned tie, scuffed up leather shoes.

Anderson, thinks Longthought.

"You don't know what you're interfering with, mutant," the dazed man mumbles.

The screen shows blurry scenes from Before, hazily intercut like an experimental film. A lawnmower across a lawn. Hopping birds on a sidewalk. Fall leaves piled by a curb. A brick house with brightly painted porch. A yellow-brown shape on a tiled floor—part of a dropped muffin, maybe? Sound effects are eerie sharp but also in some odd way distorted. There's a faint hiss where you might expect music.

HDMI cables lead from the back of the plasma to a reconfigured streaming media box. Its guts lie open, alligator clips and naked copper wire fed through its chips and circuit board. These in turn lead to a nearby table, and to Smoky.

Anderson has restrained the crying dog, wrapping it in a blanket and encircling that in duct-tape. More rolls of tape pin the blanket to the table. The top of the dog's skull sits in a glass jar filled with alcohol. The wires from the media box terminate in a network of pins jutting from the animal's exposed brain.

Longthought goes to free the dog.

"You can't do that," says Anderson.

Longthought directs the feeling of query at him.

The man responds as if not noticing the strangeness of Longthought's communication. "You'll destroy everything. No one likes to see that happen to a dog. God knows I sure don't. But it's our only way back, don't you see? Please don't touch that. I'm on the verge of breaking through."

Longthought hesitates.

The dog regards him pleadingly.

Hands held in surrender, Anderson slowly rises. "Catastrophic climate change. Starvation of the phyto-planktons. Bio-engineered pandemic. The closing of the antibiotic window. When I was younger, global thermonuclear war. An asteroid hit, even. These were the end times we anticipated. A semiotic apocalypse? Who was ready for that? No one. The rebellion of signs and signifiers. The vengeful outbreak of a poisoned collective unconscious. You're Longthought, aren't you?"

His captor nods.

"I thought of contacting you, but then learned the trick of achieving dominance over the montags. And others besides. I can save us all. Retrieve the essential data from reality's corrupted hard drive. Reboot. Return us to those days. Halcyon. That was a word I never used in a sentence, Before." He gestures to the screen.

A family now sits on the porch. They drink lemonades. A boy in the foreground sets up a sprinkler to water the lawn.

"We can't remember it straight. We're all mutated up here." Anderson points to his temple. "The animals may be altered elsewhere, but not in their minds. From their memories, we can get a clean enough reality read to...well, I haven't got to that part yet. First we get the clean read, then we figure out the reboot. An exercise of collective will, I'm thinking. Something ritual or ceremonial? The key is, we have to get the clean read. This dog remembers the old times pure, purer than anyone sapient can possibly hope to. It's special, high-functioning, keen senses. There will be others like it, which you and I must collect. The data must be extracted. Then we can have it all back. Safe homes. Abundant food. Medicine, surgery. So many other vital technologies. And with it, yes, perhaps the vapid insanities of celebrity culture, too.

Fun things. Video games, espresso on a Sunday morning, an evening at the symphony. We can get it all back. All of it, I promise you."

Longthought takes his memory of Anderson from a few seconds ago, pointing to his head and saying everyone is mutated there. He beams that image into Anderson's mind.

Anderson seems puzzled. "You're asking me what?"

Longthought repeats it.

"How can I know I'm not crazy, like I'm saying everyone else is? Is that it?"

Longthought nods.

"I can't be crazy. We have to be able to get back. We were bad, but we weren't that bad. We don't deserve this, none of us." His sentence slams to a stammering halt.

Longthought ponders. He looks at the dog. He takes his image of the dog, the pins in his brain, the pain he's in. This image he scatters into a hundred duplicates and telepaths into Anderson's head.

Anderson comes nearer, excitement rising in his voice. "Yes yes we'll have to do it to many more dogs. Which we'll have to carefully find. Perhaps breed for this purpose. But that would take too long. The important thing I said already. We can get back!"

Longthought beams him cartoon images. A bull. A plus sign. A curled and steaming turd.

He draws his sword. His other sword. Its blade glows red. He flicks it across the top of Anderson's hand. Barely breaking the surface of his wrinkled skin.

Anderson drops dead at his feet.

In the echoing distance, montags wail.

He plucks the pins and wires from the dog's brain. Fishes the top of its skull from the jar. As best he can, he fits the skull piece back in place.

He draws his first sword, his most important sword, and plunges it through the top of the skull and into Smoky's damaged brain. The wakizashi glows orange. It heals the wounded animal, fusing his skull back shut.

Longthought wraps the dog in a blanket—a different blanket—and carries it out of the lab and down to the retail floor. Montags, kardashians, lohans and headless mansfields circle. He projects his rage at them. He projects his memory of Smoky's pain. Clutching their foreheads, they shuffle back, making way. Longthought takes Smoky out of the Baby-Mart.

He returns the dog to Cripple, who waits back in the mall's good end. The dog leaps up on his master's legs as if nothing has happened. Tears fill the old man's red eyes.

The community has gathered around him. They view the old man's happiness with closed and hardened faces.

Laws claps a hand on Longthought's shoulder—a difficult reach. "Shame he can't stay with us. That he has to go right back out to where he got ambushed. But hey, the community voted. And you and I were in the minority."

Longthought beams an image to everyone. A community meeting. With slumped and guilty shoulders they convene. No way they're going to reverse themselves, to let a dead weight like Cripple eat through their larder. They appreciate the sentiment of it, and are grateful for all that Longthought does for them. But in the end, this is a democracy. Not many of those out there, but that's what this is. One person, one vote. Longthought gets no more votes than anyone else. Carries no more weight.

Speakers speak, according to their modified rules of order. Laws presents Longthought's case for him, to the extent that he can intuit what it is. He throws in a few arguments of his own to sweeten the pot. After he repeats the pros, North and Detector team up to give the cons. Community members nod sagely as they speak.

When Longthought gets up, they're surprised. They sit back on their metal folding chairs, ready for what he gave them last time: feelings of fellowship, compassion, mutuality.

This time he beams at them another image: an image of him, framed in the doorway, his body dark against the light of a rare bright day. In the image, he abandons them, trudging off alone toward the violet horizon.

"You can't..." says North.

"That's blackmail," manages Detector.

Longthought nods.

Laws keeps a smart ass look off his face, mostly. He asks if anyone else wishes to speak. They don't, so the vote is called.

This time Cripple is accepted, by a solid majority.

Laws goes to break the news to him. North and Detector follow along, to lay on the old man the community's rules and conditions. They heavily stress the probationary period.

Longthought leans down to scratch Smoky behind the ears.

They're gonna need that fucking dog.

Footsteps in Limbo

John Scott Tynes

When Satan fell, he was accompanied by a host of angels who likewise had raged against God. God threw them down into Hell. He chained them to the shore of a lake of fire where they struggled and cried.

Professor died alone, resolute, eyes dry, his heart a cold stone. He lay slumped in a chair and dragged razors down his thick wrists. His blood pooled at his feet. A chill set into his flesh. His eyes grew dull and distant. The room became dim.

Professor did not believe God existed at all. He was wrong.

He was sure that neither Heaven nor Hell awaited his miserable soul. He was right.

◇

Jaclyn was on the slope. The steep incline in the heart of the city's downtown was dotted with people trudging up or quick-stepping down. The art museum was nearby, dominated by a giant animated iron silhouette of a man raising and lowering a hammer, turning the street into an anvil. The people passed directly through Jaclyn without taking notice. Their mouths moved without a sound. Their feet fell silently on the pavement. Jaclyn was dead and this was Limbo and the only noises she ever heard here were in her memories. It was late afternoon and the sun should have been warm, but she couldn't feel it. *This is your world, Professor,* she thought. *Not mine.*

Jaclyn stood short, a little stocky, about thirty-five. She'd had black hair when she lived but now her projected sense of self had the light brown hair that came to the fore whenever she hadn't dyed it for a while. Her eyes were narrow and crinkled at the corners when she smiled. No one had ever really noticed that about her—or much of anything else.

Then Terrance blinked and was there. She felt his presence before she saw him. "Jaclyn," he said, in a soul's mimicry of audible speech. The soft bubble of his essence trembled with fear, pressing up uncomfortably against her own rigid, opaque being. Her soul briefly caressed his, smoothing its surface like a cat's fur. It was a social thing you did here. He settled slightly.

Terrance stood a block uphill, a thin older man in baggy clothes whose white hair was little more than a fringe around a bare dome. He wasn't yet very precise when he blinked. Jaclyn moved near him. Proximity was only marginally relevant to a soul's speech but their humanity still demanded it.

"I found someone. Cut down. It felt like Jason. It was near his locus."

"Take me there."

Terrance's being rippled. He didn't want to go back.

"Let's get Professor. He'll know what to do."

Her essence glowed with warmth briefly, lessening the chill he felt. Below the warmth she had an unbending will.

"Take me there. Now."

They blinked.

◇

Jason took an overdose of sleeping pills. His marriage of forty years ended three years ago and he'd lost his home. He lived in a broken-down car near a park when he found the pill bottle. Saturated with fortified wine, he'd taken them all. His last thought was of a dog he'd had as a boy. When he stirred next, he was in Limbo.

That was where all the suicides went.

Jaclyn and Terrance regarded the bedraggled mass of black and green matter lying in the road. It looked vaguely fetal in pose, although of adult size. The outlines of its form were already vague and the mass was seeping into the street. Cars and trucks drove through it without a disturbance—and through the two insubstantial souls who had come to see it. Nearby, huge old trees wreathed the large expanse of grassy green parkland Jason spent his final days in. Loitering, as they called it, when they hauled him in for being drunk and disorderly. He'd loved that park. It was all he'd had to love, anymore.

"Jason?" she asked.

"I think so. His locus is around the corner and I can't find him. I thought maybe Professor could make sure, you know."

"I'm already sure. Did you see it happen?"

"No. I think I got here just after."

"Okay. There's nothing more you can do. I'll take care of this."

A large truck drove through them. They didn't even notice.

"Are you going to get Professor?"

"Terrance, I know you think Professor is going to make it all better. He's not. Professor is on a bender. He's in no shape to deal right now."

"But—but I *heard* something."

"What do you mean? You felt someone else?"

"No. I mean I *heard* something. Footsteps."

"That's impossible. There's no such thing."

"I know."

"So you're wrong."

"Just get Professor, please. He'll know what to do." Terrance's

Footsteps in Limbo

essence had firmed up. Jaclyn could feel it both resolving and retracting from her at the same time.

"All right. You'll come with me."

"Thanks, Jaclyn."

"See if you still feel that way in half an hour."

◇

Professor's home lay north of downtown. Since his suicide the 1930s bungalow had been sold, remodeled, refurnished, and occupied by a young family. When he came here, which was not often, he would pad silently through the rooms and eventually lay down. The people who lived here now would pass through him, unknowing. He didn't notice. He didn't notice anything when he was here, not the new paint on the walls or the fashionable marble countertops in the kitchen where he used to chop carrots on scarred Formica or the kids that slept in the room where he graded papers year after unchanging year. Everything was so different and it didn't matter in the slightest. When he came here it was not to look. It was to *feel*.

What Professor felt here in his old home was misery. Absolute misery. From the moment he blinked in his being folded in on itself, forming an existential pocket dimension of agony. He would slide down inside and even the feeble pull of Limbo receded like a dark moon glimpsed from within a deep ocean. Blackness. Blackness and an impacted density of suffering. Years of heartache flaked off and settled slowly to the bottom, a thick sediment, and when he stood in this house the walls of his diving bell cracked and shattered and he sank limply down into that morass.

Professor was on a bender.

Jaclyn and Terrance blinked and were there. Jaclyn took them right to where Professor was. Terrance's relief turned to horror. He reached out his hand but it shook violently, an echo of the palsy that afflicted him in life.

Professor was only partly coherent. He lay slumped on the floor, legs curling, and his skin was the color of cremains. His face and hands were melting, their definition sloughing into a dark, slick mass. The transition was slow. He would not fully dissolve for days at this rate. But if he did, he would drop through Limbo and plunge silently into the molten core of Hell. It would be a second suicide.

"Professor!" Terrance cried. His essence was as wobbly as his hands. Professor was his rock, as he was for most of the souls who transited Limbo and ascended. Few ever saw him like this. It wasn't Jaclyn's first time.

Professor didn't respond.

"He won't go," Jaclyn said. Her tone did not exactly reassure: certain but scornful. "He does this sometimes. Comes back here and just drowns himself for a while. He always comes back."

"But why?"

"Why do you think he spends so much time around people like us? He's a junkie for suffering. And sometimes he needs the really good stuff. His stuff. Homebrew."

Terrance resisted, firming up again. His hands steadied. When he spoke it was almost childlike. "Professor helps us. He saves so many."

"Then don't tell them. When they go on about how great he is you just take this memory and keep it for yourself. You know the truth. He's a goddamn vampire."

"Can we wake him up? What do we do?"

"He's waking already. Look."

Color came back into Professor's skin. The seeping mess of his face and hands paled and slowed.

"We'll wait in the library," Jaclyn said. "He won't talk to us here."

◇

The downtown library was a many-angled obelisk of steel and glass, a squat post-modernist toad with pointy edges. In the late day's sun it glinted and shone.

Inside, above the cavernous main level intersected by angled steel beams, there was an upper floor where every surface was painted a glistening red. The walls were curved. It was like standing inside a human heart.

That was where you could find Professor.

Jaclyn and Terrance waited for what used to be an hour. Few library patrons ventured into this red heart. Come evening, the meeting rooms would be used for twelve-step groups and ardent practitioners of felting. Then he was there.

"Jaclyn," he said. "Terrance."

Seen away from his locus, out of his bender, Professor was medium height and heavy, with a bushy grey beard and thin hair, in his fifties. His students in freshman English called him Santa Claus, and not kindly. In life he had grown taciturn and snappish, a once good man whom life had slowly, methodically curdled. His funeral was poorly attended.

His years in Limbo had sweetened his being into a kindly fire. He stoked that fire now and extended it to his companions, reaching out with a mastery of control and empathy far beyond what either of them had learned. Terrance's essence received the warmth and expanded slightly, smoothing out and becoming firm, Professor working his soul like a glassblower. Jaclyn's rigidity softened and elevated, buoyant. When she was near him like this she was glad. When she left his presence she hardened and sank as his residual warmth cooled. Her own inner fire burned well but cold.

Jaclyn, disarmed, answered first. "Professor, Jason's gone."

"Let's go there," he replied, glancing briefly at a small group of students who walked the red hall.

"Professor, wait," Terrance said, looking a little nervously at Jaclyn. "Are you okay? In your house, I mean, you didn't look so good."

"I'm fine, Terrance. We all have our moments of weakness. Now let's go attend to the dead."

◇

Jason was an oil slick. He had continued to dissolve and now the rendered remains of his essence were spread widely across the road. The sunlight here guttered slightly, filtered by the spiritual residue of his sadness. But he was long gone, plunged into Hell for eternity.

Professor and Jaclyn were there. Terrance stood yards away, not comfortable getting close. Succumbing in Limbo happened all the time. People came here, tried to get it together, failed, and fell, even some of the ones Professor managed to reach. But this was different.

Jason had help. Terrance stayed back.

Professor knelt in the street, heedless of the cars that drove through him.

"You're sure he didn't just succumb?"

"I saw him this morning," Terrance insisted. "I mean, he wasn't great but he wasn't like this. There hasn't been time, right? Since then?"

"No," agreed Professor.

"Plus I heard footsteps."

Jaclyn looked at him sharply. "He *thinks* he heard footsteps."

"I heard footsteps."

"That's ridiculous," she said.

"It's not ridiculous," Professor interjected. "Just metaphysically unlikely."

"But there's no sound in Limbo, Professor."

"You think so? I suppose you haven't met Asphodel."

The name resonated. Jaclyn and Terrance quivered for a moment. A wave of unease passed over them, as if a distant horn sounded and would shortly be followed by the baying of dogs.

"Feel that?" Professor said. "He's looking at us now. Which is good, because I have some questions for him."

When he spoke next the word reverberated with a clamor.

"Asphodel."

And then he was there.

The angel glowed so brightly Jaclyn and Terrance shielded their eyes at first. Eight feet tall and luminous, Asphodel folded

Footsteps in Limbo

his wings with an audible rustle. He stepped forward. The sound of his feet on the pavement was that of a heavy man and his armor made a bright grinding whine of metal on metal. They were real sounds, the sounds of a being who brought his own domain wherever he went, a domain not subject to the rules of Limbo. He towered over Professor. A circlet of pale white flowers lay atop his dark hair and classically beautiful face.

"Hello, Asphodel," Professor said respectfully.

"Still here? No matter. You may shun God's grace / a thousand years yet still assume your place. / Though self-murder may not be your final crime / for pride undoes even the best in time."

"This man isn't guilty," Professor said, indicating Jason's black remains. "He was reasonably well just hours ago. Now he is long gone. No one succumbs that fast."

"You think you know another's soul? / Only the bearer is in control. / He above and They below may jostle / but the choice it lay with your apostle." He spoke the last word with a tinge of mockery.

"I'm no messiah. And Jason was not this far gone. You call it self-murder—I would remove the 'self' from that statement. Someone *took* him."

Asphodel gave him a withering look.

"Neither I nor you wrote the laws / we only suffer their every clause. / Souls leave Limbo up or down / and every day are more to be found. / 'Tis a net suspended above Hell / for a fisherman to fill full well. / Some may leap overboard / and add their puny tally to the score. / What's more— / a suicide's fate is no great thing / so Professor, find another gong to ring."

"I like the one I strike. Why don't you help them, Asphodel? Isn't that your job? You just sit in your damned meadow day and night. These people need your help. They can be saved!"

Asphodel did not deign to reply but his lip curled slightly. With a sweep of his hand, the final remains of Jason atomized and disappeared. No sign of him remained. The angel departed without even bothering to glare at them.

"My God," Terrance said. "That was an angel?"

"Great guy, wasn't he?" Jaclyn said. "If they're all like that Heaven must be a real paradise."

"It is," Professor said.

"You've got a lot of faith for a suicide," Jaclyn retorted. "All we've really got to count on is ourselves. Look at that angel! He's no help. Make it or break it, it's up to us."

Professor looked thoughtful. He carefully thinned an outer layer of his essence, shedding emotion and identity and becoming a soap bubble of subtle sensation. Then he expanded it, growing in volume until, unnoticed by the others, it encompassed all three of them. Within his sphere of profound awareness he could observe them deeply, if briefly. He did not know their minds but he knew their souls and in probing Jaclyn's he discovered a lattice of swollen, painful scars. She had suffered like no human he'd ever met—and by an order of magnitude at that. He recoiled from the archive of pain encased in her being and the fragile sphere of his distended awareness collapsed. He sighed. "Well, even Paradise has its meliorists."

"So the footsteps I heard," Terrance said. "That was him?"

"I doubt it," Professor said. "I don't think angels are in the business of murder. But maybe someone who was once like him. Tell me, how long has Jason been in Limbo?"

"Not long," Terrance said. "Maybe a few days. I've been helping him."

"I'm glad you tried. Please make the rounds, both of you—see how the other recent arrivals are doing. I think whoever is doing this is picking off the weakest, those whose sense of self is too fragile and wounded to resist. See who is the most in jeopardy of succumbing."

"So where are you going?" Jaclyn asked.

"I'm going to check in on a new friend."

"Professor, wait," Terrance said. "What do I do if I hear footsteps?"

Professor thought for a moment.

"Blink," he finally said. "Keep blinking. Don't stop until you find me. And above all, don't doubt in yourself."

Footsteps in Limbo

◇

Maurice was sixteen and skinny, with frizzy hair and sloppy clothes. Gay. His family told him he was going to Hell. The guys at school didn't bother with theology—they just hit him, tripped him, shoved him in his locker, pulled his pants down in class, scrawled graffiti about him on the walls, left gay porn magazines on his desk, made a Facebook group devoted to wild estimates of how much cock he sucked. The assistant principal told him maybe he should try dating a girl. His life was Hell on Earth and then he killed himself.

Professor had been working with him for a couple of weeks. The first part was the toughest—just unrolling Maurice from his tight little ball of shame and self-hatred, getting him to open his eyes and understand where he was.

Professor knew the key was projecting confidence. Confidence that a suicide could be saved. Confidence that each person could find their own forgiveness. Confidence that Limbo was a second chance. These souls needed that, required his confidence as a foundation for their own.

Maurice responded. Slowly, grudgingly, he accepted his reality and took ownership of what brought him here. Professor intended to move him onto the next step in the path: getting Maurice's help with another new arrival. Nothing puts your own problems in perspective like someone else's, and taking some responsibility for another human being builds confidence in yourself. And when you succeed in helping, it gives you hope.

That was Professor's playbook. It worked about half the time. The rest of the time these bedraggled suicide souls flailed, faltered, succumbed. And then they went to Hell.

Professor went to see Maurice because Maurice had been slipping. The guy Maurice was trying to help had succumbed. Professor asked Jaclyn to work with Maurice but he wasn't optimistic. He'd put a lot of time in with this kid and if Maurice was succumbing, he might be the perfect target for whomever was doing this.

He might be bait.

Maurice stayed near his locus. He'd hung himself in the basement, suicide note posted online. Today Professor found him there, on the floor, curled up and wailing.

Nearby, Maurice's mother folded laundry. She couldn't hear him. There was nothing new about that.

As a soul in this place slowly succumbed, the loss of self manifested as a failure of the body. It wasn't a real body anyway, just a projection of self-image. Maurice's self-image was starting to collapse. His face was a mass of sloughing tissue leaving a gaping red hole where his mouth had been. That remnant of a mouth keened, tongueless, lipless, unable to speak any language but pain.

Then Jaclyn was there. Professor scowled briefly at the interruption.

"Professor?" she said.

"I asked you to make your rounds."

"I am."

Professor remembered tasking her with Maurice and nodded. "Of course."

"Let me work with him, Professor. There are others you can help."

"Shh," Professor said, growing still and quiet. For a minute no one said anything.

"Maurice," he finally said, gently. Maurice's being was a white dwarf star of compacted torment, the size of a small stone but as heavy as the world. Professor tried to warm it, embrace it, unfold it. It didn't yield.

Professor closed his eyes. He needed every ounce of awareness and will he could muster. He probed Maurice's essence until he found a tiny fissure, a slight opening where hope might get in.

"You will never be alone," he said. "When you get where you're going you will always have friends. They will understand you. They will accept you."

The fissure widened just a little. Something resembling a consciousness seemed to become aware of Professor's presence. The wailing faltered.

Footsteps in Limbo

Jaclyn was astonished. She knew Maurice very well by now and she didn't expect that Professor could make any progress with him. She pushed her essence out a little farther, trying to observe the miracle Professor was starting to work on this poor young man's soul.

Upstairs, a heavy footstep fell.

Professor's soul wobbled a little. He wrapped Maurice in his own being, trying to shield him, disguise him, anything.

"Professor, we should go," Jaclyn said nervously.

Another footstep, a heavy tread. Maurice stirred uneasily.

Then the footsteps had a voice. Loud and guttural, like a trumpeting elephant.

"MAURICE," it bellowed. "FAGGOT."

"Professor, now," Jaclyn pleaded. "We can't stay here. It's coming!"

More footsteps.

"Come with me," Professor pleaded with Maurice. "Come with me. We'll go away from here. Right now. Come with me."

No response. The pebble at the center of Maurice's being shuddered with fear and shame. The tiny fissure snapped shut.

"Professor, let's go!" Jaclyn cried.

"WE'RE COMING, FAGGOT," the voice bellowed. "KICK YOUR ASS, FAGGOT."

The footsteps came down the stairs. The wood creaked.

The demon turned the corner.

It resembled an angel—as seen in the broken shards of a mirror. Once it stood eight feet tall and regal. Now it was stooped and hunchbacked, legs permanently bowed and bent, feet deformed, plates of once-holy armor painfully embedded in gnarled, warty flesh with patches of exposed muscle and bone. The wings were long gone, painful stumps left behind that were eternally inflamed and oozing, wounds that could never heal.

The face, though. The face still shone with beauty.

"PROFESSOR," the demon rumbled.

"Go away." He willed it. He willed it as hard as he could. He *pushed*.

The demon just laughed. From its labyrinthine being emerged a darkness that knew no limits. It found that dense, tiny stone inside Maurice that was now utterly sealed, perfectly compressed, and the demon just squeezed until that stone shattered.

All at once Maurice's body went slack and slick. He began to pour onto the floor. Hell-bound.

"Why?" Professor demanded. "What is this poor boy worth to Hell? Why?"

The demon lowered his voice from a bellow to a whisper.

"True, he's no prize. Not like some. Some souls are worth more than the rest."

"That's not for you to decide!"

The demon gave a sly smile. "Well, we do rely on the counsel of others."

Professor nodded, stricken. "You're talking about Jaclyn."

"What?" Jaclyn said, surprised. "That's bullshit, Professor, and you know it!"

"You didn't last long in Limbo, did you? We never even met when you were here," he said. "You succumbed and went to Hell. And then somehow ... somehow, you came back."

The demon chuckled. Jaclyn's essence shriveled into an irregular mass. Tears welled up in her eyes, her soul's projection of the rush of emotion that overtook her.

"You've suffered more than anyone I've ever known," Professor continued. "I've seen your soul and it's a library of misery. And yet now you're working for your captors, betraying the poor souls of this place and consigning them to join you in eternal torment. How could you?"

"You have no idea, Professor, no idea what it's like." Tears ran down her face. "You'd do anything to get out of there. *Anything*. I'd snuff out the sun for just an hour away from that place."

"Really, Jaclyn? You'd send these souls to Hell forever just for, just for, I don't know what, a *vacation*?"

"Yes! So would you. So would anyone. You put Jesus down there, he'd piss in God's eye for relief, Professor. Why do you think they call it Hell?"

Footsteps in Limbo

Professor shook his head. "You did good things in your life, Jaclyn. Everyone does. You have to be strong. You have to let those things sustain you, even in the darkness."

Jaclyn shook her head, her tears slowing.

"I tried."

The demon growled. "I've heard enough of these barking dogs. Open the door."

"Yes, master," Jaclyn whispered. With a thought she sliced open a wound in the air. The demon snorted twin wisps of black smoke and stepped through it, a few final footsteps sounding before he vanished.

Professor watched this thoughtfully. He looked at the remains of Maurice, slowly dissolving on the floor.

"Well I'm very disappointed."

"You're *disappointed?*" Jaclyn sniffled. "I'm the one that's condemned to Hell, you arrogant son of a bitch! Did I hurt your feelings? After seeing you wallow in your misery like you were earlier I'm amazed you have any left!"

Professor shook his head. "I'm not talking about you, Jaclyn."

"Well I'm talking about you! You talk such a good game about helping people find redemption but you're just a goddamn leech. You're addicted to human suffering!"

"Is that what you think?" He looked genuinely sorry for her and how wrongly she saw the world. "Jaclyn, you're right about one thing. I do need to suffer. I need to suffer because if I didn't, I would have been lifted out of Limbo a long time ago."

Jaclyn was silent for a moment as this sank in.

"I have to keep myself tethered here. Limbo is the land of unfinished business. I have to wallow in my sorrow now and then, keep coming back to the scene of my greatest mistake. Digging into it. Ripping off the scab every time it forms. Killing my pride. As long as I keep doing that I can stay here in Limbo and I can keep helping people. People like you. That's what I was doing earlier."

"You mean you could just leave? You could ascend to Heaven? Just like that?"

"Just like that."

"If you knew what I know of Hell, Professor, you wouldn't wait another minute. You wouldn't risk staying here and succumbing."

"I already know all about Hell I need to know, Jaclyn. Hell was my life. I built my Hell brick by brick, year on year. And I killed myself to escape it. I don't deserve a single day in Heaven. Not yet."

Jaclyn's being was turgid and shimmering. Something welled up within her, some great emotion. She wasn't ready to release it, to feel it. It waited within her like a promise.

"I didn't know," she finally said.

"You didn't ask."

His essence touched hers, barely, their souls verging for the slightest moment. She trembled.

"Now Jaclyn, I need to ask you something. Something very important. You couldn't just come to Limbo freely, could you? That demon needed a human soul here to open the way for it and in turn that means you needed someone else to get you in."

"Yes. You're right." She didn't speak the name but they both knew it. If she spoke it he'd hear.

Professor shook his head. "Your masters aren't after suicides at all. The demon said some souls are worth more than others. They're after bigger game, aren't they?"

Jaclyn said nothing.

"Well, it's not too late," Professor said, resolute. "It's never too late. I can stop this. Goodbye, Jaclyn."

Professor blinked and was gone.

"Oh, Professor," Jaclyn said hoarsely. "They said you'd say that."

◇

Asphodel's meadow was strewn with his namesake flowers. He spent almost all of his time here. Cut off from heaven except for the very occasional summons, he abided as lord of Limbo. He had all the time in the world and he spent it tending his garden.

Footsteps in Limbo

Today he sat in the grass, working his grudges like a tongue on a loose tooth.

Then Professor was there, standing amidst the flowers. He stunk of brimstone and dead soul.

"Asphodel," he said. "It's not too late."

"Too late for what, oh clay? / Be quick lest you spoil my day."

"I know," Professor said, "you've been letting them in. They're doing your dirty work. Purging the unworthy."

Asphodel rose to his feet. The wind picked up and all the flowers shuddered. Professor couldn't perceive Asphodel's essence—the angel was too different, too tremendous—but the meadow told him everything he needed to know.

"Unworthy? Thus are you all. / You slay God's greatest gift and fall. / I would sooner save a flower's stem / than all the souls of suicide men. / A good gardener knows to prune / those shoots that too early swoon."

"Listen to me," Professor said. "I know what you think you're doing. But Hell doesn't play your game. They don't care about us. Our souls aren't worth this transgression."

Asphodel cocked an eyebrow. For once he seemed to actually be considering what Professor was saying, the way a lion might see a hyena and pause. A gust of cold wind blew through the meadow and Professor shuddered.

"Very well, what prize is worth / striding this close to forbidden Earth? / I thought my plan was crystal clear / but now it seems I need to hear."

"Asphodel, I said it's not too late and I meant it," Professor said. "You've done wrong here, terrible wrong. Repent now. Ask forgiveness."

The sky darkened with grey clouds. "You dare to lecture me / on matters of eternity? / Why should I ever repent / of the duty for which I was sent?"

"You weren't sent here to make deals with demons!" Professor barked. "Don't you understand what you've put at risk? Ask forgiveness! Before it's too late!"

A bolt of lightning struck a nearby hill.

Then Jaclyn was there, her cheeks still streaked with tears. Professor reached out and found her being a boiling mass, something inside fighting for release from the lattice of scars and sorrow.

A shadow fell across Asphodel's face. Jaclyn saw his expression and knew. The demons said it would happen like this.

They wouldn't need her to open the door this time.

"Go, Professor!" she pleaded. "Get out of here!" The wind ripped flower petals from their stems and they tumbled in the air, then were lost. Rain began to fall.

"I'm not going anywhere. There's still time!" He struggled to keep his being resolute but at the same time, he was afraid.

"Professor, go! They're almost here and I can't control them!" She had to shout now above the storm.

"Your fellows ... come?" Asphodel asked. "Why?" Then he heard his own words and looked startled.

"LOOK HERE AND BEHOLD THE ANGEL WHO CANNOT RHYME," bellowed the demon, stepping through a fresh tear in the world. With every step he took, the remaining white flowers at his feet wilted and died. "AND THE LITTLE SUICIDE WHO WOULD SAVE HIM." It was the same emissary of wrath Professor had encountered in the basement. He moved aside and three more demons followed.

"What is this?" Asphodel blurted, lost for a rhyme. The meadow stilled and grew listless, the trees shedding their leaves. Even the rain stopped.

"Ask God's forgiveness," Professor pleaded, his portly face red from emotion. "Ask it now or never!" He tried to extend his spirit out to the angel but he couldn't. Staggered by the effort, he took a half-step back, faltering slightly.

"What has happened to my voice?" the angel pleaded—and then fell.

The demons were on him the moment they sensed the change. They ripped his wings from his shoulders and golden blood sprayed across the trees. They snapped his spine and bent

Footsteps in Limbo

him crooked, broke his legs and made him hobble, scourged his flesh from his innards, and ground his armor into his gut. When they stood back, Asphodel, bloodied and broken, reached pathetically skyward.

"My God," he whimpered, "My God, forgive me!"

"TOO LATE," the demon growled. "THE PRIZE IS OURS."

The second demon eyed Professor and when he spoke it was quietly, not with brute force but with a cruel dispassion. "I know we play the long game with this one. But I am still hungry for triumph. He is the king of the suicides—let us take him now and Limbo shall be nothing but an unceasing engine of Hell to feed our hunger."

Professor blanched. He backed up slowly. Try as he might, he could not blink. Jaclyn looked on in horror and despair. Her soul roiled. Professor realized what was in there, in her.

"YES," the lead demon said. "TAKE HIM."

Professor felt the cold pressure of absolute loathing compress around his essence. He looked at Jaclyn, all but helpless. "Try," he commanded. "Just try."

Jaclyn was terrified, and not just of the demons. She balled her hands into fists and closed her eyes.

"*I'm sorry,*" she whispered. Then again, louder: "I'm sorry. I'm sorry!"

Deep within the lattice of pain that contained her there was a power. Something ancient. Something only she could let loose.

Professor could not keep his eyes open. His skin grew pale. His features sagged. The demons were too strong for him. But he felt what was happening inside of Jaclyn and, half-crazed, his identity in tatters, he remembered a line from the first book he ever read. He spoke it aloud and when he did it was a scream.

"HERE IS ANOTHER ENGINE COMING!"

Jaclyn repented. Professor forgave her. She forgave herself. Something else did too. The pure fire of redemption scorched the lattice of scars and they fell away, threads and ashes. And with that Jaclyn freed herself from Hell—forever.

She looked as surprised as anyone.

Asphodel wept at the sight. The other demons stepped back, raising their claws before their faces. Their mighty wills collapsed.

Professor cohered. He drew himself up. His soul filled with joy. He threw off the faltering weight of the demons.

"IMPOSSIBLE," cried the lead demon. He almost sounded hurt. "A LOST SOUL MAY NEVER RISE!"

"Go," Professor said, growing strong again. "Get out of here. Take your prize and go."

"YOU DO NOT ORDER US—" the demon started to shriek. Professor's essence erupted with a confidence he'd never felt before. He beat them back, a man with a soul's hammer, and they staggered with every blow. Then they turned, cowards all, and ran for the tear in the world, dragging Asphodel with them. Professor reached out and closed the hole.

"Didn't know I could do that," he muttered.

Jaclyn came to him and took his hand. The sky turned blue again but the flowers and trees were still bare. They would await a new master. At least the sun was warm.

"All this time we thought Limbo was a net below Heaven," Professor said. "I guess it's more than that. It's also a ladder out of Hell."

"Let's go," Jaclyn said. "It's time. Come with me." The radiance of the sun grew. It was a light and it beckoned. "Heaven is waiting."

Professor smiled sadly. "Only for you."

"That's bullshit, Professor, and you know it."

"True. But I'm not leaving. Especially now. I've got a new mandate."

Jaclyn shook her head. "You're the most stubborn man I've ever known." She smiled. "Keep it up."

"Goodbye, Jaclyn."

"Goodbye, Professor. And thank you."

She became light. He watched her go. This was always his favorite part, the soul loosed and ascending into paradise. He thought of the paper airplanes he'd made as a child and how they always fell to the ground. This was the opposite.

Footsteps in Limbo

Then the meadow grew still. Pensive. He knew how it felt.

Limbo was waiting. People there needed his help. And beyond that, maybe now within his reach, were all the souls of Hell, writhing at the bottom of a ladder they never knew existed.

Could he really storm damnation and set them free? He suspected he'd need an army.

Professor had work to do. He blinked, and was gone.

Guns at the Hellroad

James L. Sutter

It started with screaming.

The bar's patrons stirred and muttered. Two got up to peer out through rips in oilskin windows. A third cracked the swinging door and poked his head out.

Jacob took another drink, straining the sediment out with his teeth. He didn't turn. A little commotion was nothing new from a whorehouse, and Miss Catherine had plenty of militia boys to handle any rough stuff.

Then came the gunshots.

The first muffled crack whipped Jacob's head around. By the second, he was out the door.

Kennet was no different from a dozen other flyspeck towns. Clapboard shacks and storefronts stood with sides bleached gray by alkaline dust. Most days, wagons rolled through carrying wilted crops, and men too old to work sat playing cards on covered porches.

Nobody was playing now. Across the empty street, half a dozen militia men huddled just below window level on the bordello's porch, wooden truncheons tiny and impotent in their hands.

The man closest to the door looked up as Jacob approached. He tried to shoo the newcomer away, then stopped as he caught sight of the revolver on Jacob's hip.

"Inside?" Jacob asked.

The soldier nodded.

"Yet you're out here."

The men crouched against the wall glared at him. The one in front said, "He's got a gun."

"So I gathered. Where's Alvarez?"

A younger man, barely old enough to shave, spoke up from the back of the line. "Bryson went to get him. He—"

Another shot cut him off. All six soldiers flattened themselves against the boards.

"No time," said Jacob, and pushed open the door.

The place was much as he remembered it: round tables and walls hung with red curtains. Several chairs had been overturned in the customers' rush to escape. Three terrified prostitutes clutched each other in the shadow of the big staircase leading up to the working rooms.

Miss Catherine sprawled in the centre of the floor, sightless eyes staring at the ceiling. A red stain stretched across her bodice, wet cloth clinging to weighty breasts.

The shooter was a scrawny blond man, dirty as any outlands farmer, with a beard too big for his frame. He stood with one arm outstretched, gun still pointed at the dead woman.

Jacob drew. The revolver flowed smoothly from its holster, and he thumbed back the hammer with a well-oiled click.

"Put it down, friend."

The man didn't even look at him. "Can't."

"And why's that?" Jacob strove to keep his voice conversational.

The man turned, and Jacob saw tears running through the dust on his face. His expression was confused, uncertain.

Jacob nodded for the man to go on. He kept his own face open, as if there wasn't a dead woman lying on the floor. The man tentatively returned the nod.

"Ghosts," he whimpered. "At the hellroad. We were supposed to find others, for the guns. But the demons—" He bit his lip, clipping off a chunk of flesh and sending a trickle of blood down into the haystack of his beard. "Tommy couldn't even scream."

Shit. Crazy men didn't know when they were beat. Jacob began to circle around behind the man. "What's your name, son?"

Another tear welled and ran. "Clyde."

"Why'd you kill Miss Catherine, Clyde?"

The gunman's shoulders shook, spreading until his whole body shuddered.

"She touched the gun. I had to protect her."

The man was really chewing now, blood pouring down his chin.

Jacob made a decision. Clyde would still probably hang, but he wasn't right in head, and Alvarez would want to know where he got the gun. He stepped forward.

"We can help you, Clyde. But you need to put the gun down."

The man's eyes were big and dull—cow eyes. He shook his head. "Can't protect you. Can't protect Tommy. You have to protect yourself."

"How, Clyde?" Jacob was almost within range. Three quick steps, and he could grab the man's wrist, twist until the gun dropped.

Clyde smiled, teeth stained dark with his own blood. "Like this."

Then he put the gun in his mouth and pulled the trigger.

◊

Alvarez found Jacob at the pump on the brothel's back porch, rinsing the grit of Clyde's skull from his face and hair.

"Jacob."

The general was a large man, and carried his fat with authority. Two soldiers flanked him, all confidence returned. One stretched out a hand for Jacob's revolver, and Jacob stared at him until he withdrew it.

"I wasn't sure we'd see you again, after last time."

Jacob shook his head, remembering the smell of burning flesh. "That was bad business."

"And now this."

The general snapped his fingers, and a soldier produced Clyde's automatic. He handed it to Jacob. The gunslinger racked the slide, then popped the magazine release. Empty.

"The shooter drifted into town yesterday," Alvarez said. "Claimed he'd been salvaging up at the hellroad, him and some mute partner. Came across a cache of guns—not rusted out, but fresh and loaded. That was about all anyone could get out of him before he got strange, quit talking. And then—well, you saw what happened."

Jacob handed the pistol back. "So why are you telling me?"

Alvarez smiled and produced a leather purse.

"I want to know whether those guns are real." He frowned down at his honour guard. "You saw how my men handled things. We're on our own out here. There've been three raids since you came through last. The nearest town is Salban, a few days down the tracks, and we haven't heard from them in months—the men I sent with messages never came back. It's fine to hunker down and say we'll look after our own, but sooner or later our luck is going to run out."

The general tossed the purse to Jacob.

"That's yours whether this drifter's cache is real or not. You ride his backtrail and see if there's any truth to his story. If there is, you take a gun for yourself and lead us back for the rest, at which point you get that much again."

"That it?" Jacob asked.

"Almost." Alvarez turned toward the doorway. "Olivia?"

A girl stepped onto the porch. She was no prostitute—couldn't have been more than fifteen—with long, dark hair and pale skin that said she didn't spend much time in the fields. She paused at the doorway, eyes closed and head cocked, then took several careful steps forward. Crossed arms held a leather-stitched pad of paper to her chest.

"Olivia will be going with you as my cartographer. Not that I don't trust you, but I'd like to have some verification of your route before I send a pack train out with you."

Jacob looked to the girl, who still stood with eyes closed, swaying slightly. "A blind girl?"

Alvarez touched her shoulder. "Olivia, please show Mr. Weintraub what you do."

With uncanny certainty, the girl produced a stick of charcoal and began to sketch. As Jacob watched over her shoulder, a landscape took shape. Scrub hills above a withered streambed, a dented pot hanging over a fire—

He jerked backward. "You were spying on me."

The girl's laugh was high and honest. Alvarez smiled.

"We didn't know you were coming until you arrived."

"But the campsite—"

"—is Olivia's gift," Alvarez finished. "She sees memories. And she can draw anything she sees."

Jacob looked uneasily toward the girl. Alvarez caught his expression. "It's a gift from God, Jacob. We don't truck with witches in Kennet."

"I never said you did." Jacob's attention was still on the girl. He addressed her directly. "You can read minds?"

The girl turned toward him, face weaving side to side in a seeking motion. "Only pictures, here and there. Places work best." She flipped to a fresh page. "Think of somewhere you've been."

Jacob thought for a moment before choosing another campsite, one far beyond the range of Alvarez's scouts. The girl's sticks began to scratch.

On a whim, Jacob added a five-point buck hanging from a tree. He fixed the image in his mind and held it.

The girl stopped abruptly. "It won't work."

"What?"

She waggled her charcoal at him. "Memories and imagination are different. In your memory, the whole picture is there, whether you know it or not. Imagination is like dreams—details exist while you focus, and disappear when you focus somewhere else. You can't lie in a memory."

Jacob looked to Alvarez. "So she's here to make sure I don't take more than my share."

"Precisely." The general grinned. "You leave at first light."

◇

By noon they'd seen the last of the farmers' shacks. With Jacob leading, they followed their man's trail northeast, weaving around ridgelines and patches of thornscrub. Behind him trailed the girl's horse, a plodding beast that carried both rider and supplies. Jacob had angled for a mount for himself, but animals were valuable. Unlike Jacob.

The girl was another story. While she moved with easy grace within town, fingers only rarely brushing a wall or shoulder, she made no objection when Jacob demanded the horse on her behalf. The last thing he needed was her stumbling over every unfamiliar rock.

The heat of the first day sapped their strength, and conversation was sparse even once they made camp. The girl—who insisted Jacob call her Olivia, no "Miss"—proved just as adept around the campfire, helping to curry the horse and prepare dinner. As he watched her build a frame of sticks on which to hang the cook pot, Jacob found he couldn't keep quiet.

"How do you do that?"

Olivia's smile said she'd been waiting for the question. She hooked the pot handle with a stick and levered it farther out over the fire. "You mean, how do I move so well?"

"Yes."

The girl sat back on her haunches. "You saw the drawings."

"Alvarez said you draw memories. Places."

She stirred the stew. "Places are easiest, but you're making new memories all the time. Sometimes I catch them as they're forming. They help me keep my bearings."

"So you're seeing through my eyes?"

Black hair shook. "Just flashes. I can't control it—they're there and gone. But the longer you focus on something, or the harder, the easier it is to catch."

"I see," said Jacob. Then a thought occurred to him. Squatting down, he looked hard across the fire at the girl, holding his gaze on her. Though still narrow-hipped and rangy as a month-old chicken, her body was young and strong, and her skin was clear. He focused, letting the picture settle into his mind.

"Oh!" The girl's cheeks flushed, and she busied herself with the cooking. After a moment, she said, "Thank you."

"It's nothing," Jacob said, and went to forage for more scrub grass.

The second day saw them leave the worst of the badlands, vegetation increasing as the waves of hills began to roll rather than crash. From her seat on the horse, Olivia sketched landmarks. At one point they flushed a rabbit, a little mutie with fringes instead of ears, and Jacob shot it, tying it up with the rest of their supplies.

They smelled the horse before they found it. The thing lay at the base of a gravel berm that ran between the trees in a straight line ten feet high. The way its limbs were twisted, the horse had clearly lost its footing, yet Jacob had a feeling the animal was done for long before it took its final stumble. The flesh on its bloated, fly-covered sides had been whipped bloody.

"Somebody rode it to death."

Jacob half-expected tears, but Kennet was a farm town. With one hand over her mouth to shield against the stink, Olivia asked, "Was it him? Clyde?"

Jacob was already digging through the bags lashed behind the saddle. Most were empty, yet in the last one he found what he needed. He held it up to the light.

"Cartridge," he said. "Right calibre, and never reloaded." He stood and pocketed the shell. "Yeah, it's him."

"What do you think he was running from?"

But Jacob wasn't listening. Instead, he grabbed her horse's reins and pulled all three of them up the berm. At the top he stopped and peered down its length, to where its narrow corridor disappeared into the woods.

"What is it?" Olivia asked.

Jacob kicked one of the metal rails, making it ring. "Railroad tracks," he said. "Most of the hellroads were connected by them, to supply the siege castles. They should take us northeast though Salban, then on to where we need to go. Our man must have tumbled off the rails and just kept running in a straight line."

"But what was he running *from*?" Olivia repeated.

Jacob looked down at the dead horse, festering in the midday sun.

"Let's hope we don't find out."

◊

The tracks made travel quicker, and miles churned by. Late in the day they came to a river. Above it, the rails stretched across the rushing current, but the ties between them had all rotted away, and their quarry's tracks turned south for more than a mile before the river widened out and shallowed.

They crossed the waist-deep current with Jacob in the lead, guiding the horse with one hand and holding his gun belt overhead with the other. The girl rode, despite protests that she was better suited to finding footing on the invisible river bottom, and held the rest of their gear above water, dress tucked up under her legs.

The sun was getting low by the time they reached the far bank, and as soon as they regained the tracks, Jacob opted to make camp. As hot as the days could be in these parts, nights were equally cold, and he had no desire to spend this one freezing in waterlogged clothing. He set to work dragging deadfalls to the river's edge, and soon they had a fire burning.

Jacob hung his shirt up to dry. He was prepared to suffer through the time it took to dry his lower half—then remembered the girl was blind. Feeling unreasonably exposed, he stripped down to his smallclothes and hung his trousers up, taking the opportunity to wash in the river. Afterward they sat on opposite sides of the fire, Olivia drying out the hem of her dress, Jacob enjoying the fire on his front and the cool breeze on his back.

James L. Sutter

"What do they mean?" Olivia asked.

"Eh?"

"Your tattoos. What do they mean?"

Jacob startled. "How do—?"

She smiled. "You were looking at yourself in the river. I didn't see anything else, I swear. Just the tattoos."

Jacob realized he'd crossed his arms. So much for propriety. He let his hands drop, exposing the black bird shapes that marked each shoulder, wings spread toward biceps and neck.

"They're ravens," he said. "Huginn and Muninn—the names mean 'thought' and 'memory.' Their story is very old."

"Will you tell it to me?"

Jacob shook his head. "Not tonight. It's a long story."

"Where did you get them?"

Jacob's stomach tightened. "That's an even longer one."

The girl slumped back. Rather than press the issue, she pulled out her pad and began sketching. After a few moments, she held it up, displaying a perfect rendering of the decaying railroad bridge.

Jacob made an approving noise. Mollified, the girl turned to a new page and began tapping the charcoal against her lip, leaving a stain.

"Will you tell me about the Rapture?"

Jacob tested the cooking meat with his belt knife. "I'm no scholar."

"Yet you know about the hellroads."

Jacob shrugged. "Only enough to avoid them. You probably know as much as I do."

Olivia snorted. "All anyone in Kennet knows is how to plant crops and get drunk. We haven't had a proper priest or god-scholar since before I was born. And who teaches a blind girl?"

"A blind girl with a talent."

She waved the charcoal irritably. "A talent half the town thinks is witchcraft, and the other half couldn't care less about. If it wasn't for General Alvarez letting me stay in the hostel past my debut, I'd already be popping out babies for some farmer too ugly to find a normal girl." She began chewing on the charcoal, blackening her teeth. "So humour me."

The girl had fire. "Fair enough. What do you already know?"

Pretty lips twisted in a smirk. Olivia clasped her hands in front of her, a caricature of a child at catechism.

"Once upon a time, the world was Paradise, but people forgot their place. God sent his angels to collect those who had kept faith, then gave the world to demons, that through suffering we might prove ourselves. For seven generations we fought, forcing them back to Hell. And now we live as best we can, awaiting judgment."

She stopped and dropped her hands. "That's it."

Jacob nodded. "It's true enough. After the hellroads opened, people fought—but the way I understand it, we lost. It took a long time, but by the end, the demons had us on our knees. And then, just when it looked like they'd finish us off, they turned and marched back into their portals."

"Why?"

Jacob lifted his hands. "Who can say? Maybe they'd done what they came to do. Maybe we redeemed ourselves in the fighting, the way the priests say." He took a drink from their canteen, then spat into the fire. "Maybe they're just waiting."

The girl shivered. "Tell me about the ancients."

Jacob smiled. Maybe Olivia wasn't a child, but she still wanted a happy ending, even if it meant telling the story backward.

"Before the Rapture," he began, "people had factories that could make anything they needed. They lived in buildings twenty stories tall, and flew through the sky in hollow birds. People lived for a hundred years, and some—what?"

Olivia, whose charcoal had been drifting idly over the paper, suddenly dropped the stick. She stared at him through closed eyelids.

"What?" he demanded.

The girl was shaking. Jacob made to wrap her against the cold, but she shied away like a kicked dog.

The drawing pad caught the firelight. Sketched in light but clearly discernable lines was the profile of a city, its towers soaring above blooming tress and a wide river. In the background, an arch rose.

Jacob's gorge filled his throat.

"You've seen it," Olivia whispered.

The gunslinger struggled to keep himself under control. When he spoke, his voice was flat. "You're imagining things."

"That's not how it works. You—"

Jacob snatched at the pad, tearing the page free. His arm jerked, and then the crumpled sheet was in the fire, blackening and twisting into a red-lipped curl of ash. For a moment, the flames grew and he was somewhere else, somewhere far from the blind girl and the silent landscape.

Control returned. As gently as he could, he took the pad and closed its leather covers, then set it down on her pack.

"No more stories."

Olivia made a small sound, and the two lay down on opposite sides of the fire. Though her eyes were closed, as always, Jacob could tell from the girl's breathing that she was too keyed up to sleep.

No, not keyed up—scared. Of him.

Again Jacob saw the drawing of the towers, edges bending and blazing. His tattoos itched.

Sleep was a long time in coming.

◇

The demons caught them completely off guard.

One moment they were at the river's edge, scrubbing out their breakfast dishes. The next a demon was rushing from the bushes, catching Olivia under the arms and sweeping her up against its armoured chest.

The thing was tall—maybe seven feet—and Olivia's legs kicked as she writhed in its grasp. Above her head, a misshapen face like a crimson ant's stared at Jacob with bulging, multifaceted

Guns at the Hellroad

eyes, its mouth two tusks of bone that pointed downward in an ivory beard. The rest of the head was a mass of black tendrils and leathery flesh.

Jacob looked to his gun belt, lying on his pack a full fifteen feet away. The creature followed his gaze. Bladed fingers touched the girl's throat.

"Don't." The creature spoke without moving its mouth, voice deep and hoarse.

Jacob showed his palms. "All right," he said. "No guns."

His foot came down hard on the raised lip of his plate, launching rabbit meat and silverware into the air. His hand dipped, caught the hunting knife as it rose, and flipped it underhand in a lazy arc. The blade tumbled across the intervening distance and slammed into the demon's forehead just inches above Olivia's own. The pair went down in a tangle.

Two more demons charged from the brush.

Jacob dove. He hit the ground flat, almost knocking the wind out of himself, but his fingers touched the weathered grips of the revolver. He drew and rolled, coming to rest on his back.

The gun roared. Jacob fired twice, left hand fanning the hammer. The first shot caught a demon in the eye, spinning it halfway around. The second took its partner in the chest, the heavy slug knocking it backward.

Jacob rose up on one elbow, barrel tracking across the tree line, yet no more demons emerged. The world was suddenly and terribly quiet.

Olivia scrambled madly. Jacob bounded to his feet and caught her just as she was about to rush headlong into the fire. He held her still as she struggled, feeling her heart beat against him like a frightened bird. When he was sure she'd stay put, he let go and approached the corpse of the one who'd grabbed her.

"Don't!" she sobbed. "It's a demon!"

"No," Jacob said. "It's not. Look through my eyes." He reached down and tugged his knife free of the creature's insectile skull.

The thing's face came away with it. Underneath the blackened wire of the eyes and the stained wood and bone of the mask, the sallow features of a man stared up, blood trickling down to pool in his eye sockets.

The girl recoiled further. "I don't understand."

Jacob cracked the cylinder on his revolver and replaced the two spent shells, dropping the empty brass into his pocket. Fully armed again, he reached down and pulled off one of the corpse's bladed gloves, handing it to Olivia wrist-first. He kicked the thing's shin, then used the toe of his boot to lift stained canvas, revealing wooden stilts.

"Cultist," he said. "Demon worshiper."

The girl placed her own hand inside the glove, feeling her way around the finger blades. "But there haven't been demons in hundreds of years!" Never mind that such history had seemed irrelevant a moment before.

On the other side of the fire, the cultist who'd taken a round in the chest was still struggling to breathe. Jacob moved to his side and knelt over him, removing his mask.

"Who are you?"

The man's voice was a whisper, air whistling through the new mouth in his chest. "Praise Belial, Lord of the Bleeding Host, for he—"

"Wrong," Jacob said. With one hand he reached inside the man's armoured costume and found the entry wound. He plugged it with his finger.

The man screamed, limbs convulsing weakly.

"Let's try a different one," Jacob said. "Why did you attack us?"

This time the cultist's voice was stronger. "Guns," he gasped. "The salvager got away. His idiot partner couldn't tell us where they found them, so we followed."

"How many of you are there?" Jacob demanded.

But the man was already gone. Jacob swore and stood. On the other side of the fire, Olivia was running her fingers over her attacker's features.

"Why do they do it?" she asked. "Worship demons, I mean."

Jacob holstered his gun. "Why does anyone do anything? Power. Scare people into service. Or maybe they thought they could summon the demons again with sacrifices."

Guns at the Hellroad

"But that's crazy!"

"Crazier than any other priests?" Jacob bent and began collecting their gear. "Get moving and douse that fire. I want to put some distance between us and the smoke. From now on, we stay off the tracks."

◇

They slept that night in the woods, and were glad they did so. Less than an hour after they started walking the following morning, the forest thinned and they caught their first glimpse of the column rising in the distance.

Centred directly on the tracks, the funnel cloud whirled and slashed at an otherwise blue sky. Iron-rich dirt from the surrounding plain gave the whole thing a blood-red hue.

"What is it?" Olivia asked.

Jacob squinted. "A tornado. Except it's not moving."

It was true. Though it wavered like any such storm, the twister's base remained firmly in one spot, as if tethered.

"Is it magic?"

Jacob shrugged. There were bubbles of strangeness all over—regions where landscapes shifted and time slowed, or babies were born speaking, or people sickened from walking through certain fields—but there was no way to know whether it was the legacy of the demons or the ancients. "Doesn't matter," he said. "We'll go around."

Curiosity kept them from swinging too wide, however. Before long Jacob could see not just the tornado, but the ramshackle town that straddled the tracks beyond it. Scrub hills provided plenty of cover, and Jacob couldn't resist a look. Olivia refused to be left alone—a reasonable position—and Jacob settled for leaving girl and horse at the base of the last hill while he lay flat on the crest and peered out from the bushes.

This had to be Salban, yet there was nobody in it. Instead, a mob of perhaps fifty people stood on the tracks between town and tornado, gusts whipping at their clothes. The wind carried their voices to Jacob, but not enough to make out the words. Then several familiar figures stepped forward and began to address the crowd.

All three wore the same costume as the men who'd attacked them. In a group, the illusion was even more impressive. Arms rose and fell in rhythm, and the crowd moved with them in eerie synchronization.

One figure broke the choreography. Twisting and flailing, a man was dragged forward. He was small and misshapen, with a bulging skull and wide-set eyes. Though his mouth stretched wide, no sound emerged.

He couldn't even scream. Jacob knew he was looking at Clyde's mute partner, Tommy.

The man's arms were tied behind his back at wrists and elbows, a length of rope connecting them to hobbles on his shins. As two burly townsfolk held the prisoner still, the foremost cultist reached out a bladed finger and carved a mark into the man's broad forehead.

Then the whole crowd split to reveal a new oddity in their midst—a wheeled metal cart. The prisoner's captors jerked his bonds tighter, hogtying him into helplessness. Reverently, they laid him on the cart's flat front. Behind it, townsfolk formed into two lines, taking up heavy ropes.

Jacob understood even before the two largest men began pushing the cart toward the funnel. The contraption moved slowly at first, then picked up speed as the winds began to take it. The men jumped back out of the way and joined the lines of people hauling on now-taut ropes, playing out slack and slowly feeding the cart into the tornado.

A chant began. Wind slapped at the man on the cart, and only a slim tether kept him from being rolled off the apparatus entirely.

The chant grew louder, and now Jacob could make out two words.

"Red Whirling! Red Whirling! Red Whirling!"

Guns at the Hellroad

The cart was shaking, straining at its ropes. Jacob could see where the thing had been clamped onto the rails. Above, the man thrashed violently back and forth, caught in the storm's rush, his helpless body slamming into the cart over and over until his face was a mass of red.

With a jerk, the cart plunged full-on into the funnel. Through the spinning dust, the prisoner levitated, straining against his restraints like a kite.

The tether snapped. The man vanished, thrown upward into the tornado's depths. The townsfolk broke into a cheer as they began to haul the cart back out of the hungry winds.

Jacob had seen enough. He climbed back down the hill, placed the girl on the horse, and got them moving. It wasn't until they were on the tracks again, well out of sight of the town and its pet storm-god, that the girl spoke.

"So that's why nobody's heard from Salban."

Of course she'd been able to pull images of the sacrifice from Jacob's memory.

"Do you think they planned the same for us?"

Jacob said nothing.

"At least now we know why our man rode his horse to death."

It made sense. Yet less than a mile later, they came upon a muddy break in the railway ties and found hoofprints, deep and wide-spaced. There was no mistaking the pattern.

Clyde and his partner had already been running.

◇

They were another day north when they saw the pursuit.

At first it was just a thread of smoke, a thin trail in the sky behind them. Then the tracks climbed a hill, and Jacob scaled a tree. Two minutes later, he was back on the ground.

"About twenty men," he said. "Five dressed like demons, and all on horses."

"Twenty!" Olivia paled. "Do you think they found the ones you killed?"

Jacob shook his head. They'd rolled the bodies into the river. "More likely they found our tracks, or Clyde's. Maybe they're making an educated guess that the guns come from the hellroad. It doesn't matter." He grabbed the horse's reins and ushered Olivia off the tracks. When they were a hundred yards into the trees, he stopped and tied the lead to a branch. He shrugged off his pack.

"Stay here," he said. "Don't come out unless you hear me call your name."

"What? No!" Olivia grabbed at his arm. Jacob gently unclenched her fingers.

"They have horses," he said. "Which means they're going to catch us unless we slow them down."

"Can't we just stay off the tracks?"

Jacob squeezed her hand. "We're all going to the same place now. Even if they don't catch us, they'll get there first. Think about what that lot could do to Kennet with guns."

Olivia said nothing, but she let go and settled down beneath the horse's tree.

"Be careful," she said.

Jacob touched her hair.

"Always."

◇

The cultists may have dressed like demons, but they slept like men. They camped on the tracks, their fire a beacon visible from miles away. With so many men, they clearly thought themselves invulnerable.

Their lone sentinel sat with his back against a tree just outside the firelight, eyelids drooping. For a moment, those eyes grew wide. Then they glassed over and quit seeing altogether. Hand over the man's mouth, Jacob carefully lowered him the rest of the way to the ground, then withdrew his knife.

The horses were well away from the fire, tied to a single line running between two trees. That made Jacob's job easier, and he quickly sawed through the rope, pulling it through the horse's leads until all stood free. The nearest horse was a fine mare—still saddled, he noted reproachfully—and Jacob slid easily onto her back.

Still the men didn't wake. Jacob drew his revolver.

The first shot split the night and sent the startled horses breaking for the trees. Jacob kicked his new mount into the centre of the herd, scattering it. He sent a second shot back into the huddled figures by the fire, then a third.

Men woke, shouting and scrambling for weapons. There was the twang of a bowstring, and a whine as a bolt sailed past Jacob's ear.

Time to go. Jacob made one last circuit, slapping the haunches of those horses who hadn't already disappeared into the forest, then leaned low over the mare's neck and sent her thundering north down the tracks.

Behind him, the shouts continued—and then became something worse. As one, a score of throats opened in howls. The baying of human wolves.

Jacob dug his heels into the mare's flanks. He'd done what he could to slow the cultists, and gained a second horse. Now he could only hope that he and Olivia could maintain their lead.

Behind him, the hunting cries continued.

◊

Jacob's first glimpse of the hellroad was of stone structures squatting like mountains on the horizon, a bunching of the parched and cracking earth. The bunkers stood shoulder to shoulder, bereft of decoration.

"Siege castles." Jacob looked to each in turn, letting Olivia piece together the image. Beside him, the girl leaned down, stroking the neck of her exhausted horse.

Jacob stood in his stirrups and looked back the way they'd come. Far down the tracks, where the forest had given way to bare earth, Jacob could see the plume of dust, no more than half an hour behind them.

They were out of time.

As the railroad guided them in, the gaps between castles became more visible, revealing the parallel line of structures just beyond. At the switching station where the tracks divided into tributaries leading to each fortress, Jacob lost several minutes searching for hoofprints, finally finding them beside the line leading toward a middle castle, its three-story keep studded with turrets and empty gun emplacements. Instead of following the rails straight to the great steel gate, the prints circled around to the side, into the gap between fortresses.

Now they could see the hellroad in earnest. Here the two lines of fortifications created a shooting gallery a thousand feet apart. In front of each lay a buffer of ashen dust. And beyond that...

The air above the hellroad shimmered and distorted with a heat that was more than physical. The road itself was unpaved, yet the ground within its boundaries twisted and wavered, undulating in strange directions. At one end, clearly visible down the narrow avenue, the illusion of movement faded and gave out onto normal ground. At the other, where the fortresses were largest, the road bulged and pressed until it seemed to burrow through reality itself, tearing the air in two and opening onto — elsewhere.

Figures walked the road. Indistinct even where the heat-wavering was weakest, they marched in jerky marionette motions. Their bodies were featureless, little more than oily smudges, with the grotesquely thin limbs of stick men. Silent, seemingly unaware of the humans or each other, they appeared at the narrow end of the road and marched in solemn procession toward the pulsating rip of the portal's mouth.

Olivia's hand found Jacob's. "What are they?"

"Shades. Souls of the dead." Jacob squeezed once and pulled her away from the macabre parade. "Spirits marching down to Hell."

The hoofprints ended at a sally gate in the castle's curtain wall. Beyond it was a paved courtyard, empty save for a week-old pile of horse dung next to a door leading into the keep proper. Jacob tied the horses' leads to a hinge, then led the girl inside, drawing his revolver.

Guns at the Hellroad

It wasn't hard to see where their quarry had gone. The place appeared to have been sealed until recently, and clear trails cut through the dust. The hallways beyond the doorway were dark, and Jacob lit a lantern, instructing Olivia to hold onto his belt so that he could hold the light with one hand and his gun with the other. Together, they advanced into the keep.

Once, the fortress would have been full of soldiers pouring fire down onto the hellroad, trying to kill as many demons as possible before they reached the end and manifested. Now there were only a few bent shell casings, some crumbling scraps of garbage. Whatever hadn't been removed following the demons' withdrawal had almost certainly been stripped by generations of looters. The larger chambers echoed with their footfalls.

The trail led straight and unerringly down passage after passage, up one staircase and then another. At last, on the top floor, they came to an open doorway overflowing with light.

The room was not an armoury. Jacob would have expected that to be a vault, a sealed place. This was a turret, its tall firing slits admitting bright shafts of sunset.

The guns lay in a heap where the sunbeams converged, a pile of black and blued steel. There was no order—military rifles lay jumbled at all angles with holstered pistols and tattered boxes of ammunition. Bronze glinted from the tops of crescent-shaped clips, and cloth bandoleers tied the whole mess into a great knot. Some pieces were stained the rust-brown of old blood. Others looked brand new.

Olivia spoke for both of them, voice tense.

"This isn't right."

Jacob grunted agreement.

"Could it be bandits? Raiders?"

It wasn't unheard-of for outlaws to set up camp around hellroads. That made more sense than a pile of guns lying untouched in an open room for centuries. And yet they hadn't seen any signs of habitation.

Jacob reached down and picked up one of the pistols.

honour the fallen we are you are the fallen you are we

"Jacob?"

Jacob's arm was stiff, muscles tightening of their own accord. The rush of voices was a cold wind inside his skull.

carry us carry the blood avenge defend your brothers fathers mothers sisters children

"Jacob? What's wrong?"

He struggled to speak, but his jaw was clenched too tightly. In his hand, the pistol pulsed, throbbing in his fingers like a living thing.

the road the maw the road war to the warmakers smoke them out burn them in their holes

His vision narrowed. The throbbing was coursing up his arm, through his chest, out into his brain, his balls, his legs.

bring others find brothers form ranks bringfindcallmake—

The leather-bound drawing pad swung in a perfect arc, connecting edge-on and knocking the pistol from his hand. Jacob staggered back as the tide of words cut off. A leg gave out, and he sank to one knee.

Olivia was at his side, one hand on the wall, staying safely clear of the pile of guns. She touched his shoulder.

"Jacob? Are you all right?"

"I'm fine." His head felt like it was packed with sawdust, and his limbs were water. He coughed. "I think we know what Clyde was running from."

"What happened?"

Jacob closed his eyes. The images accompanying the voices still burned brightly behind his lids, the hellroad streaming with armed men and women, warriors charging through the portal at its end.

"They're a press gang," Jacob said. "The spirits of those who fought here. They want a new army, to march to Hell and take the fight to the demons."

"And they want you to lead it?"

Jacob gripped her hand. "I think they'd be just as happy with you. They're not picky."

Grunting, he pushed himself upright and tottered over to a window. Outside, the dust of the pursuing cultists drew steadily closer.

Jacob smiled.

◇

In the predawn light, Kennet was a tiny huddle of boxes against a featureless plain. White smoke drifted from chimneys, creating a lightness in the sky.

"Are you sure you won't come?"

Jacob finished adjusting his new saddlebags and looked to the girl.

"I don't think it would be wise. You can give Alvarez the drawings if he insists. But I doubt he'll be pleased."

"But your money!"

Jacob patted her leg. "Money's only good if you're free to spend it. If Alvarez is still feeling generous once he learns about the guns, you're welcome to the other half. But I'd rather not wait around and see." He turned his horse.

"Jacob, wait."

He expected a plea to come with him. Instead, Olivia's voice was thoughtful.

"If the hellroads are still open, why haven't the demons come back and taken us all to Hell?"

Jacob thought of the cultists. From the casement of a neighbouring castle, he and Olivia had watched as the pursuing demon-worshipers stormed past their horses and into the building—then came streaming out again, weapons high. For long minutes, the cultists had flickered silently as they scrambled in slow motion down the twisting earth of the hellroad, toward its invisible maw. And then they were gone.

Afterward, Jacob and the girl had carefully bagged up what guns remained—never touching them directly—and dropped them at the edge of Salban. If all went as planned, the remaining demon-worshipers were already carrying the last of the possessed weapons down to Hell, where both belonged.

The girl was waiting for an answer. Jacob shook his head.

"Maybe we don't need the help."

Before Olivia could respond, Jacob slapped her horse on its hindquarters, sending it trotting forward. From his low hill, he watched until beast and rider entered the cluster of buildings.

The girl never looked back—but then, she didn't need to.

Jacob turned and spurred his mare east into the rising sun.

Stalking in Memphis

Jean Rabe

The fire for the most part out, smoke pulsed from what had been a furniture warehouse and stretched toward Confederate Park and Wolf River Harbor, joining the early-morning fog that clung to the banks. The stench warred with exhaust fumes from cars that inched by as the lookee loos inside them strained to absorb the destruction. Everything was all grotesquely concatenated, Sabine thought.

The bitter odors settled heavy like cement on her tongue. She couldn't work up enough saliva to get rid of it, and yet, mesmerized, she couldn't leave to find cleaner air. She perched on the corner, just beyond the barricade, ice blue eyes peering into the smoldering wreckage and watering with the sting. A tall, hooded man loomed behind her, statue like and seemingly oblivious to the bustle of firemen and police and the coroner's people who were bagging a half-dozen bodies.

Sabine had summoned the man too late. Her calculations had been wrong. She had expected the fire hours from now, close to noon, when she and he would be ready, waiting.

"What did I miss?" she wondered aloud. At least she'd gotten the building correct, but people had perished because she'd misjudged the timing.

They stood there until her legs were stiff and her toes cramped and she'd sucked so much of the acridness into her lungs that she struggled for breath.

"Follow me," she ordered the tall man.

They wound their way through the crowd on the sidewalk—men and women dawdling on their way to work, shopkeepers come out for a gander, and the street people who held out paper cups and hats for coins, relishing the donations that seemed a little more generous this close to a tragedy.

Sabine's bookstore was on Peabody Place, just north of the historic district, narrow, but deep and wedged between a resale shop where she bought most of her clothes and a delicatessen that catered to the health-conscious with its tofu burgers and organic bean puree.

"Won't be able to look around until dark comes," she said. "Fire marshal will be poking through it all day. He won't find anything, though. He's a smart one, but doesn't know what to look for."

The man stood just inside the entrance, watching her turn on the lights, flip the closed sign to open, and rearrange a few books on the front display table. Sabine busied herself with the routine of work for several minutes, pausing to wait on a customer who came in, a young woman with a bulging backpack who gave the tall man only a passing glance.

"Here's the book you were looking for, Miss Swails," she said. "*King Leopold's Ghost* by Hochschild, first printing, 1998. Near to mint as I could find. It covers everything—his incursion into the Congo, the dismemberments, mass murders, burnt villages. Grisly, but it should help with your history paper."

Miss Swails paid for it and left.

"The fire marshal is thorough, I know," Sabine continued. "I've seen him work the other fires downtown. He just doesn't understand the pattern." She pulled out a city map, spread it on the counter, and motioned the man join her. "I'll show you."

He brushed back his hood and leaned close. He wore a skull cap so black that it seemed to absorb the fluorescent light cast from above. His short beard, braided and pointed, was shot through with gray, his eyes intense pinpricks. His skin was dark, but he was not a black man, it was all over walnut brown, looking burnished and oiled, his muscles well defined beneath a tunic that resembled a sleeveless T. In his right hand he clutched an ankh made of gold and inlaid with lapis lazuli in symbols representing life, the sun, and rebirth.

She stabbed her index finger at Xs she'd marked. "Here and here. These were the first two. I hadn't thought anything of them at the time. The first dismissed as a grease fire in the kitchen, and from this old hotel a man they'd guessed was smoking in his cot in the basement." She jabbed at a few more. "But then there were three more fires, all downtown and close together, and the buildings total losses. Something niggled at the back of my mind, and so I mapped them. Do you see?"

The man shook his head and growled from deep in his throat. "I see colorful, thin papyrus with markings I cannot fathom." He stood away from the table, seeming even taller than before. "So you have called me for this? For ink scratches? You have ripped me from my comfortable sleep for burned buildings?" That he could speak her language was part of the magic in the summoning, but that magic did not extend to the written words. "Scratches on papyrus, inky insects that mean nothing to me. Worthless."

"I summoned you, Ptah, he who the Egyptians called the creator god, because I haven't the power to stop the fires myself." She paused and brushed her fingers over two more Xs. "I need help."

"And I have the power you need?" He looked down his long nose at her.

Sabine was barely five feet tall, and slight, a woman who appeared to be in her middle years, but who was far older.

"This is Memphis," Sabine said. "Memphis was made for Ptah."

"This may well be Memphis. But not mine."

Jean Rabe

"Your Memphis was the first capital of united Egypt. It remained the capital of Egypt for at least eight dynasties."

"During the Old Kingdom."

"Yes, I read extensively of it." She waved a diminutive hand at a section of bookshelf crowded with titles about King Tutankhamen, Giza, the pyramids, and various translations of the *Book of the Dead*. "In the sixth dynasty it was the center of worship of you, Ptah, the deification of the primordial mound, god of craftsmen and potters they called you, builder and regenerator."

Something that passed for smugness lit his face.

"But you were not a god, just a being with immense power, you and your kind, members of a race that was ancient when the Egyptians arose."

"They worshiped me," he said.

"They built for you an alabaster sphinx to guard your temple."

"It still stands," Ptah said, "unlike your ugly buildings that appear so easy to burn. That Memphis was for me."

"This is *my* Memphis, and though not so large and imposing as your great city was, it is far more important in that proverbial scheme of things. I felt it fitting to summon you to it."

"Ptah in Memphis. But your Memphis is not a capital of anything."

She shrugged. "That would be Nashville, but that is not so crucial a place—"

"—as your Memphis," he finished.

"Yes. This Memphis is vital to all mankind."

He chuckled, the sound like pebbles rolling down a hill. "Ptah in Memphis once more. I will tell my consort Sekhmet and my son Nefertem of this when we are done, *woman*—" The word sounding like a piece of spoiled meat. "When this is done and you dismiss me."

"Sabine. My name is Sabine Upchurch."

"Sabine. It means?"

"I was named for the Sabine River that runs through Louisiana."

"Which is—"

"A ways from here. We don't have time for this, Ptah. We—"

"—will take time, for I will know of you before I aid you. I will know the loins you sprang—"

She gripped the corners of the counter, squeezing so hard her knuckles turned bone white. "My father was a preacher, the fire and brimstone kind."

"Does he still live, or is he relegated to—"

"The fires, Ptah, are what concerns us this day, and—"

"What concerns me, Sabine Upchurch, is the *woman* who summoned me. I will know of you, or I will not help." He closed his eyes and stood still, as if he was listening to a voice from elsewhere.

She relaxed her grip on the counter. "My parents came to Louisiana about the time it became a state."

"A considerable while ago," he pronounced, his eyes still closed.

"My father had a fierce sense of right and wrong, shared by my mother, who had ... gifts ... that she passed to me, their only child. That's all you need know of them."

"These gifts? The ability to summon?" He'd opened his eyes and was studying her.

"Yes," she said. "I have dealt with otherworldly threats all of my life, Ptah, traveling throughout the south and settling here because the ley lines cross and the energy is strongest. There is something special about this ground."

"This Memphis."

"Yes, Ptah."

"And you are its keeper."

She stepped back and let her hands relax and drop to her sides. "I intervene when the threat is beyond the ken of the people who live here."

"Such as this threat, the fires."

"Yes."

"To this Memphis."

"Yes."

Ptah smiled, showing an even row of pearl-white teeth. "My son must see this place. Perhaps you will bring him here now to help and so that he might see this garish and stinking new Memphis for himself. And so that he might hear the cacophony that—"

"—passes itself off for music." A restaurant had opened across the street, and a bluesy piece, Wynton Marsalis' *Deep in the South*, poured out the open door and found its way inside Sabine's shop. "I haven't the power to bring more of you. Not for a while. Summoning magic is taxing and difficult."

"It weakens you."

Sabine nodded and pointed to more of the Xs. "Do you see the pattern?"

"How is it you summoned me?"

She let out a breath that whistled between her teeth. "Truly, I don't have the time to discuss the intricacies of my ... magic I guess you would call it. Others I have summoned—"

"From Egypt?"

"No. Genghis Khan, Thomas Jefferson—"

"I know of the former, Sabine Upchurch, daughter of a fire and brimstone preacher. This Thomas Jefferson, I have not heard—"

"Edward Rickenbacker," she went on. "Julius Ceasar—"

Ptah's eyes lit up in recognition of the last name. "That spirit I have met in my otherworld existence, and I—"

"—have asked more questions than any of them. Suffice it to say that with effort I pull beings from the past, those who have skills to assist me."

"Skills the people of this Memphis lack."

"Perhaps I am the last of my kind, Ptah. And I use my abilities to safeguard—"

"Your Memphis. You have told me."

"Yes, and thereby the rest of the world."

His eyebrows rose in question.

"And so I ask you again, do you see the pattern? The symbol the fires are creating?"

He shook his head, and she took a marker and connected the Xs like a child would connect the dots in a coloring book.

"Now?"

"Yes."

Stalking in Memphis

At first glance the line looked like sword that had bent over at the tip, as if made of a noodle. Then she connected the side points, what would be the pommel's crosspiece. "The first two fires," she said. "It took me more than a little while to realize what the symbol was ... is becoming. Familiar to me, but in that faraway manner, something I'd read or looked at and had nested itself at the back of my mind. And so I traced this into my computer."

The last word had no meaning to Ptah.

"And it came back with this." She retrieved a printout from under the counter.

It was not a sword but a khet, a hieroglyph that represented a lamp or brazier, the "bent blade," fire arcing away.

"Fire is the embodiment of the very sun," Sabine said, "and the symbol for that is the uraeus—"

"Which spits fire," Ptah finished.

Sabine looked up as the bell chimed, announcing customers, these two older men who always came here together, a couple, she guessed. They favored her offering of mysteries. They headed toward the back, aiming straight for her section of Mary Higgins Clark.

"Odd that this Memphis, so far removed in time and distance from my Egypt, would have a khet carved out of burnt buildings in its landscape."

Sabine met his gaze. She realized he had no eyelashes, and she could not discern pupils. "Fire was key, Ptah, in your time. And is still dangerous in mine. It played a role in ancient Egyptian's concept of the underworld."

"The fires of the underworld," he said. "Where souls went if their heart did not balance with the feather of truth."

"Fire is the commonality between Egypt's old religion and modern Christians' belief of hell."

"Fiery lakes filled with fiery demons."

"Yes, eternal suffering in flames."

Ptah watched the two men pull down one book after another until their arms were loaded. They shuffled to the counter and deposited their treasures, barely registering the creator god's presence.

"Ought to last us a month or so," one said as he handed over the bills.

"We'll buy all of your Connollys next," the other told her. "When it's my turn to do the picking. Police procedurals with a bit more zip."

"They ignored me." Ptah said after they left, not hiding the offense in his voice.

"They don't see you for what you really are," Sabine explained. "Part of my summoning magic."

Ptah looked even more offended.

"You don't need the people of my Memphis to worship you," she said. "People today are more skeptical, iconoclastic and—"

"Oblivious to the destruction they face." He traced the line that formed the khet. "It is not yet complete. If the mark were to continue to here—" His finger touched the intersection of Second Street and Beale. "The khet would be complete."

"And what would that mean?" She rocked back on her heels. "That all of my Memphis will burn in the fiery pits of hell?"

"The End of Days," Ptah pronounced. "Even my people knew of that. I believe if the khet is finished, it will mark the end of this world."

"The fire marshal, he's a smart man," she repeated. "But he doesn't see this symbol. And if he did, he wouldn't understand it. The End of Days, I thought that a possibility, the indications point to that. Oh, I suppose I might have this all wrong."

"You would not have summoned me if—"

"Summoning is serious magic, reserved for critical events and—"

Ptah pointed straight up. "This was critical?"

An old building, Upchurch Used Books had a high ceiling, roughly sixteen feet. It was covered by a detailed painting that the fluorescent lights hanging from it did not properly illuminate.

The creation of Adam was in the center, God stretching out a finger to touch him, the colors predominantly beige and peach, eggshell and tan. Unlike in the Sistine Chapel, Adam's loins were swathed in a rosy cloth, the same shade used in the rendering of the separation of land and water and the section depicting the separation of light and darkness.

"My ceiling needed to be redone two summers past," she said. "His technique improved since his previous ceiling work. A painted ceiling was crucial to me."

"Your customers—"

"The astute ones notice it." A pause. "And appreciate it."

"Who have you summoned to tidy your shelves? To catalog your books?"

She scowled at him, but said softly: "William Shakespeare and I have discussed literature."

Ptah made a snorting sound. "When I am returned to the land of spirits I will search for others you have summoned, and we will talk. I am not limited to conversing with only the dead from my time. We will talk at length, Sabine Upchurch." He returned his attention to the map. "You thought this morning's fire would not come so early."

"No. I thought I understood the time within the pattern."

"Tell me when each of these fires occurred."

The pair spent the next few hours going over details of the fires—when they were called in, what the fire marshal had noticed and had subsequently reported to the press, how many people were killed, how long it took to put each blaze out.

"Your fire marshal is a fool," Ptah decided. "That he cannot see this ... that he cannot see the ultimate danger ... that—"

"I don't think he's studied ancient Egypt or can read hieroglyphs, and he likely knows nothing about the End of Days beyond a handful of thriller movies made to capitalize on supposed Mayan myth."

"You summoned me for my great wisdom, yes?"

"And for your power." She rubbed at the back of her hand.

"I am wise above strong." He thrust out his chin, his mien haughty.

"Ancient wisdom is clearer. It is not cluttered. People in this Memphis are—"

"My time was no less complicated. My race, and the Egyptians that sprang from us, were not primitive. Their deeds are unequaled even in this day. I challenge the residents of ... this Memphis ... to build pyramids so great and perfect. Their language, mummification, and—"

"People today rely on computers." Sabine smiled, enjoying that she used a word he could still not comprehend.

His eyes glimmered darkly, showing that perhaps he did grasp it. "They let other things do the thinking for them, and in their reliance they have grown dull. And so the people of this Memphis will never be as wise as the people from my Memphis."

"And so I need your help, creator god, to save them."

"And thereby all of mankind."

"Please."

She closed her shop at sunset and they melded into the exodus of people leaving work. Music came from a variety of sources now, second and third floor apartments that offered jazz, hip-hop, and oldies rock, and the taverns that provided live fare, all of this one incarnation of blues or another. Sabine thought that Ptah was actually enjoying the clamor.

They kept to the shadows when they reached the site of this morning's fire. Two police cars and a fire department van remained. Traffic was slow around it, more lookee loos taking in the aftermath.

"Perhaps around the back."

Ptah followed Sabine.

There were more police there, walking from one corner of the lot to the next, as if patrolling the place. When Sabine had their predictable pattern memorized, she clung to the opposite side of the property and slipped inside.

The air was warm, and not from the summer. Heat oozed from what was left of the structure and threatened to siphon her moisture. Her throat went instantly dry. Ash filtered down like fat snowflakes, landing on her face. Despite the stench, she inhaled deep.

"Do you smell it?" she asked.

Ptah had edged ahead of her. In the half-light that spilled through melted windows he looked like he was carved from a piece of stone, his form dark and perfect and his chest rising and falling almost imperceptibly. She could understand how he could have been taken as a god, and that his bearing only added to the notion.

"Wood and metal and char. I smell these things."

"Nothing more?" Sabine smelled evil.

"Pig," he said. "Crocodile. I smell these creatures. I smell the dragon."

Sabine picked her way toward him. "A dragon?"

"*The* dragon," he corrected. "He is hungry and he will feast again soon."

"In two nights I believe another fire will—"

"In less than two hours," he corrected her again.

She shook her head and he whirled, bringing his face down to hers. The angles and planes of his visage were sharp like a sculptor had chiseled them.

"You summoned me for my wisdom, Sabine Upchurch, daughter of a fire and brimstone preacher. The dragon will eat again very soon. You do not understand the ..." He drew himself up to his full height and searched for a word. "Timing. It was why you missed this morning's blaze. My people, and the Egyptians who sprang from them, far better understood time and the position of stars."

She knew Egyptian calendars had been incredibly accurate, and their buildings positioned just so that when the sun rose or certain stars were high the light glimmered through openings.

Ptah looked past her, as if he was seeing something far beyond this burned warehouse and Memphis. "And you will need more than my power to stop the dragon."

This time, Ptah led Sabine out onto the street. He wove through alleys and paused only to watch a homeless man urinating in a garbage can.

"It will be this building or the next," he pronounced. "Either will finish the engraving of the khet."

Sabine looked from one to the other, the first an older office building that had a scattering of lights on. She saw shadows moving across a few of the windows, cleaning people perhaps. The second building was ornate and older, a white façade with the carvings of men's faces and vines. Memphis Repertoire Company, the sign read.

"That building." Sabine felt a tugging to it. People were filtering in the front. It was seven, the performance starting in an hour. "The dragon will strike here."

"Where the damage will be greater," Ptah said.

"A greater loss, this building." Though she supposed that factor didn't really matter if its destruction meant the beginning of the End of Days.

They found a way inside around the back and took the stairs down into the bowels of the theater.

"I miss the music of the street," Ptah admitted. He had to crouch in places, the beams from the low ceiling brushing his skull cap. He cocked his head as the timbers above groaned under the weight of actors and stage crew moving around. "The dragon could strike anywhere in this building." He batted at a curtain of cobwebs.

Sabine stretched an arm up and pulled on a cord, an old bulb shed a buttery light.

"All of the other fires started in the basements."

"If this building is the correct one."

She could smell the evil, the taint not as strong as the building they'd left. That she could smell it meant that the dragon was coming. Sabine sat cross-legged under the bulb and pulled vials from her pockets, uncorking them and spilling the colored sandy powders in front of her in a pattern that looked like a series of hieroglyphs but were something entirely different.

"I am not sure I have the strength for this," she told Ptah. "So soon after bringing you here. But I will try to call your son. Perhaps he can—"

"Not my son."

"I understand that you would want to protect him. Your ... wife ... then. Sekhmet. I will—"

"As much as I desire that they see this garish and stinking Memphis, their power is not enough. You must call Horus. Only he, and perhaps not even he, will be strong enough."

"Horus."

"You claim to have studied ancient Egypt, *woman*, Sabine. Horus is—"

"Horus the falcon," she supplied. "The son of Isis and Osiris."

"Son of Hathor," Ptah corrected. "God of the sky of war, god of protection and—" Ptah turned and faced the far corner, where the buttery light did not reach.

The scent grew stronger and nearly choked Sabine.

"I smell it," Ptah said. "The pig and the crocodile and the dragon. Hurry, Sabine Upchurch, daughter of the fire and brimstone preacher."

Her fingers danced inches above the powder, the movement stirring it into new patterns. Her unblemished skin sprouted age spots and the lines deepened at the corners of her eyes. Her smooth skin became rough and brittle looking, as if she were having the life drawn out of her. She breathed shallowly and continued her work, her shoulders hunching and her back rounding, her hair turning wispy and her ice blue eyes taking on a rheumy cast.

The shadows darkened, and a patch of blackest black glided forward to face Ptah. The darkness snarled and released a gust of brimstone.

"Dreamer of creation," the blackness rumbled. "I will dance upon your corpse."

Sabine's fingers whirled faster and she gasped for air. Her chest felt tight, as if a constricting band had been placed upon her. "Come Horus," she implored. "Join Ptah in Memphis." She'd never called two such powerful beings to her time at the same juncture. The farther back in time she stretched, the more of her energy it took, and the stronger the being pulled, the more of her soul lost. "Come Horus, god of war."

The powders swirled and rose as if picked up by a tiny whirlwind. They separated, then coalesced, became diaphanous and sparkled like miniature stars. Sabine seemed to fold in upon herself, becoming smaller, more hunched, more of a husk of a woman.

The powders took on a manlike form with a falcon's head, and grew larger and more substantial now. Opaque one moment, and then bright solid with colors, the dark, polished skin shining in the light from the lone bulb.

"Set," Horus pronounced. The god of war was not quite as tall as Ptah, but he was more imposing. His chest impossibly broad and rippling, his arms long and deeply muscled, the veins standing out on them like thick cords.

"Set," Sabine whispered. "I should have realized."

In a faraway part of her memory she'd placed what she'd read about Set. Worshiped as the god of the wind and desert storms, the Egyptians had prayed to him asking for strength. Portrayed as dark and moody, he was not always thought evil. But that had changed a long time ago, when he chose to conflict with Horus.

"Apep," Horus said. "Set and Apep in one."

The blackness took shape, first becoming a monstrous boar.

The pig Ptah had said he smelled.

Then transforming again and taking on the aspect of a man with the head of a crocodile.

Ptah had said he smelled that, too.

Sabine inched back, her body aching and her breath coming ragged. The second summoning had sapped nearly everything. What little energy she had left she used to hold the two gods in this Memphis.

The darkness changed again. This time it was a snake, so great it took up nearly the entirety of the basement, as thick as an elephant and with a head that resembled a Chinese dragon.

"Slayer of Osiris," Horus said. "My eternal enemy. Deification of darkness and chaos, contester of light and life."

Sabine recalled that according to ancient Egyptian history, Set had slain Osiris and scattered pieces of the body throughout Egypt, claiming the god-throne as his own. Horus had struck him down then, and he was working to do so again. Set-Apep was believed to hold sway in the underworld, called the Eater of Souls. The devil,

Sabine's father would have called him. Egyptian priests built effigies of Apep and burned them every year. They had a guide for fighting him, called *The Books of Overthrowing Apep*. Sabine had read the version called *Book of Apophis*, the translation in Greek. In it was an explanation for dismembering the god. Horus was trying to do just that, ripping at the darkness.

But this Set, or Apep, or whatever he was called, was not falling.

It spat fire, the flames incinerating Horus's tunic and burning Ptah's chest. The once-smooth walnut skin bubbled and oozed. Neither cried out, though Sabine was certain they must have felt intense agony. The heat alone pained her and she tried to scoot farther back, but she stopped when she bumped into a stack of crates.

Sabine smelled an intense evil now, but she also smelled char. The dragon had caught something on fire. Smoke roiled along the basement's ceiling, its tendrils reaching toward her like living things. Tears spilled from her stinging eyes. Sabine closed them and prayed.

The world was filled with the crackling, popping sound of fire and with thrashing—the great beast fighting Horus and Ptah. Things stored in the basement splintered and caught fire, props were bashed into pieces and chunks of the ceiling fell. Flames licked up crates, flowing like water, Sabine saw the brilliant red-orange of them through her closed lids.

The conflagration was at the same time horrifying and obscenely beautiful, the heat blistering and the air so thin there wasn't enough of it to sustain Sabine. She drifted mercifully into unconsciousness.

And awoke to the sounds of sirens.

She was on her back in an alley, the pong of urine and spoiled things nearly overwhelming and mixed with the scents of ash and burned wood. Ptah propped her up and pointed to the alley's end, where she saw the glow of red from a fire truck's light.

"It was not within us to stop the fire," Ptah told her. "The building is lost."

"Set-Apep."

"But it was within Horus to stop him. Slay him. I scattered his pieces, a fitting tribute to Osiris."

Dismembered him, like the ritual, Sabine thought.

There was little light in the alley, some filtered down from the stars overhead, some came from the lights of the fire trucks and rescue vehicles. It was enough to tell that the once-beautiful creation god was so scarred his skin looked wet.

"Horus, is he—"

"Forever dead. Died in the struggle, Sabine Upchurch, daughter of the fire and brimstone preacher. Gave his life that the End of Days could be stalled."

"Stalled. But not stopped."

Ptah helped her stand. She was healing, the age spots vanishing, her skin becoming soft again, her shoulders straightening, years melting.

"Summon me again, *woman*, when the threat arises once more, when another source of evil seeks to fulfill the ancient prophecies. Ptah belongs in Memphis, and though this is not *my* Memphis, I have found that it will do." He cocked his head and listened. Music seeped out an open window above and behind them, an old Elvis Presley tune. "And summon Sekhmet, too, I would have her see this amazing, stinking place."

Killing Osuran

Christina Stiles

Killing the priest would not be easy, but he *would* die soon; Kaja Dawne would see to it. She just needed to get him alone in his magically warded temple, kill him away from the eyes of the innocent people of Farik. Then she could steal his last breath and eat his heart, forever freeing the citizens of Farik of the despicable man who had inflicted a plague on them in order to set himself up as their priest-king redeemer.

Lamps and torches bobbed down the street below Kaja, breaking through the morning's gray light. The townsfolk were flocking to the temple to hear their cunning priest's morning proclamation, to discover what their savior bid them do this day. In preparation for her attack on Osuran, Kaja had observed this morning ritual for the past three days. She watched Farik's people walk, ride, and even limp to the temple's heavy, wooden, well-guarded gates. The town's grimy, skinny street folk in their smelly, tattered rags arrived first. The bathed, sweet-smelling rich in their fine garments of deep reds and purples, high headdresses nodding above the crowds from atop their mounts, soon followed. The townsfolk's intermingled scents, like pomegranates rotting under the heat of the midday sun coupled with the strong reek of horse, wafted up to Kaja Dawne as she perched atop a roof across from the temple. When the day's heat chased away the cool desert winds, the worshippers' smell would be a hundred times stronger. To Kaja's superior senses, the smell would be overwhelming. She intended to be long gone from the square by that point.

She focused her eyes on the man who had brought her to the town: Osuran Malul. The Dark Priest. Her target. He stood a few inches over six feet tall, towering over his fellow priests. His face was handsome, strong, and confident. A dark beard and mustache, both neatly trimmed, framed his features. He wore a white turban, and his blue tunic and trousers looked clean and well-made. They weren't overly opulent, but they appeared finer than the clothes his companion priests wore. Those others hovered behind him as awestruck, she noted, as the followers gathered before the man-god. Four well-muscled men flanked the priests. Two held crossbows with quarrels nocked, while the others held gleaming spears. Kaja could feel their desire for a fight; let just one man touch their priest-king, and the guards would gleefully spill blood.

The guards' craving for bloodshed flowed through her, awakening her own *maraqaze*, her bloodlust. She could already taste the coppery liquid on her tongue. She savored it. Knowing she needed to remain in control at that moment, however, she closed her eyes, took a long breath, and quelled the inner beast with a promise: *Soon*. She had only recently learned to control the *maraqaze*—and "control" was really not the right word for it. Hers was an eternal struggle against this hunger for death and destruction. She had succumbed to its wishes for many years now, powerless to do anything else, for she was Marathuk, the Killer. The Twelve Faceless Ones had forged her, brought her back from death, in fact, to serve them as a shape-shifting assassin. She was the Deathbringer. And although she had freed herself of their yoke a few years before, her purpose remained the same: to bring death to her targets—only now *she* chose them.

Lying flat on her stomach on the building's roof tiles, she continued to watch the priest, her eyes boring into him. He raised

Killing Osuran

his hands to quiet the crowd, and he began to speak. Her hearing was keen, and his voice loud, but still she angled her head toward the scene below to ensure she heard every word of his putrid lies.

"Citizens of Farik," he boomed, his voice deep, melodic, attention-getting. "Last night I conferred with the Others to learn of events outside your realm. They tell me that beyond our walls, in every direction, trouble brews. War rides the winds in the north. Its blood seeps closer to our doors. Bandits haunt the merchants' trails to the south and east, also spilling blood and destroying entire families' livelihoods. And a murderous bird creature is on the rampage from the west."

Me, thought Kaja. He's warning them about me. But he did not invoke the name Marathuk. No, that would cause panic. He only wants a controlled fear—a fear that leads to faith and trust in him.

"I have asked the Others to aid me in my continuing protection of Farik. When I arrived a year ago, you were beset by disease and pestilence."

Disease and pestilence you brought to the people, Osuran.

"The dark plague I have saved you from has abated, no longer threatening to tear you from this world into the next, but more troubles are coming, and we must be vigilant."

The people cheered when he spoke of the waning plague. They worshipped him for saving them. They thought him one of the Others of which he spoke: the gods. And he wanted them to. Osuran would not let them forget he held great power—at least against disease and vermin, abilities channeled to him through Argave, the Eighth of the Twelve Faceless Ones, her former masters, in return for his soul.

"Your past tributes have been generous, but more such gifts are required for the Others to secure this peaceful life you have come to enjoy since my arrival. Continued work and *sacrifice* is required of you, else your town and loved ones will not remain safe. Some of you may even have to sacrifice your lives, offering them on the battlefields in the North War, helping to keep the depredations of war from storming these gates and taking the lives of your beautiful wives and children."

Christina Stiles

Yes, make them worry about their families. That always wins over the masses.

"Come. Bring your offerings to the gods."

Offerings to you, Osuran, you foul, soulless creature.

The other priests moved forward and held out large sacks for the offerings of food, coins, and valuables. Young servants gathered up any offered livestock, herding the animals to the stables and pens in the temple's courtyard. Kaja watched the god-priest's smile broaden at the abundance of offerings. Her stomach churned at the thought of the families who'd starve this day in order to feed the priest's desires. She fought the urge to extend her wings, lengthen her claws, and fly in to attack the horrid man for taking advantage of these trusting townspeople. Killing him in front of the crowd would cause chaos. They would waste their energies on the "murderous bird creature," leaving them vulnerable to the invaders from the north.

While the parade of tribute continued, Kaja's sharp eyes spotted numerous black, long-winged zeringes flying in their unusual double-V formation toward the town. A smile crossed her face. The birds had finally arrived, and soon a flock of over a thousand would join these scouts. Kaja had ordered the birds to arrive several days after her, as their presence would signal the Marathuk's enemies that she was near Farik. The factions all knew she controlled Sorengis' birds now. At one time, the birds had been sent to track and destroy her, but when she had revolted against the Twelve, killing Sorengis, the Ninth of their number, his birds had become hers to order instead. Her own killer would one day gain their allegiance.

Now that they were here, the zeringes would keep the temple's external guards busy while she infiltrated, assassinating her target.

In the meantime, she had still to figure out a way to get past the temple's magical wards.

The priest concluded his proclamation and bid the townsfolk a fine, prosperous morning. Before he retreated through the temple's gates, Osuran Malul whispered to the burliest of his guards, who then turned his attention to a nearby nobleman in a crimson tunic. Kaja had earlier seen the man and a dark-haired youth unload valuable gifts for the temple from their pack mule — the man had lavished more gifts on the priest than any others, in fact.

Surely he's provided enough to satisfy you, dark one. What more could you want?

The crowd started dispersing, ambling along as if in no hurry to start the day, but the nobleman moved more quickly, towing the boy with him. Osuran's man rushed to overtake him. "Don't leave so fast, Telthen. I need a word with you," he said, grabbing the nobleman by the arm. The townspeople continued on their way with only a few backward glances.

The guardsman turned Telthen around, forcing him to face the temple's gates. Another guard came up to relieve him of his mule.

"What do you want, Jadoc?"

Jadoc maneuvered himself behind the nobleman to block any escape. "Come inside for a bit, won't you. Telthen?"

"Don't you hurt my father!" the boy of about ten cried, pounding his fists against the guard's armored back.

"Oh, he's not to be hurt — yet — young one," the guard said, ignoring the insignificant blows. "But you may come along with your father to see for yourself. After all, Domias — that is your name, yes? — you may soon inherit his estate and all his obligations."

"We'll discuss our business in the courtyard, Telthen. There are too many ears in the streets," the guard said. Telthen stood his ground.

A guardsman at the gate aimed his crossbow at the nobleman.

Jadoc leaned near Telthen's ear and whispered, but Kaja heard it all clearly: "Of course, if you don't cooperate, Telthen, my men will gladly let your blood, and then I'll kill your family myself. Your choice."

The nobleman bowed his head in resignation and plodded toward the temple. His son followed. The gates closed behind the retreating retinue, and Kaja could no longer see them or hear their conversation. Sending a thought to her lead zeringe scout, she ordered the bird to fly toward the courtyard to be her ears, while she remained on her rooftop perch across from the temple gates. The bird broke from its high position and glided downward, winging toward the walls. Just as it was about to clear the palisade, the zeringe slammed into an invisible barrier. The force bounced the bird backwards, and the creature tumbled over several times before righting itself. Determined, it flew forward again—much more slowly this time. But again it met resistance, and could not gain entrance to the courtyard.

"Sorry, friend," Kaja projected to the zeringe. "I thought the magical wards only kept out large things. They are strong indeed."

Undeterred, the crafty zeringe circled the wall, testing the obstruction, until finally locating an unprotected fence post to alight upon. The bird then focused on the targets it had been sent to watch.

Through the bird's eyes and ears, Kaja observed the courtyard scene. Telthen was shouting at the muscular guardsman beside a pool in the temple's palm garden. "I've given Osuran gold, gems, and precious spices. I've given him soldiers. I've provided food and clothing for his men. I've even sent false information to lead my warlord brother astray in the north. What more must I give, Jadoc? When is it enough?"

"Enough?" The bigger man chuckled. "It does not end, Telthen. You will give what you are asked to give. And then you will give more. And more beyond that. You owe your life to Osuran, and that is his expected payment."

Jadoc removed a dagger from his belt, and Telthen and the boy flinched. Kaja crouched low atop the building, preparing to take wing and give herself away if she must. Maybe she could break through the courtyard's wards with the force of her speed. She had yet to try that. She pictured herself flying in, severing the man's jugular, grabbing up the two nobles, and flying them to safety. It was dangerous, but it could be done. Her *maraqaze* inched its way into her veins at the thought; her hatred for Osuran and his men was strengthening it. *Yes, blood. Spill it! Now.*

No! Be calm.

Jadoc merely chuckled again at the reactions of the nobles. "You are jittery, my friends. We are only talking business." He took the point of the blade and began cleaning under his fingernails.

"The thing is, Telthen, my master wants what he wants. He's done a great deal for this town, and for your family in particular. You owe him your life, and your wife's life. He brought you both back from the brink of death when that plague had you in its terrible throes, and now you rebuff his requests? Deny his desires?" He tssked. "That's not smart, my friend. I suggest you rethink your stance and bring that lovely daughter of yours to the temple as he requires. Bring Hesal here *tonight*. This is your last chance, you understand. Dress her in her finest, make her even more beautiful, and bring her here for Osuran.

"Oh, and afterwards, you'd best see to the assassination of that troublemaking brother of yours on his battlefield. Despite your efforts, we've heard he's won a major battle, and the tides are turning in his favor. We don't want the war to end and we don't want it at our door. We like our peace just fine."

He wants a girl? Her mind flew to the sister she'd lost to lust-filled, murderous men—men like Osuran—in her own city's streets. She'd been powerless then to stop it and could only hide. She was not so weak now. *Osuran, you will not have her!* Deep fury rising within her amplified her *maraqaze*. She trembled beneath its strength. Momentarily, she let it flow through her, bathing in its raw, primal urges. Then she realized what she had done.

Jadoc finished picking his nails, and began to return the knife to its scabbard. Suddenly he grabbed Telthen, pressing the knife to his neck. He let its tip penetrate, drawing blood. The scent of it drifted to Kaja's feathered spy and through it to her. It pulled at her. She wanted to spill more, only it would not be Telthen's; she craved Jadoc's blood, his heart. She struggled to contain it, but it was much too late. The desire was so...*very strong— overwhelmingly strong and joyous to her Marathuk nature.*

Kaja leapt from the roof, changing to her ferocious bird shape in mid-flight. She circled around the building to gain needed speed.

"Actually, Telthen, the first task may be better suited to your son," Kaja heard him say to the boy as she dived toward the courtyard. "He's going to be the man of the family soon, so let him make his first business deal."

"You said you wouldn't hurt him! You said you wanted to talk!" Domias battered Jadoc's body with his fists to no avail.

"No, Domias! No!"

"More feather-taps from you, little man?" Jadoc laughed. "Domias, as long as you bring your sister to the temple gates at dusk, I'll return your father to you. You fail to make the exchange, and I will kill him. Then, I will march my men to your house and take your sister for our master and your mother for us. Do you understand?"

The boy looked to his father for guidance, but the dejected man wouldn't meet his eyes. He merely whimpered and gave a slight nod.

A cry went up at the gates. "The bird creature! The bird creature! It's here!"

Kaja let out a loud, angry series of caws as she zoomed toward the gates. The guards loosed a dozen crossbow bolts in her direction. Some flew true, but bounced off her hard skin. One man rushed off to ring the temple's bell, to alert all within the complex—and the town—to the danger.

Jadoc lowered his knife; his jaw followed. "What in the heavens is that?" he said, as the bird creature dived toward the gates. Even with her great speed, Kaja banged against the ward's force, unable to penetrate it. She fell to the ground, momentarily stunned. Pain surged through her. More bolts rained ineffectively down from above. Kaja paid them no heed: The barrier had her attention. She needed to get beyond it to feed her *maraqaze*. She cawed loudly in frustration and raked her claws along the invisible obstacle. The futility pushed her into a berserk rage, and she lost herself to her animal nature. For several minutes, she clawed, stabbed, and smashed at it, focusing all of her anger on it in a wild, cacophonous attack.

The wards held.

Killing Osuran

Jadoc cringed at the noise at the gates, but kept his senses. "Run, boy," he yelled over his shoulder as he fast-walked Telthen toward the inner temple. "You better hope that creature doesn't get you. And be expecting a guest later today to help you set up that assassination, Domias. I think I'll have you take care of that as well," he yelled before fleeing through the doorway.

Domias ran toward the gate, fear energizing his legs.

The temple guards flung open the gates, spilling out into the streets for a better shot at her. Bolts continued to strike Kaja, as she flew to the rooftops, avoiding a direct confrontation with the oncoming troops. The poor fools didn't have the special silver-tipped bolts needed to penetrate her skin, but they might have a silver-edged sword or dagger among them.

Kaja's *maraqaze* was fading, perhaps exhausted by her tantrum against the ward. She saw young Domias safely fleeing the chaos, a zeringe scout close above him. She tamped down the last of her bloodlust, and took flight, soaring well outside the city. Osuran's men now knew she was here. With Osuran's counsel, they would soon realize what she was, and they would arm themselves appropriately.

I lost control, and with it, I may have lost my kill.

◇

At dusk, a trembling Domias arrived at the temple's outer gates with a young woman in tow. He surveyed the demure girl with his large eyes, and his hand on her arm shook even more. She was adorned in her finest silk dress. Dazzling emerald rings bedecked her long fingers. A matching necklace lay on her outer clothing, between her breasts. A full-face veil covered her youthful countenance, hiding her emotions.

"Halt!" a guard called out from above, and leaned over the wall to look out at the arrivals. He pointed a readied crossbow at them, as his eyes flitted from the murky sky to the streets beyond the pair, and back to them. "Get under the light, so I can see you better."

Domias reluctantly pulled the girl toward the gate, his knees knocking.

"You are bringing the girl for Osuran, yes? She is called Hesal?" the guard asked.

Domias nodded and whispered, "Yes."

"My but you are a tall one," the guard noted to the girl, who stood a half foot taller than her brother.

"These are Jadoc's expected guests," the guard yelled down to someone below. "They are safe to pass." He returned to searching the sky, where dozens of strange black birds circled above. Their incessant cawing unnerved him and the other men, as did their occasional dives toward the guards' heads. The birds were smart. They veered away quickly before making contact with the gate's wards. This fact unsettled the guards more.

The gates opened and the guards ushered the boy and girl inside. The men quickly shoved the gates closed, and four guardsmen surrounded the pair, while a fifth rushed across the courtyard toward the inner temple.

The boy's courage began to falter, but the girl at his side squeezed his hand to reassure him. He took a deep breath and straightened himself, trying to gather his calm.

After several moments, Jadoc swaggered up to them. He clasped Domias's shoulder and smiled. "Fine job, my boy! You are much smarter than your father, I see."

"Where is my father? You said you'd exchange him for Hesal."

"Yes, yes. In due time, Domias." He removed his arm and moved to the girl. "Let's have a look at the beauty who's had my master so enthralled." He lifted the light cloth, and stared into a heavenly oval face. He let out a low whistle. "Yes, you are indeed a fair beauty. But," he added, leering over her figure and checking her backside, "you are a little too thin—and young—for my tastes. Still, when the boss tires of you, I'll pay you a visit."

Jadoc stopped and shook his head. For a moment, he could have sworn her face was older, that of a girl in her twenties, and her bright eyes...they had stared back *defiantly*. He blinked. No. No. She was a girl, a young, dark-haired beauty of about eleven,

Killing Osuran

he'd guess, though tall for her age. Her brown eyes were very meek, really. Her face showed only compliance. Timidity rolled off of her in waves as she dropped her gaze to the ground.

"Ah, yes, you are quite a beauty, aren't you?"

She did not reply.

"Oh, there's no need to answer, little girl. You'll be talking—or making noises at least—soon enough." He replaced her veil, and then headed for the temple. "Come along." The surrounding guards pushed the pair behind the retreating Jadoc.

The other guards stopped at the inner temple doors, and only Jadoc went through with the two. After locking the massive doors behind them, Jadoc led the pair along the marble-floored corridor through a series of halls with vaulted side chambers filled to overflowing with gifts to the temple.

Finally, they arrived at their destination. "Be on your best behavior and bow your heads to Osuran. You will be in the presence of a *god-kin*, and you must show respect." He then knocked. "My great lord, your beautiful guest has arrived," Jadoc said. "May we enter?"

"Yes. Bring me my prize."

Jadoc led the girl into the room, bringing her before the seated Osuran. The priest rose from his padded armchair, anticipation twisting his features. "Finally, you will be mine, my beauty. Your father has kept you from me for far too long." He pulled up the cloth covering her face, and blinked. Confusion crossed his face.

"What foulness is this? Who have you brought me? This is not Telthen's daughter Hesal! This is a woman, not a girl! Don't you know the difference?"

Jadoc leaned around to look again at her face. "What? That's not the girl from the gates. That's the other..."

The illusion of Hesal now discarded, Kaja extended her claws, stabbed one set into Osuran's throat, and the other into his chest, piercing his heart. Her movements were inhumanly quick; whatever powers Argave may have granted him, he had no time to react. As blood gurgled from his neck and pumped out from his heart, he tried to speak.

Christina Stiles

"What's that, Osuran? You weren't expecting danger from a little girl, were you? Seems appropriate to me."

"You...the Twelve," he managed before his eyes rolled back into his head and he slumped downwards into a heap. She ripped his heart out as he slid down. She put it to her mouth, took a large bite, and swallowed.

Jadoc grabbed her around the neck with his forearm and squeezed, trying to strangle her. "You will pay for this!" He began yelling for more guards, but then remembered he'd told them all to keep their distance on Osuran's orders.

"Done?" she asked.

"Why won't you die?" he huffed, straining against her throat.

"I'm already dead," she laughed. "I don't need to breathe." In a whisper she added, "I'm Marathuk, remember? The Deathbringer is in your temple, little man. She has easily killed your *god-kin* master."

The man's grasp loosened as her words sunk in. "But...but the gates are warded. How did you get in here?"

"You *invited* me in, you fool."

She grabbed his forearm, twisted her body to get leverage, and then threw him over her shoulder. He crashed into a small table. A piece of its wood stabbed through his side. Blood pooled to the floor. The sight of it fueled her bloodlust, and Kaja completed her transformation. Jagged wings burst through her dress, her eyes darkened to obsidian orbs, and her face elongated into the beak of a carrion bird. She glanced back at the frozen Domias. She'd already warned him what would happen. She'd told him to remain still no matter what. Good. He was obeying her. She nodded, and he closed his eyes.

Then she leapt onto Jadoc, ripping his flesh with strong, razor-sharp claws. She shredded his throat to stifle his screams, and then pulled out and devoured his heart.

Good. Deserved, she thought as she fed. Farik is free.

Her *maraqaze* sated, Kaja found and freed the imprisoned Telthen, then walked the two nobleman out through the temple's main doors. Her borrowed silk clothes were blood-drenched rags, but she didn't care. The courtyard guards remained oblivious to Osuran's murder. Many still watched the dark sky for the bird creature's return; none of them looked toward the temple.

She, too, looked skyward and let out a silent call to the zeringes. She would let them feed. Osuran's staunch followers would do no good for the people of Farik. They were complicit in his crimes.

"Come to me," she ordered. "Eat. All within and on the courtyard walls are yours except the two with me."

The birds descended from all directions. The guards screamed as a mass of darkness overtook the courtyard. The birds flocked to Kaja and the two she protected; they whirled around the trio and then burst outward, one flock for each guard or priest remaining in the temple's outer complex.

Rippling, moving darkness swarmed the men, enveloping every inch of their bodies. The avian storm ripped their flesh from them and tore out their eyes. The zeringes then devoured them.

The birds sent waves of happiness back to their mistress as they fed. Like her, they were children of the Twelve, and they thrilled to death as much as she did. Their joy in slaughter always calmed her; she guessed that was part of their connection to her, a part she inherited from their former master. Their feedings sated her own bloodlust, but, as the Deathbringer, she preferred to slay her own targets.

For several minutes, she let the birds consume the priest's allies. Then she turned her gaze northward, where war raged and an assassin had been sent to kill the one true hope for the rebels, Telthen's brother. She tasted the breezes flowing from the north. There was smoke, blood…and death.

She remembered something an old ally, lover, and now nemesis had said of the Lords of Calos, the aggressors in the North War: "They truck with otherworldly creatures. They will do more harm to the people of Farik than Osuran ever would, I assure you. Osuran plays both sides of the war, ensuring it never reaches Farik's gates. He *is* evil, but if you kill him, they lose that buffer and will most definitely suffer. It's best to keep the Balance," he said.

She pictured Thoroc's face, revisiting the day he'd tried to kill her as she lay next to him. He had failed because he had hesitated, giving her time to realize something was amiss. He wanted to kill her for the sake of the Balance he believed in.

She let out a deep breath. She hadn't chosen this life—or unlife. The Twelve had thrust it upon her when they created her. That didn't matter to Thoroc; according to him, she needed to die to ensure his precious Balance.

"Betrayer," she spat to the wind. "I'll decide what's Balanced. Neither you nor the Twelve will manipulate or destroy me," she said aloud. "I'll protect Farik from anything Osuran's death will visit on them."

She winged herself skyward, leaving the noblemen behind. She glanced down at the zeringes: "Come. We have Lords to slay."

The thousands of zeringes behind her formed into their double-V flight pattern, their wings working hard to carry their full stomachs. "Happy to kill Lords with the Marathuk," they projected back.

The Rydr Express

Tobias Buckell

You've made your way through the corridors of the train and found your room, up on the third deck. Tea has arrived, delivered by a vaguely humanoid robot that balances its torso on a pair of continuously spinning gyroscopes.

Sitting down at the small table, you let yourself relax just a touch and stir in milk and sugar as the train continues to speed up. Two hundred miles per hour, two-fifty. It has just emerged from a wormhole that led downstream towards even more wormholes that eventually bifurcate. At that junction there are trains to the worlds of Fairwater and Fairhaven.

Outside your window, the purple forestry of Rydr's World whips past. The occasional city slowly accretes around the windows, then fades back away.

Now that the Rydr Express has slipped out of the wormhole at the Western edge of its lone continental landmass it is headed East toward the other wormhole on the far coast. When it hits that wormhole and passes through, it'll start jumping its way toward the Dawn Pillars junction. From there it'll head upstream through hundreds of wormholes, until it ends up in League territory when it exits a final wormhole and arrives on the world of Bifrost.

The Rydr Express is a spur that juts off in that uncertain territory of unaligned planets that all exist in between the Forty Eight worlds. They are all connected by thousands of wormholes, and it's only been in the last decade that the wormholes have been moved out of space, onto land, and hooked up by rail.

You have nine hundred miles to go before you hit the Eastern coast. Nine hundred miles of tension.

The door to your room slides open.

You drop the spoon to the table. A startling sound: metal on wood. The clattering reveals that you are surprised. It also reveals that you are a bit stunned, and overly nervous.

The tall man you're looking at is wearing a black oilskin coat, and he walks with a slight limp as he slides the door closed behind him.

Inside the small sleeper berth, he dominates the room. His steel-gray eyes flicker, scanning everything, then finish up by pinning you in place. His shoulder-length dreadlocks are graying, slightly, and with the weathered lines of his face, he looks like he's in his forties.

A far cry from the centuries that you know him to be.

You're holding your breath, and the trigger of the gun in your left hip-pocket, where it's been all along.

It's a trigger's-width away from releasing hell as the man sits down across from you on the other side of the table. From the creak of the floor underneath, you can tell he weighs double, maybe triple what a man should.

You can't say you weren't expecting this. He's that good. That's what everyone says. But this is your world, your game, and your territory. To have been flushed out before you'd even really sat down is a gut punch.

"This is a private room," you say, mustering indignant outrage. You're still trying to keep up your usual traveling businessman camouflage.

The man leans in, his elbows resting on the table and making it creak from the strain. "I'm Pepper," he says, as he holds out a hand and his locks fall forward.

The Rdyr Express

You maintain the fiction for another split second, then lean back and retrieve your tea. You're impressed at your steady hand. "Most of my friends," you mutter over a sip, "call me Vee."

"Are you going to pull that trigger, Vee?" Pepper asks, very seriously, your eyes meeting over the lip of the cup.

"I haven't decided yet," you reply, setting the tea down.

◇

Eighteen hours earlier the militia summons jacked you up out of bed with a ringing headache, leaving you stumbling around shaking your head as your partner grumbled and pulled the covers up and fell back asleep.

The klaxon sound, rigged to a bone-induction military earpiece quantumly entangled to HQ, continued on until you patched in and reported that you were on your way, goddamnit, and they could quit paging you.

But there was no trip to HQ. Head of operations was standing outside your very door with three other rail agents when you got uniformed up and burst out the door.

"We have a situation," she said.

They all forced their way into your tiny apartment.

"I have someone here," you stammered.

Operations looked over at the door to the bedroom. "Tell them to leave," she said. Then she paused slightly. "How serious is this?"

"What?" You were a bit lost for words. What the hell was going on?

"Your file shows few social attachments. Is this someone we need to take into our protection during this mission? There's a high risk component. An attachment could be a liability."

"Protection," you said, eyes wide. Even if it was only a fling, you hadn't wanted someone's life at risk due to their having the bad luck to stumble into you for a few great encounters.

Operations sighed and pointed at the bedroom door and snapped her fingers. "Make it happen."

One of the agents walked to the door.

Moments later the apartment had been vacated, and the confusion and shouting abated. Everyone'd had a deep breath, and Operations sat in your armchair as if she'd owned it her whole life.

"We have a situation," she said.

"You mentioned."

"Pepper's here on Rydr's World."

"Oh."

"We're constitutionally a neutral zone, Vee. Our economic ties are to the Xenowealth, but we still have two League-loyal worlds downstream of us, and they have peace-brokered rights of transport through us on upstream all the way back to core League territory. We can't have the Xenowealth's top troublemaker running loose. Fairhaven and Fairwater, those worlds are far more militarized than we are."

"What do you want me to do?" You'd been unsure of what all this meant.

Operations clarified that, leaning forward. "Intelligence says he's been around shipping and loading centers. We think he's planning to get weapons aboard a train. Why? We're not sure. But it can't be anything good. We need you to shadow him until he gets out of our territory. Once out, he's not our problem. But whatever he's involved in, we can't have it jeopardizing our neutrality."

You'd licked your lips. "And if he starts causing trouble, what am I supposed to do?"

"Stop him."

"Stop him? This is Pepper. The man is more alien machinery than human. He's more legend than real. I'm probably not going to be able to stop him, Ops, you know that."

She looked at you, and then nodded. "I know that," she'd said. "But we need you to at least try, to demonstrate our seriousness."

And you'd swallowed. Because you realized then that's why they chose you. No family, no attachments.

You're damn good at being a rail agent, there's that too.

But most of all: you're kinda expendable.

And Operations was watching. She'd at least done you the favor of explaining things. They're always honest. It's a volunteer job. Always was.

You could have refused.

But you'd slowly nodded.

Because in the end, how many people ever get a chance to meet a living human legend?

◇

Pepper grins at you, now, as you let go of the gun in the hip holster and put both your hands on the table. "I've haven't really done anything yet, and you're the fair sort," he says. "I like your decision-making process."

"What are you up to here?" you ask.

Pepper leans forward. "How much weaponry do you have access to aboard the train?"

Enough, you hope.

"This is neutral country," you remind him.

He slings an arm over the ledge on the back of the built in seat. "Neutral? The line's swimming with League agents."

"And with Xenowealth agents," you tell him.

He waves a hand, unimpressed. "We just follow the activity."

"Treaties were brokered. Rydr's World seceded from the League ten years ago. But we are also not allied with the Xenowealth. We host trade to both."

"And you let the League run up and down the train lines as they see fit," Pepper says. "That breeds trouble."

"It was a condition of our independence."

"The League knew it couldn't hold onto you, so it grabbed that best possible concessions. You bent over backwards."

You bite your lip. "I'm not here to argue history."

"And yet, it always walks back up the line to bite us all in the ass," Pepper says.

"What are you planning?" You ask him, outright.

"It's not what I'm planning you need to be worried about," he says, and raises a finger.

You both hear the dull thud down the corridor. Your ears were cored out and replaced with synthetics when you agreed to join the rail's security. Yes, you volunteered to defend your planet. Yes you do as part of a self-assembling militia. But that doesn't mean you aren't teched out with the latest and greatest. Quick nerves, reinforced skeleton, subprocessors in the nape of your neck.

A body hits the carpet. A hand smacks the wall. You half stand, but Pepper, expecting something of this sort, shakes his head.

Wait.

The door is kicked open, and Pepper reaches out and grabs the man standing there.

He's a bit stunned. He's holding a large, silenced pistol, but Pepper's grabbed and broken his hand before he's even had time to frown. You notice, in the split second as his entire body is violently yanked from the doorway and over your cup of tea, nudging it slightly with the tip of his boot, that there's blood splattered on the assassin's gloves.

By the time Pepper slams him into the side wall, just under the window, his neck is broken.

Yet, for good measure, Pepper takes the man's own silenced gun, puts the silencer to the dying man's mouth, and pulls the trigger.

Blood and brain tissue spray the window.

Pepper sits back down and delicately pushes your teacup back to its original location on the table. "You were saying something about neutrality, I think," he says.

◇

The dead man will be tied into a battle-net of some sort. You're not wasting time. You're kicking out the paneling underneath your bench seat and reaching under to retrieve a large black case.

Inside, nestled in foam: extra handguns, a tactical assault rifle, ammo, a belt of flash bangs.

The Rdyr Express

"Who are they after?" you ask. "Me or you?"

"They're killing passengers," Pepper says.

You pause. "I can't believe that."

Pepper still has the gun he took off the dead man. He glances around the door. "Follow me and see for yourself."

Outside, in the hallway, blinking at the bright lights, polished brass, steel inserts and other neo-modernist stylings you see the first body. It's an alien: Nesaru. Its quill-like feathers droop from its skin in death. Clear fluids are dripping, splashed against the hallway wall, and soaking into the carpet.

The slender, ostrich-like alien's neck is bent in an impossible angle.

"There's more," Pepper whispers.

Each room is a display of death. Different colored fluids. Different bodies. But all punctured, broken, run down. Still. Unmoving. Statues in their nooks, holding gory, distorted death poses for you.

But some of the rooms are empty.

That leaves you puzzled. You're mulling it over, but even as you do that, you enable contact with HQ.

It's quantum entanglement communications. Which means it's expensive. Someone has to create the two paired pieces of quantum bits and separate them. You get one bit, HQ gets the other. And once one gets used, and the information passed through, its state reverts to unpaired. It's the universe's most expensive form of limited bandwidth email.

So you telegraph HQ a summary: LEAGUE *KILLING* PSSNGRS. TRAIN HIJACK IMMNT? ADVISE.

Pepper looks inside another empty room, then back at you.

He's expecting you to notice something, but the reply flashes back, painted over your eyesight thanks to a chip in your visual cortex. WCH PSSNGRS?

Which passengers?

And the empty rooms are a puzzle that finally snaps into its proper shape.

You're only seeing dead aliens. There are no humans in here.
NON-HUMAN, you reply.
Pepper's watching your air-typing fingers.
OBSRV & RPRT, you're ordered.
"What do your masters order?" he asks, forcing another door open.
You don't answer. You don't need to. The troubled look on your face tells him everything.

◇

"So what's your plan, here?" you ask. You're keyed up. Sickened. Shaken. Trying to figure out what all this means and what it means to you. You're also relieved no one has ordered you to detain or try to stop this man.

"Plan?" Pepper looks down the corridor. "To stop it."

"Why?" You do hate yourself for asking, somewhere deep inside. But there is genuine curiosity. What's in it for this man? What is making him tick. "This isn't your fight. This isn't a world that asked you here."

"It's infectious," Pepper says as he points at one of the bodies.

You recoil for a split second, then realize stepping back won't make a difference to survival one way or another. "Biological warfare?"

"No, the violence," he says. He's looking back at you. "It starts here, but then it spreads. Consumes everything around it. Like a fire, it tries to pull in everything within reach. Borders might be decent barriers, but it tries to leap around, continue. So I come out here, to fight it before it has fuel. Before it spreads to the worlds I hold dear."

There's a darting movement, a shadow against the far door leading to the next car. Pepper launches himself forward, boots digging into the carpet hard enough to rip it and make the metal beneath his feet groan as he springs away.

You follow, a breath behind. Fast to the unaided eye, but molasses compared to the snap-speed of Pepper, who hits the steel door and rips it out of its hinges.

He pivots, keeping it to his right side as a shield that smacks into someone you can't see, just as another man bursts down the corridor. This man is dressed in dull gray armor. It's a flowing, shifting exoskeleton He looks like a knight with submachine guns in either hand. Pepper drops the door and closes with him.

When he and Pepper hit, it sounds like a padded gong has been struck. Metal colliding with flesh with metal underneath.

Pepper grapples with whining exoskeletal arms, and both men twirl and spin around the corridor, each one looking for a weakness as they grunt, shift, and struggle in their rapid tango.

Still locked together they smash through the door of a cabin.

◇

As the sounds of destruction and splintering walls fill the corridor the ripped off door shifts. A man crawls out into the corridor on his hands and knees.

He leaves a trail of blood behind from his ruined face, where the door struck him as Pepper passed. He has a large gun in one hand, which he awkwardly holds as he pulls himself along.

A new sound creeps out into the train car. Something like the scream of a can being slowly ripped apart, and then a fleshy, wet, thump.

Pepper steps out of the room holding a helmeted head in one hand, torn completely free of a body.

"Pepper!" You shout the name in warning, without thinking about it, and the crawling man raises his gun.

But before he completes the motion Pepper throws the decapitated helmeted head at the gun. The shot destroys the dead skull, creating a cloud burst of blood mist that Pepper cuts through to kill the crawling League agent with heel stomp to the back of the neck.

The two of you are alone again.

"I was hoping he'd still be unconscious," Pepper says, looking down at the corpse. "I wanted to talk with him. Find out where the human passengers are being herded to. How many League agents there were."

"And what they were up to?" you suggest.

Pepper shrugs. "That'll emerge." Then he looks up and down the car. "What do you think, up to the front, or back?"

"I can't help you," you remind him.

He looks past you, back down the train. "Are you physically prevented from helping me in any capacity, right this second? Is something literally holding you back? Neural taps?"

You shake your head.

"Then you're full of shit. You're making a philosophical choice. To follow an order. *You* are choosing to stand by."

◇

Pepper chooses backwards, and you begin to move through the cars door by door. He leads, and you follow.

OBSRV, you think. Yeah. You'll do that. You'll just fucking OBSRV.

Three more cars of death, corpses framed in their rooms, and you catch up. Five League agents ordering humans forward, killing any aliens they manage to catch.

People scream when Pepper kicks the door from the hinges and wades in. But the agents don't. They're expecting him.

They move in synchronization to turn and attack, as if sharing a single brain. Linked to each other in some deep, technologically enabled battle symbiosis. Gunfire rips through the walls as they open up, and you duck back into the space between trains and look through bulletproof glass. The thundering sound of air passing over the rubber, vacuum-proof flexible tube that connects the two cars deafens you, and mutes the sound of battle.

A multi-person ballet of death ensues. Pepper sprints into the mix, his trenchcoat flapping around him with each twist and turn. He leaps off the wall, almost hitting the ceiling, and flips around behind the first pair of attackers.

Like Pepper, these five attackers are more than they seem. Wherever the League rose up against the aliens who had once held humanity in its iron grip, they slaughtered former masters and sought to plunder their superior technologies.

Some thought the League was too far diminished, too obsessed with human-only worlds and too pushed back to the fringes. But here are their well-funded paladins, and they are faster than you, stronger than you, more vicious than you.

And almost as dangerous as Pepper.

Almost.

One is shot in the back and falls, writhing. Another's head disappears. Was that a shotgun blast? You didn't see one, but it's hard to follow.

Number three's chest is caved in when Pepper runs him through wall, and pulls him back out to use as a shield.

And then the remaining two withdraw, running right past you as Pepper chases them.

A sixth man carrying what looks like a grenade launcher melts out of a room and ghosts past you. He's dressed in a suit, the same camouflage as you, and his eyes flicker sideways as he spots you.

It was a well sprung trap for Pepper. He's focused forward, and here comes the high powered attack from behind.

But this man reads something in you. He isn't going to leave *you* in his blind spot. He's moving to pull out another weapon with his left hand.

He's faster than you. Stronger, more dangerous.

But he wasn't expecting you, and you have the drop. Simple physics.

Because, much to your astonished satisfaction, you've had your own firearm out and ready to fire, finger just outside the trigger, since you stopped by the window.

Just in case.

OBSRV!

Forget that crap now. There's only flight or fight now. And flight was kicked in the nuts the moment this man started to twist and reach for his backup weapon, realizing that the damn grenade launcher would kill you both.

You fire from the waist, just out of general principle, as you're bringing the gun up to your trained fire stance. He's hit in the core, which barely registers on him. But once you're up and ready, it's two to the chest and two to the head.

For good measure you empty the clip into his face, revealing metal chips, machine eyes, and more. The man's more metal than human. Which is why you stand over him and keep shooting until there's nothing left.

"Give me the grenade gun," Pepper says, suddenly back in the car. You wordlessly pick it up and throw it over.

He turns around and kneels.

When the door to the car opens, it reveals forty League soldiers, dressed in armor, carrying rifles. Where the hell had they come from?

Pepper fires the grenade launcher through the car, through the open doors, into the mass of soldiers. The doors close. But flame licks around the doors' gaps, the windows bow out, and explosions rock everything.

He walks over and hands it over. "Pick a position, fire on anything that comes through."

"I can't do that," you protest, even as you hold the weapon.

"You already killed a League agent," he says, moving back into the car with survivors. "You've chosen your side. You're in."

He leaves you alone with the grenade launcher, and you reluctantly drop to a single knee.

Congratulations. You're now responsible for a full-on, hundred percent, international incident.

◇

Pepper gives the civilians instructions, and returns dragging a large case. "Get dressed, we'll need these to stay on the train."

Inside are spacesuits.

He's right. Whatever the League is planning revolves around hijacking this train. Which means it's not stopping on the East Coast. It's going to dive right through the wormhole leading away from Rydr's World and keep going.

The Rdyr Express

You quickly pull a spacesuit on. It's a transparent baggy film that hangs loosely around you until you press it to the helmet and make a seal. Then the material constricts and sucks itself in to you until it's more of a second skin over your clothes.

All this time you've awkwardly kept the grenade launcher sighted on the far door of the train car.

Pepper looks at you, and a faint flicker of communications laser appears as motes drift through the air between the two of you. That makes sense, you don't want the League hearing you over radio of any type.

"I need that launcher back," Pepper says, and swaps you for a machine gun. "And this is your last chance. To get off the train. If you want."

Get off the train. Return to HQ. And explain you shot a League agent? Covered Pepper with a grenade launcher?

If you were going to go rogue, you might as well see this through.

You've got no soft spot for aliens. Rydr's World was run by Nesaru when your grandparents were your age. You saw the scars on their arms and tattoo barcodes. They told you about forced breeding programs with that aura of shame, but insistence that you know what happened.

There are still Nesaru gated compounds, complete with orbital defenses and full security.

And those aren't going away. Nesaru built those long before humanity was brought here. They won't give them up, not without a fight that would cost both sides too much.

Awkward compromises had been reached. And time had passed. And Nesaru who worked side by side with humans had always been here, and had helped when humanity revolted and demanded self-determination here, as it did all throughout the known worlds. And for a while, Ryrdr's World was a strong League of Human Affairs supporter.

But when the League began deportation, people refused. It was understandable, leaders argued, but would lead to humans acting like the Nesaru had when they had dominion. Humans would lose Nesaru technical expertise, finance, and technology. The success of Xenowealth worlds, fully integrated alien and human societies, led them to resist purism.

But you know of Nesaru that live in compounds, that despise humans as little better than monkeys. You read their sneering reviews of bumbling human efforts to deorbit wormholes and create a more directly linked system of worlds.

You understand the League, on a fundamental level.

Maybe once you agreed.

Until that single moment, when you walked through the car and saw those dead individuals. Each one, formerly a thinking being. This was the end result of League ideology. If you value one life, think it superior, eventually, taking the other does not matter.

"I'm staying on board," you tell Pepper.

"Good," he says, and behind you something detonates. The next time you glance back through the doors, the rest of the train is falling behind, emergency brakes shuddering it all to a stop.

If nothing else, you tell yourself, their lives will have been saved.

◇

The spacesuits' gloves are like gecko feet: they're embedded with pads and microscopic nano-adhesives that allow you to clamber up the outside of the car.

But you're moving along at several hundred miles per hour. It isn't wind you encounter as you crawl up to the roof, but a hurricane.

You're flat to the roof, army-crawling along a tremendous, pounding resistance that wants nothing more than to bat you off your perch. The adhesive pads hold.

AGNT: RPRT!

Just barely.

It's an exhausting, sweat-filled haul to get three cars forward from where you were. When you're done, it feels like you climbed up the side of a building.

You dig your pads into the roof and shelter behind the several inches-high protection of a vent and pant.

OBSRVNG HIJACK IN PRGRSS, you tell your superiors. SURVIVORS IN BRAKED TRAIN.

An hour later, the train is still hauling at top speed as it passes through the last stop on Rydr's World. Skyscrapers whip by, and for a while an aircraft paces the train.

You wave at it.

AGNT: RPRT!

You ignore the demands ghosting over your eyeballs.

Fifteen minutes later, you squeeze your eyes shut and feel your stomach lurch as the train hits that blank portal of darkness that is the wormhole leading out and away from Rydr's World.

◇

Pepper shouts. It's joyful.

"Open your eyes, Vee," he says happily, rapping the side of your helmet. "Open your eyes. You never see the full vista from one room window. Not like this."

When you open your eyes the train is whipping past a giant mountain chain. There is no vegetation, and you're deep in the valley. Overhead: the remains of a nebula is scattered over the entire sky. Impossibly jagged peaks rise for miles around you. You feel light.

There is no wind pressure thundering at you.

Five minutes later the train dives into another wormhole.

Right away a giant hand of wind smacks into you.

You open your eyes, and this time the tracks are on a bridge. It stands in the water, pilings driven down maybe ten feet. There is no land anywhere, you feel dizzy looking out at the horizon.

Where the sea laps, smoke wisps and rises. The pilings are burnished and polished, as if the sea is acidic.

Half an hour later you leave that behind. Plunge through yet another wormhole, and when you open your eyes you gasp. You're out in space. There's nothing but the darkness of vacuum and distant stars all around you. Track hangs in space, suspended in nothingness.

You stare at the heavens for twenty minutes, awestruck, until you realize the train is coming to a stop, and that it has been slowing the whole time.

Pepper taps you, and you turn. He points.

A starship approaches. Black paint against the black space all around you. You can see it by the stars it occludes: a darker space slipping over space as it gets closer.

Nav lights and docking lights pop on, and the frame is outlined: a giant functional cylinder strapped to a bell-shaped engine.

"What now?" you ask Pepper.

"Wait and watch," he says.

OBSRV.

◇

The League shuttles thousands of soldiers into the train after they cut in temporary airlocks near the front. Pepper counts ten thousand. That sounds right. They must be literally standing shoulder to shoulder to fit.

And to the front of the train, a sled is being prepared with a rocket attached to it.

"When we last had a full-on war between the Xenowealth and the League," Pepper says, "we had a problem. Each wormhole is a natural border. A checkpoint. When they were in space, we stacked orbital firing platforms around the wormhole. Try to shove your ships through, and you'd get hammered. That's how the Satrapy, the aliens, that's how they kept us all in check. But once we had League and Xenowealth, the only way to push against each other was to foment revolution, play secret agent.

"Then, when the wormholes get moved down out of orbit, into oceans, it's the same problem. Natural chokepoints. Then we start running track through them all, thinking of them as just subway stops, that's when the League thinks, ah, now it has a military option.

"But it only gets to use it once."

You're both ready to bet that what's on the sled is a bomb. It rockets through the wormhole ahead and detonates, and then comes the ten minutes later, delivering troops and hardware to secure the wormhole: the chokepoint.

Then comes more.

And more.

"They've probably had this starship mothballed in far orbit ever since wormholes were in orbit here, back in the day, and the League had ships out here, before it withdrew," Pepper muses. "It's not a warship, we've tracked all those and the negotiations made sure those withdrew. But that doesn't mean it isn't useful. They've been smuggling troops one by one to this location for years, staging them in a station that we would have assumed was abandoned. I followed people out here. Followed the activity. Didn't see it being this big."

The League is invading. Not Rydr's World. But the next habitable world upstream of this string of worlds connected by wormholes: Dawn Pillars. A center of trade and activity, a highly developed world. And unlike the polyglot Rydr's, Dawn Pillars has a population that is almost all human. Very few aliens.

Ripe for League take over.

No OBSRV left, really.

You sit down and tap out a report.

There is no answer.

You wonder what that's about. Is your department infiltrated with League? Are they just waiting? Are you that clueless, or ignorant?

Or are they just speechless because you dropped a bomb in their lap?

"What do we do next?" you ask.

Pepper's looking up at the starship. "They hijacked our train, Vee. I'd like to return the favor." He looks over at you. His dreadlocks are floating in the bowl of his helmet, making him look medusa-like. It's slightly disconcerting. "If you don't mind, I'd like to throw you at that ship."

◇

He's not kidding.

Pepper has a half mile of a high-tensile thread, and he unspools several feet of it and ties it off on a tiny buckle on the back of your suit, near the small of your back. Then he throws you over the side of the train, lets you out about six feet, and starts spinning you around over his head like you're a bucket on the end of some string.

The world cartwheels around you, and then stops as Pepper lets go, the timing impeccable. He's slingshot you toward the dark bulk of the starship.

You fly through space, falling in, and then Pepper slows you down, using the brake on his spool.

After you reach out with your pads and grab the hull you look back and wave.

The thread yanks at you as Pepper activates a motor on the spool. Two minutes later he lands next to you, you both glance around, and then begin crawling around the hull of the ship.

The way in presents itself: a manual emergency airlock near a set of bay doors. You move to undog the first hatch to cycle in, but Pepper stops you.

"Not yet," he says. "Not until they finish unloading."

◇

An hour later you both make your move. The manual airlock deposits you inside a cavernous cylindrical hanger. You scurry across the curved walls, weightless, using your gecko-fingers to grab any surface you can and then kick off.

"Keep up." Pepper moves like a cat in the air, loose-limbed and graceful. A natural hunter. And he knows what he's hunting. He's taking you to the core of the ship.

You suddenly get the feeling this isn't the first time he's done this.

He has a silenced gun out, and everyone you cross in the corridors of the ship ends up spinning slowly in the air, a surprised look on their face, blood slowly drifting out of punctures in the forehead.

Swift, quiet, calm, suddenly violent.

And fast. You're pushing off every bulkhead as fast as you can to keep up. You've bored down through most of this ship's bulk in minutes.

The men guarding the cockpit barely have time to register the fluttering trenchcoat, the man spinning in the air and firing, dreadlocks spread out around his face.

He's through them and into the actual cockpit of the ship in the blink of an eye, and shouts of outrage end with the silent thwack of Pepper's response.

"Shove them out and lock us in," Pepper orders. He's floating around from control pod to control pod, his head cocked, as if getting advice from someone. Maybe he has quantum entangled communications of his own. Someone's talking him through what the controls are, you think. Someone deep in the heart of the Xenowealth.

Screens flicker on, and you hear the wail of wind outside the door.

Glancing at the screens showed you what just happened: the ship vented its air. Airlock doors throughout are wide open to space, and you can see up on the screens random faces, tortured, blood beginning to leak out of orifices.

You look away.

"Any of them good about drills and who kept near their spacesuits will be trying to get back in here," Pepper says. "So stay clear of the door, they might blow it."

He's listening to instructions and moving quickly from place to place, frowning.

Then the engines thunder to life, and he claps his hands.

"Oh, they're not going to like this."

◇

There are no weapons systems on this ship. It's transport, pure and simple. Which is how the League was able to leave it behind, hidden away from Xenowealth and Rydr's World military negotiation accountants looking for just this sort of stunt when comparing inventories and current ship names and movements out of the area when Rydr's World demanded independence.

But that doesn't mean it can't be used as a crude missile. Pepper orders you into an acceleration pod to strap in, but keeps spinning around and flitting around to control the ship.

You're not moving fast when you strike the train and track. But it's fast enough to rip the outer hull of the ship and derail the train. It's fast enough to twist and rip track.

The impact throws Pepper around the cockpit, his body smashing equipment. He wearily pulls himself out and gets back to the controls, firing the engines to pull the ship free of the track and turn it about.

The ship's external monitors, shown on screens all throughout the orb of the cockpit, show cars full of soldiers and equipment hanging around the ship. The staging area is chaos.

Pepper lines the ship up and fires it up. It shudders and caroms its way down the tracks. It speeds up, heading for the wormhole leading to Dawn Pillars.

"Pepper?" you ask. "What are you doing? This thing can't go through a wormhole."

"These ships used to do it all the time," Pepper said.

"Yes, when the wormholes were in orbit. Now they're deorbited. We're going to drive this thing through that hole and out into a train station that's on a planet's surface."

"I know."

There was, you could hear, a sort of boyish satisfaction in the tone of Pepper's voice.

◇

The Rdyr Express

When you pass through, there was that familiar kick in the gut. And the sudden resumption of gravity, yanking down on you again.

And then it all turns bad. The walls flexing and bending visibly. The creaking superstructure that then began to give up creaking and just start screaming.

There is what feels like a mile of sliding, and tumbling, and then darkness as the energy systems on the ship all fail.

Someone is chuckling in the background of the debris and shaking and… yes, that's an explosion somewhere nearby crackling the air.

The next kick isn't in your gut, but to your helmet, which cracks and falls away. And then you pass out.

◇

A lot of men make a point of arresting you when you wake up in quiet, very clean and modern feeling hospital wing. They've vacated other patients and have what looks like a small military guarding you.

No one is happy.

Very grave people are making very important, and measured, but Very Serious accusations. People wearing very expensive suits who look perpetually constipated.

No one is sure what, exactly, to charge you with, but ramming a spaceship through a wormhole into an urban world has repercussions, they explain.

You ask about Pepper, but they pretend not to hear you.

On the second day, when you're able to get up and walk, you stand by the window and look out over the city. And you see the wormhole and the central train station. And you note the long furrow in the parks and space around the wormhole made by the massive spaceship, the ruined hulk of which rests at the end of the giant, debris-scattered, ploughed mess it has created.

You helped do that.

No wonder they're pissed. At least four buildings have been subject to a rapid and unscheduled demolition by spaceship.

You're going away for a long, long time.

But was it worth it?

You hear mutters from some of the soldiers guarding you that the League managed to overwhelm a couple of worlds this way. There's fighting with the Xenowealth breaking out. It's the League's last stand. And they're going for broke.

Which means that even if you helped delay them, those surviving soldiers, even without the benefit of surprise, are still going to try to shove through that wormhole any minute now.

◇

You've been stripped of your volunteer rail militia communications equipment by a surgeon who cuts out the implants. A formal letter declaring you persona-non-grata has arrived. You're stripped of rank, pay, and your pension has been scuttled.

That is your afternoon. The Rydr's World embassy liaison has you sign here, there, and here, and here again to formalize it.

They will not be helping you find legal counsel in the upcoming fun.

But after the glowering liaison leaves, one of the guards taps your shoulder. "Legal's here for you," he says, and points out a room.

Inside is Pepper, dressed in a suit, holding a briefcase.

As the door closes behind you, he sets the case down and opens it. "So, I'm here as a Xenowealth ambassador," he tells you. Inside are citizenship ID chips, a few wads of hard currency and some gold coins, and several wads of explosives.

You don't bother to ask how he got all that up here.

"You can't follow me directly anymore," Pepper says. He motions for you take everything but the explosives. "But these chips are a new identity anywhere in the Xenowealth, and starter cash. Go on a vacation. Start a business. But just one favor, Vee?"

"Yes?"

The Rdyr Express

He's shoving the explosive into the wall, careful to point the shaped charges in the needed direction. "Don't ever work for someone who demands you stand still and do nothing."

"I can do that."

"If you're not interested in a vacation, call the person on that card. Tell her I recommended you. She'll know what that means."

You nod.

Pepper walks over, pushes you behind him, and blows the wall off the side of the hospital. "Apparently," he shouted, "even the diplomats can't get these guys to let you go, so I have to get involved. I hate administrivia like this, but I wasn't about to leave you to pay the price for my little joyride."

He's holding out his hand. You're not sure what the hell comes next, but you stop near the edge and look out over the city, the wormhole, the train tracks, and the destroyed ship, and then take a deep breath and jump with him into the air.

◇

Five adrenaline-fueled hours later, you're on a train by yourself, wired, jittery, and feeling the kick to the gut as your train indolently passes through a wormhole on its way deep into the Xenowealth.

You flip the plastic business card Pepper gave you around.

Nashara, it says. And there's the contact info.

So there's the question. Do nothing? Take the starter cash. Settle in somewhere. Start a business? You can do anything.

Or make the contact.

What will you do?

Biographies

Alex Bledsoe grew up in West Tennessee, an hour north of Graceland (home of Elvis) and twenty minutes from Nutbush (birthplace of Tina Turner). He now lives in a Wisconsin town famous for mustard and trolls. Find more of his iconic hero Eddie LaCrosse in the novels *The Sword-Edged Blonde*, *Burn Me Deadly*, *Dark Jenny* and *Wake of the Bloody Angel*.

Emily Care Boss is a role playing game designer, writer and editor living in Massachusetts, USA. Through her independent publishing company, Black & Green Games, Emily publishes *Breaking the Ice*, *Shooting the Moon*, and *Under my Skin*, winner of the Audience Award at Fastaval 2009. Her essays on role playing game theory have been published in *Push Vol. 1* and *Playground Worlds*, from the 2008 nordic Nodal Point conference. Emily edits the *RPG = Role Playing Girl Zine*, annually featuring essays and articles on and by women in gaming. You can find Emily and her games at blackgreengames.com.

Jennifer Brozek is an award-winning author and editor, slush reader and small press publisher. She has been writing roleplaying games and professionally publishing fiction since 2004. She has won awards for both game design and editing. With the number of edited anthologies, fiction sales, RPG books and the one non-fiction book under her belt, Jennifer is often considered a Renaissance woman, but prefers to be known as a wordslinger and optimist. Learn more about her at www.jenniferbrozek.com.

Tobias S. Buckell is a Caribbean-born SF/F author and NYT best seller who now lives in Ohio. He is the author of *Crystal Rain*, *Ragamuffin*, *Sly Mongoose*, *Halo: The Cole Protocol* and over forty short stories in various magazines and anthologies. Pepper, from the story here, is a recurring character from *Crystal Rain*, *Ragamuffin*, *Sly Mongoose*, and several of his short stories. His next novel, Arctic Rising, is due out sometime soon from Tor, and he's working on his next book. Find him at www.TobiasBuckell.com.

Jesse Bullington spent the bulk of his formative years in rural Pennsylvania, the Netherlands, and Tallahassee, Florida. He is the author of the novels *The Sad Tale of the Brothers Grossbart* and *The Enterprise of Death*, and his short fiction and articles have appeared in numerous magazines, anthologies, and websites. He currently resides in Colorado, and can be found online at www.jessebullington.com.

Matt Forbeck has been a full-time creator of award-winning games and fiction since 1989. He has designed collectible card games, roleplaying games, miniatures games, board games, and toys, and has written novels, short fiction, comic books, motion comics, nonfiction, magazine articles, and computer game scripts and stories for companies including Angry Robot, ArenaNet, Del Rey, Adams Media, Simon & Schuster, Atari, Tor.com, Boom! Studios, Ubisoft, Wizards of the Coast, Games Workshop, WizKids, Mattel, IDW, Image Comics, and Playmates Toys. His latest novels—the critically acclaimed science fiction thriller *Amortals* and urban fantasy *Vegas Knights*—are on sale now, and his next one, *Carpathia*, ships in March. For more about him and his work, visit Forbeck.com.

Will Hindmarch's writing has appeared on the pages of *The Thackery T. Lambshead Cabinet of Curiosities*, *McSweeney's Internet Tendency*, and numerous other books and magazines. In addition to writing and designing games, Will aims to write one of everything else. When not writing, he probably should be. Find him online at wordstudio.net.

Editor and Stone Skin Press Creative Director **Robin D. Laws** is an author, game designer, and podcaster. His novels include *Pierced Heart*, *The Rough and the Smooth*, and *The Worldwound Gambit*. Robin created the GUMSHOE investigative roleplaying rules system and such games as *Feng Shui*, *The Dying Earth*, *HeroQuest* and *Ashen Stars*. He is one half of the podcasting team behind "Ken and Robin Talk About Stuff." Find his blog, a cavalcade of film, culture, games, narrative structure and gun-toting avians, at robindlaws.com.

Jean Rabe tosses tennis balls to her dogs when she isn't writing. When she isn't editing, she tugs on old socks with them. She's the author of more than two dozen fantasy and adventure novels, more short stories than she cares to count, and she's edited 20 anthologies ... yep, she's got some age to her. Among her novels are *The Stonetellers* and *Dhamon* series from Wizards of the Coast. She's currently delving into the mystery and science fiction genres. She got the idea for "Stalking in Memphis" by taking a course on Egyptian Symbolism at her local museum. Visit her website at www.jeanrabe.com.

Christina Stiles is a freelance roleplaying game writer/editor from South Carolina. Her most recent publications include Open Design's *Streets of Zobeck*, *Kobold Quarterly*, and *Dark Deeds* *in Freeport*. She is co-author of the Origins-Award-nominated *Faery's Tale*, a roleplaying game for children, and she is currently completing a game adaptation of Faith Hunter's *Rogue Mage* novel series with Faith Hunter, Raven Blackwell, and Spike Y Jones.

Greg Stolze is 41 years old and, while generally shy and sulky, he overcompensates entertainingly for crowds of strangers. His novels include *A Hunger Like Fire* and *Ashes and Angel Wings*. His nonfiction account of nearly dying from stupidity got him second runner up in the Outrider Press 2006 Anthology, but no way is he doing that again. In 2009 he won the Richard Eastman Fiction Award for his story "Regret, With Math." You can read that for free online at www.gregstolze.com/fiction_library/ along with lots of other stuff. Also, he designs games.

James L. Sutter is the author of the novel *Death's Heretic*, as well more than twenty-five short stories for such publications as *Apex Magazine*, *Black Gate*, and the #1 Amazon bestseller *Machine of Death*. His anthology *Before They Were Giants* pairs the first published stories of such SF luminaries as Larry Niven, William Gibson, Cory Doctorow, and China Miéville with new interviews and writing advice from the authors themselves. In addition, James has written numerous roleplaying game supplements and is the Fiction Editor for Paizo Publishing, creators of the Pathfinder Roleplaying Game. For more information, check out jameslsutter.com.

John Scott Tynes is an award-winning game designer and writer in Seattle. He currently designs Xbox 360 videogames for Microsoft Game Studios. He was the founder and editor-in-chief of Pagan Publishing and Armitage House and his best-known projects include *Unknown Armies*, *Puppetland*, *Delta Green*, *The Unspeakable Oath*, and *Call of Cthulhu D20*. He has served as a film critic, videogame critic, graphic designer, web designer, videographer, and screenwriter. His film *The Yellow Sign* is available on DVD from Lurker Films and his novel *Delta Green: The Rules of Engagement* litters the shelves of used-book stores worldwide. He is very fortunate to have married the love of his life, Jenny, and to have a brilliant daughter, Vivian. He smokes a pipe and drinks brandy from a snifter because by God, someone should.

James Wallis is a games designer and author with fourteen books under his belt. He's best known as the founder/director of Hogshead Publishing Ltd, the largest publisher of roleplaying games in the UK in the 1990s, but he's also been a TV presenter, magazine editor and Sunday Times journalist, a university lecturer and an award-winning graphic designer. Previous fiction includes titles for the Black Library, Puffin Books and Virgin Publishing, and his game designs include the storytelling games *Once Upon a Time* and *The Extraordinary Adventures of Baron Munchausen*. These days he runs the games consultancy Spaaace and lives in London with his wife and 1d4-1 children.

Other Publications From Stone Skin Press...

Shotguns v. Cthulhu

Pulse-pounding action meets cosmic horror in this exciting collection from the rising stars of the New Cthulhuiana. Steel your nerves, reach into your weapons locker, and tie tight your running shoes as humanity takes up arms against the monsters and gods of H. P. Lovecraft's Cthulhu Mythos. Remember to count your bullets…you may need the last one for yourself.

Relentlessly hurtling you into madness and danger are:

Natania **BARRON** • Steve **DEMPSEY** • Dennis **DETWILLER**
Larry **DiTILLIO** • Chad **FIFER** • A. Scott **GLANCY**
Dave **GROSS** • Dan **HARMS** • Rob **HEINSOO**
Kenneth **HITE** • Chris **LACKEY** • Robin D. **LAWS**
Nick **MAMATAS** • Ekaterina **SEDIA** • Kyla **WARD**

ISBN: 9781908983015
Publication date: October 2012
Available to order from the Stone Skin Press website
www.stoneskinpress.com

The Lion and the Aardvark
Aesop's Modern Fables

These confusing times of Internet trolls, one-percenters, toxic fame, and impending singularity cry out for clarity—the clarity found in Aesop's 2,500 year old fables. Over 60 writers from across the creative spectrum bring their modern sensibilities to this classic format. Zombies, dog-men and robot wasps mingle with cats, coyotes and cockroaches. Parables ranging from the punchy to the evocative, the wry to the disturbing explore eternal human foibles, as displaced onto lemmings, trout, and racing cars. But beware—in these terse explorations of desire, envy, and power, certitude isn't always as clear as it looks.

ISBN: 9781908983022

Publication date: December 2012

Available to order from the Stone Skin Press website www.stoneskinpress.com

The New Hero
Volume 1

Older than the written word and more popular than ever today, the hero story crosses cultures as an eternal constant. *The New Hero* gathers an unexpected team of writers, celebrated and emerging, to deliver fourteen thrilling and distinctive variations on this classic theme.

Bending genres and crossing boundaries are:

Maurice **BROADDUS** • Monte **COOK** • Richard **DANSKY**
Graeme **DAVIS** • Julia Bond **ELLINGBOE** • Peter **FREEMAN**
Ed **GREENWOOD** • Kenneth **HITE** • Adam **MAREK**
Johnny **NEXUS** • Jeff **TIDBALL** • Monica **VALENTINELLI**
Kyla **WARD** • Chuck **WENDIG**

ISBN: 9781908983008
Publication date: June 2012
Available to order from the Stone Skin Press website
www.stoneskinpress.com

BITS AND MORTAR

BITS AND MORTAR is a pro-retailer, pro-bricks-and-mortar, pro-PDF, pro-ebook initiative backed by several tabletop game and fiction publishers. We love real, physical bricks and mortar game and book stores, and we want to see them survive — and thrive — even as the digital content options for traditional publishing become more prevalent.

WHAT WE DO

If a customer buys a book published by a Bits & Mortar publisher from their local game or book store, and that book is available online as a combined print and PDF bundle, we will give them the **PDF at no additional charge**. It's a free value-add and a thank you from the publisher for supporting their local store.

Better yet, we will make it possible for that local store to give the PDF to the customer directly, keeping the sale completely "in house".

For more information and a list of participating stores, please visit the website

www.bits-and-mortar.com